THY BROTHER'S KEEPER

iBooks

Habent Sua Fata Libelli

iBooks
Manhanset House
Shelter Island Hts., New York 11965-0342

bricktower@aol.com
ibooksinc.com

Library of Congress Cataloging-in-Publication Data
Bethel, John David
Thy Brother's Keeper
p. cm.
    1. FICTION / Thrillers / Psychological. 2. FICTION / Thrillers / Crime.
3. FICTION / Crime
Fiction, I. Title.
ISBN: 978-1-955036-96-2 Trade Paper

November 2025

iBooks are published by iBooks, an imprint of J. Boylston & Company, Publishers
Manhanset House, Dering Harbor, New York 11965 •www.ibooksinc.com•

THY BROTHER'S KEEPER

2024 Awardee

John David Bethel

Note

Thy Brother's Keeper is a work of fiction. Perhaps the biggest fiction is that a Democrat could get elected to a statewide political office in Oklahoma.

Then the Lord said to Cain, "Where is your brother Abel?"
"I don't know," he replied. "Am I my brother's keeper?"
—Genesis 4:9

"So we beat on, boats against the current, borne back ceaselessly into the past."
—F. Scott Fitzgerald, *The Great Gatsby*

Table of Contents

Dramatis Personae

Major

Declan Ryan:	Sheriff, City of Owen
Connor Ryan:	Brother of Declan
Jim Smolders:	Deputy, City of Owen
Joseph Berger:	Agent, Oklahoma State Bureau of Investigation
Maria Luna:	Victim
Maybelle:	Owner, Maybelle's Eagle Pub
Whalen Jones:	Oklahoma State Senator
Marco Jones:	Brother of Whalen
Raymond Lee:	Investigator, Oklahoma Senate Public Safety Committee
Lincoln Stephens:	Governor of Oklahoma
Noreen West:	Oklahoma State Legislator, Speaker of the House
Len Slade:	Director, Oklahoma State Bureau of Investigation
George Layton:	Eyeball Killer
Dr. Drew Cranston:	Director, Ottinger Wellness Center
Senator Roy Evans:	United States Senator, Oklahoma
Gary Iglesias:	Communications Strategist and Principal, Iglesias Group

Recurring

Monica Filer:	Aide, Office of Senator Evans
Nancy Wilcox:	Executive, WindServ
Merl Thaxton:	Former Sheriff, City of Owen
Paul Linares:	Chief of Police, Wichita Falls, Texas
Marty McDowell:	Major, Texas Ranger Company C
Milton Leonard:	United States Congressman, Oklahoma

Twenty-Five Years Ago

The boy sat at the base of the south wall, his knees pulled up in front of him, his arms wrapped around his legs. He remained still, a small figure in a sliver of shade created by the roof overhang on the square, two-story, red-brick town hall.

Beads of sweat slid between the boy's shoulder blades and soaked his shirt where his back met the wall. He leaned forward, repositioned the gun from the belt line at his side to a more comfortable spot near the small of his back. He made certain his shirt covered the weapon, then rested his chin on his knees and stared down the shimmering ribbon of highway running through Owen.

Rachel Beasley and Wanda Richardson were seated on a wooden bench under a large elm tree shading a small patch of green in the dried, yellow lawn bordering the town hall. The lawn, which had been fried by thirty consecutive days of temperatures hovering near 100 degrees, was divided in the front of the building by a sidewalk leading from the curb to the front steps. The women fanned themselves languidly with their broad-brimmed straw hats.

Daniel Watts, Warren Nader, and Buddy Williams huddled together in the shadows of an iron monument dedicated to four soldiers from Owen killed during World War II. Watts, Nader, and Williams moved only to dab their glistening foreheads with white handkerchiefs.

Mary Upton and Laura Ivers stood on the sidewalk staring at the highway. Every so often one of the girls would giggle excitedly or reach out and touch the other, pushing gently to make a point.

"Flashing red lights up the way," Upton announced, jabbing her arm toward the highway, and bouncing on the balls of her feet.

The boy watched as the separate knots of people coalesced into a crowd at the curb. He stood slowly, shifted the weapon to his hip, and made his way to the front of the building. He climbed three cement steps to the porch that wrapped around the first floor and positioned himself next to the large double doors opening into the town hall.

A black and white car approached shimmering in the liquid illusion rippling across the surface of the baking asphalt. As it broke through this illusion, the outlines of the car became clearer and it appeared to pick up speed.

"I see him! I see Connor," Mary Upton screeched, her red curls bouncing as she hopped with excitement.

The boy could distinguish four figures in the car. Two in front, two in back. His concentration was broken by the smell of spiced cologne. Ned Travis rounded the corner of the building and stood next to him. The scent caused the boy to draw his shoulders up around his ears, as he did every third Saturday when Travis put the finishing touches on his haircut by slapping a stinging blue liquid on his freshly shaved neck. Travis took a handkerchief from a pocket in his white smock and wiped at beads of sweat trickling from his bald head into his eyes.

"Morning," Travis said to the boy, his eyes trained on the road. "Gotta say, I'm surprised to see you here." He studied the boy carefully. "You okay?"

The boy nodded.

"Merl," Travis called over his shoulder into the darkened entrance of the town hall, keeping his attention on the highway.

A large man stepped from the shadows onto the porch. His light brown shirt, the buttons straining against the bulk of a massive chest, was sweat stained under the arms. He held a ten-gallon Stetson in one hand, and with the other, wiped the inside hat band with a red bandanna. As he walked to the porch banister his leather holster cradling a pearl-handled Colt 45 bounced against his thick thigh.

From the corner of his eye, the boy saw Travis nod in his direction as Sheriff Merl Thaxton shared a "Good morning" with the barber.

"Morning, Declan," said the sheriff, acknowledging the boy. "Come to see Connor one last time before they carry him off to McAlester?" He adjusted his holster. "To the Big Mac."

The boy shrugged a response as he watched the black-and-white cruiser negotiate the town square and head for the town hall.

"Sure enough, it's Connor and they got three men guarding him," Travis said toying with a pair of scissors in the front pocket of his smock.

The boy moved away from the doors and approached the weathered wood banister. He shifted the gun closer to his belt buckle as he walked up next to the sheriff, pulling his shirt away from his body to keep the weapon hidden.

As the car pulled to the curb, the officer in the passenger seat waved the people away. "Give us some room, please." He watched intently as the group retreated and reformed, lining both sides of the walkway leading to the town hall.

Mary Upton bent at the waist, peered into the car, and clapped her hands excitedly. "I went to school with Connor Ryan," she said.

"I know that," Laura Ivers replied, pretending exasperation. "So did I."

"Yeah, but I sat right next to him from first grade right on 'til high school," Upton declared. "Ryan was always next to Upton. R, S, T, and then U," she clarified.

The boy squinted into the bright sunlight and watched closely as two officers emerged from the front seat of the black and white. They positioned themselves on either side of the car and the one on the curb side opened the rear door.

"We got the prime spot," Travis said proudly, sliding up next to the boy. "Connor'll have to go right past us."

The sheriff glanced at Travis and the boy, shoved the bandanna into his back pocket, and sauntered down the steps to the sidewalk. He stopped, put on his hat, adjusted it carefully, then made his way toward the car.

A small, skinny man swung two chained legs out of the rear door and set his unlaced boots on the curb. He hesitated, his eyes dancing across the faces of the greeting party. The officer standing nearest the door reached down and grabbed the prisoner's shoulder, pulling him into a standing position. The man's orange jumpsuit was at least two sizes too large and he swam in it. The pant legs fell over his boots and dragged on the ground. Although buttoned to the top, the neckline stretched to his shoulders. The sleeves hung loose covering the handcuffs. Thick chains showed from the cuff line.

The officer who had been on the far side of the car came around the front and signaled the group forward. The prisoner was sandwiched between the men in front and followed by one behind.

Mary Upton grabbed Laura Ivers by the wrist. The girls were wiggling with excitement.

Warren Nader, standing across from the girls, waved awkwardly at the approaching phalanx. "Hey, Connor," he called as the prisoner passed through the gantlet. "Welcome home. Can I get you a soda or something? Remember you used to shop in my store?"

"Course, he remembers," Laura Ivers said mockingly. "You got the only store in town. Where else would he go?"

The prisoner ran his tongue nervously across his thin, liver-colored lips. His cheeks were hollow, his skin so pale it was luminous, and his eyes deep-set, giving him a skeletal look. His attention darted from one side of the sidewalk to the other without settling on anyone. He lowered his head and pulled his chin to his chest.

Daniel Watts stepped in front of the foursome and backpedaled as they approached. "Connor worked at my gas station when he was in high school," he informed the officers. "Worked for gas for his truck."

The group stopped abruptly and one of the officers demanded, "Sir, get out of the way." He placed his hand on his holster. "Right now."

Sheriff Thaxton came up behind Watts and gently eased him onto the grass. He leaned forward and whispered to the officers leading the procession. The one who had been following the group came around and stood in front. The prisoner leaned into the conversation. His eyes saucered, and he moved as close to the lead officer as he could. The group, with Thaxton following closely, veered away from the sidewalk and cut across the grass toward the side of the building.

Ned Travis stiffened. "Hey, what're they doing?"

The boy's knuckles whitened as his grip tightened on the banister.

"But..." Travis left the word hanging, scurrying down the steps, and following the assembly around the building.

The others stopped at the point where the officers detoured and watched the tight squad enter the building, trailed by a skittering Travis.

Wanda Richards asked no one in particular, "How long is Connor gonna be here?"

"'Bout two hours. That's how long they usually stay," Warren Nader answered.

"Funny how you don't pay attention until it means something special to you," Rachel Beasley remarked thoughtfully. "I never gave any thought to how long they stayed in town. Most of the time I never even knew when they came through."

Ned Travis was pushed from the darkness of the town hall's entrance. He stood hands on his hips, clearly annoyed, waiting until the officer retreated into the building, then scowled at his back.

Mary Upton hurried toward Travis. "Did Connor say anything about us being here to see him?"

Travis shook his head. He jabbed his thumb in the direction of the entrance. "Locked him up before I could say hello or anything."

"Isn't it neat how things worked out?" Mary Upton exclaimed. "I mean with Owen being on the way to McAlester from Eureka and all. Gives Connor a chance to stop at home before he has to go into that horrible place."

"Seems like they should let us say hello to him," Daniel Watts said indignantly. "He's a neighbor." He shrugged. "Used to be anyway. Not like we don't know him."

"Yeah, it'd give him a pick-me-up, I imagine," Buddy Williams added. "Be nice to know friends still care when things go bad."

"If he was tried here, he woulda got off," Laura Ivers declared. "Too bad Owen isn't the county seat 'stead of Eureka."

"Well, I know I don't believe he robbed all those banks," Mary Upton said. "And if he did, it's only 'cause the bank was tryin' to take his farm away." The girl balled her hands into fists and bounced them off her thighs. "Why, I bet Connor was robbing those banks to help other people, too."

When this remark drew blank stares, she added, "You know, to give money to other folks so they wouldn't lose their farms."

"Could be," Daniel Watts said, nodding. "I read once that Pretty Boy Floyd did that and they shot him for it."

"Connor did kill his parents," Ned Travis noted, breaking the mood. "That's what he's going to jail for. Didn't hear much in Eureka 'bout the bank robbing part of it. And," he said with a smile bordering on a smirk, "I was there for the whole trial."

"Oh, we all know his daddy beat him somethin' awful," Rachel Beasley said. "His lawyer said so at the trial. I read that in the *Eureka Sentinel*. And I remember he'd come to school all beat up. Black eyes. Scratches."

Mary Upton matched her with, "He had a broken nose once. Had to go to the nurse."

Travis clicked his scissors nervously, coughed to get the girls' attention, widened his eyes, and pursed his lips in a "shut up" signal.

Laura Ivers caught Travis's gestures. She poked Rachel in the side and jerked her head toward the porch. "Declan's up there."

The group fell silent. Mary Upton fanned herself vigorously with her open hand.

Rachel bent her head toward Laura. "S'okay, he didn't hear anything."

The boy stared into the middle distance.

Warren Nader approached the group after a quick pass by the side entrance. He stood a moment collecting his thoughts, then offered, "How 'bout I go to the store and grab some sodas, some stuff for sandwiches, and we wait right here 'til they take Connor away? Let him know we...well, that we care." Another pause. "Okay?"

"I'll run over to the diner and get us some pie for dessert," Rachel Beasley offered.

"I've got a coupla card tables and some folding chairs in the shop," Travis volunteered. "We can set 'em up under the tree." He nodded toward the elm.

The boy came down the steps as the group dissolved. He pulled his perspiration-soaked shirt away from his chest and returned to the shade along the side of the building. As he settled, the side door swung open and slapped against the brick wall, startling him. One of the officers stepped from the doorway. He lit a cigarette, shielded his eyes with his hand, and glanced up at the sky before turning toward the building, where he saw the boy huddled in the shadows.

"Got enough shade there to share?" he asked, tilting his head and blowing a stream of smoke into the air.

The boy nodded.

The officer squatted and pulled hard on the cigarette. The end of the butt fired red, then grayed. An ash fell on the man's pant leg. "You here to see Ryan, too?" he asked, wiping away the ash as he sent smoke billowing from his nose and mouth.

"Guess so."

The officer flicked his spent butt into the grass. The two sat in silence as if surrendering to the heat, their energy sapped.

Travis and Nader shuffled across the lawn lugging a card table they set under the elm tree.

"I heard'em say they're gonna wait on Connor," the boy said in response to a question in the officer's eyes.

The man raised his chin in the direction of Mary Upton and Laura Ivers who arrived and were busily removing items from two brown grocery bags lined up on the now-assembled card table. "What're they doing?"

"Gonna make sandwiches."

"Sandwiches?"

"Yes, sir. And Mrs. Beasley went for some pie. Like a picnic, I guess."

"In this heat?" The officer's voice pitched high in disbelief.

"Gonna get comfortable 'til Connor leaves, I guess."

The officer stood and pulled his dampened shirt away from his body. "He was nervous about coming back here. Doesn't look like he had reason to be, you think?"

"What was he nervous for?" the boy said, leaning into his question.

"I don't know. Like some of these folks might not be real happy to see someone back in town who murdered his own parents."

The boy's mouth hardened, his lips thinning. His eyes shifted to the activity under the elm tree. "They don't care nothin' 'bout that."

The officer pushed away from the wall and looked down at the boy. "Really? Why do you say that?"

"Never cared before." The boy felt the man's eyes on him and began scratching his finger in the dirt. "But Connor got his name in the paper and he's famous."

"Famous?" the officer said with a note of disgust as he stared at the activity on the lawn. "He asked us not to stop, but this is the place we stop to rest, get some gas, and eat. Always the same when carrying prisoners cross state from Eureka to the Big Mac."

The man shifted his weight. "Said he didn't care about eating, going to the bathroom, nothing." He took a final drag on his cigarette and tossed the butt to the grass, where a thin wisp of smoke curled into the air. "He wanted to keep going right on past. The man's a coward. Not worth the effort those folks are making."

The boy flicked a look at the officer. "Why didn't they send him to the 'lectric chair?"

"Can't say. I'm not the judge, but if I was him, I would've begged for the chair. He's going to be in hell for the rest of his life. He'll wish he was dead before he's spent his first week in the Mac. Those boys there will make mincemeat out of little Connor Ryan."

A beat of silence passed, and the officer looked at the boy. "Maybe the judge knew exactly what he was doing."

"What about those banks he robbed on top of the killings?"

"Banks?"

"Yeah, maybe the judge let him off easy 'cause he was gonna give the money to other people so they wouldn't lose their farms."

"Lose their farms?" The officer's face was a mask of disbelief. He took a few steps away from the building, stood and pointed at Travis, who was handing a sandwich to Rachel Beasley. "Is that what this is all about? They think he's some kind of Robin Hood?"

"Jus' tellin' you what I heard."

The officer laughed loudly. Mary Upton and Laura Ivers looked in the direction of the laughter, then returned to their lunches.

"He *tried* to rob a bank. One bank, and he screwed that up. Dropped the money all over the floor as he was running away, tripped over the bag he was carrying, and begged the bank guard not to shoot him." The officer looked down at the boy. "It was such a fiasco the whole bank thing was dismissed so they could get at the murder charges quicker."

"Did he kill anyone?"

"Besides his parents?"

"Yeah."

"Like I said, he's a coward. His kind goes after people he knows can't hurt him back."

"Yeah," the boy agreed. "He's a coward."

A note of recognition lit the man's eyes. "You his brother? The sheriff said his brother was here. Didn't want to parade Connor in front of him. That's you, right? I saw you on the porch."

The boy didn't respond.

"Gotta name?"

"Declan."

"Irish like your brother."

The boy gave the man a look. "I'm an American."

"No, I mean your name is Irish. Declan. That's an Irish name and so is Connor. So is Ryan." He tapped a nameplate above his left breast pocket. "Berger. French."

The side door swung open. "Joe," a voice called.

"Be right there." The officer stared in the direction of the elm tree. "Seems to me like your friends have way too much time on their hands."

"Ain't my friends," the boy replied.

The officer looked intently at the boy. "Connor'll get what's coming to him. Cowards like him who kill their parents have a real tough time in prison. Yeah, a real rough time." He winked and disappeared inside the building.

***

It was his father's hoarse voice that woke Declan. The old man was standing over Connor's bed on the opposite wall of the small room. The early morning chill hardened the packed dirt floor, but the cold could not stem the stench from the waste bucket the old man kicked over when he walked into the room.

"I ain't askin' again," he spit out angrily. "It's already six and we hafta deliver what little we got to the market 'fore the others beat us there." He jabbed at Connor's shoulder. "I don't have time for your back talk."

Connor fended off the man's jabs; his face contorted in anger, his eyes wide and alive. "I ain't goin' nowhere with you."

The boy pushed himself to the corner of his bed and squeezed against the wall. It was always bad between them, but this morning their anger was roiling. The battle of wills had crossed a line.

"You never been good for nothin' and you never will be," the old man yelled with his face close to Connor's ear. "If you ain't goin' to work for your keep in this house, then get the hell out and find a place of your own." He yanked the thin hopsack cover off Connor and tossed it on the floor into the stinking puddle of waste.

Declan turned his back to the anger. He knew his father needed Connor to drive the truck. The old man was almost blind. Once he offered to drive and that caused both of them to turn their fury on him.

Curled into a ball, ears covered, his face pressed against the mud-packed, rough-hewn log wall, Declan began humming a tuneless ditty to drown out the white heat of angry voices. He was managing to divorce himself from the chaos when he felt his father fall on top of him. The old man was making sounds curdled by fear and twisted into a wailing that Declan felt to his bones. He turned enough to see Connor holding the old man down with his knee and beating him with his fists.

"You won't ever hit me with that strap again," Connor was yelling, his face red, veins popping at his temples.

It was then Declan saw the thick belt in his father's hand.

Connor yanked the old man up from the bed and shoved him through the bedroom doorway onto the wood-plank floor in the front room. He raced after his father, who was scuttling across the raw boards on his hands and knees.

Connor picked up the belt, which had fallen from his father's hand, and was about to hit the old man across the back, when his mother grabbed his arm. "Don't you dare do that," she forced through clenched teeth.

Connor shoved her away and swung the belt at his father, who was trying to push himself off the floor. The old woman came at Connor again. He struck her with the back of his hand sending her hurtling toward a wall.

Declan raced into the room and saw his mother slam against the wall and begin to crumble. He reached her in time to keep her from falling face forward. As he walked her away from the wall, Declan saw a red streak smeared against the logs. His hand went to the top of her head and came away covered with blood.

As Declan lowered his mother into a chair, her eyes widened, and she raised her arms over her head. Declan heard his cheekbone crack before he felt a sharp, hot pain sear the side of his face. The blow spun him around and he faced Connor, who was swinging a piece of firewood. A flash of bright lights exploded in front of Declan's face. There was a terrible ringing in his ears, and then blackness.

He was surprised to find himself on his stomach and pushed his upper body off the floor. He stared down at a puddle of blood. It was expanding as a red stream poured from his nose. This tide was fed by blood coming from a gash that ran the length of his left cheekbone, ending under his ear; the lobe was hanging by a thin piece of skin and swung freely splashing blood on the floor.

He struggled to his feet but could not maintain his balance and fell onto his knees. He took a deep breath, fighting the urge to be sick, and stood, his hands resting on his thighs. He widened his stance and slowly straightened.

His mother was sitting in the chair, her back to him. He approached and put his hand on her shoulder as he came around the side of the chair. He was having difficulty focusing on his mother's face, which was cocked at an awkward angle. Finally able to wipe and blink away his own blood and tears, Declan saw his mother's head was nearly severed from her neck.

He whirled away and staggered to the middle of the front room. He was having trouble breathing and either passed out or slipped on the blood-slickened floor. The next thing he knew he was staring into the open, blank eyes of his father, who was sprawled next to him at the base of the wood-burning stove. Declan crawled to the front door and pushed it open. He tried to stand but couldn't and rolled into the dawn.

The first thing he remembered when he regained consciousness after three days in the hospital were the stars he was staring at as he lay on his back in the yard. He was thankful for that because the second thing he remembered was the ugly red slice across his mother's throat.

***

Warren Nader gestured toward the town hall. "One of them officers just peeked out. Betcha they're getting ready to leave."

"Let's put some of the food together for Connor to eat on the way to McAlester," Mary Upton suggested, gathering up a sandwich, soda, and piece of pie.

"There they are," Laura Ivers announced shaking her hands in front of her face excitedly.

The party of five men, Sheriff Thaxton in the lead, stepped away from the front door of the town hall. Before starting down the steps, one of the officers checked Connor's handcuffs and leg irons.

Mary Upton and Laura Ivers walked hurriedly toward the building, the others following in their wake.

Thaxton and the officers moved in a tight formation, walking across the porch and down the stairs. Connor, head bowed, pinned himself close to Thaxton's broad back.

"We got some food for Connor," Mary announced, holding a wax paper coated bag toward the advancing men, who ignored her.

Declan positioned himself at the end of the sidewalk and watched the huddle advance toward him. As they neared, he yelled, "Connor, I'll come to see you at the Big Mac. Wanna make sure you're doin' good."

The officer who had been talking to Declan jabbed his chin toward the grass and the boy stepped out of the way.

Connor, his eyes wide, and head swiveling, tried to locate Declan. When he saw him, he hesitated, almost tripping on the chains joining his leg irons. He held his brother's gaze and opened his mouth but made no sound.

"Don't let nothin' happen to my brother before you get him there," Declan called to the officers as they passed.

Mary was still waving the bag in the air as if pleading for someone to take it from her.

Berger pushed Connor into the backseat of the cruiser and turned to Mary. "He doesn't need anything from you." He glanced around and found Declan. "We'll take real good care of him."

Mary stood, her arm hanging in the air, a look of confusion on her face.

Berger tipped his hat, smiled, and got into the car.

Today/Monday-April 23

She was a pretty woman. Stunning figure. Narrow waist. Shapely hips. Long legs tapered perfectly at the ankles. Ample breasts. The kind that created cleavage without being heavy. Her hair was raven. So dark it shined. If it was not for the bloody gouge where her right eye should have been and the slice across her throat that caused the pillow to be soaked with blood, she would have been perfect.

"That's ugly," Sheriff Declan Ryan said as he turned away from the bed. The manager of the Sleep Inn, his face ghostly, stumbled backward as Ryan stepped toward him.

The smell of cigarettes accompanied Deputy Jim Smolders into the room. His short, heavy stature was in stark contrast to the tall, thin, gray-haired man who followed him. "Oh, shit," Smolders said and stopped short, causing the man behind to half-step and pivot away from the deputy.

"Yeah," Ryan agreed and nudged past the manager who stood stiffly, a large ring of keys in his hand.

Smolders raised his chin in the direction of the tall man, now at his side. "This is Agent Joe Berger from the State Bureau of Investigation." He directed Berger to Ryan. "Sheriff Declan Ryan."

Berger smiled. "Irish, right?"

"I'm an American."

Smolders looked from one man to the other, a question in his eyes, and made a weak gesture toward the bed trying to refocus the conversation.

Berger reached out his hand. "You've sure grown up."

"That was the best way to go. Up."

Berger nodded at the badge attached to Ryan's thick embroidered leather belt holstering a Glock. "And you're the sheriff here?"

Ryan answered with a nod. "And you're with the SBI? What are the odds?"

"Not long, I guess."

Ryan turned his shoulders toward the bed without looking at the carnage. "How did you know?"

"Someone caught the radio chatter."

"Someone?"

Berger walked to the side of the bed and stared down at the body. "This isn't the first. We have people with their ears to the ground. Alert to the possibility of..." He paused before adding, "This."

Ryan attempted a question that was lost as his voice cracked. He cleared his throat. "More? Like this?"

"Similar."

"How many?"

"Three."

"Three," Smolders blurted.

Ryan asked, "Around here?"

Berger waited a beat before answering. "No, and that's what's strange."

"That's what's strange?" Ryan asked incredulously. He pointed at the bed, not looking at the butchery. "No, *that's* what's strange."

A thump caught their attention and they turned toward the collapsed figure of the motel manager. He was on his back; his eyes were open but unfocused. Ryan and Berger lifted him onto a floral-covered easy chair as Smolders ran into the bathroom returning with a glass of water.

Berger pointed Ryan toward the door, and they stepped onto a breezeway fronting a line of rooms. This single wing extended from a small brick building where guests registered at a window thickened by bullet-proof glass; they slid their cash or credit cards into a drawer, and never got out of the car.

Berger studied the surroundings as he and Ryan ducked under yellow caution tape strung from pillar to pillar along the breezeway. "Not the kind of place people spend more than a night," he mumbled and gestured at the empty parking lot. "No one else here?"

Ryan shook his head. "No one. The manager said a man checked in. He never saw the woman. He noticed the car was gone this morning and went to clean the room and found the body."

Berger looked into the eaves of the single wing of the motel. "No CCTV."

"I think that's likely a perk of the place. Anyone who comes here probably doesn't want a record of it."

"Anything in the way of a description of the man?" Berger asked, his eyes going to the open door of the room. "Make of the car?"

"No, nothing. The thing he remembers was the man paid in cash."

"Of course he did."

Ryan took a deep breath. "You have three more like this one?"

"Similar to this one. Started about two years ago. The first one was in Wesper. Second in Laramie. Third in Mannix. They all have similar MOs and signatures." He squinted at Ryan. "You know what I'm talking about? MO and signature?"

Ryan gave him a look.

"I don't mean to be disrespectful but..."

Ryan raised an open hand. "No, I get it. Not your standard investigation. It's just that I spent a couple of years in the service as an MP and we got some training on this kind of thing." He paused. "Stranger murders."

Berger titled his head, amused. He smiled. "*Stranger murders*. That's fallen out of use."

"What can I tell you? I was trained by the Army. It's a tradition-bound organization and usually one or two steps behind whatever's current." Ryan pressed his thumb and index finger into the corners of his eyes, massaging the bridge of his nose. "Christ, a serial killer here in Owen. Big city problems are coming with what's called progress these days."

"I'm not so sure."

Ryan peeked at Berger around his still massaging fingers. "What?"

"I mean, yes, this has some of the earmarks of the other murders. That's why I'm here, obviously." Berger raised his chin toward the building. "But there's a problem with that one."

"How?"

"The other victims were found in their homes, or, in one case, their parents' home. And they were all in upscale neighborhoods. The hands and legs of the victims were tied to the bedposts and their throats were cut so violently they were almost decapitated. None of that is evident" – he pointed at the entrance to the room – "in there."

"Don't these guys generally change their MOs from victim to victim? They learn what works for them, what gets them off, what leaves fewer clues to chase, and that changes what they do?"

Berger nodded. "You do know something about this. I know each one can be slightly different. The violence can be jacked up to satisfy his escalating fantasies. And they improve how they do what they do to keep us off their scent. That" – he again pointed at the door – "is a de-escalation. For one thing all the other victims had their nipples bitten off. For another that poor person's eye was, uh…well, it wasn't removed with the surgical precision like others were. That's a mess. And this one was bound with plastic zip ties, not with curtain tiebacks used in the other cases. Plus, she wasn't bound to the bedposts. Some important differences."

"Maybe he was in a hurry. Out of his element so he didn't feel comfortable enough to spend time with this victim."

"Which goes back to my point about the difference in the scenes. This is nothing like the others."

Ryan stepped away from Berger and stared at the empty parking lot. He let his eyes roam the warehouses and razor wire protected storage units surrounding the Sleep Inn. "This is definitely a long way from an upscale neighborhood. The definition of a rent-a-bed. Didn't notice, but I'm betting there are no bedposts in those rooms, and definitely no fancy curtains with…what did you call them?"

"Tiebacks, but even without those, if it was the same person, I'd have expected him to use the cords from the Venetian blinds to maintain some symmetry to the other scenes."

"I didn't even notice the Venetian blinds."

"I knew what to look for."

"Anything else?" Ryan asked.

"The room is a mess. The sheets are pulled off the mattress like there's been a struggle. I think I remember a lamp on the floor."

"There was," Ryan agreed as he walked back toward Berger.

"The other scenes were not in disarray. It's as if the victims cooperated with the killer. There was no indication they were coerced. Like they cooperated with being bound up. No mess. The violence was all to the bodies. The breasts. The near capitation. In this one, it's almost the exact opposite. The violence to the body is controlled. *Too* controlled."

"So, what do we have?"

"No idea, but I have serious doubts this is the same guy I've been chasing."

"About that. How come I haven't heard anything? No alerts. No bulletins."

"Between us?"

"Okay," Ryan agreed, a question crossed his face.

"I got called into this after the incident in Laramie. Looking into that one, I found out there'd been something like it about six months earlier in Wesper, and by the time there was a third in Mannix, I had already come to the conclusion that we had a single offender."

"But in three separate cities?"

Berger nodded his answer.

"That's unusual, right?"

"Very. These offenders usually confine themselves to a comfort zone. Usually near where they live or work."

"Okay, so back to my question on why I haven't heard anything about this."

"It gets complicated. After I concluded that we're dealing with a serial murderer, I met with the local cops, and the families. In a first for me, the families asked us not to say anything publicly. They asked us to work the case quietly."

Ryan narrowed his eyes and tilted his head. "Why?"

"They were concerned how something like this would blow up in the press."

"I'm not following at all."

Berger held up his hand, palm out. "There's more to this. Like I said, it's complicated. I mentioned the victims were killed in upscale areas. *Upscale* is way shy of accurate. These are families of consequence as it was put to me by people above my pay grade."

"'High value constituents,'" Ryan said with a note of disgust.

Berger smiled tightly. "Yeah, and their daughters had histories of, shall we say, risky behavior? Drug use. In one case, time in a juvenile facility for incorrigibility. In another, time in a mental institution instead of incarceration. Other stuff, too, and the families didn't want to expose any of that, which would have happened if we went public. The serial killer thing would have brought the press into this in a big way. A huge way. From everywhere. Think Ted Bundy. Ed Kemper. BTK. It's like a magnet for people who have to fill their networks with chum twenty-four/seven. That would include taking the victims and their families apart."

"So?"

"So, we're working the case without fanfare."

"Fanfare? Warning the public about a serial killer is fanfare? Getting the press involved to spread the word that might dig up something you could use to help you is fanfare?"

"You're preaching to the choir, man. These families have sway with the powers that be. They have ties to the state house, and beyond. We were asked to investigate quietly, which we're doing; and until this one, the killings had stopped for two years. Haven't had another one since the cluster of three, all of which happened in a ten-month period. And that's strange because once these offenders get started, they usually keep going until they're caught, die, or go to prison for something else. Anyway, here we are."

"How have you managed to keep the other jurisdictions quiet about this? I'm guessing everyone knows what everyone knows."

"I don't know what everyone knows. I do know everyone is working their own case. And I know what I need to know to do my job. I have no idea how the lid stays on, but if I were a betting man, I'd say you'll be getting a phone call from someone about this."

"How is someone going to find out? Or put two and two together and see that" – he nodded in the direction of the Sleep Inn – "as part of your investigation?"

"I do my job, make my reports, enter them into the system, and..." Berger shrugged the balance of his thought.

"You said this one's different. If she's not like the others, and this is a whole different thing..."

Berger spoke over Ryan. "I didn't say this was a whole different thing. There are similarities. I'll be noting the similarities and the differences."

"How're you working with the other jurisdictions? Or are you?"

"I am. We share the information we develop."

"What have you developed?"

Berger took a deep breath. "Not a whole lot. I'll send you everything I have found so far."

The men watched an ambulance park in front of the room. Ryan pointed at the EMTs. "Coroners. CSIs. Those guys. All of them touch these investigations. You're saying no one's picked up on similarities or evidence tying them together?"

"They occurred in different jurisdictions which is what kept this from morphing into a huge deal. Murders happen everywhere. Sure, these got some coverage because of who the victims were, but it was all local. But even if all of them happened in one place... Think about it. Everyone has a job to do. Separate links in a chain." He pointed at the EMTs dragging a stretcher toward the room. "They have a single job. Pick up the body. The coroner looks at one body. Crime scene people are focused on the incident they're investigating. That goes for the local cops. Speaking of which" – he pointed at Ryan's badge – '*Sheriff* Ryan. How long?"

"A few years. Came home, went to the academy and here I am. It isn't an elected position. I don't have the stomach for that kinda shit. Remember Sheriff Thaxton? The sheriff when you stopped here?"

"The guy with the cowboy hat? Never forgot that John Wayne vibe. You know he was worried about parading your brother in front of you? I was never sure if he thought you might do something stupid or if he didn't want to cause you heartache."

Ryan curled his mouth in an imitation of a smile. "Heartache? He could have cared less about that. He and some others were worried I might do something."

"Like?"

Ryan shrugged. "It was a long time ago."

"I wondered what happened to you. Your parents killed. Brother in jail." Berger waited a moment before continuing. "Wondered if you stayed with relatives. Friends."

"None of the above. Foster homes," Ryan said flatly dismissing the subject. "After Amazon built a distribution center here, the town became this," he said lowering his head in the direction of warehouses and budding skyline behind. "Owen became the county seat. Needed a larger police force. I moved up the ladder and when Haskins retired, I got the job. What about you. SBI?"

"I went to law school at night while I was with the state police. Halfway through, I decided I didn't want to be a lawyer. It hit me while I was trying to put the bad guys away and had to work around lawyers to do that. But I didn't want to waste two years of my life so I found out about the SBI and here I am."

"What's the saying? 'Man plans, God laughs'?"

"Hear anything from your brother? He was the first guy I escorted to the Mac from county jail."

"Nothing."

"Not in touch?"

Ryan shook his head. "No, not in touch."

Berger stared as the EMTs wheeled out the stretcher and body bag. "Assuming I'm right, and this isn't the same guy, we have another problem."

"Just what I need to hear," Ryan said, pain in his voice.

"How does the killer know how to stage this?"

Wednesday-April 25

"Welcome," Ryan greeted Berger who followed Deputy Smolders into his office. Smolders plopped down in one of two thinly padded gunmetal grey office chairs facing a steel desk with a faux wood top. The desk was bare except for a computer screen and keyboard, and a green plastic nameplate identifying Sheriff Declan Ryan.

Berger stood next to the second chair and studied the empty white walls. "Just move in here?"

Ryan followed Berger's scan of the room. "No, just not real big on interior design."

"Interior design is one thing. A few photos, one of a dog even, would warm up the space."

"Don't own a dog," Ryan said and pointed at the chair.

Berger handed Smolders a file and slid one across the desk to Ryan. "Short histories of each of the victims."

"Thought you were going to send these along. You hand deliver to everyone?"

Ignoring the question, Berger said, "Read through them, and I'll add a few details."

"Now?" asked Smolders.

"No time like the present. It's only a couple of pages. I scaled back the details to the important stuff and wrote it in English. Took out the jargon. It's chronological from the first victim to the one at the Sleep Inn. Maria Luna. I appreciated the quick ID and coroner's report."

"Courtesy of Jim. He has all the right contacts in this building."

Smolders smiled thinly. "Old friends."

NAME: Sarah Churchill
AGE: 24
OCCUPATION: Lawyer
HEIGHT: 5 feet 3 inches
WEIGHT: 165 pounds
CAUSE OF DEATH: Exsanguination. Throat cut violently through to the spine almost decapitating the victim.
OTHER SIGNS OF VIOLENCE: Nipples bitten off/sodomized with lotion bottle (vagina) and shampoo bottle (rectum).
CRIME SCENE: Victim was found on the bed in the master bedroom with her wrists and ankles bound to the bedposts by curtain ties. There were no signs of a struggle or of forced entry into the house.
LOCATION: Single family home
                             217 Laurel Lane
                             Wesper, Oklahoma

NAME: Maryanne Smithson
AGE: 27
OCCUPATION: Doctor (GP)
HEIGHT: 5 feet 2 inches
WEIGHT: 172 pounds
CAUSE OF DEATH: Exsanguination. Throat was cut violently through to the spine almost decapitating the victim.
OTHER SIGNS OF VIOLENCE: Nipples bitten off/sodomized with handle of shower brush (vagina) and shampoo bottle (rectum).

CRIME SCENE: Victim was found on the bed in the master bedroom with her wrists and ankles bound to the bedposts by curtain ties. There were no signs of a struggle or of forced entry into the house.

LOCATION: Condominium
23 Willis Circle
Laramie, Oklahoma

NAME: Laura Regent
AGE: 22
OCCUPATION: Commercial Real Estate Broker
HEIGHT: 5 feet 4 inches
WEIGHT: 157 pounds
CAUSE OF DEATH: Exsanguination. Throat was cut violently through to the spine almost decapitating the victim.
OTHER SIGNS OF VIOLENCE: Nipples bitten off/sodomized with knitting needles (vagina and rectum)
CRIME SCENE: Victim was found on the bed in the master bedroom with her wrists and ankles bound to the bedposts by curtain ties. There were no signs of a struggle or of forced entry into the house.
LOCATION: Home on the estate of Mr. and Mrs. William Regent
Victoria Gardens
Mannix, Oklahoma

NAME:	Maria Luna
AGE:	36
OCCUPATION:	Unemployed
HEIGHT:	5 feet 9 inches
WEIGHT:	128 pounds
CAUSE OF DEATH:	Exsanguination due to cut throat.
OTHER SIGNS OF VIOLENCE:	None
CRIME SCENE:	Victim was found on a bed. Sheets and blankets appeared to have been torn from the bed during a struggle. Wrists and ankles of the victim were bound by plastic zip ties. Gagged with a hand towel.
LOCATION OF BODY:	Sleep Inn Room 7 Owen, Oklahoma

"Okay," Ryan said as he looked up from the pages. "There are some distinct differences between the first three and the one we found here."

"Which are made even more distinct when you consider these," Berger said and slid another file to Ryan. "Churchill, Smithson, and Regent are not attractive women."

Ryan flipped through a series of headshots of the women and handed the file to Smolders. "And plus-sized."

Berger nodded at the photos Smolders held. "And Luna was brown. The other three were as lily white as you can get. White as in more than appearance. White as in way upper crust. The country club set. The women who shop as a hobby. Join the Junior League."

"Didn't you say all of them had problems?" Ryan asked.

"They did. Churchill was arrested a few times in college for public drunkenness. She was kicked out. She got it together long enough to get back into school, and made it through law school. Her father, a prominent oil broker, arranged to get her a job with a downtown law firm by giving them his business. I'm guessing it was this influence that got her through law school. Passing grades in exchange for donations. That kind of thing. Anyway, she had a thing with one of the married partners at the law firm and…" Berger waved his hand in a circle. "And she was 'on a sabbatical' when she was killed."

"Smithson had a nervous breakdown, or something, before she was killed. Never got a complete handle on it since the details aren't available. Doctor-patient thing. Her parents said she was stressed to the breaking point during her residency. She was working up to eighty hours a week and some of her shifts lasted twenty-eight hours."

"Why would they feel the need to cover that up?" Ryan asked.

"She was self-medicating. Stealing Adderall from the hospital pharmacy. The administration agreed not to press charges if her parents got her help. Also, she's the one I told you about who was in the mental institution. It was more like an intense rehab. When she was in high school."

"Okay," Ryan said. "Got it."

"Regent was a freaking mess. Drugs from high school on through a short and failed time in college. Multiple high schools and colleges, I should say. Her parents kept the lid on that. Hired lawyers to 'settle' with the schools and others to bury her records. She did work periodically for her father's development company and leased out space in his buildings. Did pretty well from what I can tell when she didn't have her head buried in a pile of cocaine."

Ryan leaned back in his chair, an ergonomic black mesh design, and the only remotely contemporary piece of furniture in the room. He stared at the acoustic paneled ceiling. "The first three were killed in a short span. Less than a year, right? Then he stops."

Berger nodded. "There are a lot of things about this that don't make any sense." He gestured toward the pages on Ryan's desk. "Three from well-to-do families. As Waspy as you can get. Professionals by education in two of the cases. All killed in their homes. Not attractive women. Then we have Luna. Not white. Older. Prettier. She was rough around the edges, but a saint compared to the other three. Kill sites completely different, and the MO and signature in her case don't match up with the others."

"A little rough around the edges," Ryan said, still focused on the ceiling. "You got my email on her."

"I did. Hard to believe her parents had no idea where she'd been for the last three years."

Ryan let his weight fall forward and pulled himself close to the desk. "Before Amazon moved in here most of that lovely real estate where we found her was farmland. Had a lot of migrant workers coming and going, and a large community of Hispanics stayed on. Luna's people. Rough life for many of 'em. I know. I worked alongside the few my father could afford to hire to help with our planting and harvest." Ryan took a deep breath. "Anyway, things got worse for most of them when the farmland was taken over for development that became the warehouses and industrial properties you saw. According to Luna's parents, they lost their livelihoods when the land was paved over. Not much of a transfer of skills from a farm to Amazon. She ended up leaving home right after high school. Lost touch completely the past few years."

"Okay, so she's nothing at all like the others," Berger said. "And that muddles things even more. These guys always have a victim type, strict MO, and signature. They need all that to satisfy their fantasies. There's a lot different with Luna."

"Wait, wait," Smolders said, looking from Berger to Ryan. "I've been left in the dust here." He waved the photos and pages. "You're saying they're not related?"

"My bad," Ryan said apologetically. To Berger: "I've been so focused on Luna, I haven't briefed Jim fully." To Smolders: "Agent Berger..."

"Joe," Berger said.

Ryan nodded his understanding. "Joe told me he's been working on what might be serial killings."

"Yeah, I got that part when he went through the description of the causes of death and crime scene stuff. I'm confused about the direction this is taking with Luna. So, she's not part of it? Not killed by the same person who did these?" Smolders said, waving the photos again.

Berger replied, "No sodomy in Luna's case. The signature – the biting of the breasts – isn't there. He didn't bind her to the bedposts. All that tells me she wasn't killed by the same offender who did the other three."

"Okay," Smolders said. "What's next?"

"I'm not altogether certain," replied Berger.

"Sheriff?" a sing-songy request came from the doorway.

"Yes, Nelly," Ryan acknowledged a short, heavyset woman who stood shoulders slumped, face screwed up in a pained *I'm sorry to interrupt you* frown.

"Can I have a word with you? It's kinda an emergency," she said, her inflection a mix of urgency and apology.

"Sure," Ryan said, giving Berger and Smolders wide eyes of question as he pushed out of his chair.

Nelly backed into the hallway and was wringing her hands as Ryan stepped toward her. She handed him a yellow sticky note saying, "This man called and said it was important that he talk to you immediately. He was insistent about the *immediately* thing."

"Okay," Ryan said, accepting the note.

"And, Sheriff," Nelly squeaked, appearing pained, "he said he was your brother. I know..." her voice trailed.

Ryan put a reassuring hand on the woman's shoulder. "Thanks, Nelly."

"What was that?" Smolders asked as Ryan returned to his desk.

"This must be old home week," Ryan answered, studying the yellow sticky.

***

Ryan pulled in front of Maybelle's Eagle Pub and sat a moment studying the tricked-out trucks. Running boards. Stove pipe exhausts. Many hiked up on 48-inch wheels. Tucked between were motorcycles. High handles. Harley Davidson Shovelheads. Heavy D&D exhausts. Tricked out two-seater Indian Scouts. His police cruiser was the only standard vehicle in the parking lot.

Maybelle's was a redneck bar. Pub was ironic. Swinging Western saloon doors were set in a barn façade fronted by a faux hitching post to which a large plastic horse was tethered, strapped with a worn leather saddle. Ryan pushed through the doors. A rare visit. He generally came in response to a 9-1-1 call about a public disturbance, when things got so out of hand the bouncers could not handle the problem.

Ryan passed between two dead-eyed, thick armed, bull-necked men sitting on stools inside the entrance, eyes glued to their cellphones. "Connor?" he asked. Without looking up, both pointed toward a room-length dark wood bar to the left of the door. Round-topped tables and straight-backed wood chairs were scattered around the space between the entrance and the bar. Few were occupied. A room at the rear of the building, behind closed double doors, was where the drivers of the trucks and owners of the bikes filling the parking lot were spending their money on slot machines. Indian gaming thrived in the state. Maybelle's was not an Indian casino. Hence, the slots hidden behind closed doors and the colossal guardians at the entrance.

Ryan walked slowly toward the bar, studying the man who was polishing a mirror that took up the space on the wall behind shelves holding scores of bottles. He worked carefully, removing the bottles and polishing behind them, surveying his efforts before replacing the bottles on the shelves. Ryan stood next to a stool watching. He could see the man's face reflected in the mirror. It was not familiar.

The man stopped and stared a long moment at the figure visible in the mirror he was facing. "Been a while," he said, turning slowly.

Ryan narrowed his eyes, straining to bring up a memory of this face. "Connor?"

"I got old."

Ryan pulled a stool away from the bar and sat down. "It isn't that so much." He leaned forward and took in the man from his feet to his head. The physique was solid. "You're, uh..." He struggled, finally settling on, "You filled out."

Connor smiled and held his arms away from his side. "Gotta be able to protect yourself inside or you're toast."

A scar ran across the man's nose, under his left eye, across his cheek, ending low on his jaw. Healing had distorted his features, pulling the left side of his face downward, giving the appearance of someone who had suffered a stroke.

Noticing Ryan's eyes scanning his face, Connor rubbed his scar. "Yeah, pretty ugly. This is what got me into the weights and other stuff. Almost killed me and it happened my first few days in the Mac."

Ryan felt the tug of memory. It was physical. He felt a flush of anger, something he thought had died years before. "How about a glass of water?" he asked struggling to remain calm.

"Sure," Connor answered and moved down the bar to a faucet where he filled a beer stein, returned, and placed it on a coaster in front of Ryan. "You look 'bout the same."

Ryan drank deeply, put the stein down, and stared at his brother drawing an explanation from him: "I mean you ain't changed much since I saw that picture of you in the paper. When you was 'lected sheriff."

"Appointed. Not elected. I was *appointed* sheriff."

"Yeah, appointed. Kinda funny. You the sheriff and me, well, bein' in prison."

"Yeah, funny," Ryan said bitterly.

"Who'd you live with? I mean after it all happened?"

"Whoever would take me. Foster homes."

"I know 'bout how you was a big star runner and football player in high school. Read all that in the papers, too."

"Long time ago," Ryan answered dismissively, the anger at the surface. He finished the water and pushed the stein toward Connor. "Thanks."

"People said you was gonna go to OU or even Texas and then..." Connor looked at Ryan a question on his face. "What happened?"

"Seriously?" Ryan said. "You really want to go over all that? Fill in the blanks?"

Connor shrugged. "Just askin' is all."

"What're you doing out?"

"Don't wanna know why I called?" Connor asked and wiped the area in front of Ryan with a tattered red rag. He stopped and looked hard at Ryan. "You must or you wouldn't've come."

Ryan stared coldly. "Answer my question."

Connor laughed, truly jubilantly.

"That's funny to you. That you got out?"

"No, not that. Well, kinda, I guess. The reason's funny. Overcrowding. Can you believe that shit? They gotta let some go to make space for more. I had *good behavior*' goin' for me, and my lawyer told'em I had been abused. He told'em that's what caused me to do what I did, and I wouldn't be a threat now that I'm older. He said I was *mature*. I'm surprised they didn't tell you I was bein' let out." He cocked his head. "Did they?"

"No. How long have you been out?"

"'Bout a year." Connor stepped back and leaned against a prep sink. "I didn't call. Knew you didn't wanna hear from me. You didn't visit all those years I was there."

"What do you want?"

"Help findin' someone. Maria Luna."

Ryan pulled his head back. "Who?"

"Maria Luna. I need your help findin' her. We was kinda engaged and she disappeared a few days ago."

Ryan peered into the mirror behind Connor and studied the pieces of his own image fractured by a line of bottles. A confusion of emotions was complicated by the random introduction of a dead woman into a surreal conversation with his brother, a man he had been convinced he never wanted to see again, ever. A man he hated. Wanted dead. All this accompanied by the sounds of pinging and chirping slot machines escaping from the nearby double doors. "Engaged?" was all he could manage in response.

Connor nodded. "She's disappeared and told me stuff that's probably related to that. She even said she knew stuff people didn't want her to know and she was worried. Well, not 'xactly worried but at least, uh..." He searched for a word. "Concerned."

Ryan placed his forearms on the bar and leaned toward Connor. "This woman told you things you think contributed to her disappearance?"

"Yeah, and I knew you are" – he waved his hand in a circle – "a sheriff and all, so I called."

Ryan turned around on his stool and gestured toward the room. "And it seemed like a good idea to meet me about this in here."

Connor made a show of wiping a spot on the bar. "Made better sense to me than comin' to you. Didn't wanna bring up..." He bobbed his head. "You know. Figured this was best."

Ryan spun halfway around and asked, "When can you come to Owen and talk to me there?"

"Yeah, well that's another thing. I ain't never goin' back there."

Ryan sat still and silent a moment before asking, "Is there somewhere we can go to talk?" He glanced around the room.

Connor followed Ryan's eyes. "What? You afraid someone's gonna listen in?"

Ryan stood and walked to a door to the left of the bar and knocked. The two hulks at the entrance came off their stools and quick-walked toward Ryan, who pulled his badge off his gun belt and held it in front of him. They stopped short and recoiled like vampires threatened with a cross.

A tall, broad-shouldered, horse-faced woman, at the door, looked past Ryan at the two hulks. "He's good." She returned her attention on Ryan. "What the hell you doin' here, Declan? False alarm or somethin'? It's quiet," she said, nodding in the direction of the room. "Not that I'm not glad to see you."

"Always good to see you, too, Maybelle, when it's not to sweep out some trash," he said to a bottle-blond, who still had the bones of a good-looking woman. She needed a bit more make-up these days to cover the ravages of age encouraged by years of cigarette smoking and as many pouring alcohol into her system. A strong foundational bra and Spanx kept a figure together as it fought gravity, but, all-in-all, still a woman who caught men's attention.

Ryan canted his head toward Connor. "Can I borrow your bartender for a few minutes?"

Maybelle looked at Connor. "Hope he hasn't done anything wrong. He's still on probation."

"Nothing like that." He pointed at the room behind her. "Can we talk privately in there?"

Maybelle crooked a finger at Connor. "Sure. I'll take over behind the bar while you do what you need to do." She stood in the doorway as they passed. "You two are brothers, right? How do I know that?" she asked the air and closed the door behind them.

The men squeezed into a small area made smaller by boxes of napkins and toilet paper, cases of beer, two battered file cabinets, a card table doubling as a desk, a folding chair behind, and a bar stool in front.

Ryan pointed Connor to the bar stool and sat behind the card table. His line of sight was interrupted by a pile of papers on the desk, which he carefully moved aside. Connor hiked himself atop the bar stool.

"Tell me about Maria Luna."

Connor blinked rapidly and played a tune with his fingers on the stool area exposed between his legs. "Okay, so I met her here at the bar like 'bout a week after I got out. She knew Maybelle. Used to work here herself; she got me this job. Well, she recommended me to Maybelle."

"This is before you two had a relationship?"

Connor nodded. "Yeah, she told me later she liked my eyes and thought I'd do a good job." He smiled. "Can you believe that? 'Thought I'd do a good job.' Anyway…"

"Hold up. She used to work here? What was she doing when you met her?"

"Working at that uh…" Connor struggled for the words. "Not a rehab place but more for" – he gestured at his head – "mental problems. Kinda like a hospital for rich people."

"The Ottinger Clinic? I think it's called a wellness center, not a clinic."

"Yeah, there. In Owen. She was like an orderly or somethin'. I think it's called that. Basically, cleaned up 'round there but she was thinkin' 'bout goin' to nursing school."

"Okay."

"We got friendly and one thing led to another. You know," he said, looking at Ryan as if expecting a response. When none came, he continued. "Maria talked about knowin' some stuff that could embarrass some important people."

"Knowing some stuff," Ryan said with a shake of his head. "What does that mean?"

"It means she recognized someone in that place."

"In Ottinger?"

"Right. She knew someone in there and found out it was a secret."

Ryan spread his hands in question. "A secret?"

"This person was like a prisoner."

"Kept there against their will?"

"Yeah."

"Okay," Ryan said, exasperation evident. "How's this a secret if she could find out?"

"No," Connor said with a shake of his head. "No one told her or nothin' like that. She recognized him and checked some kinda files or somethin', and it turned out this guy had a different name."

Ryan placed his elbows on the table and leaned toward Connor. "He was being kept there under a name other than the one she knew him by?"

"Yeah, said she used to see him 'round Owen. Not friends or nothin', just knew who he was."

"Did she talk to him? Confirm he was who she thought he was?"

"No, she was afraid if she did, if she asked questions, he might say somethin' to her bosses and she'd lose her job. People like her weren't supposed to talk to the people there. They called 'em 'guests' and sayin' much more'n 'hello' was what she called 'frowned upon.'"

"Did he recognize her?"

"Guess not. She never said that."

"Who is he?"

Connor shrugged. "I don't know. She never said. I never asked."

"Really? Never asked? She told you she thought someone was being held against their will…laid that out for you, but never said who it was, and you never thought to ask?"

Connor shook his head. "Learned never to ask too much. If someone wants you to know somethin', they'll tell you. If they don't, leave it alone. A prison thing, I guess. Also, I got the feelin' she thought it was better if I didn't know."

Ryan pushed away from the table, his frustration chuffed out in an exaggerated sigh. "You said some people would be embarrassed about him being there. How'd she know that? And how'd she know for sure he was there against his will?"

"First off, why would he be there under a name that wasn't his? And she said he had someone watching him. Like a guard or somethin'. All of that caused her to wonder what was goin' on."

"How did this get to the point she was aware there were people who weren't happy about what she knew? That caused her to be concerned? How did they even know what she knew?"

"She went and talked to someone in the guy's family 'bout it."

Ryan straightened. "She went to his family?"

"Yeah."

"And?"

"And I don't know much else. Yeah, yeah, I know," he said, anticipating Ryan's response, "but that's the way it was. I didn't ask. All's I know for sure is Maria talked with someone and they made some promises to her. They didn't like that she knew 'bout him and was willing to give her what she was askin' for."

"You're telling me she was blackmailing his family?"

"Guess so," Connor said with a shrug.

"What was she asking for?"

"Don't know."

"You don't know?" Another huff of exasperation. "But she was okay with telling you all this other stuff? That she was blackmailing someone to keep her quiet about a family member they had stashed in a mental hospital. Someone who didn't belong there is what I'm getting from all this."

Connor stiffened, rolling back his shoulders. "I'm tellin' you what I know 'cause Maria is gone. She's gone and there's something wrong. There's reason for me to be worried."

"I'd say so if she was blackmailing someone. And you have no idea who? You said it was someone important."

"Yeah, she said it was someone important, but never said who."

"There's nothing she ever said that might provide some clue about who it is? Did she say where they met? How many times she talked to them? Did she ever get anything from these people?"

"I've told you all I know. Look..." Connor paused and slumped, his shoulders going soft. "I never woulda bothered you." He looked up. "I wasn't gonna call you. I was gonna stay outta your life. I made a mess and...well, it wasn't right. But" – he blinked rapidly sending tears streaming down his cheeks – "she was my angel." He wiped his cheeks. "That don't sound right. It sounds stupid. She was a good person, and I cared about her. I couldn't let this go. That's all. I had to do somethin' and you're a sheriff, so..."

"Yeah, okay." Ryan stared at his hands which he had folded and rested in his lap. "You asked what happened with going to college."

Connor sniffed and reached for a box of tissues resting on the edge of the desk. "What?"

The surprise in Connor's voice brought home to Ryan how abruptly he had changed the conversation. He did not know where this left turn came from. He had to level the emotional playing field. "You asked about the whole track and football thing and what happened."

"You don't hafta say nothin'."

"No, it's okay. One morning I woke up and the anger was gone." Ryan waved his hand. "Just like that. Gone. I ran mad. I played ball mad. Hell, I lived mad. When it was gone I wanted a new life. A different reason for going on." He took a deep breath. "I'm not mad anymore, Connor."

"You didn't look real happy to see me. You *looked* mad."

Ryan smiled. "I wasn't happy. It dragged up some of that anger, but I moved past it and I have to stay past it." He took a deep breath and sat up straight. "Okay. This thing with Maria."

Maybelle announced herself with a knock on the door. "You boys 'bout done?" she asked, leaning her head and shoulders through the doorway. "The after-work trade is comin' in and I need my bartender."

Ryan asked, "Can you give us a few more minutes?"

The woman nodded and shut the door.

"There's something I have to tell you about Maria."

Friday-April 27

"I'm Chairman of the Public Safety Committee," Senator Whalen Jones screamed. "Of course, I'd find out. We're the oversight committee for the SBI and have an influence on their budget. Slade has been hounding me for more funding. This" – he picked up a file from his desk – "is red meat for him. It came hand-delivered to show exactly how hard they're working and why they need more money."

Raymond Lee shot forward in his chair catching the file pushed across the desk toward him by Jones.

"I can't believe we're having this conversation," Jones said, his face contorted in anger. "I said take care of it, not..." He slammed his fist down on the arm of his chair.

Lee gently placed the file on the desk.

Jones pushed out of his chair and began pacing around his office stopping to gaze into the aquarium that filled the west wall. On his return to the back of his desk, he ran his hand along the bottom of the fringed silk American flag standing to one side of the bookcase behind his chair. He stopped as if considering sitting down before starting his second lap around the office.

"Okay," Jones said, sitting heavily on a couch along the far wall facing the entrance to the office. "Tell me exactly what we're dealing with."

"Not a good idea," Lee responded with a shake of his head. "The reason I didn't say anything is the less you know the better."

Jones spit out a sardonic laugh. "I *know* everything." He pointed at his desk. "I have that goddamn file with the gory details. Jesus, man, it never occurred to you this would make its way to me? That I'd be put on the spot?" He cradled his head in his hands.

Lee opened his mouth to respond and Jones stopped him. "A rhetorical question. Slade included a note asking if I wanted to maintain radio silence." Again, pointing toward the desk. "On all of it."

Lee spread his arms in front of him and turned to his left to face Jones. "Then it worked out fine. He's talking like they're related. Exactly what I planned. Tell him it looks like the guy is back and you think the SBI should pursue this one as part of that investigation."

"Presumptuous, don't you think? Injecting myself into this? I'm not a cop."

"You're giving him a nudge in the direction he already wants to go."

Jones shook his head. "No, he's not necessarily going down that road. A note in the file says his people have doubts about it being related. He's suggesting, I think, that that one" – another nod toward his desk – "should be investigated separately from the others. Another way to show how diligent and busy they are. More work. More man hours. More money."

"Wait," Lee said, leaning forward in his chair. "Doubts? Like what?"

"Like…" Jones slingshot off the couch, walked briskly across the office, sat down, opened the file, and scanned the contents. "Like here. 'The victim wasn't sodomized. She wasn't bound to the bed. This does not match the results found at the other scenes.'" He looked at Lee and slammed the file closed with the flat of his hand. "And a lot of other details his investigator pointed out."

"But apparently not so different that Slade is *completely* discounting a relationship or he wouldn't be mentioning the…uh… Wouldn't be asking about the radio silence thing."

Jones stood up and returned to his path around the room. "What the fuck were you thinking?"

Lee hesitated before responding. "Taking care of things like I was ordered."

Jones stopped in front of the office door, stared intently at Lee, and with effort, said evenly, "No, no, don't do that. Nothing was said, or even hinted at along those" – he pointed toward the file on his desk – "lines. It wasn't even a fleeting thought."

Mimicking Jones's deliberateness, Lee replied, "I dealt with her patiently and politely. She started out making demands to keep her quiet about something she knew. *Something.* We didn't even know at first what it was. She kept threatening to take this *something* to the press. To ruin you."

"Well," Jones said, "I suspected then it had to do with Marco. I didn't think it *was* Marco."

"It took a hundred thousand dollars to find out. It took another two hundred thousand to keep her quiet until we could come to some final understanding. Before we could do that, she came back at us for another five hundred thousand dollars. You were a spigot she kept turning on."

"But that didn't mean..."

"Then," Lee said with a burst, "when I said 'no,' she went ape shit. I mean *ape-fucking-shit*. She kept demanding the money. Screaming like a banshee. Hit me when I tried to calm her down. Said she was going to call the cops and say I was trying to rape her. It was a shit show." Lee raised his hands. "I didn't mean for it to go the way it did, but once it happened, I made a decision, and I still think it makes sense. It was a split-second thing."

"Enough," Jones said emphatically. "About the money we gave her. Where did it come from?"

"WindServ is already in for the three hundred thousand dollars. How many more trips could I take to that well? Another reason to end this."

"What did you tell Nancy? About why we needed the money?"

"I didn't say anything. And she's way too savvy to ask. She said she considered it a donation to your political PAC. Bottom line, we couldn't keep going back, and Luna wasn't going to stop. So..." Lee let the balance of his thought float away.

"What'd she know? I mean other than Marco was at Ottinger? We never talked about that."

"And you think it's a good idea to get into it now? You still have some plausible deniability."

"Oh, for Christ's sake. I know a woman is dead. I know you were talking to her. Tell me what else she knew."

"That was it. She knew it was Marco at Ottinger."

"You're sure? Nothing else?"

"She figured out he wasn't there voluntarily."

"Figured it out? How the hell did she figure that out?"

"From what she told me, she looked at his chart and saw he was there under an assumed name. Not the name she knew him by. She also noticed Marco was shadowed everywhere he went by what she called 'a bodyguard.' She put the pieces together."

"If she could find all that out, who's to say someone else couldn't do the same?"

"No," Lee said adamantly, "the coincidence of her being assigned to do whatever she did in the building where he was, and them having gone to high school together, are not likely to be repeated."

"Not likely?"

"Won't happen. I'll tell Cranston before anyone new is hired for that wing, we want to know who it is. I want to vet them."

"We should've thought of those details before this happened." Jones ran his hands through his hair and dropped his arms to his side. "You're certain she didn't know anything else? Why he was there?"

"If she had an inkling of anything else, especially why he was there, she would've been asking for a hell of a lot more than she did."

"She could've told other people. Family. Husband. Boyfriend."

"If she did, we'd have heard about it. Either from the cops or whoever she told. The silence, for us, is golden."

Jones walked to the middle of the room and stood on the ornate Turkish rug running under his desk and covered most of the dark wood flooring. He put his hands on his hips and stared ahead, his brow furrowed. "You're comfortable, then, no one else knows about Marco?"

"No, no one at Ottinger. Not the cops or any of her people. What about your family? Does anyone ever ask about him? Want to know where he is?"

"He's been an embarrassment for so long that no one wants to put me on the spot by asking. Voyeurism; exposing himself; he even burned down a house as a kid. Then this...uh..." Jones struggled to find the words. "I can't even let myself go there. I don't know how to process it."

"Beyond family. What about friends? People who knew him, or about him? Anyone ever ask how he's doing? Where he's been? Anything like that?"

"Look, there are people who know about Marco. They know I have a 'strange' brother. They don't know any more than that. No one has ever said anything to me about him. There's never been anything raised during my campaigns, even when things went negative. There's some honor among thieves." Jones chortled. "Not so much honor as an understanding that no one opens Pandora's box."

"There is a loose end."

Jones narrowed his eyes in question. "A loose end?"

"The families of those women. How long do you think they'll stay quiet?"

"It's not like they know, or even suspect it's Marco. That would be a 'loose end.'"

"So, they'll stay quiet? Won't get frustrated and push this into the open?"

"They don't want to expose their dirty laundry. The press would have a field day." Jones raised his arms, palms up. "The priorities for them are different than for most people. They've spent a lifetime and a fortune keeping the family secrets in the closet. And the noise would hit their pocketbooks in a big way. Sounds harsh but there are different considerations at play here. Closure would be good, but not if it means the dog and pony show that usually goes along with these things."

"Okay, then we have to push for a continued blackout and hope it goes cold. Tell Slade to keep it quiet."

"Christ, this whole thing is a real shit show."

"Every cloud has a silver lining."

"A silver lining?" Jones said peevishly. "You found a silver lining?"

"Marco has the perfect alibi for Luna. He's locked away. A good lawyer could massage that to create doubt about the others."

"We're talking lawyers now?"

"I'm just saying if it ever got that far...what I did works for us on a number of levels."

Jones pursed his lips. "I still have to deal with Slade's questions. I'm convinced he's looking to work them as separate cases. Like I said, he's setting the stage for his next budget request."

"I can't speak to the politics of this, but I can tell you as a former cop they want to confirm it's the same person. It makes their lives easier. They don't want to add any complications. And right now they got nothing. Zip. Zero. Nada. If we bide our time it will go cold."

"Well, I don't know much about being a cop, but I know a play for funding when I see it. How do I respond to what he's given me here?" Jones said, jabbing a finger at the file.

"Hell, you hold the purse strings. He's a bureaucrat. He'll go whichever way you blow the wind at him."

"This whole thing was going away," Jones said angrily, "until you stoked it. I hadn't heard a word about it from anyone for months." He waved the file at Lee. "Now this."

"I see the bigger picture," Lee responded evenly.

"That picture better not include me."

Monday-April 30

It was after ten p.m. The budding skyline twinkled.

Declan parked on the upper floor of the garage. As he got out, he pointed Connor toward a bank of elevators. Their footsteps echoed in the empty space.

"Thanks for agreeing to this," Declan said as they approached double glass doors.

"After what you tol' me 'bout Maria..." Connor coughed his constricting throat clear.

"After that, well, I gotta do what I gotta do."

"You're going to be a big help."

"I can't believe I'm back here," Connor said, a nervous tremor in his voice. "Sure don't look nothin' like it did."

"You have Amazon to thank for that. Coupla hundred jobs in a hundred thousand square foot warehouse. A lot more jobs with independent truck delivery companies. Even the post office has opened a regional center here to compete with Amazon. Last I heard that was fifty more jobs. Got a Walmart. Lots of smaller businesses cropped up. Some a real pain in my ass. Package stores. Strip joints. Incredible a single industry can have that effect."

"I didn't know what Amazon was 'til I got out. I mean I heard 'bout what it was but didn't *know* know. Heard some stuff when I watched TV, and just learned how to work a computer a few years before I left the Mac. Kinda leaves you in the dust on what's goin' on, but I didn't care since I never expected to be out."

Declan opened the door leading to a bank of elevators. Connor stopped, turned toward the view from the top floor of the parking lot, and took in the expanse. "This is where the town hall used to be. Right? The square is still there. I thought I recognized that when we drove into the garage. Just put it all together lookin' out over it all."

Ryan nodded. "Tore down the town hall and built this after Owen became the county seat." He guided Connor toward the elevator. "Federal offices are here also."

A dark cherry wood door faced them when the elevator doors slid open. Connor hesitated a beat before stepping toward the doors. He waited for Ryan to move past, following him into a large reception area that was still and quiet except for the sound of the air exchange humming softly.

They walked toward an empty reception cubicle. Couches fronted by coffee tables were arranged on both sides of the room. Mirror images. The settings included two large paintings on backing walls that caught Connor's attention. He approached one and read the plaque on the wall to the right of the painting: *The Fighting* Temeraire *by the English artist Joseph Mallord William Turner, painted in 1838 and exhibited at the Royal Academy in 1839. This painting depicts the 98-gun* HMS Temeraire, *one of the last ships of the line to have played a role in the Battle of Trafalgar.* Connor backed away from the canvas. "That's really good."

A door opened to the left of the receptionist cubicle and Berger greeted them with "Thanks for coming." He stepped aside and motioned them into a conference room. A window filled the wall opposite the entrance where the night lights of Owen showed ribbons of streets snaking from the burgeoning business area into spreading suburbs.

"Thanks for agreeing to see us after hours," Declan said and turned toward Connor. "My brother."

Berger reached out his hand. "I appreciate your coming in to talk to me, Mr. Ryan."

"Mr. Ryan," Connor said with a laugh. "I ain't been called that in, hell, I can't ever remember being called that, and definitely not by a cop." He stared hard at Berger. "Declan tol' me you was one of the cops who took me to the Mac."

"I was."

"Sorry, don't remember a lot 'bout that. I was scared and jus' tryin' not to shit my pants."

"It was my first time transporting someone to prison." Berger took a step back. "I'd never have recognized you. The person I remember was about half your size."

Connor smiled. "Like I tol' Declan. Bulkin' up was about survival."

"This is definitely a small world," Ryan offered, looking from Berger to his brother.

"And it gets smaller every day," Berger said. "We're all in almost the same spot our paths first crossed twenty-five years ago."

"Just as soon forget 'bout that day and those twenty-five years," Connor said. "A lot of other stuff, too."

Berger pointed to the highly polished oblong conference table that filled the room. "Coffee? Water? Something else?"

"Coffee would be good," Ryan said and looked at Connor. "You?"

"Yeah, coffee."

Berger walked to a credenza on one side of the room and slid open a panel, removed three mugs, and placed them next to a silver urn. "Black?"

"Black is good," Ryan replied.

Connor nodded. "Black."

"Good," Berger said. "I don't know where the cream and sugar are kept." He reached across the table and placed the mugs in front of Ryan and Connor.

"I'm sorry about Maria," Berger said and sat down.

Connor wrapped his hands around the mug. "Me, too."

"He told me about your thinking she was caught up in something that might have gotten her killed." Berger waited for Connor's nod of agreement before adding, "Did he also tell you about what I'm working on? The serial murders?"

"Yeah."

"There are similarities between how Maria and the other victims were murdered, but there are differences. Significant ones."

"There's more," Ryan said. "Connor's got another twist."

Connor looked from his brother to Berger. "We got the Eyeball Killer at the Mac. You know that?"

Berger nodded. "Yes, George Layton."

"He killed three people, right?" Connor asked.

"That we could prove," Berger responded. "We think he killed at least eight others. We could only develop enough evidence to convict him on three counts."

"He took their eyes like this guy you're after."

Berger let a beat pass before answering, "Not exactly. The offender we're looking for takes one eye. Layton shot his victims. Our guy kills them by..."

Connor held up his hand. "I know."

Berger glanced at Ryan and then settled back on Connor. "I'm not sure where this is going. Layton's in prison. Has been there for ten years."

Connor nodded. "Yeah, and I remember when he came in. It was a big deal. He got a lot of attention. TV people there all the time doing interviews. Writers who was writin' books 'bout him and what he did. Some actor even came to talk to him 'cause they was doing a movie and he was goin' to be George and wanted to talk to him 'bout everything."

"Okay?" Berger said.

"You know George gets letters from people askin' questions how he did it, why, and all that stuff?"

Berger nodded. "Most of these offenders have admirers and people who are curious about them. Most have pen pals. Serial killer John Gacy sold paintings to people. For a lot of money. Sickos."

"After each of the ones Declan told me you was investigatin' I remember George got a letter from a guy who said he did it. Tol' him what he did. How he did it. That stuff. Like he was lookin' for a grade on a school paper or somethin'."

Berger pulled himself closer to the table. "How do you know that? How did the letters get past the prison censors?"

"Don't know about how they got to him, but I know they did 'cause I was his cellie for a few years and he bragged 'bout it. To me and anyone who would listen. He loved the attention and loved to talk 'bout what he did. Guys usually got their asses kicked for killing young girls but people was 'fraid of him. So, he talked and talked and talked. I listened. It passed the time. The important thing is he didn't get any letter after Maria was killed. That should clear up some stuff, right?"

Berger looked at Ryan and back at Connor. "I'm not getting this. How do you know he didn't get a letter? Maria was killed...what, a week ago? How long have you been out?"

Connor waved off the question. "I went to see George and he told me he didn't get a letter."

Berger placed his elbows on the table, clasped his hands, and looked at Ryan. "Going to see Layton. Your suggestion?"

Ryan shook his head.

Connor interpreted the look of skepticism on Berger's face. "I did it because I was...*am* mad. After Declan tol' me 'bout Maria, I wanted to do somethin'. I remembered the letters he got and went to see him. To see if he got a letter. To see what it said. There's no letter this time. That means what she said 'bout her knowing somethin' 'bout the person bein' kept in that clinic, or whatever it is, could be right. It could have something to do with what happened to her. But she ain't part of what happened to the others." Connor looked at Declan. "Right?"

"What person?" Berger asked. "What clinic?" Berger let out a "Jesus," after Ryan filled in the details. He spent a moment absorbing what he had heard before offering, "That adds all kinds of possibilities, and confusion, to this."

"And it looks like we're chasing a copycat," Ryan said.

"A copycat who knows things no one else does," Berger said. "Before we settle on any of this, we need to talk to Layton. What do you think, Connor, will he talk to us?"

"He likes attention so I'm guessin' he will."

"Would you go with us? He might be more comfortable if you're there."

Connor sighed deeply. "I swore I'd never come back to Owen, and here I am. I said the same about the Mac, and I been back once. If you think we can get more from him, sure, I'll go."

***

"Governor," Whalen Jones said as he stepped into the office and offered his hand to Lincoln Stephens.

Stephens made a show of looking around the room and then spread his arms wide. "I don't see anyone else here, do you?"

"Okay, okay, Lincoln. I was trying to be respectful."

"Only need the 'governor' thing when we're being formal," Stephens said as he walked to a setting of armchairs circling a small round table on which sat a silver tray with two cups. "Willa, I asked specifically for cream, not milk or half-and-half," he said loudly enough to summon a tall, stout woman who rushed in, scooped a creamer off the tray, and disappeared.

The men sat on opposite sides of the table and each had poured himself a cup of coffee when the woman reappeared, placed the creamer on the tray, and was gone.

Stephens took a sip and stared at Jones across the top of his cup. "So, we have a meeting with Nancy? Saw it on my schedule. Imagine my surprise. The reason I didn't cancel was I saw that you had arranged this happy little occasion."

"I appreciate your agreeing to meet with her."

Stephens lowered his cup slowly, his face unhappy. "You obviously missed my meaning. I didn't agree so much as feel obligated. What's going on?"

"Nancy has an 'ask,' but there is an easy fix."

"*Fix*?" Stephens said and placed his cup on the saucer. "I don't know what *the ask* is and you're telling me we need a fix? I knew I should've cancelled this."

"Bad choice of words." Jones poured cream into his cup and added a teaspoon of sugar. "We can take care of this easily and make her happy."

"*We*?" Stephens said. "*We're* going to offer this fix? Why do *we* need to make her happy?"

Jones raised his hand. "*Me*, I'll take care of it, but the optics of you being involved carries weight."

"Optics," Stephens said, smirking. "Okay, I got it. We're talking about those leases WindServ is going after in Washington."

Jones nodded. "WindServ wants our blessing...well, more like needs our blessing before going to BLM. WindServ wants to be able to say it has the okay from the governor and the leader in the senate. If we aren't okay with it, BLM will never approve the request."

Stephens lifted and then held the cup suspended in front of his mouth. "I know all this, Whalen. Why exactly are we here? We could've signed off on this in a phone call or via email, or something. A meeting? What the hell? Why call attention to this? We could've taken care of it without the formality. Without the optics, which we sure as shit don't need."

A knock on the office door came with a voice announcing, "Mrs. Wilcox is here, Governor."

Stephens put his cup on the tray, gave Jones a look of disgust, and stood. "Send her in, please."

Jones pushed himself up and turned toward the door. A tall painfully thin woman marched in extending her hand stiffly toward Stephens. A silk Hermes scarf draped loosely across the shoulders of a dark pant suit jacket accentuated her long, thin neck and added a dash of color to a dull palate made duller by her pale, makeup-free face. She carried a black portfolio. "Thank you for seeing me, Governor."

"My pleasure, Mrs. Wilcox."

A sliver of a smile pulled at the corners of her barely-there lips. "Nancy, please."

Stephens lowered his head toward Jones. "You know Senator Jones, of course."

"Yes," she replied, turning her attention away from Stephens. "Good to see you, Senator."

Stephens gestured to a chair and he and Jones waited until Wilcox sat before seating themselves.

"Coffee, if you'd like," Stephens said.

"No, thank you. I know your time" – she smiled at both men – "is limited. I'll get right to it. Next week, WindServ is going to submit an application to lease federal lands from the Bureau of Land Management in the south-central part of the state." She pointed at the tray. "Do you mind if I move this?"

Jones moved toward the tray but was waved off by Stephens who called for "Willa." The large woman appeared at the door. Stephens nodded at the coffee service. "You can take this."

With the table cleared, Wilcox pulled a large sheet from the portfolio and laid it on the table. She traced her bony fingers across a map landing at an area encircled in red marker. "Here. We are going to request these leases from BLM."

Stephens nodded. "I don't see a problem. Do you, Whalen?"

"Nope."

"Good to know," Wilcox said as she slid the map back into the portfolio. "But what I want to know is will you actively support our bid?"

"As I just said, I don't have a problem with your request and I won't oppose it," Stephens responded. "Where does the Congressional delegation stand on it?"

"We're split in the senate. Clifford for. Evans, the esteemed 'Senator from Oil,' is, of course, opposed. The one from the House who matters is Mooney whose district is where the leases are located. She's not saying."

Stephens shifted to the edge of his chair. "So, you need us to line up with Clifford, which would tilt the scales and likely get Mooney onboard? Then you'd signal the consequential political weight is with you? That about it?"

"You ran on a platform supporting green energy solutions," Wilcox said. "You can't get any greener than wind energy, Governor. We already generate thirty-five percent of the state's electricity. That reduces emissions and water consumption by fossil-fuel power plants by…"

Stephens held up his hand. "No need to go into the song-and-dance on the green thing, Nancy."

"So, let me do the song-and-dance on the business side of this proposal," Wilcox said. Before Stephens could object, she was launched. "Wind energy has made fifteen billion dollars in capital investments in the state. We have created more than six thousand jobs and pay 107 million dollars in state and local taxes. That's a lot of green. And speaking of green." She turned her attention toward Jones. "We've recently contributed generously to your PAC."

Stephens threw back his head and laughed freely. "Okay, I have a much better picture of what's going on here. Right to the heart of it, Nancy. Good for you."

Jones smiled at Wilcox. "You have and we'll continue to see that those funds get to candidates who recognize the value of meeting the energy needs of our state in environmentally sound ways."

"Shit, Whalen," Stephens said. "Nancy doesn't beat around the bush and that's the best you can do? Platitudes. She's looking for a commitment."

Wilcox said, "The senator and I understand each other, but I would appreciate a full expression of support from you both."

Stephens shot forward in his chair. "Here's the bottom line, Nancy. You go ahead and request those leases from BLM. We have no reason to oppose them. We're going to get pressure from Novins and the others on this. From what I can tell, they have an interest in leasing those same lands for oil exploration. We haven't heard anything from them yet, but I'm guessing we will the second after you've made your request formal. Whalen and I will figure out a way to handle them."

Wilcox stood and brushed her hands across her lap smoothing wrinkles from the cloth. She picked up her portfolio. "Thank you for meeting with me. Frankly, I would have preferred to leave with a much stronger expression of support, but I understand the pressure you're under."

"And we appreciate that you appreciate," Stephens said as he walked Wilcox to the door. He started to open the door and stopped. "Privately, let me say that I plan to stand by my pledge to seek green solutions for the state's energy needs."

"Thank you," Wilcox said, a broad smile showing small, white teeth.

Stephens opened the door and ushered Wilcox into the reception area. "Have a good day."

Stephens returned briskly to his office and stood over Jones. "How much did you take from WindServ?"

"Not a lot."

"How much?"

"A few hundred thousand."

"What did you do with it?"

"What are you asking, Lincoln?"

Stephens' face reddened. "What did you do with it?"

"Exactly what I said. We're going to support our candidates."

Stephens loomed over Jones a moment before retreating to his chair and sitting down heavily. "Do you have any idea how thin a line I have to walk on this thing?" He leaned forward resting his arms on the edge of the table. "Wind energy? Are you fucking kidding me?" He raised his hands. "Check that. It's important. We have to look ahead. Clean energy and all, but comparing what we get in terms of jobs, revenues, taxes, and all that other shit from oil and gas to the returns from wind? There is no comparison." He pointed in the direction of the door. "Six thousand jobs," he said, his voice straining. "She made a big damn deal about six thousand jobs. Our friends in the oil fields provide around fifty thousand. Add another hundred thousand employed in related jobs. And two billion in taxes when you include state and local."

"I know, I know," Jones said.

"I've managed, very skillfully," Stephens continued intensely, "to paint myself as a friend of the environment while keeping the oil guys from jumping down my throat. You know how I've done that?"

Jones remained silent, understanding Stephens was not looking for an answer.

"First of all it helps that I come from a background in the industry, what with my family producing drill pipes and mud pumps. That gives me a little armor. But lately more by working wind and solar into the conversation without overwhelming anyone with this stuff. The line is thin given we have nutcases in the party talking about sidelining fossil fuels altogether by taxing and regulating them out of existence. And with the reality of climate change beating the hell out of us..." Stephens shook his head and took a deep breath. "It's exhausting. I get ambushed by this scarecrow because you want to get people elected who will support you when you run for governor?"

Jones raised his hand to make a point.

"Oh, fuck you, Whalen, I know you've talked to some people. The same people who talk to me. I also assume you're planning on waiting until I'm outta here, but let's start dealing straight up with each other." Stephens smiled. "And that'll teach you to think you can have private conversations in our business."

"Of course, I'd never challenge you if you decide to run again. I'm not into suicide missions, and, besides, I sure as hell wouldn't challenge someone in my own party."

"Good to know because ambition can cause people to lie to themselves. But you're safe to move ahead. I'm going to announce for Evans's senate seat."

"Speaking of confidential, that's not exactly a secret, and knowing that is the reason I've said anything about running for governor."

"The timing fell into place. Novins and the others have had their fill of Evans. 'The Senator from Oil' has seen his final days. He's embarrassing them. He's had his head so far up their asses for so long, it's getting uncomfortable for them."

"There's an image I won't be able to forget. Does Evans know anything?"

"He barely knows what day it is. Deadly mix of onset dementia and being drunk most of the time. Even that wouldn't be a disqualifier if he was making a minimal effort to do the job everyone wanted. If he showed any competence at all. He doesn't even bother to make a case for his votes anymore. Never counters in committee or on the floor when he should be bringing some balance to the scales. On those rare occasions when he does stand up he sounds like a blowhard. No subtlety. No factual information. Just noise."

Stephens shook his head in frustration. "Nancy mentioned Mooney was on the fence about WindServ's request for the leases in her district. Do you know why she's straddling that fence?"

"She's between a rock and a hard place. WindServ would bring jobs into the district but piss off the big dog on the block."

Stephens nodded. "That's the politics. On the ground floor, let's call it, her people are beginning to complain about the noise from the turbines. They welcomed those giant windmills at first. They brought a few jobs and there was the self-righteous satisfaction of being part of the clean energy thing. Reality is sinking in. The noise. Headaches. Vibrations are shaking the land and dropping land values, and people aren't happy. Evans could have used that during the recent hoopla over the Green New Deal. He just had to point out that these issues should be considered. He didn't bother."

Stephens spit out a sardonic laugh. "No one takes him seriously. He's a vote for whatever they want but doesn't carry anyone with him. In fact, people are starting to run in the other direction. They don't want to be associated with 'The Senator from Oil.' Plus, he's an expensive vote. Wants the treatment. Special considerations. Stupid shit like Super Bowl tickets. Invitations to speak at conferences sponsored by the industry. And he expects an honorarium. He's a pain in the ass."

"I take it you have the go-ahead from everyone to challenge him."

"Shit, they came to me."

"When are you going to announce?"

"Not sure." Stephens got up and walked to the office door, which he opened. "Can we get some sandwiches in here, Willa?" He went to his desk and shuffled through a stack of papers, pulled one from the pile and scanned it as he walked slowly back toward Jones. "And there's this. Hendricks wants me to consider chairing the Democratic Governors Association." He handed the letter to Jones. "He followed up with a call yesterday."

"Senator Hendricks?"

"Yeah, that Hendricks. Out of the blue he volunteered to nominate me." Stephens leaned toward Jones. "I never said a word to anyone about wanting the chairmanship. In fact, I don't, but if Hendricks asks, you don't say no."

A knock on the door preceded the entrance of a cart pushed by a man in butler livery.

"That was quick," Jones said eyeing a platter with an assortment of cold cuts, cheeses, lettuce, slices of onion and tomato, small cups with a variety of dressings, and a choice of beverages.

Stephens nodded as the delivery was completed. "Thanks, Bill." As the man left and closed the door behind him, he said, "They know what I like and have it ready to go. I'm going to miss this." He filled his plate and lifted a bottle of water from an ice bucket. "Although I've eaten in the senate dining room and it ain't half bad."

"I'll have you back for lunch," Jones said playfully. "Chairmanship of the Governors Association and Hendricks on your doorstep? Not bad. What I'd call a head start on the road to D.C."

"I don't want to think too far ahead, but Hendricks is suddenly my friend and I don't even know the guy."

"That's one hell of a guy to have in your corner. Majority Leader in the senate. Means he's confident you're going to be joining him and he wants your vote so he can remain Leader."

"Which gets me back to this pile of shit you've gotten me into."

Jones cocked his head. "How have I gotten you into a pile of shit? We smiled at Wilcox, made nice with her, and made a minimal commitment. That should be good for a few bucks."

"You're running for an open office and I'm challenging an incumbent. A coupla hundred thousand from Wilcox and friends isn't going to do the trick. We can't be seen as compromised. We can be magnanimous and make some gestures but a full leap across the divide isn't in the cards."

"A few hundred thousand doesn't mean I've jumped the divide," Jones countered. "But the reality is we're an anachronism. We're paddling against a green tide. No pun intended. We need to show some flexibility."

"I know that for Christ's sake. Like I said, I've managed to keep an even hand in this. I've accepted the fact that if we want to go somewhere beyond" – he spread his arms – "this statehouse, we'd better make like we care about the alternatives. Wind, sun, and whatever else they're talking about. Hydroelectric power. Biofuels. The money and influence aren't on their side yet, but it's coming. And a measured nod in their direction makes good sense."

"So" – Jones wiped a splotch of mayonnaise off his chin – "maybe, I haven't gotten us into a pile of shit after all."

"I said measured. Three hundred thousand is on the edge of 'all in.'" Stephens shifted his weight and dipped his shoulder toward Jones. "You could take your lead from Novins."

"Novins?" Jones said, pulling his head back in surprise. "I should take my lead from the biggest oil and gas company in the Southwest? Seriously?"

"Watch those commercials on television carefully. Novins and the others have that 'we care about the earth' stuff shoehorned into their messaging. They can point to it as their responsible stewardship of the environment while they continue to do what they do. Subtle. Receptive. Balanced. That's the approach I'm suggesting."

"Speaking of which, you know Novins is going to oppose WindServ's request. Strenuously."

"I'm sure they will, and here's where we can be more receptive to Nancy and friends, while remaining balanced. Doing just enough to stay within the prescribed limits so we don't piss off Novins, while giving a slight nod to the other side."

"*More* receptive? Beyond not opposing the lease request?"

"Here's where subtlety comes into play. We don't have to make any public displays. Novins is going to oppose the leases on cost-benefit grounds. Their case is that the amount of energy generated is not worth taking land out of circulation for other purposes, meaning for their purposes."

"And?"

"And you're the leader in the senate. Get your caucus to support WindServ and that gives us the cover we need without leading the charge. We wouldn't have to say a thing."

"That's nuts." Jones said animatedly. "I'm going to ask my caucus to walk the plank for WindServ? You made a case for subtlety. That's not subtle."

"Be creative. You don't have to lock arms with them or anything. Or even mention WindServ. Pass a senate resolution recognizing the majesty of the Wichita Mountains Wildlife Refuge, or some such shit. Hell, include some wildlife management areas in the resolution. Throw in the importance of protecting the indigenous wildlife, or whatever; that kind of thing, with an added sentence or two about how we need to support efforts to keep these places pristine."

"And that accomplishes what?"

"That lets me, and you, and anyone else with the sense God gave them, support the resolution and bank the vote as support for environmental stewardship. That's a subtle plug for WindServ. We make sure WindServ knows ahead of time we're going to be waving this flag and suggest they use it as validation for their petition in Washington."

"Might work."

"You make it work. Use some of that money WindServ has rained down on you and round up those votes. Promise your caucus campaign cash if they do the right thing."

Jones and Stephens sat in silence considering the dessert plate. Chocolate chip cookies. Brownies. Small cups of yogurt. "And I want Noreen on board," Stephens announced as he picked up a cookie.

Jones shot forward so quickly he almost pushed over the food cart. "Noreen *West*?" he said steadying the cart.

"The one and only. The House Speaker."

"I'm going to have to work serious magic to get our people on board and you want me to cross the aisle and bring her along, too?"

"I have full confidence in your abilities to persuade, but if she balks, ask her about Ralph's contracts with fleet management."

"Her husband?"

"Yeah, *that* Ralph," Stephens said with a tinge of a smile. "I'll send over some information for you to arm yourself, but he's been making a healthy living from no-bid contracts, which aren't supposed to be no-bids."

"That's a helluva chip to play."

"A chip that could not only help us get where we want to go, but it adds legitimacy to efforts. Makes them bipartisan. Also, spreads the responsibility. So, yeah, I think it's worth playing.

"I'll make it a voice vote so no one has to go on record, but if asked, we have the names that count."

"I'm assuming you want this resolution or whatever we're going to call it to be a 'Sense of the Legislature' kinda deal. What about the minority side of the senate? I'm going to have a hard enough time with my own people."

"You take care of yours, I'll deal with the rest. I'll twist some arms; offer some goodies; use some chits I've stored."

Tuesday-May 1

Ryan and Berger sat on one side of a battleship-gray steel table bolted to the bare concrete floor facing a single chair. Connor sat to their left at the head of the table.

The men remained still in the windowless room. The only sound being a hum from the HVAC unit stirring the stale air.

The room color matched the table and chairs. A single light hung low over the table; the shade a thin aluminum cap with the bulb protected by a mesh cover. The walls were scarred with scratches and gouges, a disturbing reminder that some conversations in this room did not go well.

Shouting could be heard through the thick steel door. Obscenities strung together without any coherence.

"Loud," Connor said. "Always like this. Twenty-four, seven. It took me a long time to get used to the quiet when I got out. Even when Maybelle's is full the noise don't match that," he said with a nod toward the door. "I still can't sleep unless the TV is on."

Berger slid manila folders in front of Ryan and Connor. "We have a few minutes before they bring him in. I've put together some information that should give you a sense of the man."

Connor opened the file. "I don't need a sense of him. I spent three..." He looked up from the pages in front of him and stared at the wall. "No, more like four years. Spent four years in a cell with him. He never shuts up. Caused me to learn how not to listen. To close my ears. And all he talks 'bout is himself. Taught me to be sure I had something worthwhile to say before I opened my mouth. Talked about awful shit. Made me think I wasn't such a bad person. 'Course that was like comparing bad apples to worse ones."

"You know him pretty well, then," Berger said. "You know what he likes, what he doesn't like, what keeps him talking?"

"Anything keeps him talking. Just show signs of life and he'll talk. There's not much that'll make him shut up."

"Meaning there are some things that will?"

Connor nodded. "If you act like you don't believe him or laugh or something."

"I wish we had had more time to prepare for this." Berger leaned toward Connor. "If there's anything I say that you think might cause him to shut down, cut in and say something you know he'll respond to. That'll keep him going."

Connor snorted a laugh. "You have a pulse, he'll talk. There is somethin' you should know I bet ain't in here." He put his hand flat on top of the file folder. "Sometimes when he gets goin' about those women he killed, he'd get real excited and jerk off."

"Shit," slipped from Ryan.

"There's not a lotta places you can go in a cell so I'd squeeze up against the wall in my bunk and put on my earphones."

"Do me a favor," Berger said insistently to Connor, "and read what I've put together on Layton. I've used what I found to frame what I'm going to talk to him about. If there's anything wrong, or anything else you think I should know about, tell me before I take a wrong step."

Connor took a moment before opening the file and removing the pages which he arranged in front of him.

Layton was described by friends and relatives as a happy-go-lucky person. He was talented. Could play the piano. Quote poetry by heart. A good artist. A good carpenter.

In high school Layton was a star on the football team, vice president of the senior class, and voted "Most Likely to Succeed." He was popular with the girls. But he did have a mischievous side. He broke into the rival high school and cut the head off their mascot, a wooden Indian like the kind found in front of tobacco stores, and left a note that read: "No one here uses their heads anyway." He stole a copy of the final test from the Algebra teacher's desk and made copies for everyone in class. He was caught when everyone made an A.

Over time his crimes escalated. He formed a burglary ring that broke into and stole from local department stores. Layton sold the property to pawn shops and used the money to buy beer and food for parties.

He was sent to a psychologist by the juvenile court and years later the judge still remembered Layton. He described him as being completely without a value system and a person who convinced himself that the lies he was repeating were the truth.

He was kicked out of college his junior year after he snuck into the records office and forged transcripts and diplomas for a number of his friends. He awarded himself a master's degree in biology and another in psychology. He later used the false documents to get a job teaching and counseling in a high school. After he was caught, the high school and college agreed not to prosecute because of the embarrassment that would be caused if it became known he had fooled both institutions.

After college, Layton inherited money from his parents allowing him to work odd jobs, including as a plumber, an electrician, a window installer, and car mechanic. He even worked in a beauty salon cutting and coloring hair calling himself Mr. George. He had no training in any of these fields and he was successful in each one only leaving when he "got bored" (his words).

Layton visited red-light districts in Tulsa where the murders took place. He is known to have killed at least three prostitutes. He shot each of them in the chest and removed their eyes with surgical skill. According to the coroner's report: "The killer had to know how to slip a knife around the eyes, making sure not to injure the adjoining skin, and then cut the six major muscles holding each eye in the socket, as well as the rope-tough optical nerve."

There was no evidence of "unusual" sexual abuse on any of the bodies and the women he paid for sex described him as "a gentleman." They were shocked to learn he was the Eyeball Killer.

When asked why he killed the women and removed their eyes, Layton said he had a fascination for eyes that came from a course he took in taxidermy when he was a young boy. His mother enrolled him in the course. He would go into a wooded area near his house and kill birds and squirrels with his pellet gun, bring them home and clean them and stuff them. According to Layton, the best part was cutting around the eyes with a scalpel and using forceps to pull them out. He loved going to the taxidermy shop to check out the boxes full of iridescent fake eyes. He loved their gleam. But they were too expensive, so his mother gave him buttons to use for eyes. It frustrated him and he pointed at this frustration as the reason for taking the eyes. As to the killings, he said, "I liked to watch the light go out of their eyes."

"Okay," Connor said as he placed the pages into the file folder and pushed it toward Berger. "I didn't know a lot of that stuff. I just know what he told me."

"Which is?" Berger asked.

"That he killed whores 'cause his mother was one and he hated all of 'em. Said they didn't care 'bout nothin' but gettin' drugs and shouldn't be mothers."

"That adds a different perspective to this. Nothing I found about his mother indicated she was a prostitute or even promiscuous. In fact, what I found was the opposite. Very strict and religious."

"He liked killin'," Connor said. "Sometimes I think all that studying 'bout guys like Layton is a waste of time. They're evil and want to kill people. They like it so they do it. Not much more complicated than that."

"Did he ever say anything to you about the eyes?" Ryan asked. "Why he took them?"

"If you believe him," Connor answered, "'cause of the bad shit they'd seen. Like I said, he liked killin' and messin'em up. No other reason."

Berger said, "Here's what's going to happen. Declan and I are going to be talking to Layton, asking questions, and listening as cops. Taking it all in from our perspective." He tapped the table in front of Connor. "Like I said, if I start going in the wrong direction, you jump in. Also, I need you to listen and separate out the bullshit. Not right here in front of him. Don't challenge him. Just tell us later if you think any of it was bullshit. We" – he nodded at Declan – "don't know how it works inside here." He motioned around the room. "And I'm sure lying and holding things back and playing with words are part of the culture we can't see through. You can."

Connor registered a knowing look. "There's a way of doin' things in here. Culture sounds funny. It's more like coverin' yourself with armor or somethin' so no one can see inside. See any weakness. Buildin' up the bullshit is part of that. Layton was big on that, I think. He wanted to keep people scared of him, and he did. Makin' himself out to be a real scary guy was part of that."

The door to the room opened and two uniformed men stood to each side, and one behind, a large man whose ankles and wrists were bound by thick iron cuffs, connected by chains wrapping around the man's waist.

The man cocked his head and squinted at Connor. "What the hell? You don't visit for a year and now twice in a couple of weeks?"

George Layton shuffled to the open chair and sat heavily. His round, fleshy face and bright eyes were Sunday school benign. His hair was groomed and although overweight, Layton looked strong and healthy. He shared a beatific smile with Ryan and Berger and raised his cuffed wrists. "Not being rude but it's difficult to shake hands when they're bound."

The guards released the chains connecting the handcuffs to Layton's waist belt and secured them to an iron loop soldered to the tabletop. They carefully checked the leg irons, and before leaving, one of the guards asked Berger, Ryan, and Connor, "You all okay?" to which he received assenting nods.

"I'm Joe Berger, special agent with the Oklahoma State Bureau of Investigation. This is Sheriff Declan Ryan. You know Connor Ryan. We're here..."

"At least this won't be the same old shit," Layton interrupted and began a sing-songy delivery: "'Why did you kill those girls?' 'Why'd you cut out their eyes?' 'Why do you think you did it?' It's always the same." He stared hard at Connor. "This is about that letter I didn't get, right?"

"And more," Berger answered.

"Fire away" Layton said, a gentle, half-smile animated his lips.

"We know you've heard from someone who's been killing women and cutting out an eye."

"And you're telling me they're real? There is someone doing that?" Layton raised his chin in Connor's direction. "He came asking whether I got one recently, but I still didn't believe they were from someone doing any killing. I haven't read about anything like that or seen anything on the news. I figured a nutcase was getting off on writing to me about his fantasies. I truly thought they were fantasies because the letters weren't 'letters.' They are more like short stories. Love stories with bad endings. He starts out describing all about how they met, why he fell in love, and that kind of thing. Then, it would turn bad. The girl, or woman, I guess, wouldn't want to do certain things he liked. In bed, I'm talking about. And that would lead to him killing her."

"He described what he did in those letters?" Ryan asked, leaning in, and thinking better of his proximity to Layton, sat back slowly.

Layton answered, "He described what he did. Liked getting into the nitty gritty."

Berger asked, "How did these get past the prison censor? That kind of thing should have been separated out and never gotten to you."

"I wondered about that but I'm guessing since more than half of what he wrote was like the beginning of a romance novel, whoever was reading got bored, or wasn't a romantic, and stopped reading and let it go."

"Can I see them?"

"Didn't save 'em. Our cells are tossed every few weeks. Guards looking for porno, weapons, whatever, and they throw everything out onto the landing. Afterward I retrieved what I needed, and that didn't include the stories, letters, whatever you want to call 'em. Whatever we don't haul back into our cells is considered garbage and gets thrown out."

"And you got three of these?"

"Yes, but nothing about his friend," Layton said with a nod at Connor. "What'd you say her name was? Maria?"

"Maria," Connor agreed.

"You should be glad." Layton laughed boisterously. "Means she wasn't going out on you."

Making an effort not to react to the cruelty of the remark, and marveling at Connor's self-control, Berger asked, "That's one of the things we'd like to talk to you about. We're trying to get a read on what you think is going on. Any thoughts on whether it's possible the first three aren't related to the most recent one?"

"What? Not related because I didn't get a story about this last one?"

"There's more to it than that."

Layton smiled. "Like?"

"Like the details of the murders differ significantly."

"If you want anything from me," Layton said, his smile fading, "you're going to have to give me something."

"Such as?"

"Next time bring me photos of the crime scenes. The more details I have the better I can help you."

"We don't need any of that to get started," Berger objected.

"I do." Layton called out to the guards, "Ready to go."

In a reverse of the routine that bound him to the table, Layton's wrist chains were slid from the iron loop and locked around his waist. "Always good to see you, Connor," he called over his shoulder as he was led from the room.

Berger, Ryan, and Connor sat a moment before Connor broke the silence. "Those crime scene pictures. It's like porn for him."

As the trio started out of the room, Ryan put his hand on Connor's shoulder and stopped him a few feet behind Berger. "I had no idea," he said looking around at the surroundings. "This is hell."

"Supposed to be hell, I guess. I deserved to be here. It saved my life, as weird as that sounds. In the world," Connor said with a wave of his hand, "I couldn't deal. Woulda died tryin'."

Wednesday-May 2

Marco Jones stood in the library looking out at a bank of floor-to-ceiling windows onto the travertine-surfaced patio protected by a redwood pergola. A gap in the waist-high stone balustrade surrounding the patio allowed a view of the manicured lawn extending to a stand of pine trees. Azalea bushes planted along the sides of the balustrade bloomed in red, pink, and white.

The cherry wood shelves in the library held first editions which were one of the prizes of the West Wing of the Ottinger Wellness Center where the privileged patients spent their days. This wing, an appendage to the main building, was twinned by an East Wing where those needing more serious care were housed. West Wing residents met with health professionals and psychologists on a regimented but not onerous schedule. They were not subject to drug therapy and enjoyed a "guest" status akin to staying at a five-star hotel. Spa services, gourmet dining, an Olympic-sized pool, workout center, and jogging path were available. Marco spent a good deal of his time in the library with its eastern exposure allowing the morning sun to warm the room.

Marco walked to the large working fireplace and laid his book on the coral mantle. He poked at the last embers of a dying fire started earlier in the morning to help chase the early hours chill from the room. With the remnants of the logs again orange and smoking, he picked up his book, walked to the opposite end of the room and sank into a down-filled armchair. It was one in a setting of three around an antique Regency Rosewood table.

The only other person in the room was Marco's minder who stood at the entrance. The two men rarely spoke but were always together.

Marco's morning routine ended with an hour in the library. It began after breakfast with a walk around the gardens reserved for the "guests." This one-and-a-half acre plot was surrounded by a ten-foot, ivy-covered brick wall.

During his daily walks, now going on for almost two years, Marco noticed the West Wing landscaping crew arrived and left through an opening in a hedge hiding the service entrance and delivery bays behind the main building. Access to the main building was protected by a wrought-iron security gate opening to a driveway circling a large fountain.

Marco had enjoyed his time at Ottinger. It relaxed him. He loved to read and as he studied the bookcases lining the wall facing the windows, he ticked off the books he had read. At least fifty. Perhaps more as he tried to read one every other week. Hemingway was his favorite, followed closely by Fitzgerald. He also enjoyed Aldous Huxley, even contemporary writers, Stephen King and John Grisham among them.

He had taken advantage of the services provided and opened up to the psychologists. Not about everything, but about some of his frustrations. He was an old soul in a world entertained by Instagram and Tik Tok; a world where social media established cultural norms. A world in which he never felt comfortable. He could not find his place. And not finding a place was not good in a family where "place" was everything. Another frustration. That one he did not talk about. He knew full well he was not ever to talk about that.

Most beneficial of all, he enjoyed a sense of control. A sense of being in control. As counterintuitive as that might seem upon an initial consideration, in a place where one was controlled, he established his own routine, his own pattern of behavior that gave him comfort. Of course, it was predicated on telling people what they wanted to hear, what they expected to hear. But that was also expected outside the walls where he never managed to find his place; a life in which he always felt insecure. The demands were too great. The demands to understand what people were thinking and how to respond in ways that made everyone happy, or, at the very least, not unhappy. It was exhausting and frustrating, and he never fully succeeded. It often made him extremely angry. Here the demands were lessened. He found a place. A comfortable niche.

He understood he needed to be here. Whalen made the right choice. He had to be away from what he did. He also understood Whalen needed him gone, which he could accept even if it upset him. Still, there were always the urges. They tugged at him. And that tugging was becoming difficult to resist. He felt the urges dig deep into his bones, then gather, slither up his spine, up his back and into his head. It took hold of his being. It became him.

Resisting was a daily struggle. Hourly struggle. He fought it with the routine, the control he learned to bring to his life. And now it was time for lunch. Not that there was a set time. He could go when he wanted, and this time every day he decided he would have lunch. Later than most of the others which ensured a largely empty dining room.

As he left the library and walked into the quiet hallway, he could hear his minder following close behind him. Again, he understood why, but more and more his understanding, his acceptance, his control were being tested. The hallways were closing in on him. The immaculately cleaned red rugs and highly polished maple walls were making him anxious. He could smell the rug cleaner and the wood polish, and it was making him ill. The portraits of the men and women who served as board members of the facility stared down at him with the same dead eyes every single day.

As he preferred, the dining room was almost empty. Two others were there and they sat at a table on the far side of the room in the alcove overlooking the pool and the outdoor recreation pad that included basketball and volleyball courts.

The minder stood inside the entrance with his back against the wall facing the dining room. He pretended not to watch.

Marco sat at a table in the center of the room under an elegant chandelier. The draft from an air duct drifted across the crystals creating a chiming he enjoyed. The tablecloth was starched with a sharp "just ironed" crease down the center. The attendant filled his water glass. No ice. Never ice. He promised to return with hot tea, which Marco always had with lunch. Marco studied the menu printed on heavy stock and embossed with the Ottinger crest, a lion standing on its haunches, a crown perched between its ears, a shield in it paws. On Wednesdays the starters were wedge or mixed green salad or soup of the day. Today the soup was minestrone. Entrees options were an eight-ounce filet with béarnaise sauce, prime porterhouse, crab cake, or Chilean sea bass. All the entrees were served with creamed spinach and grilled asparagus. Cheesecake, apple pie, or ice cream for dessert.

The attendant returned with the tea and the mixed green salad. It was always the mixed green salad followed by the filet, medium well, and ice cream for dessert. That was Wednesday lunch for Marco and had been for two years.

Cutting into his filet, Marco jabbed the steak knife deep into the fleshy part of his palm near the thumb on his fork hand. The blood washed down his hand to his wrist, dripped onto the tablecloth, and stained his khaki pants. The attendant, positioned behind Marco, saw the blood and rushed to Marco's side. The commotion caught the attention of the minder who rushed to the table grabbing a handful of napkins along the way which he wrapped tightly around the wound. He talked into a shoulder microphone extending from a receiver attached to his belt and notified the clinic he was bringing in a resident who had a wound needing attention.

***

"Thank you," Marco said to the nurse who put the final touches on a wrapping of tape and gauze.

"That was nasty," she said. "But stitches aren't necessary. You will have a little scar though."

"Clumsy of me but you've done such a good job, I don't feel any pain."

"That wasn't me. It's the Tylenol-plus I gave you." She turned toward a mirrored wall cabinet behind her and removed a small bottle. "Three more in case you begin to feel some pain later."

Marco put the bottle in his shirt pocket and asked, "Would you mind giving me more cotton and some more tape in case I need it? I know, I know, I can come back any time, but just in case. Middle of the night, you know."

"Sure," the woman answered and opened a drawer in a supply cart under the cabinet. She lifted the lid off a glass canister and pulled out a wad of cotton balls, then opened another drawer and removed a roll of tape. "Here you go. I'd like to see you in a day or two, but if you feel the need to change the dressing before then, this should do it."

Marco popped off the examination table causing the paper lining to rip as he did. "Whoops, sorry."

"I'd be putting a new one on anyway."

The nurse walked Marco to the door of the office and nodded at his minder who stood and waited for Marco to walk ahead of him toward his room. He followed.

Thursday-May 3

Whalen Jones walked briskly down the wide corridor, his heels clicking on the marble floors of the Capitol building and skipped through the open doors of State House Speaker Noreen West's suite. He glanced at the receptionist who smiled and pointed him toward the closed door of West's office.

Jones knocked and pushed open the door, peeking his head in. "Anyone home?"

Senator West waved him in. "Welcome to the dark side."

"Your words," Jones said and made a show of looking around the office. "Haven't been here in a while. You've changed things, right?"

"Have to freshen it periodically to stave off boredom."

Flanked by an American and state flag, West sat in a high-backed brown leather chair behind an oak desk, her legs visible through the open design.

"You have more crap cluttering up your walls than I do." Walking along one side of the office, Jones pointed at a line of plaques. "Rotary. Moose. Elks, and, shit I don't have one of these. Shriner's Person of the Year." He turned toward West. "Bet it was 'Man' of the Year before you. Had to reboot the engraving process."

"Deserved recognition for attending to the needs of the good people of our communities."

"Yeah, right," Jones said sarcastically as he walked to a bookcase. "What's this? A football from Stoops? I don't have one of these either."

"That's from the national championship team a few years back."

"Like twenty years back."

"As you said, I got one, you don't. Senator, to what do I owe this honor?"

Jones sat in a leather upholstered wingback armchair facing the desk and set his arms on the rests. He crossed his legs and took in the imposing figure of Speaker Noreen West. She was one of the first women elected to the State House where she wrested the speaker's office from a twenty-year veteran in her second term. Once a handsome woman, she was now fearsome. Her steel blue eyes were deep set in a face giving evidence of both wariness and steadfastness. A perpetual smirk that could disarm. A woman confident in her appearance, she wore little makeup and let her hair go snow white. There was no pretense to Noreen West; among her colleagues, that is. With constituents and supporters, especially those with deep pockets, she was all pretense and successfully feigned the warmth of your favorite aunt.

"I need your support for a resolution I'm going to propose. It's innocuous enough. Naming a week of the year – I haven't decided which one yet – to preserve a natural resource." Jones waved his hands in a broad circle. "Something along those lines anyway."

"If we spent half as much time on things that mattered instead of this crap, we might get something worthwhile done around here. What are we preserving this time?" West asked, the smirk growing into an insincere smile. "The elk? Trout?"

"I don't know yet."

"What's this all about?" she asked, hiking herself straight against the back of her chair, as if preparing for trouble. "You didn't have to pay a special visit to tell me about some stupid resolution."

"I'm thinking we find something to" – he curled his fingers around the word – "'preserve' and use it to give a nod to alternative sources of energy."

West started to come out of her chair.

"Now, hear me out, Noreen. I'm not saying we make this about that specifically, but we use a resolution including something in fine print acknowledging wind and solar energy have a place in the lineup."

The smirk returned to West's mouth. "I know WindServ is planning to make a run for more land. So, you're thinking we use the resolution as code for we're okay with that." She squared her shoulders and placed her arms on her desk. "Are you out of your mind? Have you not noticed working oil derricks surround this building? Hell" – she said forcefully, pointing toward a window in her office – "we have one right out front in the middle of a flowerbed. You think your code, no matter how small the print, isn't going to be picked up by the people who keep us alive economically? Not to mention who keep you and me sitting in this building?"

"I think we can do this without causing the roof to fall in if we handle it right. You know me well enough to know I'm not going to run out into the street screaming about climate change or the evils of fossil fuels. This isn't about being green. It's about, well...covering our asses. It's smart politics not to close ourselves off to the possibilities. We stake a claim quietly. We don't have to ever mine it." Jones chuckled. "Not exactly the best analogy."

"Now, you're being insulting," West said, a challenge in her voice. "You're itching for a go at Evans and you need to create some distance from 'The Senator from Oil.' Not too far, but a crack at least if you want national support from your party. That's what's going on here, right?"

"Distance? I could just stand where I am and be in another zip code from Evans. But, no, this has nothing to do with that." Jones smiled broadly. "For me, anyway. You're getting your political intelligence from the wrong sources, which would worry me if I were you. That's always been one of your strengths, Noreen, getting the word first and agreeing to play kingmaker for a price, or cutting people off at the knees before they can get out of the blocks." He shook his head. "No, I have no interest in his job. This truly is about the bigger picture. Later on if it turns out the sky is falling, we can say we were on the right side and helped save the planet. We have to show we were willing to see what WindServ and the others could do. I'm not saying we're on the wrong side of history yet, but there are some strong signs that if we stand still, we're going to get run over."

"And this resolution of yours is a step in that direction?" West said skeptically. "On the right side of history?"

"A very, very small step."

"Not so small that it's likely to go unnoticed, but that's the point, right?"

"That's the point."

"And that's exactly why I'm going to decline your offer. The time might come when what you're suggesting makes sense, but this isn't that time. The industry still keeps the engine running. Jobs. Taxes. Everything. No, thanks."

"I'm not saying any different. What I'm proposing isn't going to deny any of that, or even suggest anything should change." Jones moved forward in his chair. "How about you just tell your folks not to object to the resolution and slip it by without a vote. Not even a voice vote. 'Sense of the legislature' thing."

"That doesn't disguise anything." West shook her head. "No one is gonna want to bite the hand that feeds them."

Jones stood, walked to a window. "It always gets me right here" – he patted his chest – "whenever I walk by the Veterans Memorial and stare up at 'The Big Guy.' Impressive. A fitting tribute to those who made the ultimate sacrifice and didn't come back." He turned toward West. "I wonder how much effort it took to convince our esteemed predecessors to accept a Native American as the symbol on that memorial."

West scoffed. "First off, you know as well as I do the figure is based on the sculpture's nephew. Who wasn't a Native American."

"Ha," Jones scoffed loudly. "That never has washed; only used when the obvious is pointed out to the...oh, shall we say the 'less accepting'? When they balk at the prospect of someone other than a white man fighting for this country."

"Oh, for fuck's sake, Whalen, what's your point?"

Jones walked to the edge of the desk, looked down at West, and extended his hand in the direction of the window. "How hard a sell do you think it was? To have 'The Big Guy' look like that?"

"Are you forgetting the Guardian who sits on top of this building is a Native American? Why are you trotting out the race card?"

"I'm saying time marches on and we'd better march with it."

"Not working. I know there's more to this. You've got something up your sleeve. Someone in your crosshairs."

Jones sat down and leaned forward, resting his arms on his thighs. "Okay, cutting to the chase. Ralph..."

West raised her hands off the desk, palms out. "My Ralph?"

"Yes, *your* Ralph. He's been successful winning contracts to supply cars and trucks and vehicle maintenance services to the state. He's got some great contacts at Central Purchasing and Fleet Management." Jones paused and stared at West. "You'd think he was being handed no-bid contracts."

"You're a real SOB," West said through gritted teeth.

"What's doubly interesting is there has been a push to lease electric cars and trucks. Last time I checked that wasn't happening through our leasing programs. Can't Ralph meet that demand? Doesn't deal in that type of vehicle?" Jones sat up and folded his hands together resting them in his lap. "There are all kinds of irregularities in the program."

"You truly think we can sell this resolution of yours to our people without everyone coming unglued?" West asked calmly.

"Oh, we'll get pushback for sure, but if you and I lock arms, I think we'll be fine. For sure everyone is going to have to step out of their comfort zone. We have to make them see taking that step is hedging a bet, a bet we might not ever have to call, but if we do, it'll pay off."

"I'll tell my people not to object, but I can't promise that some won't take the opportunity to polish their credentials by expressing 'doubts,' 'misgivings,' whatever."

"One other thing. I need you to issue a statement in support of the resolution." Jones held up his hand as West began to sputter an objection. "Nothing about the small print. You only need to mention the preservation part of the resolution, but I'm guessing your general statement of support will bring along a few of your people. Enough of them anyway. We need that."

"*We* need that? *I* don't need that."

"You really do."

West's face was flushing. "You sure as shit better have the governor on board with you. He needs to sign this thing."

"He's good. Speaking of which it's Lincoln who has his eyes on Evans," Jones said with a wink. He stood and added, "Always a pleasure doing business with you, Noreen. I'll show myself out."

***

Running, Ray Lee almost collided with Jones who was stepping into the hallway outside West's office. The marble floors did not allow much purchase and the men held onto each other to keep from falling.

"What the hell?" Jones said releasing Lee who bent over breathing heavily.

Lee held up a hand and squeezed out. "We need to talk right now."

"So, talk," Jones answered, his response clipped.

Lee shook his head and pointed at a door leading to a portico. As the men stepped into the warm afternoon sunlight, Lee looked around carefully before focusing on Jones. "Marco escaped."

"Escaped?" Jones said loudly, then did his own reconnaissance of the area before continuing. "How is that even possible? The place is like a fortress, which is one of the reasons we put him there. And he has people watching him, or they're supposed to be."

"No," Lee said, shaking his head. "The wing you put him in is not the high security one. Where he is...was...staying put is voluntarily. People can come and go as they please. They do have to check in and out, and Marco did have someone keeping him company, but, still, it's an open facility."

"This person who is supposed to keep an eye on him...?"

"He's there twelve hours. From nine until nine. From when Marco's let out of his room until he's locked in. And Marco's the only one in that part who's locked in and has to be let out."

"So, how did he get out?"

"He used some cotton or something to stuff into the lock and..."

"Cotton? Lock?"

"He cut his hand and stuffed some cotton he had into the latch and it didn't catch. The door didn't lock."

"You mean the building isn't locked up? Not secured? No alarms go off when doors are opened?"

"I don't know about alarms. We should've had him in the other wing. It's locked down twenty-four/seven."

"There are hundreds of people going in and out of that one. Patients. Visitors. Doctors. Attendants. Someone would've seen him and recognized him."

"Someone *did* see him and recognized him."

Jones stared malevolently. "Hindsight is twenty/twenty. Isn't there a goddamn wall around the place?"

"The wall is mainly to keep people out, not keep them in."

"So, what? He just waltzed out?"

"They think he used a gate the landscapers use. It's like a hidden entrance, or exit, in this case."

"And apparently not so hidden."

Jones walked to the edge of the portico and looked out across the grounds of the Capitol. He laughed at the absurdity. One minute he was playing political hardball with the Speaker of the state senate, the next he was considering the immediacy of finding an escaped psychopath.

"How far can he go?" Lee asked. "They said he didn't take anything, and he doesn't have any money."

"Shit," Jones said and began stabbing at his phone. "Good afternoon, this is Senator Whalen Jones, can I please speak to Mr. Chartoff?" A nod. "Thank you." Jones paced across the portico and leaned against one of the fluted columns supporting the roof overhang three stories above his head. "Gene, thanks for taking my call. I just got off the phone with a friend who is looking for a pretty sizable loan to invest in an expansion of his business and I recommended he talk to you." Jones nodded as he acknowledged the response. "My pleasure. I told him my family has been longtime personal and business clients and we did all our checking and savings with you as well as having a few safety deposit boxes. That about covers it, right?" He listened and doubled over before straightening up and mouthing *goddammit*. He looked at Lee. "So, he came by this morning and closed out his savings account and turned in his safety deposit box keys? Yes, he does look well. He had been gone a while, yes. Well, the rest of us are still with you. The rest of the family. Yes," he said listening. "What? Oh, right. My friend. He'll use my name. Do what you can for him. I'd appreciate it. Thanks."

"How much money does he have?" Lee asked.

"I don't know," Jones said irritably. "He had a trust fund that I assume was what he took from the savings account and he kept cash in the safety deposit box. I always assumed it was so if we tried to attach his savings he'd have cash. I could never get at it." Jones threw his hands in the air. "I thought about attaching his savings when we put him away, but I didn't want to have to explain why we were doing that. It would've been a whole big legal thing I didn't want to get into. At the time we just had to get him gone without any questions."

"We'll find him," Lee said reassuringly.

"You go to Ottinger and talk to Dr. ..." Jones waved his hand. "You know, the guy we've been dealing with."

"Cranston. Dr. Cranston. The director."

"Tell him not to say anything to anyone."

"I think the law says he has to report this."

"Report what?" Jones exclaimed angrily. "No one knows Marco was there. There's no Marco Jones in Ottinger. He wasn't registered. Who would they say left? There's nothing to report. Convince him we have this under control." He took a deep breath. "Tell him Marco has contacted us and we're dealing with it. Remind him, without hitting him over the head, that the family has been and will continue to be generous benefactors." He raised a finger. "If."

"There's got to be some trail. Maybe he told someone what he was planning. One of those people he talks to, or one of the other patients. Maybe one of the maintenance people, which would explain how we got into this mess in the first place."

"Really? You think he told someone he was planning to sneak out of the place?"

"Not in so many words but maybe he mentioned he wanted to get out." Lee shrugged. "Or something. There has to be a trail of some kind."

"Then find it, and let's hope it doesn't lead to another body."

***

Connor stepped into the apartment. "What the hell?"

Ryan laughed. "What can I say? I don't need much."

Connor walked over to an aluminum-framed chaise lounge, the lone piece of furniture in a large living room. "This and that flat screen," he said, pointing to the wall-mounted unit, "definitely are not much. Why even get this place? A nice, fancy building with a doorman and all." He pointed at the hardwood floors. "Maybe get a rug."

"I've ordered one to protect the floor from..." Ryan nodded at the chaise.

Connor took a step toward a door to the right of the living room. "Do you have a bed?"

"I do."

"I mean a regular bed. Not a mattress on the floor."

"A regular bed with a box spring and everything. I'm planning to furnish the place. Been busy."

"How long have you been here?"

"Shut up," Ryan said playfully, gesturing for Connor to follow him. "I do have a dining room table and a couple of chairs in the kitchen."

"You cook?" Connor asked. "I smell food, right?"

"You do, and 'yes' I cook."

In stark contrast to the rest of the apartment, the kitchen was fully furnished. An oval pot rack hanging above a marble-topped island displayed an assortment of gleaming copper pots and pans. Three teak stools lined the island.

Across from the island was a Wolf stove sided by counters holding a wooden storage block displaying a set of Miyabi knives, a Cuisinart, toaster, library of cookbooks and Jura Espresso machine, all competing for space. Cabinets lined the walls on either side of the stove.

A Sub-Zero glass-doored refrigerator and wine cabinet sat against the shorter wall in the L-shaped kitchen .

"Here's where all the money went," Connor said, admiring the surroundings.

"Sit." Ryan pointed to a polished wood table surrounded by four chairs in a spacious breakfast nook. Two places were set. Plates. Napkins. Silverware. Glasses filled with water. "Like sirloin?"

"'Course," Connor said, eyeing a large bowl of salad embellished with tomatoes, cucumbers, carrots, and sliced onions. "Love this. We never got much of it inside. Mainly bread, pasta, potatoes. More pasta. More bread. More potatoes. Sometimes tuna but always mixed with the pasta. Stuff to fill us up on the cheap. Can't get enough of this," he said, his eyes feasting on the salad.

"Start," Ryan said. "Steaks are almost ready." He opened the broiler and stabbed at a thick, thinly marbled Angus steak. "This is done. I'll turn off the heat."

Connor filled the bowl and stared into it, a huge smile radiating across his face. "I never even knew how much I liked tomatoes until I got out."

Ryan sat down across from his brother and filled his bowl. "Dressing?" he asked, offering a bottle of Paul Newman's Creamy Caesar.

"Nah, I don't want nothin' 'tween my tongue and the taste of this stuff." Connor forced a large helping into his mouth; a slice of cucumber did not make it and dropped onto the table. He mumbled a "sorry" as he stabbed at the errant vegetable. Swallowing, Connor said, "I gotta learn that I don't have to eat everything in ten minutes. Also, no one is gonna try to take anything away from me. That was always something you had to watch out for. If someone wanted something you had, and they thought they could take it, they would."

Ryan laid his fork on the table next to his bowl and took a deep breath. "That's something I want to talk to you about."

Connor gave Ryan a look.

"The trip to the Mac was..." Ryan took another deep breath. "I knew it wasn't a nice place."

"A nice place?" Connor said with a laugh, shooting pieces of salad and carrots across the table. "Sorry, man." He wiped at the morsels with his napkin.

"I didn't know how bad it was," Ryan said. "I know that sounds lame, but the truth is I never thought about it. Didn't want to." He shook his head. "I'm not saying this very well."

Connor laid his fork on the table and swallowed. "What're you tryin' to say?"

"I guess I'm saying I'm sorry."

"For what? It wasn't your fault."

"I know, I know, but I should've at least thought about what you were going through. The noise. God, that was awful. And the smell."

"Funny, I never noticed any smell."

"And that," Ryan said, tracing a line on his face from his nose down to his ear.

Connor touched his scar. "Just what happens in there. Happens to a lot of people."

"You asked about my playing football and running."

"Yeah."

"I was mad about what happened and playing ball and running helped me release that anger. Living with people who didn't want me and were doing it for the money. Having people look at me and know what happened." Ryan stared at the top of the table. "Running faster than everybody. Hitting people without getting into trouble for it. That was what I did."

"Smart," Connor said.

"Why'd you do that to Mom?" Ryan asked, feeling his face reddening.

Connor took a sip of water. He looked at Ryan intently. "You didn't find out 'bout that?"

"What?"

"You don't know what happened? Know what I was sentenced for?"

"Of course, I do."

"I mean the details?"

"I put it out of my mind." Ryan wiped his hand through the air. "Never asked any questions. Never read anything about it. Never talked about it."

"When I was fightin' with Dad, he got hold of a knife and in swingin' it around caught Mom across the throat when she tried to break us up. I never even knew what happened to her 'til I read in the paper they was after me for killin' both of 'em. I had figured I might be able to get off for self-defense, or something like that, but when I found out 'bout that I knew I was in trouble. That's why I tried to rob the bank. To get money to get away."

Ryan got up and pulled open a drawer under the stove. He lifted out a platter, opened the broiler, and filled it with a slab of meat. He checked the oven and looked at Connor. "I made a couple of baked potatoes. You just said you got tired of them."

"They was always boiled or mashed. I'd like one baked."

Ryan put on an oven mitt and placed two foil-covered potatoes on the platter. He went to the refrigerator and grabbed a tub of butter. As he placed the abundance on the table, he pointed at a dish. "Sour cream."

The men each cut themselves a portion of meat and gingerly pushed the tinfoil-wrapped potatoes onto their plates. Salt, butter, and sour cream came next.

Connor began cutting his meat into small cubes. "Anyway, I was accused of killing her even if I didn't do it 'cause it happened during the commission of another crime."

"Dad?"

"That and I stole some stuff from the house so I had all that goin' 'gainst me. I can't believe for all these years you thought I killed Mom. That you didn't know the particulars."

Ryan shook his head. "Built a wall."

"You wasn't at the trial. I wondered 'bout that. Thought they would have you testify."

"The prosecution thought it wouldn't help their case to badger a kid on the witness stand. And the defense knew anything I'd say wouldn't help you."

"I was always real sorry 'bout hittin' you. I was so mad at him, I was outta control." Connor pointed at Ryan with his fork. "If you look close you can see a scar. Guess we both got souvenirs to remember that day by."

Ryan nodded. "I'm betting we don't need souvenirs."

"True. Curious 'bout something. You said you took care of being angry by running and playin' football. Why'd you stop?"

"There's more to that story." Ryan looked intently at Connor. "I had another reason for being angry. More like frustrated. Well, angry about this particular thing, too. A lot of anger and frustration. Bad combination."

"Okay."

"I'm gay."

Connor looked at Ryan as if expecting more. "And?"

"And I didn't know how to deal with it. Didn't even know what I was dealing with. At first, I was confused. I knew I was different. For a long time, I thought it was something that would go away. That I'd grow out of it. Anyway, it was something else I had to deal with."

Connor nodded. "Man, you had a lot of shit to handle, and you did. Better 'n me." He laughed. "Runnin' and playing ball beats the hell out of prison."

Ryan laid his arms on the table and smiled wryly. "This isn't what I was expecting."

"What *was* you expecting?"

"I don't know. Shock, maybe. Disappointment. Even disgust."

"Really? I was in prison for twenty-five years. There's gay sex in prison, you know? And most of it ain't voluntary."

"Wait a minute," Ryan said, his voice edging toward anger.

"No," Connor said, raising his hand. "I don't mean to say what you're sayin' and what I said are the same. What I'm sayin' is you're doing what's natural to you. I get it. I seen other stuff. I know all about it and some of it was, what do they call it? Consensual. A lot wasn't. Whatever," Connor said. "I'm just sayin' it's no big deal far as I'm concerned."

"It was to me."

"And you handled it. You are handling it. That's what I'm tryin' to say. You're being *you* and that's a good thing."

"For a long time I didn't handle it, at all, which gets back to why I stopped the football and running. I decided I am who I am. Accepted it. I just got up one day and said, 'Fuck it.' The anger slid away."

"No anger, no football?"

"No anger, no football, but" – Ryan sat back heavily – "I haven't made any announcements, and no one's ever asked."

"Isn't that what's called 'don't ask, don't tell'?"

"That was a policy used in the service not so long ago. I mean, I don't go out of my way to say anything and no one's ever asked."

"Your life is your life. No need to say nothin'."

Ryan smiled. "The fact is I'm not ready to come out. I'm okay where I am and it isn't perfect, but it's way better than where I was."

"Not ever lonely?"

Ryan considered his response a moment. "I have friends, just not around here. You want to know anything else?"

"Hell, I didn't have to know that. Pass the salt."

Monday-May 7

Layton smiled broadly as he entered the room, his eyes fixed on the file folder in front of Berger. "Wasn't sure if I'd see you again."

"Really?" Berger said, both hands on the folder. "Worried we weren't going to take you up on your offer?"

His smile broadening to show a line of perfectly straight white teeth, Layton waited until the guards secured his cuff chains to the heavy iron ring bolted to the tabletop before responding. "It's your lucky day. I have something for you, but first things first." He nodded at the folder. His chest began to heave. "Want me to share my wisdom? I'll need to take a look at what you have there."

Connor glanced at Ryan and Berger and rolled his eyes.

Berger slid the file toward Layton keeping his hand pressed on the material. "No games, George. I'm giving you what you want and I need to know what you see." He slowly lifted his hand.

Layton kept his eyes on Berger as he opened the file. Shifting his weight so his upper body was leaning over the folder, his smile faded. He let his head drop and pulled his shoulders up around his neck. He shuddered. His face slackened causing it to narrow and appear gaunt. The color drained from his cheeks and his complexion went waxy. The liveliness in his eyes disappeared, replaced by a blank stare concentrated on the photos as he slowly shuffled through them. His brow hooded and his lips protruded. His breathing increased causing his nostrils to broaden.

"My, my." Layton slurred the words. In a whisper more to himself than to the others: "This is good work. Some of it anyway." He trembled, his shoulders shook. "My girls."

Unnerved by Layton's physical transformation and his reaction to the photos, Ryan pushed away from the table, stood, and walked to a corner of the room where he leaned against the wall.

Berger waited until Layton had reviewed each of the images before asking, "Are those what he described in his letters?"

Layton arranged the photos in a row and carefully reconsidered each one. As he raised his head, his eyes brightened, and the smile returned to his face. "Some of them. I have to say that based on what he said about them" – he let his eyes go briefly to the photos – "I was expecting something else. These aren't exactly beautiful women. He has a thing for bigger bodies, doesn't he?"

Layton paused allowing time for a response. Not getting a reaction he said, "Come on, you all were thinking the same thing." Then, without looking down at the arrangement in front of him, he tapped three. "Them. Those were done by the same person." He stared at the fourth photo. "Not that one and she deserved some attention. There's no care there. Whoever did that is an animal. A butcher. He showed no respect. No care."

"The other three were not killed by an animal?" The words were out of Ryan's mouth so quickly he heard them before he had time to consider what he was saying. He surrendered to his disgust, approached the table, and jabbed a finger at the first photo. "She had her throat cut so deeply she's been decapitated." He leaned in. "The other three had an eye cut out of their heads. But only this one" – he pushed the photo of Luna at Layton – "was killed by an animal?"

Layton looked at Ryan, squinting. "You came to me and asked what I think. That's what I think." He repositioned Luna's photo and straightened it carefully. "The person who did this is a piece of shit."

"You're saying we have two different killers?" Berger asked.

Layton nodded. "Yes. These" – he separated the three from Luna – "were done carefully. With care. Real concern. He took his time. He knew what he was doing. I'm talking about the eyes. This last one was just someone killing someone."

"But trying to make it look like the others?" Berger asked.

"Could be, and if so, it was a sloppy job. The other three have no signs of trauma, I mean other than the obvious. No bruises, and there was sex, but not violent. The biting came post-mortem. Not a lot of blood. Right?"

Berger nodded.

"But her..." He tapped the photo of Luna. "I can see she was hit at least once, probably more, right?"

Another nod from Berger.

Layton spread his arms out in front of him as far as the chains would allow. "It doesn't take a genius."

"Okay, I have to ask those standard 'why' and 'what' questions," Berger said.

"Why'd he do it?" Layton said mockingly. "What made him into the person he is? Those questions?" He sat back and shrugged. "You know those answers. Or at least you can guess at them as well as I can. Hell, I wasn't abused growing up. Sure, I had a mother who might've been smothering." He stared at Berger. "I know you know all about me. I'm guessing you've been to Quantico and talked to those experts at the BAU, right? You've been to the seminars that dissect people like me. Like Kemper. Like Bundy and all the rest. Organized. Disorganized. And this guy" – he pushed Luna's photo aside – "is organized. No frenzy with him. Careful job on those eyes. Admirable work." He studied the photos. "In the end though, who knows why anyone does anything? Bundy said, and I memorized this for people like you who come around poking at me. 'Society wants to believe it can identify evil people, or bad or harmful people, but it's not practical. There are no stereotypes.' So, don't try to pick me apart or use me to understand any of this. There's nothing new you can learn from me."

"'New'? Maybe not," Berger agreed. "But you can provide some insight on this guy." He jabbed his forefinger at the photos. "The one who did this."

"Sound like semantics to me." Layton smiled and shook his head. "Insight? Okay, fire away. Pick at me."

"He killed three women in a span of about ten months and stopped. If we agree the last one isn't him. Why did he stop?"

"I'd say he's been locked up somewhere."

"Or dead?" Berger asked.

"No," Layton said, leaning down toward his right foot. "And that's not insight talking." He removed a folded piece of paper from his sock and held the small square in front of him like a prize. "He's back."

Berger straightened; he squared his shoulders. "He wrote to you again?"

"He did. I got it this morning. Talk about good timing. And not like the others. Just a regular letter."

"Can I read it?"

"Shit, you can have it," Layton said and waved it teasingly. "But only if I can have these." He laid his hand on the stack of photos.

"You know I can't do that."

"Oh, yes, you can. Who's going to know?"

"The guards who find them in your cell the next time it gets tossed," Berger said sharply. "Then, I'll have a big problem."

Without looking at Connor, Layton said, "Tell 'em, cellie."

"Yeah, there are things the guards never find," Connor answered. "We put stuff around in places we know they'll get at. Once they find the obvious stuff, they don't look no further. It's real easy to hide shit."

Layton put the prize on the table, gathered up the photos, slid them into the folder, and leaned forward securing it in the elastic of his pants at the small of his back.

Berger pulled a pair of surgical gloves from his pocket, slid them on his hands before touching the letter.

"Give me a break," Layton said. "You know how many people in this prison have handled that before it ever got to me? And like I said, this guy is organized to the point of being clinical. He didn't leave any fingerprints or anything else that's going to be useful to you."

"The envelope?" Berger asked.

"Tossed it. No return address, if that's what you were thinking." Layton stood. "One other thing, and I'm guessing you've thought of this. To be a copycat you have to know there's something to copy. From what I've seen, and what you've more or less admitted, you've kept the wraps on all of this. So, how does this copycat know what to do? He did screw up some, but he knows enough. Maybe you're going about this all wrong. Find the copycat who is definitely not as careful as this guy" – he pointed at the note – "and he'll lead you where you want to go."

***

As Layton left the room, Berger carefully unfolded the page. Ryan and Connor scooted close. The three men leaned over the table and read:

Sorry about not writing sooner. I had nothing of interest to report, but things have changed.

I'm back out in the big wide world. Everything seems brighter, fresher, and sweeter. That's probably insensitive of me to say given your situation. Or perhaps you enjoy hearing what it feels like to be free. Although I wasn't incarcerated in the same way, and I enjoyed the peace and quiet where it wasn't necessary to do anything, say anything, or prove anything, it was still confining. I couldn't be fully myself.

I am once more on the prowl. That sounds so cliché-ish. Better said is that I have options I can pursue. And pursuit is the operative impulse. The challenge for me has been that I always truly hope every time that the pursuit will result in the purest satisfaction. It never does. There's always something missing. I don't know what that is, but I have to keep chasing the satisfaction in the hopes that one day I'll find it and that will soothe my soul. (Again, cliché-ish, but apt.) So far, I've succeeded in keeping the yearning at bay for a time and then it slowly builds back until it is too strong to contain.

And that is where I find myself at the moment. I'm both elated to be able to scratch my itch and frustrated that I have to.

But I ramble.

I look forward to getting back to you with news of my latest adventures and the results.

Best.

When Ryan and Connor lifted their eyes from the page, Berger slid it into an evidence bag.

"You carry those with you?" Ryan asked, less out of curiosity and more to break the silence feeding the malevolence Layton left in his wake.

"Yeah," Berger answered blankly as he patted the air out of the bag.

"I'm having trouble wrapping my mind around any of this," Ryan said. "Layton called Luna's killer an animal. He saw art or skill, or whatever he called it, in the way the others were killed. Like it was okay if the victim served a purpose. I think that's what he was saying. I don't know how to process this."

"If you understood it, or could process it, you'd be in pretty bad shape yourself. There's no understanding what makes them tick. Even they don't know what drives them. Layton said that himself. So, we're left to figure out 'what' urges are driving them; 'why' they do what they do to satisfy those urges; and 'how' they do it. The MO. We identify a signature and then hope..."

Connor asked, "What's a signature?"

"Taking the eyes and biting the breasts is the signature of our guy. He does that to each of his victims. It's part of his fantasy, his compulsion, and he has to do it every time to satisfy an urge. And most of these offenders take souvenirs to remind them of the kill later on so they can relive it. I'm guessing he keeps the eyes as his souvenir. So, for our guy, his signature is tied to his souvenir. Then, we put all the pieces together – the 'why,' the 'how,' the kind of signature – and hope we have a profile to follow.

"We've also learned control is another primary motive driving most of them. They have little control over their own lives, or had none when growing up, and thrive on the fear they cause; the control that comes from instilling fear. They see murder as the ultimate form of dominance. Of control. Ted Bundy said he felt like God when he killed, and Dahmer said he wanted to find a way to keep the people he killed with him forever."

"Yeah," Connor agreed. "George used to talk all the time about *his* girls and by killing them and taking out their eyes he was the last thing they ever saw, and it made him like immortal, or something. It wasn't the killing that turned him on, or that's what he said. He said he wanted to make sure they had a 'good' death. That he gave them a reason to die."

Ryan heaved a full sigh. "So, Layton considers himself to be a better person than whoever killed Luna because he thinks he gave his victims a *better* death? They contributed to his being immortal?"

"Don't even try to figure it out," Berger said insistently. "Ed Kemper – one of the worst of the worst – he killed his own mother and grandparents, along with ten others, was in a cell next to Herbert Mullin, another despicable killer who abused his victims in every awful way imaginable. Kemper called him a creep because he said Mullin killed indiscriminately. Described him as subhuman. There's a supreme form of irony in there somewhere."

"My God," Ryan said, "and we have one of these maniacs running around in our city."

"Two," Connor said. "We're talkin' 'bout two of 'em."

"If Layton is right, and I think he is, Luna was not a random victim," Berger responded. "She was targeted and then 'dressed for the kill.'"

"You're saying Maria *was* killed for something she knew," Connor said.

"I'm saying it's possible," Berger answered, staring down at the evidence bag. "And whoever killed her has to know about the first three victims."

"It's gotta be a cop," Connor said. "One of your guys who knows what's goin' on."

"That would be me. I'm the one who's been working all the cases."

Connor raised his arms in surrender. "My bad, then."

"No, your line of reasoning makes sense," Berger said, nodding at Connor. "There's something I'm missing." He stared ahead and tapped his index finger metronomically. "Hell, there's a lot I'm missing."

"Let's push past that," Ryan insisted. "We know from the note the writer was away somewhere he didn't want to be."

"Prison, maybe," Connor suggested.

"No," Ryan said, sliding the evidence bag in front of him and pressing on the plastic so he could read the passage he wanted. "He wrote, 'Although I wasn't incarcerated in the same way, and I enjoyed the peace and quiet where it wasn't necessary to do anything, say anything, or prove anything, it was still confining.' Doesn't sound like he's describing a prison."

Berger did his own pat down on the plastic. "He said he's back on the prowl. Those are his exact words. 'On the prowl.' Where? Most stay close to home. They hunt where they feel safe. Usually not more than a twenty-five-mile radius from where they live or work." Berger massaged the bridge of his nose. "But our guy spread out his kills. Wesper, Laramie, and Mannix. Hundreds of miles apart."

"And?" Ryan asked.

"And I don't know," Berger said in frustration. "I was thinking out loud. Okay, throw out the 'comfort of home or work' part of this profile. Maybe we can go with another attribute these people share. They all have a record. Thefts. Assaults. Something. They never go from zero to sixty. There are signs."

Berger pulled his cell phone from his briefcase and stabbed at the face. "This is Agent Berger for Director Slade." He scooted his chair close to the table. "Thanks for taking my call, Len. We've got a situation. I'm here at the Mac and I've been talking to George Layton about our case." He listened. "Yes, that one."

Berger spent five minutes bringing Slade up to speed and ended the summation with, "I need you to okay opening this case up to the public. We desperately need to get the word out via the press, warn people we have a problem, and get more eyes and ears on this thing."

Berger listened and a broad smile crossed his face. He nodded at Ryan and Connor. "Yes, sir. We'll go public. A serial killer. The attention will give us the boost we need. Someone out there has to know something. Unofficially, I'm thinking we have a copycat on the fourth one, which raises the question: 'How would he know what to copy?'" He listened. "Yes, Luna. It's less organized and might give us more to work with. We have nothing at all to go with on the first three. If we do find who killed Luna, they could lead us to the other one. They have to know who it is to copy the MO." He listened. "Thank you."

Berger put his phone on the table. "He agrees."

"Good," Ryan said.

"Yeah, good," Connor added. "So, you're gonna concentrate on finding who killed Maria? All this stuff about comfort zones and radiuses is real complicated, at least to me. If Maria's killing wasn't random, that should be easier to work on, right?"

"Out of the mouth of babes," Berger said.

Connor scowled. "What's *that* supposed to mean?"

"It means you're right. Find the copycat and find the other guy. Logical, but we don't have much to work with. Maria's parents weren't any help and you told us she was closed-mouthed about what was going on with her, so we're thin on information to follow up on. But I guarantee you as soon as we open up to the media about a serial killer, that's going to change in a big way. In fact, we're likely to have more information than we'll need, and that can be as frustrating as having too little. You don't know where to start. But when those floodgates open something is likely to flow through that will give us a place to start with Maria."

Berger closed his briefcase and stood. "This is the wrong place to be having this conversation." He looked around the sterile room. "Let's get the hell out of here. It's giving me the creeps."

"There is one other thing," Connor said and motioned for Berger to sit down. "Maria has a kid. She's living with her grandmother. Start with the grandmother, maybe?"

"What the fuck?" Ryan said. "Don't you think that's something you should have told us before?"

Berger followed up with, "A grandmother? Her parents never said anything about grandparents."

"I know," Connor said, a look of pain furrowing his brow. He spread his arms. "She made me promise not to ever say anything 'bout the kid. She was paranoid someone would find out 'cause she had to fight to keep her out of the system. Those child protection services people was always on her back. She had some problems with drugs a long time ago and it was always coming back on her. I promised." He shrugged. "And the whole 'don't snitch thing' was put in me real deep in prison. A code I lived with for a long time. It's hard to break that hold, you know? It takes time to get away from all that."

Berger asked, "Do you know where we can find the grandmother?"

"Sure. It's Maybelle."

"*Maybelle*?" Ryan spit out in disbelief. "*That* Maybelle?"

"Yeah, *that* one. Well, she ain't really her grandmother. Just called her that 'cause they was so close."

Berger said, "That explains why her parents never mentioned grandparents." He looked at Connor intently. "There aren't any other children, relatives, or friends I should know about, are there?"

"If there are, Maybelle'll know."

Tuesday-May 8

"Son-of-a-bitch," Jones exclaimed as he slammed down his phone.

"What?" asked Ray Lee who had come into the room, his hand still on the doorknob which he felt being pulled from his grasp.

"Is there anything I can do?" a voice came from behind Lee.

Jones waved dismissively. "No, Eileen, but thanks."

"What?" Lee repeated, walking to the chair facing Jones's desk.

"Slade told me he's going public with the investigation."

"Why now?"

"Well," Jones responded, intense irritation in his voice, "offhand, I'd say the recent murder played a role. It re-energized a case that was going cold. So, thank you very much. That and Marco has been writing letters to George Layton which..."

"Wait, wait," Lee said, his hands in the air. "Marco wrote to the Eyeball Killer?"

Jones took a deep breath. "Not as Marco. He didn't identify himself or we'd be having another conversation altogether. Like how to minimize the damage."

"Then how do you know it's Marco?"

"Slade got a call from his agent working on the case who went to talk to Layton about the letters."

"How'd this agent know about the letters?"

Jones huffed in frustration. "Someone told him, but let's focus on the real issue, shall we? Layton's got a letter after each murder. And that would have to be Marco, wouldn't it? He drops Layton a line letting him know who, what, and how."

"When you say 'who,'" Lee asked, "you mean 'who' was killed, right?"

Jones rubbed both hands across his face. "Yes, lovely things like that. And the latest letter announced his reemergence, I guess you'd have to call it."

Lee shot forward in his chair. "Did he say where he was?"

"I would have led with that. No, only that he was out. Have you talked to Cranston?"

"I have an appointment with him this afternoon."

"This afternoon? What the hell? It's been, what, three, no, four days since Marco took off?"

"I didn't want to blow in there like we were in a panic. Remember, this is a place where people can walk out anytime they want. They have no idea why you parked Marco there, do they?"

Jones shook his head slowly as his thoughts coalesced. "Said it was nervous exhaustion and there was a concern he'd harm himself."

"Cranston was apologetic. Embarrassed that he just walked away. No explanation for how he was able to do that, but said he wasn't shocked Marco left. Said he appeared 'fully competent,' his words, and figured he had gone home."

"Not to our home. Not in my lifetime." Jones sat forward and squared his shoulders. "And when we get him back in there, make sure Cranston understands he'll be a permanent resident."

"That might entail putting him in the other wing. The one for the, uh...more challenging cases, which means you might have to say more about why you want Marco to stay put.

"Okay, that's for another day. Right now, find someone who knows where he went. He must have said something to someone."

"I'll speak to everyone he dealt with. But, like I said, I don't want to raise any red flags. I sure as hell don't want to leave the impression we think he's going to do anything nuts."

"Just find him."

There was a soft knock on the door and Eileen announced, "The governor is here for you."

***

Ryan, Berger, and Connor squeezed into Maybelle's office-cum-supply closet. Ryan sat on the bar stool to the side of the card table she used as a desk. Connor leaned against a tower of boxes holding toilet paper and Berger sat on stacked cases of beer.

"This can't be good," Maybelle said, letting her eyes roam from man to man. "Two cops and an ex-con." She kept her eyes on Connor. "I have a feeling I know where this is headed."

"We want to find out who killed Maria," Ryan said. "That's it. We have no interest in saying anything about her daughter."

Maybelle glowered at Connor.

"I know you, Maybelle," Ryan continued, "and I know the girl is being taken care of and will get the best you have to give. We just want to get the SOB who killed Maria."

"I told'em," Connor said, "what Maria said 'bout being caught up in something. How that might be tied up into what happened to her."

"Oh, it's tied up in that all right," Maybelle said intensely.

"If you believe that," Ryan responded, "why didn't you come to me and say so? You could have said something when I was here talking to Connor."

"My first priority is taking care of her daughter. If I said anything right off you'd have found out about her and I promised Maria, and swore on her daughter's life, I wouldn't say nothin' 'bout the girl." She stared at Connor. "I'm surprised he said anything."

"They need to know everything we know," Connor said. "If we're going to find out who killed Maria, we can't be hidin' stuff."

Maybelle lowered her eyes and slumped. Her shoulders sagged and dropped forward. She let a moment pass before offering, "I wanted to say somethin' real bad." She looked up and blinked tears onto her cheeks. She rubbed at them with the back of her hand.

"What can you tell us?" Berger asked.

"Probably no more'n what you already know from Connor."

"Tell us what you know. Everything."

"Maria said she found out something that might be embarrassing to some people. Some important people."

"'Xactly what I said," Connor concurred.

Ryan held up his hand and gave Connor a look.

"Embarrassing?" Berger probed. "What do you mean by that?"

Maybelle shrugged. "I don't know. I'm saying it like Maria did. I got the idea it was 'someone' not 'something.'"

"Yeah," Connor agreed eagerly. "She told me it was *someone*." He looked at Ryan and Berger. "She knew some people wouldn't like her knowin' she saw this person. Like they wanted them gone."

"Gone as in dead?" Berger asked.

"She didn't say that."

"At the beginning," Maybelle said, "she asked me if she should find out if these people were tryin' to hide something. Like if she should say something to see what happened."

Berger pushed himself off the cases of beer and approached the desk which he started to lean on until it threatened to topple under his weight. "You're saying Maria was thinking about blackmailing someone."

Maybelle nodded sending another torrent of tears rolling down her cheeks.

"Where was she when she found out whatever...?" Ryan waved his hand as if to churn his thoughts. "Where was she when she found out about this person? Where was she working?"

"At Ottinger."

Connor nodded in agreement.

"So, you" – Ryan looked from Maybelle to Connor – "think she saw someone there and assumed it would be embarrassing to this person's family? Is that what you're saying?"

"I never put it to her like that," Maybelle answered, "but that's the way I think it was. I listened to what she said, and if she asked me for advice, I gave it."

"Did you tell her she should go to these people and feel things out?"

"No," Maybelle answered with a shake of her head. "I told her she was playin' with fire." She wiped her face with tissues she removed from the pocket of her apron. "People that got people at that place would not want to be answerin' the questions Maria would be askin' for the reasons she would be askin'em."

"And?"

"I know she was leanin' toward talkin' to'em. She was buildin' up her courage, I think."

"I told'em what she said 'bout the name thing," Connor said to Maybelle. "That the name this person had in that place was not the same as their real name."

Maybelle nodded. "That's what got her thinkin' 'bout all that she was plannin'."

"But she never told you this person's name?" Berger asked. "Their real name?"

Maybelle took a deep breath and shook her head. "Like I said, we never got into any detail. I always figured she thought it best if I didn't know."

Connor raised his chin toward Maybelle. "Yeah. She came right out and tol' me it was better if I didn't know. And that means I should probably not say this next thing, but since we're all tryin' to find out what happened to Maria…"

He paused and glanced at Maybelle who nodded for him to continue. "She did go to these people and they was not happy. They was willing to…as Maria said, 'help her out' to keep quiet."

"When was the last time you saw Maria?" Ryan asked Maybelle.

"Maybe two days before she went missin'. She came by every day to see Lisa so when she didn't come, I wondered. Not worried but wondered."

"She never said anything that caused any alarm bells to go off?" Berger asked. "She didn't appear concerned or afraid? I'm talking about after she talked to the people who weren't happy with what she knew."

Maybelle cocked her head toward Connor. "He knows a lot more'n me. Only thing she ever said to me was things was gonna get better for us, and they did. She bought Lisa some nice clothes and gave me more money for food and whatever I needed."

"That didn't cause alarm bells?" Berger asked, disbelief in his voice. "You never wondered about that? Where she was getting the money? That it might have something to do with this mystery person?"

Maybelle considered Berger a moment before answering. "You still askin' questions to find out what happened to Maria or accusin' me of somethin'? Tryin' to make me feel like I shoulda done somethin' different and Maria wouldn't have been killed?"

Berger shook his head. "Not at all. I don't think you could have done anything to make this turn out differently. It looks like Maria was determined to do what she did. And if I had to guess, I'd say she didn't say anything to you or Connor to protect you and to protect Lisa. She knew she was taking a risk."

Ryan jumped in. "We have pieces of a puzzle, Maybelle. We're trying to put them together. If Maria had more money than usual and we can trace back where she got it that should help us find out who she had been seeing and..."

"No," Maybelle said with a wave of her hand. "I got all that. I don't like the way he's askin' his questions."

"You're right," Berger said, "and I apologize. I guess I'm frustrated. As Declan said, we have a puzzle and it's a complicated jigsaw puzzle."

"Yeah, she had more money than usual. Yeah, I wondered. No, I didn't ask 'cause I was scared for her and I couldn't do nothin' 'bout it. She woulda told me if she wanted me to know. So, I put it aside."

Berger to Ryan, "You searched Maria's place, right?"

"Of course."

"Didn't find any money? I mean an unusual amount?"

Ryan gave Berger a look. "If I had, you'd know."

"Just setting the table for everyone. Okay," Berger said, "here's what we have." He raised his index finger. "Maria identified someone at Ottinger she knew and found out they were there under an assumed name." He lifted a second finger. "She figured someone must be trying to hide the fact this person was there. Three," he said, presenting a third finger. "She went to see someone who, apparently, paid her to keep it quiet. That about it?"

Connor and Maybelle looked at each other and nodded.

Berger and Connor were up and out the door where Ryan stopped before crossing the threshold. He asked, "What's the situation with the father? The girl's father?"

"There is no 'situation,'" Maybelle responded.

"Meaning?" Ryan persisted.

98

"Meaning it was a mistake. She got pregnant. Tried to do the right thing. He lived in Galveston and she moved there. Had the baby. He got killed in an accident. He rode a cycle so I guess it was that. She never said."

"Really?" Ryan said in surprise.

"You've not gotten that Maria kept her business to herself?" Maybelle asked.

"Okay, so she came home with the baby."

"And had some problems bein' a single mother and makin' ends meet. Caused her to do stupid things and she got in trouble with Child Services. Look, she did what she did to take care of her child. Her choices weren't the best and I'm thinkin' that's what got her killed. Unfortunately, it fits a pattern, but she was a good person with a good heart," Maybelle said, tears streaming down her cheeks. "That's all I gotta say."

"Thanks for that," Ryan said.

"Well," Berger said, "that would explain why we never found out anything about the child. Our searches didn't take us to Galveston."

"It also takes the father off our list and we can move ahead in the direction we're going," Ryan said.

***

"Always nice to be chauffeured," Jones said as he got out of the backseat of the limousine. "Don't have to drive around looking for a parking space."

"I call bullshit," Stephens said as one of his security guards held open the door of the federal building. He pointed Jones ahead of him. "When was the last time you had to drive yourself anywhere?"

Jones gestured at the phalanx of security guards. "Just saying. All of this is a nice perk. Very comforting."

"In a rather uncomfortable way. Keeps the need for security top of mind."

"Relax. You only need security when you do things that piss people off. When you don't do anything, you reduce those odds."

"Fuck you," Stephens said playfully as the elevator doors closed. "Do we need to rehearse this?"

"No, let it flow. I'm sure we can make our point convincingly."

"So, we're not concerned with subtlety, being sensitive? Showing the man some respect? He's been a public servant for, what, forty years?"

Jones laughed. "I'll leave all that to you."

When the elevator jerked to a stop two gray-suited, sun-glassed large bodies positioned themselves shoulder-to-shoulder. They stepped forward together as the doors slid open and peered down the corridor. One looked left, the other right. The third man in the detail hit the Stop button, waited until he received a nod, and then gestured at Stephens and Jones, who walked into a marble hallway.

The corridor echoed with footsteps as the five men marched toward the far end of the hall. As they neared a door festooned with the state seal and a plaque to the right of entrance identifying the office of United States Senator Roy Evans, a young man who had been standing to one side of the door, smiled. "Welcome," he said and stood aside as the group passed into the reception area.

A collection of photographs covered the wall directly to the right of the entrance. Jones stopped, leaned close, and read, "The scissor-tailed flycatcher. Says it's the state bird. I didn't know that. I mean I know we have a state bird but didn't know it's this one. Never heard of it."

"Shame on you," Stephens said.

"Yes, shame on you," agreed Roy Evans who had stepped into the room from a doorway behind a cloth-covered reception cubicle.

"But this I did know," Jones said, pointing at another framed photograph. "The red rose is the state flower."

The three men clasped in shoulder bumping hugs. Big smiles all around.

Jones broke away and bent close to a framed newspaper clipping. "Christ, Roy, how long ago was that? You look like you're twelve."

Evans walked over and stood behind Jones. "That's the night I won my first race for political office. County commissioner in Tulsa. I was twenty-four."

Evans tapped the glass front of another photo. "Me the night I was elected senator." He patted a prodigious stomach that threatened the buttons on his shirt. "A few pounds ago."

"And that's Barry, right?" Stephens asked, stepping toward the wall. "And Stoops."

"Shit," Jones exclaimed. "Is that Howard Schnellenberger? I forgot he was at OU."

"Brother," Stephens said. "First not knowing about the state bird and now this. You'd better bone up on this stuff if you're going to run for governor."

Evans jerked his head toward Jones. "What?"

"The reason we're here," Stephens said. "Why don't we go on into your office and talk?"

A young woman appeared from behind the cubicle that fronted the door to the office and asked, "Coffee? Water? Something else?"

"Monica Filer," Evans said, presenting the young woman with the proud smile. "This is Governor Stephens and Senator Jones."

"My pleasure," the woman said, her Stepford Wife smile showing a flawless set of gleaming white teeth. The perfect smile was enhanced by beautifully formed, full lips, and bright, clear blue eyes that nearly sparkled. She stepped toward Stephens and placed her hand under his elbow, tucking his arm close to her full breasts, and escorted him into a sunny office. Remington prints lined the walls, and reproductions of the artist's well-known sculptures of The Bronco Buster and Off the Range stood sentinel on either side of a large desk.

"You've changed the motif," Jones noted. He spread his arms and turned in a slow circle. "Not a single picture of a derrick or oil-covered rouster."

"Monica," Evans said to the young woman as he gestured to a small, round cherry wood table in the center of the room. "Why don't you bring us a carafe of coffee?"

She dropped her hand from Stephens' elbow, but not before squeezing it tightly and bending her chest into the gesture. "Coming up," she said cheerfully and left the room, closing the door behind her.

As the men settled into cushioned captain's chairs, Evans smiled broadly and slapped the top of the table to emphasize: "So it's the executive suite for you, Whalen? I always knew you would move up. Frankly, I was worried you had your eye on my seat."

"No," Stephens said. "That's me."

Evans drew back his head, blinking as if trying to bring something into focus, the smile still animating his face, but his eyes had lost the joy. His attention darted from Jones to Stephens, the smile slowly fading. "What?"

"We're going to throw you the biggest, baddest retirement party ever known in Oklahoma politics," Stephens said, leaning forward and patting Evans on the shoulder.

As Evans absorbed the words, Stephens jabbed at his cell. "William Ricks, please. This is Governor Lincoln Stephens. He's expecting my call."

Stephens placed the cell on the table and pressed "speaker" and "Lincoln" roared through: "You there with Roy and Whalen?"

"I am, and we're giving Roy the good news about the bash we're planning for him with the help from you at API. And I got word Norman Ledbetter at the Cattlemen's Association, and all the gaming people are onboard. In fact, the Hard Rock Casino right in Roy's hometown has agreed to host the soiree. It'll be a night to remember."

Evans leaned forward to say something. His lips moved but there was no sound.

"Roy, congratulations from everyone here in D.C.," Ricks said. "We're grateful for all you've done to keep our great American industry alive and thriving. And I'm speaking for oil producers across the country. You're a damn legend."

Evans's lips continued to move without result.

"He's speechless," Jones said. "Thanks, Bill. We'll keep you posted on the details as we get everything nailed down."

Just as the phone signaled the disconnect, it buzzed in another call. Stephens peered at the face of the cell, jabbed "accept" and said loudly, "You're late to the party, Norman."

"Sorry," a high-pitched voice apologized. "Got caught on another call but better a little late than never. What about Bill?"

"Just got off with him."

"I wanted to be sure and add my thanks on behalf of the ranchers and say no one has ever done more for our people than you have, Roy. You certainly deserve some time for yourself and the wife."

"Thanks for joining us," Jones said.

"My pleasure."

Evans stared at the cell, looked at Jones and Stephens and back at the cell as if wondering what to expect next.

"Okay," Stephens said, his tone now serious. "With the elections being next year the timing is perfect. Sometime early this summer we'll announce this thing for you, Roy. We won't say anything about your retirement. We'll call it a...uh..."

"An appreciation dinner," Jones offered.

"Good," Stephens agreed. "That's perfect. Then when you give your remarks, you'll announce your retirement, and endorse me for your seat. Surprise, surprise! Then, I'll accept your endorsement, formally declare my candidacy, and announce my support for Whalen, who will do his thing. All neat and tidy."

Evans was staring at his hands which he had placed flat on the table. His pallor had gone gray, drained of its alcohol-ravaged orange tinge. The red and purple canals of the broken veins in his bulbous nose were more prominent than ever against the graying of his cheeks.

Stephens and Jones looked at each other, eyes widening in realization Evans was in crisis. Stephens jumped up from his chair so violently it tumbled backward. "Monica," he yelled loudly as he turned toward the door. "Help!"

The woman barged through the room with the carafe in hand. Seeing the catatonic Evans, she dropped the carafe and ran to the desk at the far end of the room, yanked open the top drawer and began tossing items on the floor. Rubber bands. A mail opener. Pens. American flag lapel buttons. Finding a pill bottle, she ran toward the table spinning off the top, pills scattering along the floor and tabletop, and forced one into Evans's mouth. She demanded "water" and pointed to a small bottle on the desk. Stephens ran, grabbed it, raced back, stood over Evans, and yanked his head back by the hair. He poured water down the man's throat, which Evans regurgitated along with the single pill. The woman shoved the pill, which had settled on Evans's chin, back into his mouth and took the bottle from Stephens. She tilted Evans's head gently and poured a small amount into his mouth, then massaged the man's throat. Evans swallowed and Monica, Stephens, and Jones took a step away from the table. The man's color began to return.

"What the hell was that?" Jones asked.

"Dysrhythmia," Monica answered.

"English," Stephens demanded.

"Abnormal heartbeat," she said. "It happens sometimes when he gets excited or gets stressed."

"Is he going to be okay?" both men asked simultaneously.

"Yes, it usually takes a minute or two for him to relax after he takes the pill." Monica looked intently at both men. "What were you talking to him about?"

Stephens and Jones exchanged glances. Stephens offered, "Nothing bad."

Twenty-Five Years Ago

The shack was in the fields not far from the house. Whalen and Marco rode their bikes there almost every day. Whalen tolerated his younger brother because there were no other children his age in the new tract being developed by his father.

The Joneses were among a handful who had moved into the neighborhood surrounded by a vast green moat. The high grass, wild shrubs, and trees offered a continent of adventure for young boys and within days of arriving, they had declared it their domain. The fields became their province, their refuge. There wasn't a far corner they didn't investigate or a square yard left unexplored, with the exception of the shack. It was a lure, but the wood-boarded windows, rust-stained walls, collapsing rain gutters hanging from a makeshift roof of plywood and tarps, and remnants of a flagstone path leading from a misshapen, unkempt hedge to a door askew on its hinges, made them wary.

Still, the hovel was a draw luring them back each day they spent in the fields, but always from a distance, where they considered their options. Approaching the shack and knocking on the door was way down the list. Marco's preference was to throw rocks and run. He was insistent, and annoying, until Whalen stopped him with: "It looks like that place in Hansel and Gretel where the witch lived and wanted to kill and eat them."

"Let's tell Dad, then. This is his land. What if there is a person in there and they're bad, like a witch?"

"And if the witch is magic? And they all are," Whalen said, continuing with a theme he found far-fetched, but it altered Marco's focus from rocks to witches. "She comes and kills us."

"They burned her up," Marco responded. "Remember? We should do that. Burn it down," he said, nodding at the shack. "We can get some charcoal starter Dad uses for the grill and use those long matches he has. It'll be easy."

Whalen yanked his brother away from the trees. "Start a fire where Dad is building houses?" He turned in a small circle, gesturing at the space around them. "That's crazy."

It wasn't until the boys had retraced their steps around the fields for weeks, completely exhausting the unexplored areas, that they dared approach the shack, crawling toward it on hands and knees. About ten yards from the door they ran into a rusty gated fence hidden by the ravel of weeds.

Whalen tinkered with the latch. It had oxidized solidly in the paddock. Marco lay on his back and kicked at the gate; Whalen added his weight. Nothing.

Whalen pointed down the hedge line, which they followed to a bare spot, slipped through, waded the high grass, and stepped to one of the boarded windows. All they could see through the openings between the planks was the outline of a single chair. They moved quickly around the shack trying with no luck to find a better spyhole.

"Let's get outta here," Whalen whispered, his voice wavered, perspiration dripping from his face.

As the boys sprinted away searching for the bald spot in the hedge where they had entered, they were yanked off their feet – gripped by their collars – and held suspended, legs churning. They twisted wildly, flailing, screaming; they were dropped to the ground, scrambled to their feet, and without turning around, stumbled away.

A booming voice called after them, "Knock next time."

Hearts pounding, keening in terror, the boys ran at the hedge, bounced off the thicket in their panic to escape before falling through and running into the field where they reconnoitered. Together, they sprinted another twenty yards before turning back toward the shack. Both boys had tears streaming down their cheeks, and Marco had wet himself.

A thickly bearded old man stood watching, his thumbs hooked in his belt. He spit a stream of brown liquid at his feet and wiped residue from his lower lip with the back of his hand. A brown stain showed in his gray beard.

The boys turned and raced to a mound of brush beyond sight of the shack, slid under a wedge of bushes and lay there trying to fit the pieces together.

"Where'd he come from?" Marco asked.

"I don't know. We barely got close enough to see inside before we got caught."

"I told you we shoulda burned that place down," Marco said angrily.

"Stop talking about that," Whalen said and poked his head from under the cover of the bushes. He surveyed the surroundings carefully before leading Marco into the open.

The boys walked in a crouch, their heads on a swivel. Whalen stopped at the base of a large tree and looked into the branches. "Up there."

Marco followed Whalen's eyes. "What? You're gonna climb up there?"

Before Marco had finished his question, Whalen was hiking himself up to a Y-split in the trunk just above ground level. "Come on. We can probably see the place from up there."

"Why do we wanna do that?"

"'Cause," was Whalen's shorthand covering his curiosity about the old man and that shack.

Perched on the highest branches that could support their weight, the boys peered around the field. The chirping of birds along with the faraway sound of chugging machines and muffled voices provided a soundtrack.

"I can't see it," Marco said.

"Me, neither."

As the boys began to climb down, the tree shivered. Below, leaning against the trunk, arms folded across his chest, was the old man.

"Used to be you could see a good-sized pond in the other direction," he said, without looking up, "but they filled it in to have more land to build on." He walked around the tree to what had been the pond side. "Better come down before you fall down. Tree's dead. Mostly hollow. It ain't real sturdy."

Marco shook his head. "I'm not going down."

"Come on, boy," the man said gruffly. "It's gonna be dark soon."

"You go away first," Marco managed to blubber through a torrent of tears.

"I want you gone as much as you want to go. You're a bother, but I don't want to see you fall outta that rotten tree. That'll just bring more of you out here."

Whalen and Marco exchanged glances. Whalen moved down the tree stopping just above the Y-junction.

The old man sat down at the base of the tree. "Were a lot more trees to climb, too," he said, his eyes focused on the middle distance. "I climbed'em all," he said, punctuating his words with a stream of tobacco juice, much of it settling in his beard. "Every single one."

Whalen moved down slowly and stopped at the junction in the trunk.

The old man grabbed his boots around the ankles and rolled forward, sling-shotting himself upright. His faded denims were patched neatly in the back; his blue work shirt was cut into short sleeves just above the elbows. He walked a few yards from the tree.

Whalen jumped to the ground as Marco screamed, "No, he's gonna get you."

"Jesus, boy," the man said, looking up at Marco. "I ain't gonna *get* anyone. Sorry if I scared you, but you can't be sneakin' around like that. You scared the hell outta me."

"Come on down," Whalen said to Marco, keeping his eyes on the old man.

He was big, tall as well as broad. A wild shock of gray hair streaked with ribbons of dark brown framed what could be seen of a long, narrow face, straight nose, and thin lips. His eyes sparkled, clear green. Large hands hung at the end of muscled arms. A huge wad of chewing tobacco pressed against one side of his cheek, and constant use had stained his teeth.

"Like fishing? Could've fished in that pond that ain't there now." He pointed toward a large circle of red dirt. "You don't talk much, do you?" he directed at Whalen. "Your parents tell you not to talk much? Good advice. Learn more by listening."

Marco slid down the tree and stood behind Whalen.

"You two brothers?" Not getting an answer, he offered, "Yeah, brothers." He gestured toward the pair. "Same yellow hair and brown eyes. Usually with yellow hair you get blue eyes. And same bowed legs." He laughed. "Gotta a lotta years to grow and straighten those out."

"You a criminal?" Whalen asked.

"Or witch?" chimed Marco.

The old man spit a brown stream, wiped his beard with the back of his hand, and laughed. "Been called lotsa things. Never a witch. Guess I could be a criminal. Done some things that coulda landed me in jail, but never got caught."

Whalen and Marco both took a step back.

"Long time ago," the old man said and started to walk away. "You'd better head back home," he said over his shoulder. "Be dark soon."

***

Over the next few days, the boys combed the area looking for the old man, but carefully avoided the shack. They were testing their courage...and failing.

By the third or fourth afternoon, after spending hours roosting in the dead tree, they argued about their next move. Whalen was for returning to the area around the shack to conduct surveillance; Marco favored throwing rocks and running. Whalen prevailed. They carefully snuck up to the passage in the hedgerow, screwed up their courage, and duck-walked to the front of the shack, where they squatted and listened.

"I hear you sneaking around out there," the old man yelled. "Come in or leave."

Marco took off. Whalen turned to follow but resettled into a squat and studied the rundown shack. He stood, walked slowly to the door, and stared at a hole from which the knob had been removed.

"Push hard. It doesn't open easily."

Whalen struggled with the door, which scraped across a concrete floor.

"Put your weight behind it."

Whalen leaned his back against the door and pushed with his legs sliding it open enough to squeeze into a dark room. He blinked rapidly as his eyes adjusted. A flickering light created shadows on the wall at the back of a single room. The old man sat in a large, threadbare upholstered chair, puffing on a pipe, a book in his lap. A candle rested in an ornate, silver holder on the arm of the chair. The room smelled of sweet tobacco and burned wood.

"Where's your brother?"

"He got scared and ran."

The old man, jabbing his pipe, pointed at a cot against the wall to his right. "Take a load off."

Whalen inspected a bedroll laid out on the cot. A Coleman lantern, a pouch of tobacco, and a heavy glass ashtray shared space on an adjacent chair. "Why do you live here all by yourself?"

"'Cause I want to."

Whalen picked up movement under the old man's chair. A cat emerged, then flattened to the floor. Watching Whalen carefully, it bellied cautiously to a rug between the chair and cot and circled slowly, settling. A bookcase sat against the wall opposite the bed. It was built of heavy, dark wood. Books and magazines were scattered along the shelves. A large fireplace filled the wall behind the old man. Reflections of light played along the ceiling prompting Whalen to turn his shoulders toward the door. The flickering light from the candle was reflecting from the glass surface of a large, framed photograph leaning against the front wall.

"What's your name, boy?"

"Whalen," he answered, trying to keep his voice from quavering. "Whalen Jones."

"Whalen?" the old man said, a question in his voice. "Don't know that I ever heard that name before."

"Means 'young wolf.'"

"Does it now?" He considered this a moment before adding, "That's quite a name. And your brother. What's his name?"

"Marco."

"I heard of that one before. Italian."

"Whalen is Irish."

"Italian and Irish. One of your parents is Irish and the other's Italian, right?"

"My mother's Italian. Don't know about my father."

"My guess is he's Irish. You and your brother are different."

Whalen cocked his head in question. "What?"

"You're here. He ain't." The old man leaned back and blew a puff of smoke toward the ceiling.

Whalen turned his attention back toward the photograph and made out the figure of a man. "Who's that?" he asked.

"My great-great-grandfather."

Whalen stood and walked over to the photograph of a bearded man, his head covered by a wide-brimmed Stetson hat. He held a rifle across his chest on which was a bevy of medals over the pocket of a uniform. Brass buttons lined the front and cuffs of the jacket. "Looks like you."

"Bring it over here."

Whalen struggled with the heavy piece, shuffled slowly, and set it down in front of the old man.

"Turn it around and lay it on the floor." The old man scooted to the edge of his chair and held the candle over brown paper covering the back of the framed work. "You're right there," he said, pointing at a small square near the middle of what appeared to be a map sketched on the paper.

Whalen sat down and surveyed a compass icon in the lower right corner of the map. He waved his hand over the etching. "This is all the land around here?"

"Yes, and these markings," the old man said, gesturing with his pipe, "are other buildings that used to be here."

Whalen bent closer to the surface, which was cracked and torn in places making it difficult to interpret the sketches. He pointed at the largest square in the middle of the rendering. "What's that?"

"Where he lived," the old man said, tapping the frame.

"And that?"

"The barn."

"The barn?" Whalen said, wonder in his voice. He pointed at a cross-hatched rectangle taking up much of the drawing. "And that?"

"Farmland. And those are stables," the old man said, jabbing his finger at a squared marking. "Those," he shifted his attention, "were buildings where the people who farmed the land lived."

Whalen sat back and looked around the small room. "What was this?"

"The groomers lived here." Responding to a question in Whalen's eyes, he added, "The people who took care of the horses." He leaned forward and pointed at a square marking near the barn.

"And that?" Whalen indicated another impression. This one was round and set apart from the other indications.

"Cemetery. Family plots."

Whalen, on all fours, his face hovering over the surface of the drawing, studied the legend. He read: "'This is the property of Michael Nichols.'" He looked up at the old man. "That your great-great-grandfather?"

"Yep."

"What happened?"

The old man leaned back and laughed. "Life happened, boy."

"What does that mean?"

"That means everything that used to be here was sold or fell apart. My people couldn't afford to keep it up."

"Why?"

"Lots of reasons, mostly they weren't made for the times, I guess. There were also some human weaknesses involved like gambling and drinking, but I don't know much about all that. It wasn't talked about."

"Does that mean this" – Whalen circled his hand over the brown paper surface – "isn't yours anymore?"

"Right."

Whalen sat down, his attention still on the framed work. "Did you sell it?"

"I didn't do a thing. Family that came before me sold parcels. Other parts were lost by bad business decisions." The old man blew out a cloud of smoke. "It doesn't matter."

Whalen remained fixated on the jottings on the map. "All this was yours," he said, wonder in his voice.

"No," the old man said sternly. "Never was mine. None of it."

"But you're living here," Whalen said, nodding at the small square sketched on the brown page.

"Just stayed on. Living here doesn't mean I own it. The bank ended up with most of it and sold it." He waved his hand toward the front door. "And that's what happened to it. Pond gone. Everything gettin' leveled and those boxes going up everywhere."

Whalen swiveled his shoulders, taking in the entire room. "Where do you go to the bathroom?"

"Not in here." The old man smiled at Whalen's look of confusion. "There's a place out back."

"You don't have a kitchen."

The old man cocked his head toward a darkened corner of the room. "Got a potbelly stove."

Whalen stood and walked to the soot-stained piece of iron. "You can cook on this?"

"Can make real good food."

Whalen returned to his spot and sat down. "Where do you get your food?"

"Same place you do, I imagine."

"The store?" Receiving a nod, Whalen asked, "You have money?"

"Enough."

Whalen assumed his position on all fours over the surface of the rendering. "They sold all this?" he said, a touch of indignity in his voice. "Why would they do that?"

"I told you. Lots of reasons."

Whalen plopped back down on his backside. "Doesn't seem fair."

The old man looked intently at Whalen. "Life isn't fair, boy. Don't expect things to come to you."

Whalen stared into his lap chewing on the old man's words. They did not sound right to him.

Sensing Whalen was stewing, the old man said, "You want things to happen, you gotta make'em happen. I learned that too late and here I am. 'Course, I'm not sure what I coulda done, but" – he spit into a cup – "that's a whole other story."

"What happens when...?" Whalen looked up and pointed at the door. "When they come?"

A beat passed before the old man asked, "What time you supposed to be home?"

"By six o'clock."

"Last time I had to send you off, too. It's closing in on six o'clock." He stood and ushered Whalen to the door.

Whalen took a few steps away from the shack, turned, and asked, "What's your name?"

"Shane. Not as fancy as yours, but it'll do."

***

As soon as Whalen walked into the house, his mother confronted him. "Your brother tells me you're going to a strange man's house." A tall woman with the broad shoulders of an athlete, she was imposing, and threatening when she wanted to be. "You know better than that."

Whalen looked past his mother and found Marco sitting in front of the television. He refused to meet Whalen's death stare.

"He's an old man who lives in those fields. In an old house. A shack. He's nice."

"Oh, he's nice," his mother said sarcastically. "And how do you know for sure he's nice?"

"He has a cat," shot out of Whalen's mouth.

His mother looked at him quizzically. "What?"

"His name is Shane and he's old and he has a cat. He wouldn't hurt anyone."

"First of all, being old and having a cat doesn't mean he's nice. Second, there shouldn't be anyone living over there." His mother pointed at the door, still open. She walked past Whalen and slammed it closed. "It's going to be cleared for more houses."

"I told Whalen that, Mom," Marco said accusingly. "I said we should throw rocks at the house to scare the man away."

"No, Marco, no rock throwing. Your father will take care of clearing the field." She settled her attention on Whalen. "And you won't be going back to that house." She bent forward until she was eye-to-eye with Whalen, her brow furrowed. "Do you understand, young man?"

"Dad owns this land?"

His mother straightened, folded her arms across her chest, and stared down at Whalen. "You know your father builds houses for people."

"But does he own the land?"

"No, other people own the land."

"Then we have to tell them to let the old man stay there."

"What in the world has gotten into you?"

"It's not fair he has to leave. His family had a farm and stables and people living here."

"It's not his land anymore. He sold it or..." His mother grunted in exasperation. "It doesn't matter what *used* to be here. You stay away from that man." Not getting a response, she repeated, "You stay away from him. Do you understand me, young man?"

"Okay," Whalen responded petulantly, walking past his mother, near his brother, who he slapped on the head, and went into his bedroom.

***

Whalen did go back to the shack. Every day. Shane guided him through the fields and showed him the remains of the barn and stables.

"Thirteen horses," Shane said as he walked along the remains of a wood-plank wall. "This was the back of the stalls."

"Saw this before when I was exploring. Didn't know what it was. You ever ride any of the horses?"

"Gone by the time I was growing up. Just heard about it. Some of the horses were for what they call dressage. That's where they ride the horses around and show them off like when they parade dogs at dog shows."

"Any race horses?"

Shane shrugged. "Don't think so. Don't think people did a lot of racing 'round here. Got something else I want to show you." He led Whalen to the brick footprint of a large space. "This used to be the barn."

"You had cows and pigs?"

"I didn't have anything. This was mostly gone when I was growing up. Like the stables. Follow me."

He walked toward the remnants of a brick wall at the rear of the footprint, Whalen in tow. The stench began about six feet from the wall, so strong it attacked Whalen's nose and traveled to the back of his throat. By the time they passed through an opening in the wall, Whalen was gagging. He ran from the wall and settled well away from Shane.

"I need you to come here," Shane insisted.

Whalen covered his mouth and nose with the top of his T-shirt and walked to where the old man stood. Shane pointed to the wall. "You know anything about that?"

Whalen recoiled and turned away from the sight of half-dozen dead cats nailed to the ruins of the wall. All had their throats cut and eyes removed. He shook his head in disbelief.

"About a month ago, I started noticing some of the cats who used to come around for food weren't doing that." He pointed. "I found this."

Whalen walked away from the wall keeping his back to the carnage. "Why would you think I knew anything about that?"

"Just you be careful."

"What do you mean?"

"I mean be careful. Whoever's doing that" – he nodded at the butchery – "is dangerous."

***

Men and machines pushed across the fields. Piles of wood, bricks, and tools followed into large swaths of land cleared out to enable the advance. Orange-helmeted workers hurried about marking off the foundations of homes with small blue flags where concrete foundations were laid. The wooden skeletal frames of houses came next. There was an excitement to this noise and bustle.

As the activity advanced toward the shack, Shane grew quiet and sullen. Hikes into the shrinking boundaries of the fields stopped.

The last words Whalen exchanged with Shane were about Marco. "I saw your brother a few days ago. Strange little boy."

"Saw him? Where?"

Shane gestured toward the door. "Just beyond the fence. He yelled something about men coming around to tear down my house. Said your father ordered it."

"Sorry."

"You have nothing to be sorry about. Your parents wouldn't like me saying this to you but 'shit happens.'"

"Life isn't fair."

Shane laughed. "Lesson learned. You do what you have to do to get the best out of it."

***

"Progress," Whalen's father called it when he confronted him about tearing Shane's house down. "Not something I want to do, but we need the property."

"Build around it," Whalen demanded. "It's a small house."

"It's a smelly, awful house," Marco injected. "No one would want to live next to that."

"What's going to happen to him?" Whalen was in tears.

"He gonna die soon," Marco said. "He's old. That's what's gonna happen to him."

If their father had not been there to pull Whalen off his brother, Marco would have been hurt worse than a black eye and cut lip.

***

Whalen found the large, framed photo propped up against the back of the couch. "Where did you get this?" he called out loudly, desperation in his voice. He ran into the kitchen where his mother was sitting in the breakfast nook nursing a cup of coffee. That..." Whalen said, losing his voice to a tightening throat. He ran back to the kitchen door and looked toward the living room. "Where did it come from?"

"That dirty old picture? I was going to ask you. I found it next to the front door this morning when I went out for the newspaper. It had your name taped to it."

Whalen bolted out of the house and ran into the fields. The shack was gone. A large, level graded area stretched out like an empty tabletop. Men were pounding stakes into the soft, brown earth.

"Where's Shane?" Whalen shouted, running toward the nearest workmen.

"Hey, kid, you shouldn't be here," someone yelled from behind him.

He stopped and turned. "Where's Shane?" he directed at the person who was approaching.

"Who?" the man asked, grabbing his arm, and leading him away from the area. "You're the second one I've had to run off today."

"He lived there," Whalen said, twisting and gesturing over his shoulder. "In the shack. Where is he?"

"Oh, the old man. Don't know. The place was burned to the ground when we got here this morning. Saved us the trouble of dozing the junk heap. Kid, you stay off this land, away from the construction area. You could get hurt."

Wednesday-May 9

The bus station had been the worst. He bought a ticket but could not stomach the three-hour wait. The smell. Sweat with a touch of vomit and a dash of industrial cleaner. It invaded his nose and gave him a headache.

And the people. Marco fully understood the reference to "the unwashed masses."

The final push came when a woman, stinking of alcohol and cigarettes, sat across from him in the waiting area, a screaming baby in her arms, a cell phone to her ear, crying about being kicked out of her home. By her parents.

Marco picked up his shopping bag of newly purchased clothes and toiletries, and rushed through the stinking tide of humanity, out the revolving doors and across the street. He jumped into the first cab he could stop. Most drove right by his frantic signaling. He assumed they did not want to pick up anyone near the bus station. He asked if the driver would take him to Wichita Falls. No, he would not, but the company he worked for had a town car service that would.

***

Only after hours in the spa steam bath and by repeated trips to a hot shower and time in the Jacuzzi did he feel clean again. Now lying on the chaise, wrapped in a lush bathrobe, Marco surveyed the quiet surroundings of the indoor pool; the silence interrupted by the soft sound of water lapping against the sides of the kidney-shaped pool. It was still early in the season to sample the heavily advertised choice of three outdoor pools, including a lagoon with waterfalls and individual or communal hot tubs. The surrounding oak plank walls did offer a feel of the outdoors complemented by sliding panels opening to a patio and a large lawn beyond.

In truth, this was not an upgrade from Ottinger in amenities, but it did offer a more diverse clientele. To his left was a distinguished middle-aged couple that by virtue of being poolside here had obviously made a good life for themselves. A very good life. Bill and Edie. From Dallas. He was tall, thin, with sharp blues eyes, a Roman profile with a touch of gray at the temples. She was still shapely, long legs, perfectly coiffed white hair, high cheek bones, and piercing hazel eyes. Marco sat with them in the bar the previous evening. He learned Bill had sold his partnership in a law firm and she still dabbled in interior design, but left most of the work to their daughter. They were planning a year's cruise aboard the *QE2*. Lovely people.

"Another?" the poolside attendant asked lifting an empty glass from a side table.

"No, thank you. I'm good for the moment, but I'd like to take a look at your lunch menu, please."

"I'll be right back with that."

Marco took in the full scope of his surroundings and felt an uneasiness despite the comfort of the surroundings. He needed to understand what had happened. Last night was not like the others. It ended the same way, but without any of the satisfaction, no matter how fleeting that satisfaction always was.

Marco adjusted the chaise so he was sitting up straight and stared out the open end of the pool area at the green grass beyond the patio. He focused on a line of blooming rose bushes. Pink. Red. And white.

What was it?

He closed his eyes and laid his head against the softness of the cushioned matting. He catalogued his experience. On the surface everything was exactly like it had been before. Almost.

It began with his feeling a distance from his surroundings. As always. The dreamlike state. In certain ways it was the best part. His fantasies were engaged and wandered. Then the outlines sharpened. It was as if the camera eye suddenly focused. Sharp lines were drawn around the places and the people; the scene and the actors in his play became perfectly clear, iridescent. The clarity aroused his energy and sharpened his senses.

Marco sensed a presence and opened his eyes. "I hope I didn't wake you, sir," the attendant said sheepishly as he handed the menu to Marco.

"Not at all. Just resting my eyes."

"Let me know when you're ready to order," the man said, backing away from Marco, who nodded in response.

Marco resettled against the chaise and closed his eyes. It was the quickness. She hurried through everything, and in the end, she was a liar. And that made it all gross and messy. He did what he did to get rid of her. There was no...what? There was no anything. He came out of it without a result. He followed the rules. It looked exactly the same. Well, almost. In the end, with this one he just went through the motions.

Marco opened his eyes. That was it. He went through the motions. It had become rote. Except for her tongue and that was out of anger. There was no thought behind it. No reason.

"Well," Marco whispered, "she did lie."

Marco smiled at Bill and Edie. What a wonderful couple.

Thursday-May 10

The room was crowded and noisy. A platform at the rear was lined with cameras on tripods. A phalanx of cable and local television reporters were filming "teasers" in front of a banquet table on which SBI public information staffers were arranging name cards to identify speakers.

A short, compact man stuffed into a badly fitting suit entered the room through a door to the left of the table. He was followed by five men – four in uniforms identifying them as high-ranking law enforcement officers – guided to their chairs by a peripatetic young woman who placed small bottles of water in front of each setting and hustled away from the table as the men sat.

Before the group could fully settle, they were rushed by a pack of camera-laden photographers who stood in front of the table aimed and shot; a firing squad without the lethality. The young woman reappeared and coaxed the pack to the fringes of the assembly.

"Thank you for coming this morning," the short man said, brushing the tail of his bright red tie from the top of the table, where it settled when he sat, and tucking it into his beltline. "I'm Len Slade, Director of the Oklahoma State Bureau of Investigation. To my right is SBI Agent Joseph Berger. To his right is Sheriff Declan Ryan from Owen. To my left are Sheriff William Adams from Wesper, Police Chief Rolf Flipse from Laramie, Police Chief Richard Fenn from Mannix.

"Two years ago – the exact dates and other pertinent information are provided in fact sheets that will be available as you leave this morning – three women were killed. One in Wesper, one in Laramie, and one in Mannix. During his investigation, Chief Fenn consulted the Offender Data Information System and discovered the murder in Mannix had

122

similarities to previous incidents in Wesper and Laramie. He notified the SBI and asked for our assistance. Agent Berger met with Chief Fenn and subsequently with Sheriff Adams and Police Chief Flipse."

Slade was interrupted by, "You're talking about a serial killer," shouted at him.

"We'll be happy to take your questions at the conclusion of my statement," Slade said sternly. He waited a beat before continuing. "First, let me say these developments show the importance of entering information in the ODIS system. It has enabled us to extend our resources in this case. Agent Berger has been working with law enforcement authorities in these three jurisdictions for the past eighteen months or so. On April 23, we became aware of another murder in Owen having similarities to those being investigated by Agent Berger and we are working on this case with Sheriff Ryan of Owen."

As he spoke, an SBI public affairs officer entered the rear of the room, a box in hand. She placed the box on a card table next to the entrance, removed a stack of papers, and put them on the table. As quickly as she did, the attendees clambered from their seats and snatched the information.

Slade, clearly annoyed, waved the staffer out of the room before continuing. "We have put together a taskforce focusing on these crimes."

"*Taskforce*?" Berger looked down the line of men sitting with him for any indication of surprise. He could see from the body language – a subtle jerk of shoulders, a wide-eyed stare, a canting of a head in Slade's direction – that he was not the only one in the dark.

"I'll be happy to take your questions," Slade said, a wariness in his voice.

A group of reporters stood. Hands were thrust in the air. The words came in bursts.

"Please," Slade yelled, "I'll do my best to get to all of you. Sit down, raise your hand, and I'll call on you. Also, please identify who you are and your affiliation." Slade waited for the group to settle and picked out a woman at the back of the room.

"Audrey Meadows with the *Oklahoman*. You said the murders began two years ago. Why are we only learning about them now?"

"It took some time for us to understand we're dealing with a single offender...to collate information from the different scenes and identify the similarities among the victims."

"When did you determine it was one person?"

Slade looked at Berger. "Our primary investigator on this case can best answer that question."

Responding as he had been instructed, Berger said, "We were asked for our assistance after Chief Fenn realized his homicide had similarities to those in Wesper and Mannix. We reviewed each instance and did a side-by-side analysis of the victims, the victimology, how they were murdered, the modus operandi, and other determinants. A time-consuming process."

"That doesn't answer my question," the woman said. "Sounds more like you've been sitting on this for some reason."

Slade shot back, "We haven't been 'sitting' on anything. We've been working diligently with our partners." He nodded to his right and left. "The public and media in each of the affected cities were kept up to speed."

"So, when exactly did you come to the conclusion you're dealing with a serial killer?"

"Recently," Slade said and pointed to a man front and center whose carefully coiffed hair and powdered face gave him away as a talking head.

"Dan Herlihy, KOKI, Tulsa. 'Recently' still doesn't answer the question. Let me try this. Why now, Agent Berger? Is it because you haven't been able to find out anything on your own, so you decided you needed assistance from the public and the press?"

Again, as instructed: "There is a protocol to these investigations and we have been following that protocol. We made a strategic decision to move ahead carefully and confidentially. We decided to work the cases without public or media input for the time being so we could control the information coming to us. Often when we go public on cases such as this one, the media attention causes a disruption in how we proceed."

At which point the room erupted. A chorus of "bullshit" and "give me a break" floated around the room.

Slade popped out of his chair. "If you want the rest of what Agent Berger has to say, shut the hell up."

The noise level slowly dissipated.

Herlihy got things back on track. "You were saying, Agent Berger."

"The commonalities across these murders point to a single sexually motivated sadist. We have someone who is planning what he is doing. He is using preselected locations to capture his victims and subjects them to a variety of painful sexual acts, sexual bondage, intentional torture, and death by exsanguination."

"Exsanguination?"

"Their throats were cut."

"Next," demanded Slade, leaving the current questioner on his feet.

"You still haven't answered why you decided to go public," a young woman shouted before Slade could recognize anyone. As he was about to point to another questioner, she interjected, "Madeline Wicks, *Tulsa World*."

"The timing is right," Slade replied. "We've arrived at a point in the investigation when we feel you and the public can help us. It's that simple. While on the subject of media attention, I'm sure the families of the victims would appreciate your respecting their privacy. You can imagine how difficult this has been for them. I use the word 'imagine' because none of us can truly understand the grief and horror they are dealing with."

"When did you let the local police know you're dealing with a serial killer?" Wicks asked.

"As soon as we came to that conclusion."

"Did you let the families know as soon as you knew?"

"Yes. Next."

"Leslie Manday, KFOR-TV. How much danger are we in?"

Slade thumbed in Berger's direction.

"Not much," Berger said, then raised his hand in a cautionary gesture. "I don't want to be dismissive. There have been three and perhaps four women killed by the same offender, but this type of murder is estimated to comprise less than one percent of all murders committed in any given year."

"But isn't it common knowledge serial killers don't stop until apprehended?"

Berger nodded. "Yes, in most cases."

"So," Manday persisted, "we *are* in danger."

Berger considered his answer. "We are doing this to alert the public. So, yes, be vigilant."

"You," Slade selected a man on the fringes of the group who announced himself as Lymon Richards, AP.

"Agent Berger just said *perhaps* a fourth victim. Do we have three or four?"

"As I said earlier," Slade answered, "we are certain three are victims of a single offender. The most recent murder in Owen revealed similarities to the others. As soon as we have any more to say about it, we'll let you know. Have anything to add, Joe?"

"Only that we'd appreciate it if when reporting on these events you make it clear that so far we can attribute three of the murders to the same suspect. Please describe the one in Owen as not yet conclusively linked."

Slade announced, "One more question," and pointed to a woman standing on the camera platform.

"Lily Ramirez with KUOK. The first three murders came in a bunch about two years ago," she said, referring to the fact sheet. "The most recent one was about three weeks ago. Is that why you're withholding a positive link to the first three?"

Slade looked at Berger, who replied, "That is a factor along with some other anomalies."

"Like?"

"I'd prefer not to go into those," Berger said flatly.

"Serial killers follow a pattern, right?" the reporter persisted. "They act on urges. They are driven to kill. Given that, how likely is it the same offender would wait almost two years before killing again?"

Berger smiled at the reporter. "I'm still not going to discuss the recent case, Ms. Ramirez."

"Humor me," the reporter said. "Answer my question about the time factor. About the pattern these killers usually follow."

"Each one has distinctive habits, but you're correct. These offenders are *usually* governed by a need keeping them on a regular schedule. There have also been cases where an offender has a change in lifestyle causing an interruption in the pattern. The Green River Killer, for instance, got married and was happy in that marriage for a few years, and that interrupted his pattern. Some commit another crime and are incarcerated. Others change locations and before a pattern is identified, they move on. Ted Bundy, for example, traveled all over the Pacific Northwest and was finally apprehended in Florida. Any of these kinds of things could explain the gap we have here."

"What are you telling us then? Do we have an active serial killer or not?"

"We're telling you we have a laser-like focus on this investigation," Slade injected quickly. "All of these men" – he nodded in the direction of the men on either side of him – "are working tirelessly to find out who committed these horrible crimes and bring them to justice."

"Will Durant, *Duncan Banner*," a man called out without being acknowledged. "Per capita, we have more victims from serial killers than any other state. Why should we feel confident you're going to get this guy?"

Slade stood. "Thank you for coming. We'll keep you apprised as the investigation proceeds."

The others at the table, confused by the abruptness of Slade's dismissal, took a moment before filing out behind the SBI director.

***

Lee was ushered into the office by the waif-like assistant who tip-toed as she guided him to a couch and touched her index finger to her lips cautioning him to keep quiet.

Lee watched Jones leaf through a sheaf of papers, waiting until he looked up before interrupting. "I'm meeting with Cranston this afternoon."

"It's about time." Jones pulled himself close to his desk, rested his elbows on the leather blotter, and jutted out an index finger. "Point one, make sure he doesn't report this. Remind him Marco isn't on any register. And make sure he tells everyone who had any contact with Marco to keep their mouths shut. Then, find the son-of-a-bitch and take his ass back."

"I'll deal with Cranston. That's not a problem. Finding your brother is another thing altogether. Maybe he said something to someone there that'll give me a few breadcrumbs to follow. Speaking of which, tell me about Marco."

Jones pulled his head back in surprise. "What?"

"If I'm going to find him, I need to know more."

"You know what you need to know," Jones answered irritably.

"No," Lee said with a shake of his head. "We've never talked about him. We've talked about what he did. What the hell happened to the guy? What makes him do those things? I need a better feel for him; it might tell me where he'll go. Where he'll feel comfortable."

"Really?"

"You hired me because I'm an investigator. It's what I do. I have to know who he is to find him. Tell me about Marco."

Jones ran his fingers through his hair and sighed heavily. "I have some reports from therapists I can give you."

"I'll take those, but it would be helpful to get more from you. His brother. You must have some insight on him."

"I sure as hell don't understand what made him like he is. We grew up in the same house. Got the same treatment from our parents. We never spent a lot of time together, especially after I went to junior high. He was still in grade school. At that age, being two grades ahead was a huge divide."

Jones bent to his right and opened a lower desk drawer. He straightened, a pile of papers in his hand, which he handed to Lee. "This might help. From the therapists."

Lee took the material. "Were your parents strict? Religious? Any abuse?"

Jones came out of his chair. "Oh, for God's sake. You're not really going there?"

"Was Marco a bad kid?"

Jones turned away from Lee and stared out a window behind his desk. "No, my parents weren't strict, religious, or abusive. They were, for lack of a better word, 'normal.' They expected us to do our best and stay out of trouble."

"Did Marco stay out of trouble?"

Jones sat down and stared past Lee. "No, he *was* trouble. I've told you, it was one thing after another. He killed animals. He burned down a man's house."

"Wait," Lee interrupted. "He burned down someone's house. With them in it?"

"It was more like a shack and, no, no one was in it, but a man was living there and Marco burned it down to get him out. He thought he was doing my father a favor. It's a long story." Jones waved his hands in front of him. "Enough on that."

"No, not quite. Killed animals?"

Jones stood and began pacing behind his desk. "There was one occasion I know about for certain because I saw some cats he killed. The other times people told my parents..." Jones stopped and stood stock still as if collecting his thought. "Neighbors' pets disappeared and someone said they saw Marco with one of them. That kind of thing."

"You know that is a sign of...?" Lee began.

"Yeah, I know, I know. At least he never wet his bed."

"But there were other problems?"

"He was a pain in the ass. Got kicked out of school for exposing himself when he was eleven, I think it was. My parents sent him to a private school where he assaulted a girl and was hauled into court and spent a couple of years in a, uh, a juvenile home, or whatever they're called."

"Not a runaway though." A hesitation from Jones prompted Lee to add: "He didn't run away from home, or any of these places? The schools or that juvenile home?"

"Hell, no. Marco couldn't take care of himself. Well, not 'couldn't' so much as didn't want to. Still doesn't. Feels others should take care of him. I mean, he can be charming. He gets along well with others, until he doesn't. He's a manipulator. It's always all about him and what he wants. He uses people to get what he wants, and he doesn't give a shit how it ends up affecting them."

"You're describing a psychopath."

"No, shit."

"He was in therapy early on?"

"He was in therapy constantly, and he would seem perfectly okay for periods of time and then" – Jones clapped his hands loudly – "bam! Like a different person. He'd assault some poor girl or get caught by a neighbor peeking in her window. It's like it came out of nowhere."

"Okay," Lee said pensively. "He was scratching an itch."

"What?"

"An urge. He'd get an urge and it would drive him. It's what makes them do what they do. Like being an addict. They are driven. I'm guessing the therapy came and went as Marco's behavior varied."

"It came and went all right," Jones said, sitting down heavily. "I think it was more like Marco was clever enough to talk his way out of therapy. As I said, he's a manipulator and could even manipulate the therapists into thinking he had seen the error of his ways, or he could control himself, and he'd get a clean bill of health. In many ways, he's a remarkable person."

"Did you ever talk to him about any of this?"

Jones turned his chair toward a credenza behind his desk and opened a door in the center panel revealing a safe. He fiddled with the dial, lifted out thick files and several books. He spun back around and dropped the heavy pile on his desk. "How could I talk to someone I can't understand? And I tried." He gestured at the mound. "I read all that. Medical journal studies of sociopaths, psychopaths, and all stripes of behavior in between. FBI monographs on serial killers." He lifted a book from the pile. "And after the worst of it, I started in on these." He read the titles: *Inside the Minds of Serial Killers, The Anatomy of Motive, My Life Among Serial Killers.* The thing I learned is I'll never understand anything he does."

Jones shuffled through the pile and pulled out a few pages. "I found some stuff that scares the hell out of me, but probably comes close to describing what drives Marco." He looked up at Lee. "And I'm not drawing that from any conversations I've had with him, because he's way too smooth to give up anything. I'm making my judgments based on his history and what he did."

Jones nodded at a page in front of him. "This describes what I imagine goes through Marco's head. "'It was like I was in fast-forward on my own remote control. It was fast and chaotic... Afterwards, I didn't dwell on it. I had no fantasies because I was living in my fantasies, doing whatever I wanted to do whenever I felt like I could get away with it. I didn't have to think about it or fantasize about it, before or afterwards, I enjoyed doing it. Afterwards I didn't think about it, ruminate on it, or look it up in the newspapers or collect clippings.'" He picked up another page. "And I think this one nails it. 'I like killing people because it is so much fun.'

"Bottom line. I've tried to understand him. I haven't been able to and at this point, I don't care to. I need him gone from my life. That's why he's where he is. Well, where he *was*."

Jones lifted the pile off his desk, turned, and replaced it in the safe, closed the panel door, and swung back around. "So, let's dispense with any talk about 'why' or 'who.' There are no answers. Just work in the real world and find him."

"Okay," Lee said. "Some of this...what you told me is helpful. Marco can move comfortably in social situations. He isn't going to be hiding along the fringes."

"Fringes?"

"He isn't going to be hiding with the homeless or sleeping in shelters."

"Oh, hell no. That's definitely not who he is or how his...uh..." – Jones waved his hand in a circle as if trying to conjure up a thought – "sins were punished. Every time he went off the deep end, my parents provided a soft landing. Therapists. Private schools."

"How'd he hold down a job?"

"He didn't. My father tried to fit him into his company. Marco was good with numbers. He was a genius with numbers and did some accounting for my father. One time he found a way to massage the numbers and saved him a fortune in taxes. Legally. But he'd always fall off the wagon. Do something stupid."

"And he'd end up at places like Ottinger?"

"No, my parents wouldn't do that. They couldn't bring themselves to send him away. To 'abandon their child.' They couldn't see they weren't doing him any favors. Anyway, that's when the therapists kicked in. When he screwed up and ended up in one of those juvenile homes...jails... whatever they're called...my parents hired the best lawyers money could buy to get him out and sent where he could be treated and not warehoused. You see how much that helped. My parents are gone and I don't have the patience for his shit."

"But you *did* have the patience."

"Yeah, and what a harebrained mistake. I can't believe I thought I could handle him." Jones let out a sigh. "Taking him on that campaign swing was flat-out stupid. I should've known better. A vestige of my parents' failure."

"Your brother's keeper."

"Can we please move on to the 'what the fuck are you going to do about it' part of this conversation?

"Marco has money. Cash. He's smart. He won't stick around. He'll have to travel by train or bus. With those he won't be asked for an ID to buy a ticket because we could track that. I'm guessing he'll try to hide in plain sight. A city. Probably stay in an upscale hotel, given what you've told me. Doesn't sound like the Motel Six kind of guy."

"So, you've narrowed it down to him taking a bus or train to the city and staying in a nice hotel," Jones said sarcastically.

Lee stood. "It's a start and talking to Cranston should add some breadcrumbs." He stopped at the office door. "Marco left Ottinger to scratch his itch. He's on the hunt and it's unfortunate, but I'm probably not going to find him until another body turns up."

Jones gripped his hands together. "If that's where this is going, do the world a favor. Find him and kill him."

***

Lee walked into the massive foyer of the Ottinger Wellness Center. A large chandelier hung directly above the center of the room. A staircase to the right of the cast-iron and glass double-doored entrance curled along the wall to a second-story landing bordered by a polished wood balustrade. A skylight admitted a beam of sun scattered by the chandelier into a prism of colors that danced along the marble floors.

"Mr. Lee," a high-pitched voice called from the shadows of a hallway on the far side of the foyer. A short man emerged into the light, leading with his stubby arm held out stiffly toward Lee. "Dr. Drew Cranston." A large round head sat atop narrow shoulders topping a pear-shaped body. "Please," he said pointing in the direction from which he had come.

The men walked side-by-side down a highly polished pale wood oak corridor. Recessed lighting fell gently on silk-weave wallpaper. "I'm terribly sorry we have to meet under these circumstances," Cranston said with dramatic regret as he guided Lee into a large office.

Large windows were covered by heavy navy blue, pleated cloth panel drapes. A large desk sat in the middle of the room surrounded by couches and armchairs arranged on Persian area rugs.

"I know," Cranston said as he guided Lee to a setting of chairs. "Unorthodox arrangement of furniture. Theater in the round, but it fits the business I'm in. Allows me to conduct sessions with large groups of patients."

"Like the conductor of an orchestra," Lee replied as he surveyed the carousel of furniture circling the desk.

"I can't tell you how embarrassed we are about what happened. It took us by complete surprise as you can imagine. Mr. Jones was doing so well. He had participated, if sporadically, in his one-on-one therapy sessions and group meetings. He had not expressed any dissatisfaction at all. I never expected it."

"We understand these things happen and..."

"No," Cranston interrupted. "They don't happen here. This is the first time. People just don't walk out. Although they voluntarily commit themselves into the West Wing, no one has ever left without signing out, or being released to someone. Of course, Mr. Jones's situation was a little different from the others."

"Okay," Lee said with a hint of impatience. "Our concern is finding Marco and returning him to your care."

"Which will be a great deal more careful going forward."

"Did he ever talk to you or anyone here about wanting to leave?"

"No, never. As I said, he was, or seemed, content and comfortable. He didn't interact with many of the guests, but he was pleasant when he did and cooperative with our staff."

"Good to know, now..."

"But," Cranston interrupted, raising a finger in a gesture of caution, "I have to say although Mr. Jones was cooperative and engaged, he never truly revealed much about himself, his circumstances, what brought him here, or anything along those lines."

"You were told when he was admitted he would be a unique case. Our concern was to keep him safe and safely sequestered. Treatment was never a priority."

His eyes closed in concentration, Cranston nodded thoughtfully. "Indeed, we were never told much other than he needed to be carefully monitored. I have to say I believe we could have been a great deal more helpful if we had more information. More guidance."

"You could have been a great more helpful if you had kept him from leaving. I'll need to see his room."

Cranston hesitated a moment, wrestling with the impulse to respond with a reassuring word, before settling on, "Of course."

***

As Cranston ushered Lee across the immaculately landscaped grounds, he described the West Wing, where they were headed, as "Our crown jewel. We offer the highest level of services for our guests, and complete discretion. This confidentiality is not only protected by the law but by our own strict code of conduct."

"The pitch sold us in the first place," Lee said flatly. "That and the secure campus. And speaking of confidentiality," he said as they mounted a bank of stairs leading to cast-iron and glass double-doors matching those of the main building, "we don't want any reports about this. No one needs to know he walked out of here."

"Of course."

Lee stopped Cranston at the top of the stairs. "Do me a favor and reinforce the 'discretion' message with everyone here, especially with those who came into frequent contact with him."

"As I said, it's a hallmark of this institution," Cranston replied intently. "All our associates understand they have an obligation to protect the privacy of our guests. Their contracts stipulate they are not to discuss the guests or our institutional procedures with anyone."

Lee leaned toward Cranston. "I want you to *personally* remind every person who came into contact with Mr. Jones to keep their mouths shut. Are we clear?"

"Done," Cranston replied firmly.

The men stopped in an elegant foyer, this one more akin to a large living room as opposed to the five-star hotel entrance of the main building. As Lee surveyed the settings of couches, high-back, pleated leather armchairs, and small round side tables, he asked, "Do you have CCTV around the outside of the building?"

"We do. Inside as well, and we've reviewed it carefully. I'll make sure you get a copy, but I can tell you it's not likely to be a great deal of assistance. We tracked Mr. Jones from his room through an exit at the rear of this wing and around the building to the caretaker's gate where we lose sight of him."

"Where does that gate go?"

"To an employee entrance and delivery area and a side street."

"Are the grounds secured in the evening?"

"Yes, the front gate is closed and locked."

"But this caretaker's gate is not."

"It is now, and we will be putting in more cameras on the property."

"Smart," Lee said as the men walked through the foyer.

Cranston stopped halfway down a lushly carpeted hallway to call attention to, "Our library with classics as well as contemporary authors. I'm told Mr. Jones spent a lot of time here."

Lee poked his head into the room. "Smells like a library."

"We often have authors come and read and discuss their..."

Lee cut him off. "Wonderful. You said he didn't socialize much with other people."

"That's what I was told. We get weekly reports on each of our guests."

Lee jerked around to face Cranston. "See, that's the thing that worries me. Weekly reports."

"It shouldn't. He's not identified by his own name."

"He's not here to get right with the world. Weekly reports aren't necessary. They create a record and we don't want a record. I think you missed the most salient of salient points about his stay here."

Again, with eyes closed in concentration, Cranston nodded. "The necessary changes will be made."

"Let's hope we aren't closing the barn doors..." Lee let his words hang. "What about interactions with staff?"

"If you're referring to maintenance people..."

"Anyone," Lee said forcefully. "People who clean up around here. Change the sheets. Wash clothes. Anyone."

"I'd compare it to a hotel. There isn't much interaction at all." Cranston nodded at a glass fronted area. "The gym. Full service."

"I want to see his room," Lee reminded Cranston.

"The residential wing is one floor up," Cranston responded, pointing them into an elevator.

As the doors closed, Lee asked, "What can you tell me about a Maria Luna who worked here?"

Cranston shook his head and wrinkled his nose in question. "I don't recognize the name."

"The police will be around to ask about her," Lee said as the elevator doors opened.

"The police?"

"Yes." Lee motioned Cranston off the elevator.

Cranston stood, rooted in place in front of the closing elevator doors. "Is this related to Mr. Jones? Did she have anything to do with his leaving here? Did she help him?"

"No, nothing like that." Lee stared at Cranston. "His room?"

Cranston walked ahead. "But, this Maria Luna?" he stammered, still fighting to understand the context.

"She was murdered."

"Oh, my God," Cranston exclaimed, his hand going to his mouth. "When?"

"About two weeks ago."

"How do you know about her...the murder? That she worked here?"

Lee stopped short and turned to face Cranston. "I know. Now you know. You won't be able to tell the police much, since you didn't know her. And I'm guessing from what you've told me about discretion and the contracts, that extends to the staff talking to the police about her."

Cranston nodded.

"When you remind your people about the need for discretion, and cover the obligations in their contracts, make sure they understand it covers anything they get asked about Luna.

Lee took a step closer to Cranston. "*Anything*."

***

Lee stood in the doorway and surveyed an immaculate living space. The room was large. Eight hundred square feet. A four-poster bed against the wall to the left of the door faced a lawyer's desk and an ergonomic, high-back mesh chair.

Lee walked to the desk on which sat a box of stationery and a marble block pen set. He leafed through the stationery. The correspondence slots along the top of the desk were empty. He opened the top middle drawer. A roll of stamps and a letter opener.

He stepped into a small bathroom. It smelled of bleach. A toothbrush was in a water glass. A bar of soap on the side of the sink appeared not to have been used. In a neat line along a shelf in the shower was a bottle of shampoo, another of conditioner, and a third of body wash.

Back into the room. A lamp rested on a night table next to a book of short stories by Ernest Hemingway. A small closet with a neatly arranged row of brown khaki pants and collared polo shirts in various colors. Two sports jackets, one brown another navy blue, share space with a windbreaker and a down coat. The effect was a room in which no one lived.

As he walked into the hallway, Lee was surprised by a woman who stopped short in front of him. "I'm so sorry," the woman said. "I didn't know anyone was in the room."

"My fault," Lee said courteously. He decided to test Cranston's promise of staff discretion. "Did you know the person who lived...lives here?"

"Not really, no. He never wanted anyone in his room. I brought his towels and sheets and he took care of everything. Even cleaned his bathroom."

"Did he ever talk to you about anything?"

The woman gave Lee a look. "Are you related to him?"

"No, just a friend. I'm concerned about him. You know he left, don't you?"

"I'm sorry but I can't discuss anything about our guests. Mr. Cranston can answer your questions."

"Of course," Lee said, satisfied.

"Can I ask you a huge favor?"

"Sure."

She looked past Lee into the room. "I think I dropped my cell phone in there the last time I brought the sheets and towels. He was working at his desk. I put them on the bed instead of in the closet" – she pointed at a door to the left of the desk – "and left. Would you mind looking for me? We all have one to use around the grounds and in case of emergencies." She peeked over Lee's shoulder. "God, I hope it's in there somewhere."

***

Jones stopped, straightened his tie, and buttoned his jacket. The governor's executive assistant, who accompanied him to the boardroom, said, "Good luck," and walked away at a fast clip.

All eyes went to Jones as he walked into the room and faced five men and Noreen West. Not a single smile.

Stephens pointed to a chair to his right and across the conference table from West. "Whalen just came into the room," he said, directing his remarks to a conference phone. "We now have all the players. There's Whalen and Noreen, Len Martin from the Petroleum Alliance. Reynolds Comer from the Gas Association. Meyer Smith from the Independent Petroleum Association. And Gary Iglesias from the Iglesias Group. On the line with us we have Senators Evans and Clifford. Congressman Milton Leonard is representing the state delegation in Washington. They couldn't all break away at the same time and tapped Milton to represent them."

Stephens took a deep breath, which he expelled and declared, "Okay then, gentlemen and lady, we have a problem."

"Fuck yes, we do," West said aggressively. She pointed at Jones. "I told you this was a bad idea."

Stephens raised his hand. "In fairness, Noreen, it wasn't Whalen's doing. It was my idea, which he and I massaged into the proclamation approach."

"Well, then, Governor," West said, "way to go."

"This is Milton," a disembodied voice spoke. "How the hell did the *Post* get this story?"

"I talked to Nancy Wilcox this morning," Jones spoke up.

"I hope you cut her a new asshole," Len Martin said bitterly. "Give those jerks an inch and they take a mile."

"No," Jones said with a shake of his head. "It wasn't her. Someone at the American Casino Association gave the story to the *Post*."

"The American Casino Association?" a number of voices asked simultaneously.

"The casinos have been big on using alternative sources of energy. Solar. Buying power from natural-gas-fired plants. And whatever else they can do. The focus of the article is on how casinos are going green and ACA's support for WindServ's request to BLM came up as evidence of what they're doing."

"Along with a paragraph or two about the damn proclamation," West said.

"The way I read it," Reynolds Comer spit out bitterly, "the point was to show how destructive we are to the environment, and how we're responsible for climate change, and all the usual apocalyptic shit."

Meyer Smith directed to Stephens and Jones. "I didn't know anything about the proclamation."

"That was the point," Jones said. "The idea was to keep it low key."

"And we all see how that worked out," West said through a sneer.

"Why do it at all?" Martin asked.

"Our governor will be running for the senate," West answered. "The light should dawn. He has to cater to the nutcases in his party."

"Not fair, Noreen," Stephens said sternly. "And way out of bounds."

"Tell us, then," Smith asked. "What was the thinking behind this? I'm assuming there was some thought given to it."

Stephens sat up straight and rested his arms on the table. "We've been fortunate in this state to have an industry that provides jobs and wealth to millions. The taxes you pay" – he said making eye contact with Martin, Comer, and Smith – "and those paid by your employees keep the backbone of government humming along. And that government has looked favorably on your industry. More to the point, those elected to run things here have worked hand-in-glove with you to make sure your industry prospered." He paused dramatically. "To make sure *you* prospered."

Smith and Martin started to object. Stephens shook his head. "Let me finish. The wind and solar folks have no more than a toehold in this state." He held up his hand and parted his index finger and thumb slightly. "Almost nothing. Whether we like it or not, or even believe it or not, there is a growing sense across the country that we have to consider sources of energy beyond what you all are taking from the ground. We can keep fighting it tooth and nail and stand in the way of even the smallest concession, or we can agree to let WindServ and the others make their case. There is no way in hell wind and solar energy are going to replace or even make a significant dent in your earnings for the foreseeable future. It can't happen. The energy they supply can't run a city. Can't fuel transportation. Hell, not enough wind turbines can be built any time soon to challenge you or make a difference in the supply of energy. And the equipment for them isn't even manufactured in this country. You all have to calm down and take a breath."

"Practicing your stump speech?" West said.

Stephens glared at West and returned his attention to Comer, Smith, and Martin. "The bottom line is you're going to be running the show no matter what. Take a step back and look at the big picture. It'll become clear upon the most basic examination that these folks won't be able to step up and do what they claim they can, and that's going to make the case for you."

"And that's what you were trying to do?" West said skeptically. "Let WindServ step on its own dick? No thought given to your own ambitions?"

Stephens let out a laugh. "Ever the blunt one, Noreen. Of course, I was thinking of myself. And you, and everyone around this table. Let's get real. How much damage was done by that story in the *Post*?"

"And the *New York Times*," Smith said. "I don't have it right in front of me, but the headline was a doozy."

"'Wind Making Noise,'" the voice sounding like Leonard's came through the teleconference module. "That's the headline. I'm waiting for MSNBC and CNN to pick up the story and do their usual 'fossil fuel is killing us all' thing."

"Excuse me," came evenly and quietly from Gary Iglesias. The only one not in a suit, the casually dressed youngish man smiled at those around the table. "The governor is right. Sometimes it's possible to be too close to an issue. You're not seeing the advantage that's been handed to you."

The others around the conference table exchanged glances. A skeptical "What?" came from West.

Stephens pointed out, "Gary is the principal in the Iglesias Group. He handles my campaigns, polling, media relations, and all the rest of it. I asked him to sit in with us. He has some interesting ideas." Stephens nodded at the dark-haired, square-jawed man whose energy showed in his positioning on the edge of his chair, leaning forward as if preparing to spring up and give a sermon. "Go ahead."

Iglesias spread his arms to indicate his message was for everyone. "You have been given a golden opportunity."

"Pray tell," West challenged him.

"Right now it's the *Post* and *Times*. Before it's over the *L.A. Times, Huffington Post, Slate* and all the usual suspects will jump on this story. They plagiarize from each other. And, as the congressman indicated, CNN, MSNBC, along with the rest of the alphabet cable news outlets will be all over it. They have a twenty-four/seven schedule to fill. You've been presented with a perfect opportunity to tell your side of the story without coming across as defensive or aggressive, if handled correctly. These people have to – at the very least – pretend to be fair. You've been gifted with a platform. A lot of platforms."

"To do what, exactly?" Martin asked.

Iglesias furrowed his brow and squinted in a show of earnestness. "One of the pioneers in the industry here in Oklahoma was a woman. She was also a Native American. A Cherokee. Lulu Hefner was the first woman to drill for oil on her own property and the first female oil operator in the state. She was a gifted businesswoman and made a fortune."

Stephens smiled broadly. "Like I said, Gary has some interesting ideas." He puffed with pride. "Go on."

"It sells itself," Iglesias said confidently.

"What sells itself?" West demanded. "I must be dull. Where are you going with this?"

"Using Hefner's history and story, we build on her growth, the growth of the industry in Oklahoma, and the value it brings here at home and to the country." Iglesias looked around the table. "We're not going to be hitting people over the head with all of this. It's not going to be a bludgeon approach, one where we drown them in numbers and statistics about all the good things you do. The focus will be on Hefner and people like her, using that as an axis around which we build our campaign."

"What campaign?" Leonard's voice filled the air.

"Patience," Stephens counseled.

Iglesias nodded at Stephens before continuing. "Using the opening we've been presented by these recent articles, and the attention that will surely be coming, we enlist women who are successful in the field, both as owners and even roustabouts, to write testimonials and op-ed pieces using Hefner as their starting point. You know, the 'without her, I'm not a success kind of thing.' American dream stories. 'See what the industry has done for us and for our country.'"

"In response to the *Post* and *Times*?" West asked.

"Initially," Iglesias answered. "That's the first shot. We build on that to present a full picture of the industry. At that point we'll include others. Experts in the field. Economists. Labor union leaders. But this isn't a narrow response. It's not simply a response to a couple of newspaper articles or a few cable news stories."

"And that's the beauty of this," Stephens said. "Sorry, Gary, go ahead. Got caught up in the excitement."

"Texas, Alaska, California." Iglesias looked at Stephens. "Your fellow governors could get involved. The pattern will be the same. I'm guessing there are women who are prominent in the industry in those states. Maybe even some historical connections, like with Hefner here. Start there and build on that."

Iglesias directed himself to the conference phone. "Senator Clifford? Congressman Leonard?"

A simultaneous "yes" followed.

"I'd suggest talking to your colleagues and sponsoring a resolution of some kind that dovetails with what we've got here."

"Another goddamn resolution," West said under her breath.

"Sure," Clifford responded. "We can do that, right, Milton?"

"I don't see why not."

"Carefully worded, of course," Clifford said.

Jones suggested, "Use ours for your template."

West started to say something but was stopped by a clipped "wait" from Stephens.

"The daily *Congressional Record* has a section for extended remarks if I remember correctly," Iglesias said.

"It does," answered Clifford.

"You and others from the Oklahoma delegation, as well as your colleagues from the states who agree to work with us can insert remarks about the resolution. We'll get copies of the remarks framed and awarded at service club meetings around the states to...oh, I don't know...uh...to people who have 'contributed to the advancement of the industry.' Whatever. I'm blue-skying here, but the point is this is something we can do for weeks and months following the initial start of this campaign so we can extend our messaging."

Reynolds Comer asked Iglesias, "Can you give us a formal proposal, Gary, with all the details? I'd like to present it the board of the Gas Association."

"What about your members?" Stephens directed himself to Len Martin from the Petroleum Alliance and Meyer Smith from the Independent Petroleum Association.

Both men nodded and Martin said, "Send me the proposal."

"Of course. I'll have it to everyone by tomorrow."

"And be sure to include an itemized budget," West said. She nodded at Jones and Stephens. "Since the two of you are going to ride this like hell during your campaigns, I suggest you pay for it."

Iglesias frowned. "I suggest not. With all the watchdog groups out there these days, someone is going to look into the funding. If they are tied to the money," Iglesias said, nodding at Stephens and Jones, "it gets mired in partisan politics and we lose any hope of staying above the fray. I'll incur the costs. It's a 'loss leader' for me. I know we're going to succeed with this, and when we do, I'll be getting people knocking at my door. Me picking up the tab keeps it 'pure' – for lack of a better word."

"Yeah," West said with a boisterous laugh, "there's got to be a better word."

"I have an idea on how we can maintain the *purity* level," Leonard said. "Make it bipartisan. I'll work with Milton and we'll reach across the aisle to bring in a solid lineup of members on the Hill. Give us a few days and we'll get back to you."

"Do you need my help putting this together?" Iglesias asked. "I have some solid staff contacts."

"Thanks, but no. These are our people. We know what buttons to push."

Friday-May 11

Ryan leaned toward Berger as they walked through the double doors into the elegant foyer of the Ottinger Wellness Center. "You have my permission to commit me."

"Gentleman," Dr. Cranston greeted Berger and Ryan. "Or should I call you officers?"

"Declan will be fine," Ryan said. He cocked his head at Berger. "This is Agent Joseph Berger of the Oklahoma State Bureau of Investigation."

"Joe," Berger said.

As the three men shook hands, Cranston said, "This is about one of our employees? Did I get that message right?"

Ryan nodded. "You did."

"I hope I can be helpful." Cranston smiled broadly at Ryan. "I wouldn't expect you to remember, Declan, but we went to school together."

Ryan gave Cranston the once over. "I apologize, I don't remember."

"You were one grade ahead of me right through high school. Always admired your athletic abilities. Anyway..." With a slight bow, Cranston pointed the men toward the corridor on the opposite side of the foyer. As they made their way toward Cranston's office, he volunteered: "We have about 125 patients in this part of our campus." He gestured to his left. "I'm referring to the buildings on the east side as you entered. At the moment we have fewer than a dozen guests in our facility on the west side."

Pushing through a paneled walnut door that extended to the twelve-foot ceiling, Cranston stopped at the desk of a young man who popped up from his chair and stood stiffly. "Coffee?" Cranston directed at Berger and Ryan who demurred. "How about water? Soft drinks? No takers?" Berger and Ryan offered "No thank you's." The young man sat down.

Cranston lowered his chin indicating an open door opposite where they stood. Entering his office, he directed the men to a couch and double armchair setting and waited until they sat before lowering himself onto the couch.

"We appreciate your taking the time to meet with us," Ryan said to kick-start the conversation. "As you mentioned, this is about Maria Luna, your former employee."

"Excuse me." Cranston got up and walked to his desk where he opened the top drawer, removed a folder, and returned to the couch. "When a family entrusts us with the care of a loved one, I promise full confidentiality. I also give them a packet of information on how we protect confidentiality. In that packet is this." He leafed through a booklet, made a noise when he found what he was looking for, and read: "'The Health Insurance Portability and Accountability Act specifies the circumstances in which protected health information can be disclosed for law enforcement purposes. Law enforcement officers will most likely require court orders for obtaining information.'" Cranston closed the booklet. "This protection of confidentiality extends to our employees who work with our patients and guests."

Ryan nodded at the folder. "We can get a court order if you'd like, but there are reporters who spend all their time digging into what court orders are issued and why. Always digging for stories." He stared at Cranston. "What do you think will happen when they see one for this place? Could be real bad for patient confidentiality."

Cranston smiled stiffly, clasped his hands together, and settled them in his lap. "As long as we have an understanding on where we stand regarding doctor-patient confidentiality, then we're good to go."

Ryan smiled benignly. "Sure. What can you tell us about Maria Luna?"

"I'm not familiar with her." Cranston stood, walked to his desk, and hit a button on his phone. "Joel, please bring me the personnel jacket for a Maria Luna."

"I have a question," Ryan said as Cranston returned to the couch. "You called some of the people here 'patients' and others 'guests.' What's the difference?"

"The 'guests' are here voluntarily. They occupy the West Wing and are looking for peace and quiet. Maybe solace after a death in the family. A divorce. It's much like a high-end spa, although all our services are available to them."

"Like?" Berger asked.

"Analysis. Individual as well as group therapy. We also provide lifestyle counseling, and, on occasion, cosmetic services. Botox. A nip and tuck. Nothing too terribly invasive."

"And the 'patients'?"

"Our patients require much more intensive care, that is, therapy and often drug intervention. They run the gamut from mild anxiety to schizophrenia. Most have been committed, others are here voluntarily, but their movements can be restricted if our doctors suggest such restrictions."

The young man from the reception area came in, hand extended, holding a manila folder. "Maria Luna," he said.

"Thank you, Joel," Cranston said, taking and opening the folder. He scanned the contents. "Well, this person hasn't been here for a few weeks. One day she didn't show up for work."

"Where did she work, the East or West Wing?" Berger asked.

Cranston returned his attention to the folder. "West, and according to what I see here, she was one of our attendants who cleaned the rooms and kept the public areas presentable."

"Always in the West Wing?" Berger asked. "She never worked in the other parts of the facility?"

Cranston went back to the folder. This time he flipped through a few pages, backward and forward. "No, always in the West Wing."

"And to be clear," Berger said, "the patients are there voluntarily?"

"Yes, all have checked themselves in and..."

"Can check themselves out?" Ryan asked.

"There are no restrictions on their movements," Cranston replied.

Berger said, "You haven't asked what this is all about. That's usually the first thing people want to know."

Cranston let a moment linger before answering. "A vestige of the business. Our environment," he said with a sweep of his hand. "You learn to listen and let the information come to you. Pushing oftentimes causes people to hide things." He smiled. "I understand I'm not dealing with such a thing here, with you, of course, but still, call it 'muscle memory.'"

Berger decided to dive right in. "Maria Luna didn't come back to work because she was murdered."

Cranston hoped his wide eyes and surprised "What?" were convincing.

"You didn't hear anything about this? About her murder possibly being linked to a series of murders?"

"My God, that's awful. But, no, I did not. I'm so consumed with what I'm doing that events often spin right past me. Limiting, I know, but this is a heavy responsibility."

"None of your staff, doctors, nobody said anything to you about this?" Berger persisted.

Cranston shook his head. "I'm not the only one who is consumed by their work. I don't mean to sound insensitive or even patronizing, but when you deal with what we do every day, the shock that others feel at the tragedies such as the one you're describing sometimes doesn't have the same effect on many of us." He let his head drop a bit. "Not a good thing, but a sad fact of life."

"Would you mind if we took a look at the West Wing?" Ryan asked.

"Not at all. I'll take you on a tour myself." Cranston ushered Berger and Ryan out a set of French doors. He walked them into a garden brimming with flowering azalea and hydrangea bushes surrounding a rectangular square of grass split by a concrete walkway leading to a building with arched windows and a domed roof.

"Romanesque, isn't it?" Cranston said as they approached. "The towers give the building a church-like quality, don't they? There have been additions and renovations over the years, but always with the goal of staying true to the original design."

They walked into a library where a woman in a light blue uniform was vacuuming a Persian rug covering most of the floor area. Light streamed into the room through the windows.

"Looks like a college library," Ryan said as they walked through into a hallway.

Cranston stopped the parade and pointed to his left. "We have a formal dining room for our guests." He looked right. "Exercise facilities with multiple swimming options."

Berger could not help himself. "Swimming options?"

"An Olympic-sized pool. A lap pool and another for, well, I guess you'd call it relaxing and lounging."

"This way," Cranston said. He preceded them past the dining room and into a large space filled with industrial-sized washers and dryers. The room was noisy, hot, and clammy. The three hurried through and into a cafeteria.

"For our employees," Cranston said. "Three meals a day are available."

Cranston walked the group to the far side of the room that smelled of fried food and tomato soup. He knocked on a door marked "Private" but did not wait for an answer, pushing into a small office filled with folding chairs and card tables. To the left of the door, newspapers were scattered atop a coffee table in front of a pleather couch. An obese man consumed the space behind a desk. He struggled to stand but was stopped mid-effort by Cranston who said, "Don't get up on our account."

Cranston turned to Ryan and Berger. "This is Don Betters, head of Human Resources. He can answer any questions you have about Maria Luna. Within the limits we discussed."

Betters nodded at Cranston and smiled at Ryan and Berger.

Cranston held his hand toward the men. "If you want to talk to me further, stop by my office on your way out."

Ryan and Berger watched Cranston leave and turned toward Betters, who looked at them warily. Ryan reached across the desk. "Sheriff Declan Ryan and this is Agent Joseph Berger of the Oklahoma State Bureau of Investigation."

"Okay," Betters said tentatively as he shook hands with two men.

"Mind if we sit?" Ryan asked.

"Oh, of course," Betters said and gestured toward the line of folding chairs resting against one wall of his office. "Grab a couple."

"We're here about Maria Luna," Ryan said, pushing open the chair and placing it in front of Betters' desk.

"Yeah," Betters said, shaking his head slowly. "I heard about that yesterday and read about it this morning. Awful stuff."

Berger glanced at Ryan. "Did Dr. Cranston happen to mention we'd be coming by?"

Betters' eyes darted from Ryan to Berger. "Uh, he might've. We speak a few times a day about a lot of things."

"He said he hadn't heard what happened before we showed up asking about her," Ryan said.

"Then, I guess we didn't talk about her," Betters stated.

"What can you tell us about Ms. Luna?"

"Great girl. Hard worker. Always on time. Never a problem. Then one day she doesn't show up for work."

"Did you try to find out why?" Berger asked. "Call her?"

"Yeah, I tried to call her a few times on our phone and..."

"What do you mean 'our phone'?"

"We provide phones to all our people. A way of making sure we can reach them, and them us. Sometimes we have emergencies. When I couldn't reach her on that one, I tried a number she gave me. Her personal phone, I guess. Never reached her. Now I know why. Creepy."

"Did she interact with the people here? I mean the guests?"

"Depends on how you mean 'interact.' She did her job and brought somebody something if they needed it. Other than that, no. We don't encourage our people to do that. Interact. In fact, we discourage it."

"Your guests," Berger said, "how long do they usually stay? Average?"

"A couple of weeks."

"Do you have a roster of guests?"

"You'll have to talk to Dr. Cranston if you want something like that."

"Okay," Berger agreed. "The guests generally stay a couple of weeks and they can come and go freely. All of them. No restrictions?"

"Doors swing both ways in the West Wing."

Berger pulled his vibrating phone from his pocket and excused himself.

***

"They're here right now," Cranston said.

"Anything I need to know about?" Lee asked.

"They're in with my HR person. He knows to keep it short and sweet. 'She was a good worker.' Yadda, yadda. Nothing that would encourage questioning about anything or anyone else. If they do, he knows to defer to me."

"Okay," Lee said hurriedly. "Give them what they want short of anything that could even hint our guy was there."

"How would they know he was here?"

"They don't and we need to keep it that way. No slip of the tongues or any references to who she came into contact with."

"Of course. Were our security people able to help you track that phone?"

"Yeah, on that. Gotta go. Call me later with a wrap-up on how it went."

***

Lee closed the door behind him and looked down the short hallway leading into the room. He could see a woman's leg lashed to a bedpost. He leaned forward and elbowed the bathroom door open. The floor was splashed with blood. A pile of towels tossed into the shower stall was soaked red.

Lee took a step forward and leaned flat against the wall to give himself a view into the room. He could now see the woman's body. Her hands and legs were bound to the four bedposts. He did not need to examine further and turned toward the door, which he opened, his sleeve pulled over his hand. He pulled the bill of his cap over his eyes and made certain the corridor was empty before backing out of the room. The stairwell was a few steps from the door.

Impressive, Lee thought. Marco planned well enough to get a room on the first floor at the end of the hall which he could access from the stairwell and not be seen by the CCTV at the far end of the corridor.

Outside the building and down the block, Lee found a small park. He sat on a bench in the middle of the green space.

"Found him. Well, found where he's been."

"Where?"

"Wichita Falls."

"Texas?"

"Yeah."

"How?"

"He took a phone from one of the maids at Ottinger. I used that to track him."

"Bring him back."

"There's a problem. Well, there are a couple of problems."

"Fuck."

"There's a dead girl in his room. Been there a couple of days, I think. And he's disappeared."

***

"Layton got another letter?" Connor asked as he got into the back of the cruiser.

"Yeah," said Berger, turning to face Connor. "Layton wouldn't tell me much. Playing his games. Wants more photos from the other scenes." Berger lifted an envelope from the front seat. "Got'em. He said enough so I know it's not good."

"Not good?"

"He didn't go into detail, but he said 'my guy is doing his thing.' Invited us to come talk to him," Berger said as the cruiser picked up speed.

"You were talkin' to people where Maria worked, right?" Connor asked.

Berger acknowledged, "We were at Ottinger when I got the call from Layton."

"And?" Connor asked anxiously. "Learn anything?"

"We learned Ottinger's not your father's mental health clinic. Well, one part of it is. People are committed for the usual range of mental issues, and from what we were told, are treated conventionally. There's another area more like a high-end spa where people come and go, and that's where Maria worked, which complicates things."

"Why?"

"From what she told you, this person she identified was there under a false name."

"Yeah," agreed Connor.

Berger shook his head. "That doesn't make sense. People are free to come and go from the wing where she worked. Not a likely place to keep someone against their will."

"That's what the guy who runs the place told you. That she worked where people could come and go?"

Berger nodded.

"Well, maybe this person she recognized was in the other part where people can't leave. She didn't have to work there to see 'em. What about a search warrant or something to look around? You could check the list of people and see if something's not right. See how someone ended up there. If something's not right, it'll show." Connor blew out a sigh. "There's gotta be a way, right?"

"We have no grounds for a search warrant," Ryan answered. "What would we say? 'We think we *might* know of someone in Ottinger who *might* be there under a false name, and *might* have been identified by Maria who *might* have been killed by a person she *might* have tried to blackmail? Putting aside, of course, she's currently considered the victim of a serial killer.'"

"You know," Berger said, "maybe Cranston's protecting the identity of a client. Of course, it's also possible like most people who find themselves being eyed by the police, he's scared and wants us gone."

"Well," Ryan said, "that clarifies everything."

"In the meantime," Berger said, "we need your help again with Layton."

"I ain't been much help, really."

"I think he feels comfortable having you there. That's a big help," Berger said as they rolled to a stop in the prison parking lot. "I talked to the warden and told him Layton is getting these letters. He agreed to let them go through without the usual review, and he told his people to glove up before handling anything for Layton."

"You need to tell Layton that, too," Connor said. "About the gloves."

Berger shook his head. "No, I don't think he wants us to catch this guy any time soon, or at all. That would cut him off from the photographs he loves so much. If I even mention any sort of caution, he'll go in the other direction."

"Not give you the letters?" Connor asked. "That wouldn't get him what he wants."

Berger shook his head. "No, not that. I once had a snitch who wanted the money I gave him but didn't want me to find the guy I was after too quickly. That would've dried up his pay days, so he sent me on scavenger hunts to find the messages he'd leave. Told me it was to protect him from having to meet with me in person. I couldn't argue the point because I needed what he had. Point is, I suspected he was stringing me along. I'm thinking Layton might do the same if I don't play him right. Contaminate the letters even further."

"'Nother thought," Connor said. "Tell the warden to stop tossing the cells. Layton probably could hide those photos so no one can find them, but why take the chance?"

"See," Berger said, "it's the little things that make you an invaluable team member."

***

Connor stood in a corner of the room arms folded across his chest, chin lowered, staring at the floor.

Berger sat upright, both hands on the file. Ryan fidgeted with his empty holster and remarked, "You'd think they'd let us keep our weapons in a prison. Our risk is probably greater in here than it is out there."

The clanking of a heavy iron door echoed in the hallway outside the room prompting Connor to push away from the wall and sit down. "I hate this fuckin' place," he said bitterly.

Chains rattled at the door and a guard walked Layton into the room. "Good to see everyone," Layton said cheerfully.

Another guard followed, unlocked the chains connecting Layton's wrists to his waist chains, wound them through the iron ring on the desk and checked the lock carefully before retreating a step and asking, "All good?" Getting the high-sign from Ryan, he motioned his partner toward the door, which he pulled closed as they stepped into the hallway, sending up the 'you're in a prison' echo.

Layton smiled broadly. "So, whaddya got for me?"

Berger pushed the file toward him, keeping a hand pressed on the top. "What do you have for me?"

Layton reached down toward his sock and came up with a tightly folded piece of paper.

"This is a good one." He slapped it on the table. "Real good."

Berger lifted his hand off the file. He left the folded square in front of him and pulled a packet of surgical gloves from the pocket of a leather portfolio. He slipped on the gloves and pushed the packet to Ryan who took a pair, as did Connor.

Layton laughed. "I can't believe you're doing that. Got handled at the post office. Whoever brings it in here," he said with a laugh. "Intake people and the inmate who brings it to me." He shook his head. "Waste of time."

Berger did not respond. He slowly unfolded the pages, ran his palm across them carefully, smoothing the pages, laid his hands in his lap, and leaned forward, squinting in concentration.

She was a beautiful woman. Dark hair, like the others. Flawless complexion. And the most beautiful eyes. Green with flecks of blue and brown. A bit of red as well.

I knew I would not have much time with her. It was most definitely not ideal, but I was determined to make it work. If only I had known, I would not have been concerned about this, but if I had known, I would not have wasted my time with this one.

But I get ahead of myself. Again, from the top.

She was nice. We talked for hours before I offered to take her to dinner. We went to an upscale steak restaurant. I had a petit filet, creamed spinach, and potato au gratin. She had a wedge salad, surf and turf, asparagus, and seven-layer chocolate cake for dessert. She was not a large woman but ate like one. I like women who enjoy their food. I was never attracted to those who were content with a small salad or left food on their plate. This woman ate everything! And clearly enjoyed it.

Everything was going so well. We went back to the hotel and sat at the bar until the wee hours. We had a few drinks and made-up stories about the couples we saw around us.

It went terribly wrong when we got to the room. She asked me for money. "Business before pleasure," she said. It confused me. I must have looked confused and when it all fell into place, I refused, of course, to give her any money.

I was mad. Very mad. She ruined the entire evening, which, as I've said, was so nice. Wonderful conversation, wonderful dinner, nice late evening relaxation.

The usual excitement of talking them into the activity was lost. There was none of that. It was heartbreaking. Worse, it was a disappointment.

I won't even bother to go into the rest of it. There was no enjoyment. It was an exercise in frustration.

All of which leads me to this: As I reflect, I realize the satisfaction gained is not always worth the effort expended. Perhaps you experienced this. I did enjoy most of it as you know from my letters. But with each one, that enjoyment, the satisfaction, was harder to come by, and this one ruined it for me.

If my very being is wrapped up in this, but I'm wasting my time and wasting the lives of these poor girls – except for the last one who deserved what she got – then what's the point?

I have to rethink things.

As Berger raised his head from the second page and slid it toward Ryan, who put it on top of the page he had just finished, Layton said, "I had to laugh at the part about him not liking women who just ate salad." He glanced quickly at the photos in front of him. "That's an understatement. He likes'em big." Layton smiled, showing all his teeth. "When are you going to have this one for me?"

Berger took a deep breath and closed his eyes to calm himself before responding, "What do you make of this letter?"

Layton returned his attention to the photographs. He bobbed his head slowly and laid them out in a line along the table in front of him.

"What do you...?" Berger started to ask again.

Layton raised his hand. "The cop chasing the Green River Killer went to Bundy to see if he could explain what was going through the guy's head. See if Bundy could...I guess, interpret the Green River Killer's actions, or give them a heads-up on what to expect. After spending time with Bundy, the detective said what he got was veiled confessions of things Bundy had already done."

"Are you telling me this is a waste of time? I shouldn't bother coming here?"

156

"Let me finish," Layton said. He put the photos in the folder and leaned forward so he could position it in his belt line at the small of his back. "He said what he learned was Bundy didn't care about anyone. No remorse at all. That's something, right?"

"It's corroboration of what I already knew," Berger replied. "What I need from you is some information that could help us stop this one. Tell me something that gives me a handle on him."

Layton leaned forward. "No, you're trying to understand him. That's what all of you want. To understand us."

Berger shook his head. "Not possible. My ability to empathize gets in the way."

The two men stared across at each other. The clicking of the fluorescent lights and humming of the air conditioning became a presence.

Ryan broke the spell, tapping the pages in front of him. "This sounds like remorse."

"It isn't," Layton said. He looked at Ryan. "Disappointment, maybe. He didn't get the satisfaction he thought he would after being cooped up. He's frustrated."

"Guard," Layton yelled. The men came into the room and freed him from the iron ring. As he stood to be shackled around his waist, he said, "It's going to get worse. And wherever he did that" – Layton nodded at pages – "it was not around here. He's too smart for that. He traveled for that one."

"This guy's a sick fuck," Connor said as he finished reading and pushed the pages away. "Him, too," he said, pointing at the door closing behind Layton.

"Did you ask the warden to save the envelopes?"

"Thought about that but if Layton got a letter without the envelope, he'd figure out I talked to the warden."

"That's definitely a no-no," Connor said.

Berger nodded. "Yeah, and Layton might cut us off. But I did ask them to pay attention to the postmark. This one was from Lawton. I'm not sure it tells us anything."

"If we figure Layton got the letter yesterday, or even a few days ago, why haven't we heard anything?" Ryan asked. "No one's found a body?"

Berger shook his head. "Confirms what Layton said. If that body isn't around here, no one's making a connection."

"Forget a connection," Ryan countered. "I'm talking about someone finding a body, somewhere."

"If it's in a big city, it could be chalked up as just another dead body."

"Even with that MO? Eye removed and the rest of it? And the press conference got a lot of play. Should've heightened attention."

Berger said, "I'll check VICAP."

"What's VICAP?" Connor asked.

"Violent Criminal Apprehension Program. It's in the FBI. A clearinghouse for reporting violent crime. State and local cops report the details to VICAP and when we have something like this" – he waved the evidence bag and dropped it into his briefcase – "we can go to VICAP to see if anyone anywhere else is dealing with the same thing. Maybe the crimes are related, or we can pick each other's brains to find ways to deal with our own cases."

"'The Beast of Oklahoma,'" Connor said derisively. "Every time I turn on the TV, that's screamed at me."

"Blood leads," Ryan said. "The nickname was bound to come."

Connor was at the door. "Let's get the hell outta here."

Monday-May 14

"I have Gary with me in my office," Stephens said. "Who's on the call?"

"Whalen."

"Noreen."

"Len Martin from the Petroleum Alliance. I'm representing Reynolds Comer from the Gas Association and Meyer Smith from the Independent Petroleum Association."

"George Daugherty, Senator Clifford's legislative assistant."

"Monica Filer with Senator Evans."

"Okay," Stephens said cheerfully. "The gang's all here. It's your show, Leonard."

"We had a good meeting with most everyone who has a dog in the fight," Leonard reported. "A bipartisan group, believe it nor not. They're willing to consider a proposal."

"How many constitutes a 'good group'?" Stephens asked.

The sound of shuffling paper preceded Leonard's answering. "It looks like we have at least, oh…125 names on our 'get back to me' sheet. I think we're likely to pick up most of them more if we can give them something solid to chew on."

"I've got my feelers out in my world," Stephens said. "If you can get those numbers to listen to your spiel, Milton, I think I can bring a representative group of governors on board. I'm going to turn this over to Gary who has some ideas he'd like to run by everyone."

"That's a strong start, Congressman. I'm impressed you were able to get that many of your colleagues to…"

"And senators," Leonard interjected, "who made the trek from the other side of the Capitol to the House side. That's like crossing the Rubicon."

"Right," Iglesias agreed. "A solid foundation. Add to this the governors who I'm certain will be convinced to join us and we have a strong base to get the national associations on board. American Petroleum Institute. American Association of Drilling Engineers. American Exploration & Production Council. American Gas Association. Association of Energy Service Companies. And all the rest of them. We'll probably be able to bring along the National Chamber of Commerce. Mr. Martin?"

"Yes."

"I'm guessing we can count on your sister organizations at the state level to join us, right?"

"Definitely."

"We can count on the unions, the trucking associations... The list goes on," Iglesias said excitedly. "Everyone related to the industry in some way."

"When can we get moving on this?" Leonard asked. "When will we have some product to show? I want to strike while the iron is hot."

"I've given the governor a full communications plan. It includes a rollout calendar; suggested events like a kick-off press conference; follow-up press events tagged to certain milestones, like announcements of people and organizations joining the campaign; a sample op-ed article; sample press releases; a draft stump speech; letters to the editor for everyone to distribute; a fact sheet; instructions on how to keep the message active in the public domain; a design for a Facebook page promoting our efforts; Twitter and Instagram pages. A five-minute film with all the basic facts about the industry. Economic benefits. Jobs. Salaries. And there's a minute or so of information on how we're cleaning things up. Our environmental message. All of this can be used by our partners. That is, the associations and other participants. Unions. Of course, the congressional and gubernatorial partners will have access to all of this, and it will be featured on our social media platforms."

"We'd prefer not to talk about 'cleaning things up,'" Martin said. "That implies we've 'dirtied things.'"

"Of course," Iglesias agreed, "and obviously that's not how the story is told. My shorthand was badly put."

"Jesus," Leonard said, "you do work fast."

"It's what we do," Iglesias said not trying to hide the boast in his voice. "But I should be totally upfront and acknowledge a lot of what we produced – especially the short film – was edited from material provided by API and other associations who gave us permission to use what they have."

"Wait, wait," Leonard said aggressively. "If we're just recycling stuff that's already out there, what are we doing?"

"We're doing what hasn't been done before," Stephens answered. "We're assembling a significant group of influencers and opinion-makers to promote a positive message about the industry in a coordinated fashion. When was the last time you saw a positive op-ed article on fossil fuels? Or a news story like that on CNN or even FOX? That's what we're doing."

"Also," Iglesias added, "we'll be telling an entirely new story. Ours is a fully positive message. Anything smacking of being reactive or having a 'setting the record straight' vibe has been eliminated. We show an industry proud of its accomplishments and of the contributions made to the world's most successful economy. One that sets the pace for achieving the American Dream. An industry that lifts all boats. On top of that we're providing a step-by-step plan on how to stay on message and how to take advantage of a tsunami of participation we've never had before." A beat of quiet before Iglesias challenged, "Any questions?"

"Okay, I'm on board," Leonard said. "When will I have something to show my people? And what's the next move after that?"

"The proposal and products are in my hands," Stephens said. "I've worked with Gary for many years and I'm confident I'll be okaying it all today and can get it out for everyone on this call to review."

The sound of muffled voices preceded Iglesias saying, "Governor Stephens has asked me to mention one other aspect of the campaign. Rather than slide into this by appealing to the media and others to listen to our pitch, we'll compel coverage with kick-off events in every partner's state capitol. We'll gather all 'name' participants for a big party, if you will. A Fourth of July-like celebration focusing on that single individual in every state who will stand as the symbol of the industry. Here in Oklahoma that will be the pioneering female oil producer I've mentioned, Ms. Lulu Hefner. I've done research and have identified people like Ms. Hefner in most of the potential partner states who can be used as touchstones for each of these celebrations. I'll provide those names in the packets we send along to all interested parties."

"I have the perfect date for the kick-off here at home," Jones said cheerfully. "And everyone else can use that as their target D-Day."

Tuesday-May15

Ryan and Berger stood over a conference table in the office of Paul Linares, Chief of Police, Wichita Falls, Texas. The three men stared down at a scattering of photographs.

The only sound was the chopping from the whirling blades of a ceiling fan.

Linares took a moment to nod at a man who walked into the office, and quickly returned his attention to the tabletop.

A woman in the photographs was tied, arms and legs, to the bedposts. Her throat had been cut, right eye removed, and tongue cut out and set on the pillow next to her head. There were objects protruding from her vagina and anus.

"Yeah," Berger said, "that's the MO we're dealing with except for the tongue. It looks like he's escalating."

Without taking his attention off the photos, Linares introduced Major Marty McDowell of Texas Ranger Company C. "He's the one who found you through VICAP," Linares said to Berger and Ryan.

"Good to know it works," Berger said and tapped his index finger on the table. "We're dealing with three murders." He turned toward Ryan. "Maybe four." Responding to the looks of question clouding the faces of Linares and McDowell, he provided the background on Maria Luna.

"Yeah," said McDowell. "Happened to catch that press conference." He smiled at Berger. "Your guy, Slade. Not much of a stage presence."

"There's no good way for me to respond," Berger replied. "So, I'll leave it alone."

"I have some CCTV footage," Linares said, going to his desk and returning with his computer. He sat. Berger, Ryan, and McDowell huddled behind.

Linares fast forwarded to an image of a man, a hat pulled down low over his face, walking away from the camera.

"Nothing from the other end?" Ryan asked.

Linares shook his head. "This is it. The only angle. And watch. There's something weird about the way he approaches the room. Hesitant. Like he was afraid of what he might find."

"Like he *knew* what he might find," McDowell said. "There," he said, pointing at the screen. "He stops dead. Like he doesn't want to go in. The door must be open. He doesn't use a card to get in, and he's careful. Not in a polite way. More like 'I don't want to be doing this' kinda way."

Linares said, "He pokes the door open with his foot."

"I'm thinking he doesn't want to touch the door," McDowell says. "Doesn't want to leave anything of himself behind."

Ryan leans over Linares's shoulder. "Judging by the eight-foot height of the door, what do you think? Over six feet tall?"

"Watch this," Linares said after fast forwarding. "He leaves, real careful to keep his back turned, and goes out the exit next to the room. He didn't come to the room that way because he would have been facing the CCTV set up near the elevator."

Linares turned toward the three men behind him. "This is a nice hotel. One of those four-star places downtown. People who pay that kind of money usually don't want a room on the first floor with a view of the parking lot. I asked if there were other rooms in the hotel when he checked in and there were plenty. The only way he would've gotten that one was if he requested it."

"What you said," Ryan directed at McDowell, "about the way he approaches the room. Like he's concerned about what he's going to find. Are you saying he isn't the perp?"

McDowell took a moment before answering. "I don't think he killed her, but I do think he knew what he was going to find."

"So, we're talking about two different people," Ryan clarified. He nodded at the computer screen. "We have whoever that is and whoever killed the woman."

"That's my take on it," McDowell said.

Ryan sighed audibly. "Great. That adds a new level of complication. We've got someone following the nutcase around."

"Which might explain Luna," Berger said, his eyes on the middle distance.

"Which adds yet another layer of weird," Ryan said.

"Or," Berger said, "he is our perp and was being cautious because he thought housekeeping had gone into the room."

"It keeps getting better," Ryan said.

"What about CCTV in other parts of the hotel?" Berger asked. "The reception desk?"

"Nothing focused on the reception desk," Linares answered. "Too intrusive according to the management. They don't want guests feeling like they're under surveillance the minute they walk into the place, so they have CCTV set up around the lobby to – and this is exactly what I was told – 'satisfy security needs without being Big Brother.'"

"Seriously?" Ryan said.

"Seriously," Linares answered. "Plus, he paid in cash and signed the register as 'John Smith.'"

"What about...? Berger started.

Anticipating, Linares answered, "We talked to maintenance, to service people in the bar and dining room. Got nothing to pinpoint whoever it was who checked into that room. We looked at footage from a few days before this" – he nodded at the screen – "and the person who enters and leaves uses the stairs on the far end of the hall so you can't get a good look at his face.

"And there's this." Linares poked at the keyboard and the next image is a woman walking alone down the hallway. "She stops at the door to the room, looks like she uses a keycard and goes in." He fast forwards. "And here minutes later," he says, pointing at a shadowy figure emerging from the stairwell door, keeping his head low, and walking close to the wall of the corridor before slipping into the room.

"I'm thinking he sent her up and came in that stairwell door to keep away from the camera," McDowell said. "Doubly cautious, and that tells me we have two people. The other one doesn't come to the room from the stairwell. He walks right down the middle of the hall."

"Good point," Berger acknowledges.

"Then," Linares said and poked the keys, "three hours later he comes out of the room" – he gestured at the screen – "right there. Comes out and leaves using the stairwell." He fast forwarded. "Comes back later that day. Uses the stairwell to get into the hall." More fast forwarding. "Next day, he walked out and leaves the door open. This is the day he left because there is not more footage of the guy." He looked over his shoulder at the three men. "Why would he leave the door open?"

Berger said, "It's characteristic of a lot of these offenders. They're proud of their work and want to show it off. Also, a way to taunt us. A 'See, I'm making it easy for you' kind of thing. The chronology you showed us also means he spent the night in the room with the body."

"Jesus," squeaked out of Ryan.

"Also, not unusual. He's reliving the experience."

Linares walked to his desk and returned with a thick file. "These are the particulars on the victim. Eugenia Wilson from Dallas. Twenty-five. Has...*had* a record of solicitation there and in Houston but graduated from street hustler. Now an escort. High-class stuff. She's been shuttling from Dallas to Houston to Las Vegas."

"How did she end up here?" Ryan asked.

"She's from here," Linares answered. "Her parents still live here, and she comes...*came* to visit regularly. I guess she decided to make a few bucks while she was home."

"You talked to her parents?" Berger asked.

Linares bobbed his head. "Notified them. That's always fun. Worse still, they had no idea what she's been doing. They thought she was in event planning and that's why she traveled as much as she did. At first, they didn't believe me. I thought her father was going to get physical. Practically threw me out of the house, but there wasn't much to learn from them anyway."

"The people at the hotel," McDowell said, "had seen her there a few nights that week. They figured she was a guest."

"We got nothing from the scene," Linares said. "At least not yet. Forensics is still doing their thing, but they're not hopeful. Said it looked pretty clean."

Berger nodded. "That reflects what we found, or didn't find, at our sites. Did CCTV catch our guy leaving? Or the other guy, assuming we're talking about two separate unsubs."

"Nope, there are no cameras where the stairs exit along the side of the hotel, and we couldn't identify anyone resembling him. I'm talking about the stairwell guy. No one on any CCTV tape with his body type. Not the lobby. Restaurant. Nothing useful."

"How're you going to handle this?" Ryan asked looking from Linares to McDowell.

"The 'Beast of Oklahoma' crossed the border," Linares said. "Raise as much dust as we can and hope someone saw something. Marty and I have a press conference scheduled for this afternoon. Want to stick around and join us?"

"No, thank you," Berger and Ryan answered simultaneously.

"You two know about George Layton?" Berger asked.

Both men nodded.

"I have something that might interest you," Berger said and provided them with the background. "I'll send you everything else I have on our victims and what we've found to date, which, I'm afraid, isn't much. I'd appreciate being kept in the loop on what your forensics people find, and we can trade information moving forward."

Wednesday-May16

"You're where?" Jones asked in disbelief. "With whom?"

"Cranston," Lee responded tentatively, "We're walking into the Capitol Building."

"I told you I never want to deal with him directly, and I sure as hell don't want to see him in my goddamn office."

"You're going to want to hear what he has to say. It was either this way or ... well, this is the way he wanted it."

"Don't mention his name to Eileen," Jones said and walked quickly to his door, opened it, and stared at an empty chair behind a desk that looked like it had been spit-shined. A gleaming leather pad was the only item on the desk other than a small vase with a single rose.

He looked up as Lee and Cranston entered the outer door and moved swiftly to usher them into his office.

"Thank you for seeing me," Cranston said, admiring the large aquarium. "A diamond darter," he said excitedly and approached the aquarium. "The darter is rare. It thrives in the Elk River in West Virginia. Sadly, a recent chemical spill there threatens to kill it off."

Lee pulled Cranston away from the aquarium guiding him to a chair in front of the desk behind which Jones was standing, his eyes narrowed, and forehead furrowed. "I thought I made it clear Ray was the one you'd deal with," he said, standing while Cranston and Lee sat. He remained standing.

Cranston nodded. "I apologize for breaking protocol, but I wanted to bring this to your attention personally."

"Bring me what?"

"This morning we found your brother sitting on the bed in his room."

Jones looked at Lee – as if for confirmation – got the man's nod and sat down heavily.

"It's as much a mystery to us as I'm sure it is to you." Cranston waited a beat. "It is a mystery to you, correct? You didn't know he'd be returning, did you?"

"Yes," Jones answered softly. "I mean 'no,' I didn't know he had returned." He stared into his lap as if trying to process what he had been told. "This morning?"

"As if he had never left. He asked where William was, the man who kept an eye on him for us, and when told he wasn't there, Marco lay down, and that's where he's been since. Lying down in his bed. Not sleeping, just lying there and staring at the ceiling. I checked before coming here." Cranston leaned forward. "Now you know why I insisted on coming to see you."

Jones looked at Lee. "Have you seen him?"

Lee nodded.

"And?"

"Like he said. Flat on his back, in bed, staring at the ceiling."

Jones placed his elbows on the desk and clasped his hands together. He narrowed his eyes and asked Lee, "Does anyone know where he's been?"

"No, and there's nothing he brought back with him that tells us anything. I checked carefully."

Jones directed himself to Cranston. "Find William and get him back on the job."

"I think we're past having William watch Marco," Cranston responded. "I strongly suggest transferring him to our more secure facility. I'm talking about admitting him to the East Wing where we have the ability to keep a close eye on him and we can also help him with a regimen of therapy."

"And I strongly suggest," Jones forced through gritted teeth, "you fix whatever it is you need to fix to make sure he can't get out of where he is now, and everything will be fine."

Cranston jerked his lips into a quick half-smile. "Transferring Marco to the East Wing will accomplish what you want. It is fully secure and fully equipped to provide the best therapy anywhere."

"The solitude where he is suits him just fine," Jones said with a flat effect. "No therapy. The fewer interactions he has the better. No doctors. No nurses. No attendants. No group gropes. All of that has been tried and hasn't worked. You need to do your job better. Earn that king's ransom I've been paying you."

Cranston intertwined his fingers and rested his hands in his lap. He ginned up a full smile. "Marco needs more attention than we've been giving him. He's a dangerous man."

Jones tilted his head. "Pardon me?" He glanced at Lee quickly before refocusing on Cranston.

"My curiosity was piqued after I talked to those two detectives about Maria Luna." Cranston reached into the pocket of his suit jacket, removed and unfolded a few pages, pressed them against his leg to flatten the creases. "As I told the detectives, and it was the truth, I don't recall this woman. No need for me to. I leave that detail to the administrators in the West Wing. Anyway, I decided to see what was in her file" – he waved the pages – "and discovered she was assigned to clean your brother's room and provide any necessary services he might need or ask for. You know, like soap, toothpaste, and..."

"Cut the shit," Jones growled. "Where is this going?"

Cranston looked from Lee to Jones. "You'd probably be surprised to learn I'm a huge true crime fan. Watch all the shows and read true crime books. Ann Rule is a particular favorite."

"I said cut the shit," Jones again growled.

"Miss Luna died a horrible death. Like those other women and..."

Jones raised his hand, stopping Cranston. "Marco was behind your walls when this Luna person was killed."

"He managed to find his way out at least one time that we know of, didn't he?" Cranston said with a look of wide-eyed satisfaction. "And being a true crime fan, I've been following the recent developments about a woman who was killed in Wichita Falls, and the assumption is the same person who killed that woman also killed three others, and maybe Maria Luna." He folded the pages, replacing them into his suit pocket.

"Are you sure you want to continue with this?" Jones asked, outwardly calm, but his knuckles were whitening as he tightened his grip on the arms of his chair.

"We truly want to help Marco. For the past thirty-five years the Ottinger Wellness Center has served our community by providing the best and most professional care to those with even the most severe mental challenges."

Jones started to come out of his chair but was stopped short by Lee who said, "Let's hear him out."

Cranston nodded his thanks to Lee and continued, "If Marco was any other patient, I would insist, not suggest, he be housed in the East Wing. I would probably insist you find somewhere else to place him, but, given your generosity to us, and my determination to help your brother, I offer an alternative."

"Such as?"

"We brought William back, of course, who will be with your brother from seven in the morning until he is secured in his room at nine o'clock in the evening. When William has to take personal time, that is, a bathroom break and time for lunch and dinner, we will have someone take his place."

Jones squirmed and looked at Lee, his jaw taut and eyes narrowed. Lee raised his hand requesting patience.

"We will hire a second minder to watch Marco's room from nine until William returns in the morning to accompany your brother to breakfast."

"Fine," Jones said, "but I don't want you forcing him to talk to anyone, and especially none of that group therapy shit."

"If that's what you want, but I think you should be aware of your brother's condition."

"I am fully aware. Like I said, he had years of therapy and my parents and I were part of all that."

"Mental conditions evolve and change. This is where he is at present." Cranston reached into a saddlebag-like briefcase he carried with him and lifted out a small bottle of water, from which he sipped deliberately before resuming. "Marco only met with some of our counselors briefly. That's all we offer in the West Wing. Counseling. On occasion he did join group sessions. Again, these were not intensive and were more gatherings for conversation. The reports I got back indicated Marco did not volunteer much. However, from what little I have observed, and during a few sessions I had with your brother, it is clear to me he harbors a classic schizoid personality disorder."

"He's schizophrenic?" Jones asked, skepticism in his voice. "That's your expert opinion after a couple of conversational meetings, and a counseling session or two with him?"

"More a schizophrenia-*like* personality disorder," Cranston answered. "His condition is advanced and easy to recognize. He has little interest in social relationships and enjoys his own company. Like most with SPD, Marco has a cold and detached personality making it difficult for him to establish long-term personal relationships. Not being able to have these relationships means he has never learned to express his feelings, or, and this is more likely, doesn't have those feelings. SPD sufferers are often seen as terse or rude. They cannot assess their own abilities to engage successfully in social situations."

Jones sat back in his chair and crossed his leg over his knee. He visibly relaxed and focused laser-like on Cranston. "And?"

"And when someone attempts to befriend an individual with SPD, it often annoys them and causes them to retreat deeper into their fugue-like state. They tend to be most comfortable when few demands are placed on them emotionally and aren't asked to engage in social niceties. Essentially, they want to avoid any emotional attachments. They can deal with people on an intellectual, physical, or occupational level as long as no emotional intimacy is required or even expected."

"And?"

"Do you see Marco in my description of SPD?"

Jones nodded. "There's some of what you describe, but there's also an aspect of his personality allowing him to be charming and even manipulative."

"None of these diagnoses are absolutely strict. If Marco is driven by a need and he has to be social and charming to satisfy that need, I'm sure he can be. Manipulative even. But those attributes cannot be sustained.

"My experience is most with SPD understand they are different from others. They recognize while others are forming relationships, they are not. They often complain life is passing them by, and that creates a great deal of frustration, even anger, in some. They don't like 'being on the outside looking in,' a condition of life described by many of these patients. They often describe themselves as 'defective.'

"All of this often leads to the creation of a fantasy world. They even bring people into this world as long as it can be accomplished without the emotional component. Some can live contentedly in their fantasy world; others dip in and out; still others – those who see themselves as defective – often become clinically depressed. That is where I think we are with Marco right now, and to be brutally frank, that often leads to the risk of suicide."

"You still haven't laid out this 'alternative' treatment of yours," Jones reminded Cranston.

"We generally don't treat SPD with medications. We do sometimes use drugs to treat the depression, which is what I recommend. And you needn't be concerned about anyone insisting on spending time...really, wasting their time with your brother in the classical type of therapy. That is not what I'm suggesting for Marco. The classic 'sit down and talk to a psychiatrist' and undergoing periods of analysis are ineffective because those in the SPD spectrum don't form useful working relationships with therapists for all the reasons I have described. No, we can best help your brother by monitoring him for episodes of depression and treating him with medication, if necessary. We will provide him with the opportunity to engage when he chooses. Let him know he is valued, but also leave him alone when he'd prefer to be alone."

Jones tapped his hands on the armrests of his chair. "Okay, anything else?" he said and started to stand.

Cranston stopped him with, "Just a few more things. As I said, we'll need twenty-four/seven surveillance of your brother. To accomplish this safely and securely in the West Wing, where you've indicated you'd prefer to keep him, we'll need to tighten security. We'll hire a topnotch security firm to help us. You know, to install more CCTV surveillance inside and outside the building. An alarm system. And so on. I plan to spend more time keeping my eye on all of this, so we'll need to build out some office space and..."

Jones raised his hand. "Got it. You want more money."

Cranston nodded.

"How much?"

"I'll get back with you as soon as I have an estimate. And, given the amount of time I will be dedicating to the care of your brother, I suggest we set up a private account ..."

"Okay, I said I understand. I'll take care of it, but don't think for a minute I don't know what you're doing. And" – he leaned forward, lifting out of his chair and resting his hands on his desk, bringing him closer to Cranston – "don't press your luck. Good meeting. Goodbye."

Cranston took his time gathering himself and walked slowly to the office door, where Jones stopped him. "Hold on." He punched a button on his desk phone. "Eileen?"

"Yes, sir."

"Please go down to the cafeteria and get me a cup of coffee." He raised a hand as he placed the phone in its cradle. "Let's keep the circle of people who know about this meeting as small as possible."

"Of course," Cranston said agreeably and started out the door. "One other thing. I'll put the cell phone Marco brought back with him in my safe. No one has to know where he was during his walkabout."

Thursday-May 1

Deputy Smolders set up his computer on the conference table and connected it to the 65-inch flat screen. He reached for the intercom and announced, "Any time you're ready."

Moments later Ryan came into the conference room. He sat next to Smolders who tapped away on his computer keyboard. "There wasn't any CCTV at the Sleep Inn, but we found a camera in the area. At an auto junkyard up the street."

"What the hell does a junkyard have to protect?"

Smolders chuckled. "Hadn't thought of that, but fortunately there is a camera mounted on the front gate. It shows the street running in front of the junkyard. The same one that runs in front of the motel. This is what we found."

Ryan squinted and leaned close to the screen.

"It will get clearer in a second."

The contours of the street became sharper as the screen lit up.

"Headlights," Smolders said.

A white sedan rolled across the screen. The camera was askew and showed the car approaching from the left side of the frame but did not show the rear of the car. Smolders ran the video back and forth.

"The same car comes from the other direction two hours later."

Ryan asked, "That's one person in the car, right?"

Smolders paused the image. "That's all I see. Now, this is two hours later judging by the time stamp."

The approach of the sedan was again announced by the headlights. When it passed in front of the camera coming from the opposite direction the angle permitted a view of the rear of the car. "Can you make out the license plate?" Ryan asked.

"Here," Smolders said and slid a still image to Ryan. "Clipped this out. Cleaned it up and got this. A T and a W, but that's all."

"One person again," Ryan said peering intently at the still image, and then back at the video.

"This was the only car on the road the whole night," Smolders said. "And day. I went back the entire day, too."

Ryan turned to his deputy. "So, we're looking at the only car that used that road that day?"

"The only car on the road during the 24-hour period around the time the homicide was committed. The manager said he only had one customer. And it was one guy." Smolders nodded at the flat screen. "One person in that car."

Ryan studied the photo carefully. "Maria must have been in the trunk."

"Or lying down in the backseat."

"I suppose she could have been there already."

"Not likely," Smolders said. "Unless she walked to the place and even then, she would probably have shown up on the CCTV. It's the only road leading to the motel."

"She didn't have to use the road," Ryan said. "I'm guessing there are other ways to get there. For that matter, the perp didn't have to use a car. They could've walked there."

"I think we're reaching."

"Thinking like a lawyer," Ryan said and pointed at the screen. "Could you get a make of the car?"

"Probably a 2015 Pontiac G-8. Narrows it down to a few thousand, and I'm winnowing that number down by using the T and W we have from the plate."

"A needle in a haystack comes to mind."

Monday-May 21

"I owe everything to Krono Oil. My job. My future. My family's security."
William Suff
Snubbing Operator
Krono Petroleum
Elk City, Oklahoma

"It's more than a job, it's my life. Leeward has made it possible for me to improve myself, get an education, and raise a family."
Dennis Nilsen
Field Engineer
Leeward Oil and Gas
Garyville, Louisiana

"I hate to think where I'd be without the opportunities Winco has provided. I've worked my way up the ladder and my prospects continue to improve."
Karla Homolka
Protected Species Observer
Winco Environmental Services
Port Neches, Texas

"I am a skilled equipment operator thanks to the opportunities ETS provided. I went from digging ditches to being responsible for multimillion-dollar equipment.
Doug Clark
Equipment Operator
ETS Limited
Henderson, Colorado

Stephens looked up after reading the final page in the briefing book. "This is the package everyone will have in their hands this morning?" he asked Iglesias, sitting on the opposite side of a conference table along with Noreen West and Whalen Jones.

Iglesias nodded. "They'll have the entire package." He ran his finger down the table of contents. "The list of primary messages that will be used in most of the materials; the employee testimonials; press releases; speeches; third-party testimonials; sample op-eds, three of them; a fact sheet; and" – he closed the cover – "all the rest of it."

"That's impressive," Stephens said.

"I'm assuming all of this has been carefully vetted," West said. "I'm talking about making certain the facts are, in fact, facts. That the numbers are correct and all the rest of it so we don't get tripped by some reporter claiming we're feeding them bullshit."

"Everything has been reviewed by experts in the field."

"Meaning?"

Iglesias answered, "Everything has been run by professors at schools of petroleum engineering and by economists in the industry, and then double-checked by staff at API and other associations."

"I love this touch," West said, tapping the cover of the briefing book. "This is a picture of Lulu Hefner, I assume."

"It is," Iglesias responded. "The shining light on which we built our campaign for Oklahoma. She is mentioned prominently in all of the material – speeches, fact sheets, press releases – everything has some mention of Ms. Hefner."

"Pandering at its most exquisite level," West said with a smile.

"And on that note," Stephens said, "shall we get started?"

"About 250 people will be logging onto the call," Iglesias said. "Congressman Leonard has gathered close to fifty who will be with him in Washington. We have union representatives, various associations like the National Chamber of Commerce and API. State officeholders from Alaska, Louisiana, Colorado, Texas, and..."

"Oklahoma?" Stephens interrupted.

"Of course," said Jones. "I took care of that myself with" – he smiled at West – "Noreen's help."

Iglesias continued, "California, New Mexico, North Dakota, and, I'm guessing, a few more who got the word but didn't RSVP."

Stephens ran his finger down a page entitled 'itinerary.' "I start with introductions. Us," he lowered his head in the direction of the others, "and have about five minutes to explain what we're doing…blah, blah, blah. Then Whalen and Noreen do their thing and you, Gary, go through the contents of the materials."

"Right," Iglesias acknowledged. "Let's keep in mind these people wouldn't have bothered to join us if they weren't interested. What might hold them back is a concern that this will be – for lack of a better way to explain it – a shrill and defensive campaign. One that is dismissive of environmental concerns, which it is not, and ignorant of legitimate issues, which we do address. My advice is all three of you emphasize we want to demonstrate the productive role the petroleum and gas industry plays as a partner in the overall energy sector, including the alternative sources we welcome for their contributions. We're not doing this as an angry response to our adversaries. In fact, don't even mention them in any of the material."

"Okay," Stephens said. "I think we've got it. We're telling our story not using it to bludgeon anyone else in the field."

Iglesias smiled. "I think we're ready to go."

***

Smolders plopped down in a chair in front of Ryan's desk and nodded at Berger who walked in as he settled.

"Good call," Smolders said to Berger. "The hotel parking lot in Wichita Falls was chock full of cameras and we found a car that looks a lot like the one spotted going to and coming from the Sleep Inn. Unfortunately, we still couldn't get a clear look at the license plate, but we did get a shot that lets us see, I think, a T on it." He handed Ryan and Berger images from the CCTV video.

Ryan nodded as he studied the still. "Yeah, I guess it could be a T. The car does look a lot like the one we caught going to and from the Sleep Inn."

"Were you able to get anything better from other CCTV footage inside the hotel than what Linares had?"

Smolders shook his head. "The room was on the first floor so that rules out the elevator camera. He never used it. And we can't isolate anyone from what we picked up in the lobby and other public spaces."

Berger tossed the photos onto Ryan's desk. "What now?"

***

"Thank you very much for your time," Stephens said, wrapping up the session. "As Gary has outlined, the materials are yours to use as he has recommended and as outlined in the introduction and suggestion sections. I look forward to working with you on a groundbreaking campaign that will shine a spotlight on an industry that remains critical to our nation's future growth and prosperity, and on the tens of thousands of men and women who devote their lives to the welfare of the American people. Thank you."

Stephens, Jones, West, and Iglesias held their smiles and kept their attention on the red light until it blinked out. All immediately relaxed. Stephens rolled his head and gripped his neck. Jones took a deep breath and sighed heavily. West took a tissue from her purse and blew her nose. Iglesias fell against the back of his chair and tapped at his cell phone.

"All totaled, two hundred seventy-five people from twelve states," Iglesias said.

"On the call?" Stephens asked.

Iglesias nodded.

"How the hell do you know that?" West asked.

"Brother," Jones said, "you need to jump right into the new world of technology, Noreen. The abacus is out. I'm sure Gary can give you a primer on how things are done these days."

West's lips curled showing her teeth and she was about to spit a response when Stephens injected, "Leonard had a roomful with him in D.C. That will add to those numbers."

"Right," Iglesias said. "What I gave you were those who logged on directly with us. The Chamber of Congress linked their membership in on their end. I'm sure other associations did the same so we could be looking at double or triple the totals I have," he said, waving his phone.

Stephens stood and stretched. "A lot of people from a shitload of states."

"I guarantee you," West said, hand on her briefing book, "some of this is going to leak. Someone is going to say something. The haters are going to try to knock us off course before we get started."

"Of course, they are," Jones said. "I don't think any of us is under the impression something this big is going to be kept quiet. What? You think we should've sworn hundreds of people to secrecy?"

West countered. "Just thought I'd put it out there."

"That's already been factored in," Iglesias said, sliding a page of talking points across the table. "Rather than letting others control how it leaks, we'll be orchestrating our own *leakage*. That way we have some control over the narrative. As soon as you get back into your offices, call whoever you usually use as a megaphone and give them a taste. The most important messages are: 'This is a positive campaign designed to let the public know how the industry is the backbone of growth and progress in this country.' Hit the 'we're at the forefront of environmental citizenship' and" – he pointed at the page of talking points – "work Lulu into this. I'm going to email a photo of her to you and make sure you send it to everyone you talk to. That way, they'll have a graphic to illustrate their stories. They're all going to use the standard shot of an oil field, or a gushing derrick, that sort of thing. But we can soften that with Lulu."

West sat back in her chair. "Gary, you'll be running my next campaign."

"Loss leaders do pay off," Iglesias responded.

Three Years Ago

"Thanks for coming," Jones said, pointing Ryan to one of two armchairs facing a couch. "Some coffee?"

"No, thank you," Ryan said and stood in front of one of the chairs.

"We also have soft drinks or juice if you'd prefer," Eileen said as she hovered.

"I'm good," Ryan answered.

"Thanks, Eileen," Jones said, dismissing her.

Ryan waited for Jones to sit on the couch before lowering himself onto the chair.

"It's good to meet you, Declan. We have a number of connections. Personal connections, I mean."

Ryan tilted his head. "Really?"

Jones stood and walked to the credenza behind his desk. He opened a door on one side of the long blond oak piece and held up a football as he returned to his chair. He tossed it to Ryan. "That's from the state championship game my senior year in high school. There's no score painted on the side like there usually is with these keepsakes. You know why?"

"I think so," Ryan said with a smile and placed the ball on a coffee table separating the couch from the chairs.

"One of those was supposed to be given to everyone on our team after we won the game. We didn't." Jones pointed at Ryan. "You did. You ran over and around us all night long. What did you have? Something like two hundred yards?"

"I don't remember."

"I had a headache for days after you kneed me in the head, and my arms were black and blue for a week from trying to tackle you."

Ryan nodded, smiling politely.

"That was your junior year, I think. My last chance for a state title and you stomped all over it." Jones folded his hands together and laid them in his lap. "So, what happened to 'The Owen Terror'? You didn't play after that year. Disappointed the hell out of OU and a lot of D-1 schools."

"Lost interest."

"Really!" Jones said, genuine surprise in his voice. "Lost interest? That's it?"

"That's it."

Jones pointed at the ball. "I learned a valuable lesson. Never take anything for granted. We were supposed to win that game going away. What was the prediction?" He tilted his head toward the ceiling. "I think we were favored by at least two touchdowns." He brought his attention back to Ryan. "A valuable life lesson and I have you to thank."

"Glad I could help."

"It dovetails nicely with another life lesson I value. 'Life isn't fair.' Now," Jones said, narrowing his eyes, showing serious intent, "I want to return the favor. I understand you're at the head of the list to replace Sheriff Thaxton." Jones forced a laugh. "I didn't even know he was still sheriff. What? He must be eighty years old. Been there for freakin' ever."

"He's a good man."

"He *was*, but it's time for a change. You ready to take over?"

"Nothing's been settled. I'm only one of many being considered. The city council will be making a decision in a couple of weeks."

"Had your hearing with the council yet?"

Ryan nodded.

"How'd you do?"

"I think I did okay."

"As you might know, I was on the city council in Eureka before I ran for the state house. I still know most of the members in Owen. Worked closely with them on a number of things, especially when the county seat was transferred to Owen. Boy, that was a kick in the ass for us, but made sense given the growth in Owen. Anyway," Jones said with a shrug, "I'd be happy to make some calls for you."

"No," Ryan said, shaking his head. "I appreciate the offer but I'm sure they're down the road on this. Probably already decided."

"Not over 'til the fat lady sings. I'd like to help. Like I said, return a favor." Jones raised his hands gesturing at Ryan to toss the ball to him. "Let me tell you a story," he said as he caught the ball and put it on his desk. "A man told his son, 'You will marry the girl I choose.' The son said 'no.' The father told the young man that the girl was Bill Gates' daughter. Surprised, the son said, 'Okay, I'll marry her, but how did you swing that?' His father said, 'I called Bill Gates and said I want your daughter to marry my son,' but Gates refused, so I told him you were the CEO of World Bank. Gates said, 'Okay, my daughter will marry your son.' Then I called the President of World Bank and asked him to make you the CEO. He said, 'No.' I told him you were Bill Gates' son-in-law and he said, 'Okay.' That's how politics works, Declan, and you're in that game whether you think so or not. So, let me make a few calls."

Ryan stared at Jones a long moment. "A favor always begets a favor, and you'd be one up on me."

Jones held up a hand. "No, we'd be square." He waited a beat before adding. "I wouldn't mind, of course, if you took my call should I ever have a reason to call."

Ryan smiled. "And there it is."

"That's not much to ask."

"It's still an 'ask' and a hell of a way to begin my job, if I get it. Especially if I get it because you stepped in."

"Agreeing to accept a call from a state senator is pro forma. You'd probably do that even if we'd never met. Never had this conversation."

Ryan nodded. "Probably."

"Another connection. I was in Eureka when your brother was taken from the court there to the Mac."

This hit Ryan squarely between the eyes. He shifted his weight.

"I'll never forget that day. What's his name? Sorry, I've forgotten."

"Connor."

"Right. Connor. A bunch of my friends and I heard he was being transported from the jail in the courthouse to the Mac, with a stopover in Owen. He was big news back then. A bank robber and..."

"A failed bank robber who killed my mother and father," Ryan said, anger with a back note of bitterness animating his voice.

"A myth built up around him. That he was robbing banks to..."

"One bank and he was caught before he got out the door."

"Anyway, there was that myth he was robbing banks to give money to farmers who had defaulted on their loans. Never made a lot of sense to me since the banks would have known they were getting their own money back." Jones laughed. "But that was the story at the time."

"Yeah, the part about his killing my parents got lost in the telling."

"But it was the reason he got twenty-five years to life, right?" It was a rhetorical question and Jones went on. "How's he doing?"

"I have no idea."

Jones let this response sit before continuing. "I chair the Public Safety Committee and we oversee the Department of Corrections, among other things. There are serious overcrowding problems in the Mac. Suggestions have been made that some of the better behaved long-term inmates should be released to make room for the newly sentenced scum of the earth."

"Are you telling me Connor is going to be getting out?"

"I'm saying he might be one of those being considered for early release. How do you feel about that?"

Ryan took a deep breath and exhaled. "Let the system do what it does."

"No preference one way or the other?"

Ryan stared hard at Jones. "No, and so we understand each other. You call. I'll answer. I'll listen. Then, I'll do what I think is best."

"I wouldn't expect any different."

Ryan started to push himself out of the chair and sat back down. "I'd appreciate it if you didn't make any calls on my behalf."

"Those boys on the city council are a tough group." Jones rolled his eyes. "Maybe 'tough' is the wrong word. They're close-minded. Stuck in the past."

Ryan sat still.

"It would be good if you stayed away from the clubs on Pennsylvania Avenue here in Oklahoma City. Hi-Lo. Tramps. Ledo. Apothecary. Those clubs."

Jones and Ryan sat silently each waiting for the other shoe to drop. Jones dropped it saying, "I could care less but I don't think my attitude is shared by anyone on the council. Not evolved or tolerant."

Ryan stood. "You don't owe me a thing."

185

Wednesday - May 23

"This is a joint editorial?" Jones asked Ken Slade, who laid the newspaper on his desk.

Slade nodded. "That's the *Oklahoman*. It was also in this morning's *Wichita Fall Times-Record-News*. Never saw that before. You aren't going to like it."

What Happens Next?

At separate press conferences held in Oklahoma City and Wichita Falls the public was notified there is a cross-border serial killer stalking our streets. The crimes are horrific and have taken the lives of as many as five women.

We say "as many as" because – along with a lot the police do not know about this killer – they are not certain about the number of victims. So, what did they tell us?

The most startling revelations came from authorities in Oklahoma who disclosed they have known about the crimes for almost two years but decided not to make them public because it would have complicated their investigation. That was the essence of it. The public was kept in the dark so as not to cause the investigators heartburn.

Back to the number of victims. Four of the women have been conclusively identified as victims of a single killer, including the one in Wichita Falls, while a fifth was "likely" killed by that person as well. That's comforting. The best the police could do was create doubt about how many of the victims were brutally murdered by a serial killer. Which raises a disturbing question – it raises a lot of questions, but one in particular. If we have a copycat in our midst, how does this killer know about the details of the murders of other women when those details were withheld from the public?

There are no suspects.

There is no indication law enforcement is working cooperatively cross-border, sharing information, and combining resources. In fairness, we were told by the Director of the Oklahoma State Bureau of Investigation there has been an ongoing investigation within three jurisdictions in Oklahoma. We also learned the Texas Rangers are working with the Wichita Falls Police Department.

Are authorities in Oklahoma and Texas working together?

We have a suggestion. Call in the Federal Bureau of Investigation which has the resources to augment what is being done in Oklahoma and Texas. Among those resources is the respected Behavioral Analysis Unit. The BAU is a department of the FBI's National Center for the Analysis of Violent Crime (NCAVC) that uses behavioral analysts to assist in criminal investigations. In plain English, these are the profilers we often hear about. These are the people whose skills can help us.

Let's bring in the experts. And let's do it sooner rather than later.

Jones pushed the newspaper away. "The FBI?" He looked at Slade and repeated, "The FBI? Reporters would be following them around and writing about every time they scratched their asses. The feds? Brings up ghosts of Ruby Ridge and Waco." He shook his head and grunted loudly. "Plus, they love the limelight and have press conferences every other day. Having them around will make it look like we don't know what the hell we're doing. That we had to get them involved to save us from ourselves."

Slade shifted in his chair, not certain how to respond, or even if he should. He thought bringing in the FBI might be the way to go. A convenient passing of the baton in the middle of a situation spinning out of control. Let them take the heat.

Jones stood and began pacing. "And what if they find something we" – he stopped and stared at Slade" – "*you* couldn't? That'd be fucking great."

Gary Iglesias, whose meeting with Jones had been interrupted by Slade, got up from the couch where he had been sitting and walked to the desk. He scanned the editorial. "I have an idea. A way we can use this to our advantage."

***

"Look at this," Berger said. He laid three pages side-by-side on top of Ryan's desk.

"What am I looking at?" Ryan asked, turning the pages so he could read them.

"Guest lists for three political fundraisers."

"Okay," Ryan said tentatively.

"Look closely." Berger leaned on the desk, his arms supporting his weight.

"These must've been for Senator Jones." Ryan looked from page to page.

"What gave it away? His name on each page listed as 'Honored Guest'?"

He pointed. "Another name on each of the lists. Raymond Lee. I know him. He's a former highway patrol officer. Our paths crossed occasionally." He looked up at Berger. "So?"

"Look at the dates."

"Jesus," Ryan said.

'Yeah, 'Jesus.'" Berger sat down. "I left a big hole when I started looking into this. I talked to the parents of the girls. Interviewed other family and friends. All the rest of it. Once we determined the three were victims of a single killer, I went back and did it all over again, this time trying to find a connection between the victims."

"*Among* them."

Berger gave Ryan a look. "Really?"

Ryan waved him off.

"I was trying to find connections *among* the victims. I was thorough, and not finding anything, I was also frustrated. It never occurred to me to look for a connection *among* the parents." He jabbed his finger at the lists. "They are all politically active and big supporters of Senator Jones. Their daughters were murdered about a month after each of those fundraisers."

Ryan reviewed the lists again. "That's a lot of people to interview."

"Let's go in the other direction. Take the two who appear on each list and if we can eliminate them, then we start with the others."

"A state senator and former highway patrol officer," Ryan said. "Not generally 'firsts' in the box. What do you know about Lee?"

"I say we start with Jones."

"Really?"

Berger reached into his sport coat and lifted out a thick wad of papers, which he handed to Ryan, who read a headline on one of the pages: "Are Politicians Natural Born Psychopaths?" He looked up at Berger, a question still in his eyes.

"Psychopaths are perfect for politics. They have an inflated sense of self-worth. Being manipulative and charming gives them two other important attributes. They make positive first impressions. And not having to deal with remorse or much in the way of emotions, they handle stress well; aren't usually burdened with anxiety or depression."

Ryan nodded slowly. "Okay, so he belongs on our radar. What about Lee?"

"Let's see what we can find out." Berger stepped around the side of the desk and handed Ryan a web address. "Let's access his records."

Friday-May 25

Monica Filer stood at the entrance to the Sky Room at the Hard Rock Casino welcoming guests with a bright smile and a low-cut dress that threatened to spill what little it covered unless she remained standing erect, shoulders back. She handed each person a gift bag and pointed out where to find their stick-on nametag.

The floor-to-ceiling windows framed the twinkling lights of downtown Tulsa. Drinks in one hand and small plates of cheese and crackers in the other, most in the formally dressed crowd gathered at the windows, where the talk was small.

Individual tables were decorated with miniatures of posters used by Roy Evans beginning with his first campaign for city council through to his third and most recent run for the United States Senate. The room was surrounded by easels holding enlarged photos of Evans with recognizable faces: Presidents. Vice Presidents. Foreign leaders. Actors. Even one flanked by storm troopers on the set of the original *Star Wars* movie.

At the far end of the room two banquet tables sat on a low riser. Separating the tables was a dark maple wood podium festooned with the seal of the United States Senate. The guest of honor walked into the room behind the tables followed by Governor Lincoln Stephens and wife, Senator Wylie Clifford and wife, State Senate President Pro Tempore Whalen Jones, and State House Speaker Noreen West and her husband. This served as a signal to those milling about to find their seats. Stragglers were shepherded to their tables by the peripatetic Filer.

As the noise level of the room settled into a steady hum, Jones rose and moved behind the podium. He stared out at the crowd and the hum slowly receded. Static from the sound system and the occasional clinking of a water glass being filled by the waitstaff were the only sounds.

"Welcome, ladies and gentlemen. I see mostly familiar faces, but for those who are wondering, I'm Whalen Jones, master of ceremonies for the evening. My day job is herding cats in the State Senate."

A small titter of laughter.

"We're here this evening to honor a once-in-a-generation public servant for almost fifty years of service to his community, this city, and to our state. I won't go into all he has accomplished. I couldn't since we only have this room for three hours."

More tittering.

"Those gift bags you were handed on your way in this evening include a brochure we had especially prepared for this event that will let you know how much we all owe Senator Roy Evans from his days on Tulsa's city council through his legislative record in Washington. It's more a novella in length."

Monica Filer jumped up from her chair at a table in front of Jones and began to applaud sparking an ovation that spread around the room, compelling attendees to stand, and had to be interrupted by Jones who raised his arms, saying "Save your strength, folks. You'll want to wait until everyone up here has shared a story or two about a wonderful man, and then you can let it fly.

"The etiquette for most of these things is we eat first and then go into the program for the night. I'm taking it upon myself to change that order and begin the program. Seeing everyone enjoying the open bar, and given the generous pours we're getting, I think we're better off doing this now, when we can all understand and fully appreciate what's going on."

Full-throated laughter.

Forty-five minutes later the final speaker, Noreen West, finished with a flourish. True to her reputation, she caused many in the audience to cringe at her earthy language, and roar with laughter at her jibes. The best one came at the conclusion of her remarks when she asked Monica Filer to stand and remarked, "Only a man Roy Evans's age could have a young lady this healthy" – she punctuated the word healthy with a wink – "running his state office without worrying it might cause him a heart attack."

West left the podium to sustained applause causing Jones to say, "You now see why we had Noreen at the tail end of this parade. None of us wanted to follow her...but here I am. The sacrificial lamb. Of course, we couldn't, and won't, end the program without giving you all the opportunity to hear from Senator Evans. That will come after we enjoy the best food in Tulsa."

The original itinerary had Evans following West, but he pushed a note to Jones as she was completing her remarks saying he didn't feel up to speaking and asked that his time be delayed until after dinner. That was the last decision Evans ever made. He dropped dead, face first, into his dessert plate. A seven-layer chocolate cake.

***

"We need a Plan B," Jones said as he fell back onto the couch in the hospitality suite.

"A Plan B?" West asked as she came out of the bedroom.

"You go first," Jones said to her, closing his eyes and massaging his temples. "Is she going to live?"

West glanced back toward the door of the room and shook her head. "What the hell did she see in that slob of an old man?" She shivered. "I wouldn't let him come within ten feet of me and I'm a slob of an old woman. But, 'yes,' she'll live. I called his wife and..."

"He is...*was* married?" Stephens interrupted, eyes wide with surprise.

"Kind of," West replied. "Gwendolyn left him after he disowned their daughter because she's gay."

"He had a daughter?" Jones said bolting forward on the couch.

West laughed derisively. "Christ, is there no camaraderie in politics anymore?"

"Fuck no," blurted Jones who let himself drop back on the couch. "I've known...*knew* the guy for twenty years and didn't know about the daughter. I once heard something about a wife."

"They split a long time ago," West conceded. "Gwendolyn went to live with her daughter and her daughter's partner on Padre Island in a house the good senator's benefactors made possible funneling funds through his political action committee. One of many thank you's for his loyalty.

Certain irony in that, I suppose. Anyway, word was she threw him out because of the daughter, but I think it had as much to do with" – West's eyes went to the door – "a succession of those. In his younger days, Evans made Clinton and Trump look like real pikers."

"I don't think he slowed up that much," Stephens said, eyeing the bedroom door. "This is the age of Viagra."

"Roy was a scumbag," West said, "and the worst of it wasn't the women coming and going through the turnstile in his bedroom." She stared and bobbed her head as if trying to dredge up a memory. "I think it was this past election. He asked Gwendolyn and his daughter if he could see them. They thought he was going to apologize, or at least try to make amends for being such a prick. He shows up with a camera crew and wants to film a commercial for his campaign with the daughter and her partner as the centerpiece to show how, uh…" She paused, searching for a word. "Well, 'liberal' wouldn't be the right word because that wouldn't have played well. Whatever. They threw his ass out."

"How did she react to your phone call?"

"Asked if I'd talk to someone in his office and make sure her name wasn't mentioned in his obituary. Okay, it's your turn. What's this Plan B stuff?"

Stephens looked around the room, located the bar next to a fireplace on an opposite wall, crossed the room, and poured himself a drink from a bottle of Red Label Scotch. He walked to a whirlpool positioned so users could look out a large window at the "Oil Capital of the World."

"I'll get the word out in the morning that all flags should be flown at half-mast."

"Wonderful sentiment," West said. "Now, tell me about this 'Plan B.'"

Jones answered, "Evans was going to announce his retirement tonight and endorse Lincoln. That was Plan A."

"And I was going to lay hands on Whalen to be my successor," Stephens added as he sat down in a dining room facing the open suite.

West stood. "You SOBs. You were going to use me as a prop for your coming-out party. Ever occur to ask me first? Or, at the very least, let me know what you had in mind?"

"Relax, Noreen," Jones said, motioning for West to sit down. "There's a bone in this for you."

Stephens gave Jones a look.

"I've worked it all out," Jones said, nodding at Stephens. Then to West: "I'm going to tell my folks to stand down from supporting anyone for my seat."

"Meaning?" West asked.

"Meaning it's yours if you want it."

West raised her eyebrows. "What exactly are you saying? That I can run unopposed?"

"Someone will always jump in. What's the name of that nutcase who runs every year? He's a Libertarian. He'll probably run again. So, no, I doubt you'd be running unopposed, but you won't have to worry about any strong opposition from us. No one is going to say we're conceding the seat, of course. We won't formally back anyone. You'd have a clear path."

West relaxed. "I'll think about it."

"Now that we've settled Noreen's future, *we* still need a Plan B," Jones said. "And that's going to take some thought. Our Plan A guy keeled over less than an hour ago."

Stephens drained his glass and returned to the bar for a refill. "Whatever it is it's going to have to include something about the now open senate seat. "You," he nodded at West, "have this in your control. As Speaker, you pick three names and I choose from them, then the senate" – he looked at Jones – "approves my pick." Back to West: "I say you linger on your choices, that takes us closer to the election and makes filling the vacancy unnecessary."

West said, "It's good to be king, or in this case, queen."

Monday-May 28

Len Slade pulled Berger aside. "We're not going to say anything about the political fundraisers." He added, "Or the guest lists."

Berger opened his mouth, a protest on the tip of his tongue, but was stopped by Slade who raised a finger. "I'm not saying you shouldn't find out where all that leads, I'm just saying we're not going to mention it now. Let's get something solid before we open up that can of worms. I don't want this sidetracked by having to deal with the shit show it would cause."

"What are we doing here then?" Berger said, frustration in his voice. "I have no idea what this is all about."

"Look, I got the call from Jones on Saturday saying he'd been in touch with Linares and McDowell and talked to them about doing this joint presser to tamp down what he called the 'increasing hysteria' surrounding the case. You saw the editorial in the *Oklahoman*, didn't you?"

"Yeah."

"It was also in the Wichita Falls paper. Jones flipped out. Especially at the suggestion that we call in the FBI."

"What's his problem with the FBI? A little help would be a good thing."

"Political, I guess," Slade whispered. "Doesn't want the feds running around the state, plus he's chairman of our committee and…"

"What committee?"

"In the senate. Public safety. Oversees the SBI. If we call in the FBI it's like saying we can't deal with this ourselves, and that might bounce back on Jones. In a bad way. Politically. Like he's responsible for us not being up to the task." Slade looked around the room. "So, here we are."

Berger returned a nod from a man in a large white Stetson hat prompting Slade to ask, "You know McDowell?"

195

"We've met. I talked to him and Linares. Ryan and I did. Met with them about Wilson. Got the particulars on her and filled them in on what we're dealing with. I emailed you the report about our meeting."

"Yeah, okay," Slade said dismissively. "Our guy has crossed the border. No question. That's what we're doing this for. We're going to say we agree a serial killer is active on both sides of the border."

Berger waited for the rest of an explanation that was not coming. "And?"

Slade handed Berger a 'Statement for the Media.' "This is what Linares is going to say."

Berger read. "That we're forming a joint taskforce? Is there going to be a taskforce this time? You said that before and..."

"Yes, there's going to be a taskforce. I was planning to move ahead with the other one, but we'll roll those plans into..." He raised his chin in the direction of Linares and McDowell huddling on the other side of the room. "Whatever they're doing. This is all about feeding the media something to chew on so we can do our job without them pounding on us."

"What do you need me for?"

"Appearance. You're the guy leading the charge for the SBI. Well, you're the guy on the ground," Slade corrected himself, walking back 'leading the charge.' "We want to show we have this on the front burner at the highest levels, and also put a face on the person grinding away."

"Great," said Berger. "A face. What about Ryan and the others? Shouldn't their faces be here?"

"We agreed to keep this circus contained. You're the 'go-to' guy in Oklahoma."

"Small edit," McDowell said, brandishing a handful of papers as he approached Slade and Berger. He held out his hand. "Trade." He took their pages and handed them replacements. "Congratulations," he said to Berger, "you're the head of the taskforce." Reading the stunned reaction on Berger's face, he added, "More ceremonial than anything. I'll explain later."

"Let's go," Linares said and opened the door into a large room.

Microphones and tent-fold place cards were arranged on a banquet table in front of four chairs. The men sat in the order in which they filed into the room without noticing the place settings. A moment of confusion ensued when one of the reporters adjusted Linares and McDowell's name cards to identify the men properly. Slade and Berger exchanged cards.

With the line-up properly identified, the clicking of cameras went off in a barrage. The glow of pinpoint red lights on the mounted camcorders in the center of the room announced they were filming.

"Good morning," Linares said stiffly. "I'm Paul Linares, Chief of Police here in Wichita Falls. To my right is Corporal Marty McDowell of Texas Ranger Company C. To his right are Len Slade, Director of the Oklahoma State Bureau of Investigation and Joseph Berger, an agent with the SBI."

Linares cleared his throat, took a pair of glasses out of his shirt pocket, carefully adjusted their balance on the bridge of his nose, and began reading from the remarks he placed on the table in front of him. "As you know, we" – he lifted his eyes to the others at the table – "are investigating a series of murders that have every indication of being perpetrated by a single offender. To augment our individual investigations, we are today announcing the formation of a taskforce that will include the Wichita Falls Police Department, C Company of the Texas Rangers, the Oklahoma State Bureau of Investigation, and all other affected jurisdictions. This will allow us to better coordinate our efforts and increase our resources. Agent Berger…"

Berger felt himself jerk involuntarily.

"…will direct the work of this taskforce. We expect to be up and running by the end of the week. Status reports will be provided weekly, or as necessary. Thank you. We will take a few questions."

Chaos erupted and Linares shouted, "One at a time, beginning with you." He pointed to the man in front of the banquet table who had rearranged the name cards.

"This is for Agent Berger. Is the formation of a taskforce a tacit admission no one has made progress on their own, and where will it be housed?"

"Excuse me for horning in," Slade directed himself to Linares. Then to the reporter: "Please identify yourself and your affiliation."

"Richard Atkins, KFDX3, NBC."

"Thank you," Linares said and nodded in Berger's direction.

"This taskforce is being formed for the reasons Chief Linares outlined. It's a force multiplier. It will allow us to share expertise and increase our resources." Berger laid his hands on the table and sat stiffly. He had no idea where the taskforce would be housed and hoped the question would be forgotten.

"And where will you work out of?"

Slade spoke up. "Space will be provided in our headquarters."

Linares picked the next questioner.

"Rennie Haven, *Tulsa World*. This is for Director Slade. Have you determined conclusively if the murder in Owen is related to the others?"

"We are including the victim in Owen as part of our investigation of the serial murders."

Haven persisted. "That doesn't answer my question."

"Well, that's my answer," Slade said. He looked down the table at Linares who promptly pointed to a woman in the middle of the pack.

"Linda Pines, the *Oklahoman*. This is for anyone who wants to give a straight answer. Will you be asking for assistance from the FBI?"

"No, we will not," Slade responded sternly.

"Why?"

"While we respect the abilities of the Bureau, we feel comfortable with the combination of talents we've announced, we can move ahead productively."

"Does everyone agree?" the woman said, gesturing the length of the table.

"We do," Linares and McDowell offered.

"Yes," Linares said with a nod at a reporter standing on the filming platform.

"Mark Andes, KOCO, ABC. This is for Agent Berger. You've been the lead on this investigation since the beginning. How much progress have you made, and how *exactly*" – he emphasized the word with air quotes – "will the formation of *another*" – more air quotes – "taskforce push the investigation forward?"

Slade said, "I'll take the second part of your question and offer a clarification. This isn't so much *another*" – he made a show of adding air quotes – "taskforce as it is an addition of resources to the one already hard at work on the case." He tilted his head toward Berger. "Go ahead."

"As to our progress, it was no easy task identifying that a single offender is responsible for the murders. We first had to determine that the MO was consistent from victim to victim. The initial three murders were committed with what we call a 'cooling off period' separating them, so, as unfortunate as it was, we had to wait until we had the recent victims and could examine their causes of death before we could say conclusively that all were the victims of the same offender.

"We've also established we're dealing with a sexual sadist. With this information we have created a profile of the offender. He is likely between the age of twenty-five and forty; has a job providing him with an income so he can afford transportation from place to place; that job, however, is not secure employment because he has neither the personality nor ability to retain steady employment; and he is unlikely to have any lasting intimate relationships given his inability to form true attachments."

"But you still don't have a suspect?"

Oh, yeah, we do, Berger felt like blurting out and sending the assembly into a tizzy. And then it hit him like a punch to the sternum. They had much more. The letters for the partial plate identification. The T and the Z. He recognized them.

McDowell interpreted Berger's blank stare as a cry for help. "There are no persons of interest."

"Final question," Linares said and pointed to a woman who popped up from her chair swinging her arm madly.

"Given the spotlight you've put on the investigation, and with this announcement of the taskforce, aren't you concerned the killer might move on, or stop?"

Linares asked, "Name and affiliation, and who is the question for?"

"Wendy Givens, *Wichita Falls Times-Record-News.* The question is for Agent Berger."

Berger was still staring into the far, far distance and Givens said again, "The question is for Agent Berger." He blinked at the mention of his name and looked at the woman who repeated her question. "Given the spotlight you've put on the investigation and with this announcement of the taskforce, aren't you concerned the killer might move on, or stop?"

"Unfortunately, it's doubtful the person responsible for the murders will stop. They can't. They are compelled to kill. Programmed that way. It is possible he could move on. Generally, however, these offenders operate within a comfort zone that keeps their crimes near home or work. That said, the person we're looking for has exhibited a comfort level traveling to different cities, and different states, but we're not convinced he's ready to begin hiking across the country."

"That's all for today," Linares announced. He was met with a flurry of protests and demands for answers to a barrage of questions. The four ignored the chaos and as soon as Berger was through the door and into the side room, he excused himself and sprinted to the parking lot.

***

"I got something," he blurted into the phone excitedly before Ryan had a chance to acknowledge the call. "I should've picked up on it before. I was looking so hard at the forest, I missed the tree. That partial from the sedan near the motel where Luna was killed, it could be from a state government car."

"How do you know that?"

"The T and Z on the plate. Those are exclusive to official vehicles used by state government employees. I'm looking at mine right now."

A long beat of silence passed before Ryan answered. "That's something, all right."

"Ask Smolders to..."

"He's with me. I'll put this on conference. Okay, go ahead. We're both listening."

"I told Declan that the partial plate..."

"I heard that," Smolders said.

"I'm going to text you the pin number I use to get into the state fleet management site. It's the one I use to report mileage, if I need maintenance, that kind of thing. See what you can find."

"Like?" Smolders asked.

Berger stared at his car. "Like if Lee is assigned a state vehicle. And Jones."

"I can do that with your pin number?"

"I've never tried to get anywhere else on the site. Only into my own account, but see if you, or someone who knows their way around a computer, can explore and..."

"You mean hack into personal accounts," Smolders said.

"Well, yeah, if you have to. Find out if either of them is assigned a state vehicle. Specifically, white sedans."

"Sure, but how is this going to work now that we have this new taskforce? We watched the press conference. What is the protocol?"

"Screw it. They made me the leader, director, whatever the hell I am, and I don't want to deal anyone else in."

"Okay," Smolders said. "Speaking of which, I got some stuff on Lee. You have five minutes?"

"As much time as you need."

"He was with the State Highway Patrol for twenty years. Exemplary record. Lots of commendations, including a biggie for heading up an operation that brought down a major sex worker smuggling ring trucking in girls from Mexico. It went beyond Oklahoma into most of the Southwest. The feds were involved. Cartel-related stuff that included high-level military in Mexico. He got all kinds of commendations from our people and from the Mexicans. Even went to Washington for some ceremony at the White House."

"Personal life?"

"He's forty-seven. Divorced. Two daughters."

"Not the typical profile of a person of interest, but I'm constantly surprised. Prominent military types. Business owners. Doctors. Lawyers. Indian chiefs. Spreads across the gamut."

Ryan asked, "What is Lee's relationship with Jones?"

"Jones hired him to be the chief investigator for his Public Safety Committee."

"Which means?"

"I'm assuming you don't want a job description."

"No, I want to know what he does for Jones."

"According to a few highway patrol guys who provide security at the Capitol, ones I know and asked to keep my asking quiet, Lee is Jones's shadow. More like a bodyguard than a committee investigator. Goes everywhere with him."

Berger asked Smolders, "What'd you find out about Jones?"

"Nothing hinky. Decent student. Went to OU. Got an MBA. Took over the family construction business. Expanded it. Sold it for a fortune. Bought a manufacturing company that makes machinery and other stuff for the oil industry. Huge success and got into politics, where I'm sure he's making another fortune."

"Personal life?"

"Doesn't have one as far as I can tell. Never married. Has had eye candy to squire to big events. That's about it."

"Check to see if he has a government car."

***

Berger, back in the room, went straight for Slade, Linares, and McDowell. "Okay, so tell me what this is all about. Merging two groups that don't exist. And, more specifically, why me?"

McDowell picked up the question. "It wasn't fair. We put you on the spot, but you're the only one who can do this."

"I don't think so," Berger said, working hard to remain calm. "It makes more sense that any of you should be running a high-profile taskforce like this. You all outrank me by a couple of dozen pay grades."

McDowell nodded. "Which is why it makes sense for you to take the lead. We" – he turned his shoulders to the others – "have offices to run. None of us could devote time to something like this. If we announced that, it would look like we're forming a sham group. We needed someone who can devote full time to it. Someone who has a background like yours. Who's been involved from the beginning. And who has the pedigree you do, an agent with the SBI. You're the perfect choice."

Berger let his shoulders relax. "You could have let me in on it at least ten minutes before hauling me in front of that pack of jackals." He ran his fingers through his hair. "Jesus Christ."

"Entirely my fault," McDowell said. "You were my choice. It occurred to me we'd get asked who was heading this up and if we didn't have anyone, or hadn't even taken the time to assign someone, how serious could we be?"

"How serious are we about this?" Berger asked. "I mean about pulling together a functioning group."

Slade answered, "Go ahead and do what you've been doing the way you've been doing it." To Linares and McDowell: "Work up a list of a few people you have working this case and email it to Declan." Back to Berger: "You can reach out to them on your own time to fill them in on what you're doing and tell them to keep you in the loop while they're doing their own investigating." He raised his palms. "Instant taskforce."

"I'll get you those names this afternoon," Linares said. "We have four guys working the case."

"I got two," McDowell said.

Berger turned to Slade. "Have you said anything to Adams, Flipse, and Fenn?"

Slade said to McDowell and Linares, "The head cops in the other cities." Then to Berger, "I haven't, but I will. I'll tell them you'll be in touch."

"And will I? Be in touch?"

Slade took a deep breath. "Just do the same thing with them. Ask 'em to keep the lines of communication open. No need to spend a lot of time on trying to put together a formal group, or anything like that. Keep it loose and don't let anyone interfere with what you want to do."

"I promise you," Berger said. "I won't."

Thursday-May 31

It was a perfect day at the Oklahoma City Fairgrounds. A light breeze blew a cool wind across the front of the stage causing the red, white, and blue bunting to ripple gently.

The elevated stage looked across a level green space that in as little as four weeks would be an ugly brown, the grass burned by the heat and turned to dust when walked on. Today, it was a beautiful sight.

Cars were beginning to fill a large swath of land to the west of the fairgrounds where the grass gave way to gravel and dirt. Volunteers from the local service clubs, Rotary, Elks, Shriners, and Lions were directing traffic and collecting a modest five-dollar parking fee.

Hundreds of celebrants were filing into the grassy field and carving out their plots. Early arrivals got the best spaces in front of the stage. The area was becoming a patchwork of color as most brought blankets or beach towels to lounge on. There were occasional puffs of smoke from small hibachis and grills firing up and cooking hamburgers, hot dogs, and sausages. The gathering was taking on the flavor of a tailgate party with smells carried by the refreshing breezes.

The throng was drawn to a day of "celebration and thanks" by a relentless campaign of radio, television, and social media advertising beckoning people to: "Come celebrate Lulu Hefner, the First Lady of Oklahoma's oil industry." The extended message added, "This remarkable woman who had so much to do with setting the pace for our state's keystone industry will be recognized during a day of fun hosted by Governor Lincoln Stephens and sponsored by businesses small and large that make this state tick."

Balloons with Hefner's image were being handed out to every child entering the field. "Lulu" fans were also available as were banners covered with images of spewing oil derricks and the motto: "Oklahoma makes

America work." Colorful hot-air balloons hovered over the field. Some sported Hefner's image; others displayed the names of oil and gas companies.

By mid-afternoon the celebrants were in full voice. There were call-and-response choruses rising from the crowd spurred on by deejays from local radio stations who roamed through the crowd handing out song sheets with the words to "I Want to Hold Your Hand" changed to "I Want to Hold Lulu's Hand." These deejays also carried small devices that blasted music and encouraged the crowd to sing along.

The stage was built to hold the weight of two dozen people along with banks of speakers. An encircling plastic skirt was illustrated with a timeline noting significant landmarks in the history of the oil and gas industry:

1897 – Oklahoma's first oil well in Bartlesville

1901 –Red Fork Gusher makes Tulsa "Oil Capital of the World"

1928 – Massive Oklahoma City oilfield discovered

1900 to 1935 – Oklahoma ranked first among the mid-continent states in oil production

Today – More than 2,000 active producers prosper in Oklahoma

Lulu Hefner's words in swirling script lined the top of the skirt. "'I do not depend on luck. I back geological science with my own judgment and intuition. I always operate on my own money and so I cannot afford to waste time on 'dusters.' I must get producers."

In a VIP tent behind the stage, Stephens and Jones were basking in the attention of the well-heeled, the favored among their political supporters, and a select group of reporters; a group carefully vetted to ensure positive coverage of the event and the organizers.

"Gary is a fucking genius," Stephens whispered to Jones as he plucked another canape from a silver tray offered by a formally dressed server. "He keeps hitting home runs."

"No wonder you keep getting elected by double figures," Jones said. "Where'd you find him?"

"I didn't. My daughter did. They were dating in college and I had to overcome a real distaste for him – more like for anyone she dated – before agreeing to sit down and talk to the guy. He was impressive from the first words out of his mouth."

"He came straight out of college doing this?" Jones looked around the tent. "With this kind of know-how?"

"He had a few years of seasoning on my staff. I hired him to do press work and write speeches. He came up with ideas like doing a tour of the state with handicapped reporters, and anyone who had written about the ADA, to show how much my administration was doing to enforce the regulation. The articles that resulted were gold. He outgrew what he was doing for me, so I encouraged him to go out on his own. Some people just have an instinct for this sort of thing." Stephens clapped Jones on the back. "And I get a special rate for being such a supportive SOB."

"What about your daughter? How'd that...?"

"He's way too ambitious and intelligent for her. She married a lawyer who I got a job with Leonard in D.C. He does legislation or some such shit for him."

"Gotta hand it to you, Lincoln," West said, joining the conversation. "This is something. Did you see the crowd? And this here was a nice touch," she gestured at the surrounding tent. "Makes your acolytes feel special."

"You about ready to extol the virtues of Lulu Hefner?" Stephens asked her.

West lifted a page out of her purse. "Thank God I've only got to do that for" – she looked down at the page in her hand titled "Script for Hefner Day" – "five to seven minutes. And mercifully, we've all scripted for five to seven minutes, except you, Lincoln. You have to hold the crowd for ten minutes. And then do MC duties. Better you than me."

"I could do it in my sleep. It's all introductions and the usual encomiums to black gold."

"*Encomiums?*" West said teasingly. "I sure as shit hope you're not going to talk like that when you get up in front of the unwashed masses."

Stephens laughed. "No, I'll go full country. I'll make everyone my best friend."

West, eyes returning to the script, said, "Well, even if a few people get longwinded, we should be out of here in a little more than an hour. That's gotta be some record for a platform full of people who love to hear themselves talk."

"Stick around after the official part of the evening is over, Noreen," Stephens suggested. "We're going to have fireworks and lots more food and drink right here away from your 'unwashed masses.' Plus, Gary tells me he has a few hundred of those Hollywood Klieg lights positioned around the field and they'll be coming on as soon as it's dark. He's calling it 'A cathedral of light.' It should be a real show."

"A word of advice," West said, leaning close to Stephens. "Tell him not to call it 'a cathedral of light.' That's what the Nazis called the effect of those lights at their goddamn scary Nuremberg rallies."

***

"Over here," Stephens called out as he stared at the 52-inch flat screen TV mounted on a crossbar in the VIP tent. "FOX is saying tens of thousands of Americans across the country celebrated the – in the words of this bubble-headed blonde – 'social and economic benefits' of the oil and gas industry. They're showing a montage of shots from all over: Texas, Alaska, New Mexico, Louisiana, Colorado, Utah, Wyoming, New Mexico, North Dakota.

"And there we are," Stephens said, raising his voice above the din around him. Pointing at a shot of himself, he said, "Ain't he a handsome devil?" He raised his glass of scotch and water toward the screen. "Noreen, are you here? They have a soundbite from your remarks. Shut up," he yelled at those around him.

West's full-throated, deep voice filled the space. "Lulu Hefner was a great business person and a pioneer in the petroleum industry. Her determination to succeed was emblematic of the character that built our state and expanded an industry which transformed our nation into an economic powerhouse and a progressive force that lifted the standard of living for all Americans." West allowed herself a small smile. "God, who is that old woman? Gotta admit she sounds terrific."

Jones came up behind West and nudged her with his elbow. "This is the best campaign boost we could hope for."

From the other end of the tent, Milton Leonard said, "MSNBC is trashing us. As expected."

The crowd shifted in a group and listened to the commentator declare, "There was a push by the oil and gas industry today to promote fossil fuel use. Exploiting women in this industry to front their message; a few hundred people in places like Oklahoma City; Midland, Texas; Julesburg, Colorado; and Nome, Alaska turned out to show their support for continued drilling and fracking."

"Just a guess," Stephens said, "but I doubt any of our people mentioned fracking."

"I hope not," Iglesias said. "For the obvious reason, but more so because we can demand a retraction for that misrepresentation, and I'll go one further and demand equal time to set the record straight."

"So," West asked, "are we hoping they did or didn't mention fracking?"

"Yes," answered Stephens.

Sunday-June 3

An officer was leaning on the hood of his car, hands resting flat on the surface, head bowed. His hat had fallen between his hands. A second car was parked nearby, two patrolmen sat staring. One out the passenger side window. The other straight ahead.

As Ryan and Berger approached the crime scene tape, Ryan noticed no one was stationed at the door to the hotel. He veered toward the officer leaning on his car.

"Ned, is anyone inside securing the crime scene?"

The man turned slowly and for the first time in his life, Ryan understood what 'ghostly pale' meant. The man nodded slowly. "Stevens is inside and forensics is upstairs."

Ryan put his hand on the man's shoulder. "You okay?"

"No, I'm not." He looked at Ryan, his eyes brimming. "This is a bad one."

Ryan pointed at the car. "Why don't you sit down?" He waited until the officer was settled before rejoining Berger who raised the crime scene tape allowing them to cross into a parking lot fronting the hotel, a rundown building in a rundown part of Owen. A line of beat-up plastic garbage containers sat on either side of the entrance, which was strewn with bottles, most broken into shards that had to be carefully navigated. The stench, a mix of urine and rotting food, caused Ryan to cough and cover his nose.

The bones of the Clarion Hotel showed it had once been a formidable piece of architecture. Stacked stone walls with intervals of calcite crystal marble were visible under a thick layer of dirt. Elaborately designed cement gargoyles peered down from the corners of a hipped slate roof.

Ryan started to explain his conversation with the patrolman. Berger held up his hand. "I saw his face."

They walked into the lobby that, like the outside of the building, was a showcase of dilapidated elegance, adorned with chandeliers, marble columns with golden accents, frescoes, and doreé ornaments. It was bare but for two folding chairs in front of a couch that had lost its shape and bowed in the middle.

Light came from a caged reception area to the left of a stairwell. As Ryan and Berger walked toward the light, their shoes made a tearing sound as they pulled the soles away from the sticky wooden surface.

"Delightful, isn't it?" a voice came from a dark corner of the room. Ryan nodded at Officer Brad Stevens as he stepped toward them and into a rectangle of light laid across the floor in front of the reception cage.

A man sat at a desk inside the cage behind a layer of bulletproof glass. The man shot forward when he noticed Ryan and Berger approach the stairs. He tilted his head sideways and spoke through a small opening carved into the glass. "How much longer you guys gonna be here? Kinda cramping my business."

Neither Berger nor Ryan bothered to answer as they made their way up the staircase. The wood creaked so loudly, Berger, in the lead, made it a point to step carefully on the stair in front of him, testing it, before shifting his weight. Light from a series of naked bulbs lining the second-floor corridor guided their way as they approached the landing.

Habit prompted both men to slip on latex gloves as they stood in the doorway. A single pole lamp spread a ring of light across a rug so threadbare the wooden floor showed through.

A woman in a hooded paper jumpsuit and face mask approached and offered them paper booties and masks. "You'll want these," she said of the masks.

Before they could get the masks on, the stench of urine and what could have been a backed-up toilet hit them hard. Ryan retreated deeper into the hallway, where he put on the booties and mask before entering the room.

A small round table sat to the right of entrance. There were no chairs and the only other piece of furniture in the room was a bed which was surrounded by crime scene techs. The floor under a series of plastic steps arranged to prevent disturbing the scene was awash in blood.

As Berger and Ryan approached, the techs parted revealing two female bodies on the bed lying one atop the other. Their hands and feet were bound to the bedposts. Their throats cut. Each was missing her right eye. Nipples bitten off. The vaginal and anal areas of both had been savagely mutilated.

"That explains some of the smell," Berger said, studying the eviscerated intestines.

"Jesus," Ryan said and backed away.

Berger leaned in and inspected the bindings. Berger straightened and looked in the direction of the single window. "From the Venetian blinds, right?" One of the techs answered, "Looks that way."

Ryan, remaining behind Berger, asked, "Any way of determining when it happened?"

The woman who had met them at the door answered. "We'll know better when we get them into the lab, but a guesstimate would be within the last eight to ten hours." She pointed at the bed. "Still in rigor."

"Anything else you can tell me?" Berger asked.

"They both died from exsanguination caused by the cuts to their throats. They were dead when" – she gestured at the bodies – "he did that. Thank God."

"Anything else?"

"The right eyes," she said. "They were removed with surgical skill."

"Thanks," Berger said, turned away from the bed and followed Ryan out the door.

Both men hurried down the stairs, not at all concerned about the creaking underfoot, and hustled out the front of the hotel and away from the building. Ryan removed his mask and bent over, hands on his knees. He kicked off the booties. Berger took a deep breath before walking under the crime scene tape and stopping to take off his mask and booties.

***

Ryan handed Berger a bottle of water and settled behind his desk, letting his head drop against the back of his chair. Berger sat facing the desk. He leaned forward resting his arms on his thighs. Both men sipped from the bottles and stared sightlessly.

Smolders stepped across the threshold into the office. His presence seemed invasive and he stopped a few steps into the small room.

"Got the photos?" Ryan asked, waving him forward.

Smolders placed a pile on the desk and sat down next to Berger. "Lila Nethers and Cindy Athens. Pros working the area."

Ryan took another long pull from the bottle and slowly pushed himself upright. He jabbed the photos toward Berger, who put the cap on his bottle and placed it on the floor next to his chair. He picked up the photos and stood without looking at them. He walked to a window and stared out a moment, turned and began pacing as he reviewed each photo. Seven times back and forth across the office. He sat down and laid the photos on the desk, reached for his bottle of water, took a sip, and cradled the bottle in his lap.

"I think this is our guy," Berger said. "It's the eyes. That took some skill, or at least some patience. Like what I found in the first three." He took a final gulp of water and held the empty bottle in his hand. "It has some earmarks of what we saw with Luna. Chaos. Carelessness."

"The first three weren't this bad," Ryan croaked and drained his water bottle. "What he did," he said with a nod toward the photos, "to those women was way worse than any of the others."

"The basic MO is there. Binding them to the bedposts, slitting their throats, the eye, and nipples. Previously he used objects available to him to sodomize the women. He didn't have those in that room. The" – he gestured toward his stomach – "could mean he's reached a frenzy."

Smolders turned toward Berger. "That sounds bad." He waved his hand erasing his remarks. "It's all bad. I mean…"

"I know what you mean," Berger said. "And, as awful as this is going to sound, it's a good thing. When serial offenders reach this stage, they've lost total control and make mistakes. Their compulsions have gotten the best of them. They usually leave behind a trace of themselves. Fingerprints. DNA. Something. Until now, he hasn't left us much to work with. He was careful. Probably wore gloves, other protective material, and he cleaned up after himself. Not this time.

"It happened with Bundy when he lost it and bludgeoned a number of girls at a sorority house in Florida. He wasn't his usual careful self. He beat the girls with a log he found in the yard. He left a mask behind that was linked to him. He was seen in the sorority house. He was so out of control he bit the girls, and his teeth impressions were matched to the marks he left on the victims. He made more mistakes in that sorority house than he made in all his other murders combined. He couldn't help himself."

"How do you get two women in a room and kill them both?" Ryan asked staring down at the photos. "How do you control them enough to tie them up and do all that to them?" He pushed himself away from his desk. "How does that happen?"

"By doing it one at a time," Smolders answered.

"Yes," Berger agreed. "He probably brought the first one up. Did what he did and went out for the second one, which fits with him being in a frenzy. The first one didn't satisfy his compulsion. He goes for the second one and as soon as she gets in the room, she panics, and he slits her throat."

"I talked to the night manager," Smolders said. "Lila Nethers was the first one. She rented the room. The manager didn't see anyone with her. He knew Nethers and didn't think anything of it. She was a regular. He figured she was meeting a client. The guy must have come in off the fire escape at the back of the building that goes to a window opening into the hallway on the second floor. There are signs he used a knife or something to pry the window open. It looks like it had been painted shut."

"He had it together enough to do all that," Ryan said.

"He went around the bend after killing the first one," Berger said.

"He had to come in with the second one," Ryan said. "He couldn't chance doing the fire escape thing again. She might've gotten to the room before he did."

"That's gotta be how it happened," Smolders said. "The manager said he noticed someone with Athens, but she's another regular so he didn't give it any thought. Figured she had gotten a room earlier; before he came in. The guy was a real jerk. Complaining the whole time about us being there and chasing away business."

"He was like that when we were there," Ryan said.

"Asshole. I dragged him to the room and made him ID the victims. After that we had to physically restrain him to get him to stay and answer our questions. As soon as we were through, he bolted. I called the owner to tell him no one was watching the place. That SOB didn't have any reaction to what had happened. He was pissed about having to come in and work the desk himself."

The three men sat and stared into their laps.

"About that taskforce," Smolders said, breaking the silence.

Berger puffed out a sardonic laugh. "Yeah, about that. I haven't done a thing. I got some names from Linares and McDowell. I should call them, I guess. Let everyone know what's happened," he said, nodding at the pile of photos. "This one is going to be in big, bold type, and cause all kinds of hysterical reporting. 'Oklahoma Beast on another rampage,' or something like that."

"When I left the hotel, the TV trucks were lining up in the parking lot," Smolders said.

Berger asked Ryan, "Do you or any of your people know how to do one of those Zoom meetings? I can get everyone together first thing tomorrow morning, let them know the latest, and then have our people issue a press release right after. That way we can say the taskforce is on it."

Ryan drummed his fingers on the desk. "Am I hearing that all this noise about a taskforce is for show? That we're going to do what we've been doing the way we've been doing it anyway?"

"Yeah," Berger answered. "Pretty much. If I can figure out a way to work everyone else in, or if I need any help, we'll bring 'em in. Right now, we have to move on this and doing it by committee isn't the way to go."

Monday-June 4

Lila Miskey stood behind a podium facing a crowded press room. "Governor Stephens and State Senator Whalen Jones will have short statements and then answer a few questions."

Stephens stepped around Miskey, thanked her, and placed a notebook on the podium. "For the past thirty years Oklahomans were well represented by the late Senator Roy Evans. His tragic death leaves our state and the U.S. Senate poorer. As for filling his seat in the senate, we will follow the course set out by our state constitution. When I receive the list of suggested names from Speaker West, I will send my nominee to the State Senate for confirmation. I expect it will be a deliberative process.

"We must, however, move on, as I know my good friend Roy Evans would expect. Therefore, notwithstanding the chore that still lies ahead, today I am announcing my candidacy for the United States Senate." A rustle of bodies and low murmur caused him to look up from his text. He waited for the room to still before continuing.

"I know almost everyone in this room, and you know me. You have followed my career from Mayor of Bartlesville, through the State House and Senate, and into the governor's office. You know my record. I won't bore you with any of that.

"We have new and different challenges coming at us almost daily, it seems. My experience as governor, most recently, and in public office throughout my career has prepared me to meet those challenges.

"As you leave, please take a moment and pick up a packet of information from Lisa outlining the issues I will be advancing during my campaign. Thank you."

Stephens closed his notebook and stepped back. Jones stood behind the podium and removed note cards from his suitcoat pocket. He let his eyes run across the room before beginning. "When you're the governor they give you a slick notebook to read from with twenty-inch type. That's why I'm announcing my candidacy for governor. That and I get a limousine and driver." He feinted to his right, as if he had concluded his remarks, laughed, and returned his attention to an amused group of reporters.

"It's an honor to be here with Governor Stephens who has done an outstanding job for all of us. His will be a tough act to follow.

"You" – he raised his chin at the room – "and I have crossed paths, and, on occasion, swords, for many years. I think I can say without fear of contradiction that I've been square with you, and with the people I've represented in this great state.

"What's the old saying, 'A tiger can't change its stripes.' Well, I don't want to change my stripes. They've served the people I represent successfully, and I think with my stripes intact, I can serve *all* the people of this great state as they deserve, honestly and forthrightly.

"I don't have any issue papers to deliver to you today. Another reason to run for governor. I'd have a whole bunch of folks writing those for me. But I'd say if you study my record, you'll have a good idea what you can expect."

As Jones turned away from the podium, Miskey filled in behind him, her hand raised. "We'll get to your questions in a moment." She signaled to a couple of men who wheeled in a large flat screen. Miskey said something into her cell and the screen went from black to a light blue and then to an image of President Warren Silvero leaning against the Resolute Desk in the Oval Office.

Dressed casually in an open-collared leisure shirt and khakis, Silvero was clearly waiting to be prompted that he was on air. A handsome man, swarthy; gray hair set off his green eyes. He was a popular president whose Hispanic roots allowed Americans to feel self-righteous about their open-minded choice. On the cusp of announcing for a second term, he was so far ahead in the polls it was a foregone conclusion he would be in the Oval Office another four years.

Getting the signal, Silvero smiled. "Good afternoon, everyone. I appreciate being asked to join you, especially on this occasion." He pushed himself away from the heavy oak desk and ever the professional, never took his eyes off the camera as he walked behind the desk and sat.

"Two good men have agreed to continue in public service." He raised a cautionary finger. "I should say two good men have asked for the support of the people of Oklahoma so they can continue to serve.

"It's an honor for me to declare my support for Lincoln Stephens who I need here in Washington to advance my agenda for the American people. I'm proud to call Lincoln a friend and someone I trust. He and I see eye-to-eye on how we can work to remain on track promoting the caliber of government that makes certain all Americans have opportunities to succeed. I need Lincoln with me in Washington.

"Whalen is another trusted confidant of mine. I value his judgment and believe he is the best choice for the people of Oklahoma. He has an impeccable and honorable record of public service and will keep the Sooner State moving forward.

"I trust both of these men and urge everyone in Oklahoma to trust them as well. Thanks for spending a few minutes with me."

Miskey was standing at the podium when the screen faded to black. "The governor and Senator Jones will take a few questions." All reporters in the room were credentialed and known to Miskey making it unnecessary to identify themselves. Eight years had built a familiarity with an accepted routine. The scene was civil and devoid of the scramble defining most press conferences. "Bob," she said pointing to a man in the center of the seating area.

"This question is for Governor Stephens. By announcing for the senate on the same day you lay out the course for selecting a successor to the late Senator Evans, aren't you undermining any effectiveness that person will have in the senate? And doesn't your announcement make it obvious you won't select anyone who could be a threat to your ambitions? That you'd seek a placeholder only. All of this is further overshadowed by the fact you were endorsed by the President of the United States."

"I had no idea you were such a cynic, Bob." When the tittering subsided, Stephens said, "The timing for my announcement makes sense given the people will be voting in less than a year. There's that. I will be nominating the best person from the candidates I'm given by the Speaker, and I have every confidence the list will be a strong one. That person will no doubt do a good job and could decide to run themselves. I could go through a long list of 'what ifs' for you, but the bottom line is we will do what we are instructed to do legally, and we owe it to the people of our state to give them plenty of time to review candidates for all offices: local, state, and national."

Stephens stepped back and Miskey took the podium. "Joan," she said, selecting a young woman in the center of the room.

"Thank you. This is for the governor. One of the pillars of President Silvero's policy agenda is addressing issues related to climate change. Only days ago you were at the forefront of a national campaign promoting fossil fuels. How are you going to be able to support the president on climate change given your allegiance to the oil and gas industries?"

"There are two things wrong with your question," Stephens said sternly. "The effort you describe did not *promote* fossil fuels. And I don't have an *allegiance* to the oil and gas industries. The day in honor of Lulu Hefner was just that, and we laid out the facts of the industry in which she excelled. At this moment in time our economy is driven by oil and gas. That's a fact. That isn't to say, and we never did say, there is no room or need for alternative fuels. This isn't a zero-sum game. I look forward to working with President Silvero on his agenda for America. I have no conflict in doing so."

"A follow up, please?" the reporter asked, and without waiting for the go-ahead, read from a small spiral notebook. "You will have a conflict with the administration's approved EPA study of climate change. It concluded that Oklahoma will soon have three or four times as many days above one hundred degrees as we have today. The study also reported we can expect decreased rainfall and rapid evaporation reducing the average flow of rivers and streams. That's going to cause problems for farmers who irrigate their crops, and much of Oklahoma's farmland is irrigated. As a result, yields are also likely to decline by about fifty percent. Furthermore, the predicted early flowering of winter wheat brought by the changing weather will have negative repercussions on livestock farmers who depend on it for feed." The reporter looked up from his notebook. "And with the recently canceled Keystone Pipeline and halt on oil leases in the Arctic National Wildlife Refuge, both due to concerns about climate change, doesn't this put you squarely on the wrong side of history as someone who extols fossil fuels?"

"Not at all," Stephens answered confidently. "I repeat, I don't believe we're engaged in a zero-sum game. We can learn to balance the use of the energy we need, whether it comes from the earth or by wind, the sun, or water. I'll work with President Silvero to make that happen."

Miskey slid past Stephens and said, "Do we have a question for Senator Jones?" Hands shot up and she nodded at a woman in the front row. "Ruth."

"Flipping Bob's question on its back, Senator, how can you expect the people of this state to elect a man who conceived of and voted for a resolution that takes a stab at the heart and soul of our economic engine? A resolution supporting alternative sources of energy. And, related to that, in your remarks the other day – at the event Bob referred to – you made a point of encouraging the industry to clean up its act. How do you think that's going to play when your opponent challenges your dedication to the future of the industry that drives the economy of this state?"

"The resolution recognized the need to preserve the Wichita Mountains Wildlife Refuge as well as the Pushmataha, Cookson Hills, Spavinaw and Cherokee wildlife management areas. There was mention of support for setting aside small patches of land to promote alternative sources of energy. Hardly a stab at the heart and soul of our economic engine. Again, following the lead of Governor Stephens, we aren't dealing with a zero-sum game. My remarks on the prospects for alternative energy were in that vein."

Miskey identified another questioner. "Jim."

"This is for both the governor and Senator Jones. My sources tell me that you two visited with Senator Evans and strong-armed him into agreeing to resign. That opened his seat for you, Governor, and created the vacancy for Senator Jones. Is that true?"

Miskey walked back to the podium and stood beside Stephens when she realized where the question was going. She stepped in front of him in a choreographed dance both had rehearsed many times, and said, "Your sources are wrong." She selected a different reporter. "Go ahead, Wilson."

"Another one for both men. There have been two more victims of the Oklahoma Beast. When are we going to get some word on how the investigation is going?"

"I'll defer to Senator Jones," Stephens said. "He is close to the investigation as Chairman of the Senate Public Safety Committee which oversees the State Bureau of Investigation."

"Yes," Jones acknowledged, "there have been two more murders. We have assembled a taskforce with the best detective and forensic talent available. I have no doubt whatsoever this killer will be identified and taken off our streets."

"When? What progress has been made?" Wilson persisted.

"If I could tell you 'when,' I would also be able to tell you 'who,'" Jones replied not trying to hide the sarcasm. "A great deal of progress has been made as you heard the other day from the leading investigator, SBI Agent Joseph Berger. I suggest you review what he said."

Getting the look from Stephens, Miskey thanked the attendees and declared the session over.

***

A red-faced Cranston was standing at the door wringing his hands as Lee hurried toward him. "What the hell is going on?"

"He's locked himself in his room."

"What do you mean he's locked himself in? You have a key, don't you?"

"Of course, I do," Cranston whined, "but he must have wedged a chair under the doorknob." He jiggled the knob and pushed on the door to demonstrate. "We can't get in."

Lee looked at a hulk of a man standing to the right of the door, his back against the wall. Seeing Lee's attention go to the man, Cranston said, "That's Michael. He's the one who called me about the door. He takes Marco to breakfast every morning and spends the day with him, but this morning when he went to..."

"Okay," Lee said dismissively. To Michael, "We can handle this. Why don't you take a break?"

Lee stood in front of the door considering the situation before knocking. "Marco, it's Ray. Please open the door." Nothing. He tried again. "Please open the door, Marco." Silence.

Lee pushed against the door with both hands as if gauging its strength. He backed away and lifted his leg, kicked the door and bounced away. He tried again with the same result.

"Do you have something I can wedge into the frame of the door? If we can get that off, we should be able to push the door open."

Cranston looked at him blankly.

"Never mind," Lee said and started down the hall. "I'll be right back."

Cranston leaned against the door and put his ear close as he pleaded, "Marco, please open the door."

Lee returned to an open door, tire iron in his hand, and found Cranston standing over Marco, who sat on the bed focused intently on the television. "Oh, my God," Cranston was mumbling, his eyes wide but unfocused. "Oh, my God," he repeated.

Lee stumbled over an overturned chair causing Cranston to blurt out "Shit," followed by, "You scared me." He turned back to Marco. "He opened the door and sat down. He hasn't said a word."

Lee approached the bed. Marco's shirt and pants were stained. His face and arms were smeared red. Realizing what he was seeing, Lee's words came slowly. "That's blood."

Cranston backed away hurriedly, stumbled, and fell on his backside. He pushed his legs in front of him, scuttling away. "Blood," he whined.

"Close the door," Lee demanded.

Cranston struggled to his feet and peeked into the corridor, looking left then right before shutting the door. "No one there," he said to a disinterested Lee, who was running his hands through Marco's hair and checking his arms, torso, and legs.

"The blood," Lee said. "It's not his."

Cranston gulped a breath. "I think I'm going to be sick."

"Shut up and get me a garbage bag," Lee said, his attention riveted on Marco. Not hearing any movement behind him, he turned, stood, and walked to Cranston. He grabbed the man by the collar of his suitcoat and yanked him forward until their noses were touching. "Get me a garbage bag."

"Maintenance room," Cranston said absently.

Lee pushed him away. "Get some rug cleaner and rags, too."

Lee closed the door, returned to the bed, and asked Marco to stand. Marco did not respond. Lee lifted him into a standing position, unbuttoned his shirt, pulled it off, and sat him back down on the bed. He unzipped Marco's pants, untied his shoes, and pulled the pants off by the cuffs. Next the underwear and socks.

Cranston returned to the room with a box of industrial-sized garbage bags, a bucket with a bottle of rug cleaner and rags. He stood holding the bucket and box of garbage bags. "What happened?"

Lee did not answer. He raised his chin toward the open door. "Keep that closed and locked."

Cranston elbowed the door closed and stood stiffly.

"Anyone around here get hurt?"

Cranston widened his eyes, his face paled. "Oh, my God."

"If anyone had, I guess you'd have heard about it already."

Lee stood in front of Marco who was naked. The pile of clothes on the floor. "Put everything in a garbage bag and clean up anything that looks like blood or has anything else on it."

"Anything else?"

Lee spun around inspecting the room. "Yeah, anything else. Like..." He spied an open window. The sill was badly scuffed. "Clean that."

Cranston followed Lee's eyes. "Okay."

"He went out the window," Lee said non-plussed. He walked to the window and looked down at a patch of bushes. They were crushed. "He went out the fucking window," he repeated, pointing. "You said you were securing this place."

"We are, but it takes time. I told you we should transfer him to the East Wing where this never would have happened. The windows are barred."

"He jumped out the damn window," Lee said, still in disbelief, "and must've back in the same way."

Cranston held a rag and bottle of all-purpose cleaner. "Those two women in that hotel." He looked at Marco and repeated, "Those two women in that hotel."

Ignoring Cranston, Lee pointed at the pile of clothes. "Put those in a garbage bag and start cleaning." He walked Marco toward the bathroom saying softly, "Let's get you cleaned up."

As the water was running in the shower, Lee came back into the room and stood over Cranston who was wiping the windowsill. "I'm going to get him dressed and we'll take him to the East Wing. No one over there gets told who he is or that he was ever in this wing." He waited for Cranston to nod his understanding before asking. "Do you have a furnace?"

Another nod.

"Throw the clothes in the furnace along with the cleaning rags." Lee poked Cranston on the shoulder. "*You* do it. Don't give it to anyone else to do. Okay?"

"Okay."

"Only you and the men who have been watching Marco are going to have anything to do with him from now on. Double their salaries. You all change the sheets. Bring him food. Whatever he needs. He doesn't leave the room." Lee started to walk back to the bathroom, stopped and turned to Cranston. "And keep Marco happy and quiet."

"Meaning?"

Lee gave him a look. "Meaning I don't want him doing anything but sleeping or eating."

Marco came out of the bathroom soaking wet. He moved with a purpose, shook off Lee, who tried to stop him, and stepped in front of the television. The lethargy was gone. His demeanor changed completely. His eyes brightened. "There he is," he said bitterly. The midday news was reporting on Silvero's endorsement of Stephens and Jones. The anchor was talking over snippets of film showing Stephens and Jones responding to questions from the press. "The fucker's at it again," Marco snarled, his eyes dark and mouth curling over his teeth.

Wednesday-June 6

"They're calling us the Gold Dust Twins," Jones said with a laugh then looked at Iglesias who sat in front of his desk next to Noreen West. "I'm assuming that's a compliment given the way it's being used."

"It is," Iglesias said reassuringly.

West said, "I was a professor of political science before I decided to get into the game instead of just talking about it, and I can tell you the last two politicians I know of who were called the 'Gold Dust Twins' were Hugo Black and Bibb Graves. Senators from the great state of Alabama and fellow Klansmen. So, you might want to steer away from that label before someone comes across that information and uses it against you."

"That clip of Silvero endorsing us is on a news loop," Jones said and smiled at Iglesias. "That puts a good light on the Gold Dust thing. Brilliant, my man. Absolutely brilliant."

"Whaddya think people would say if they knew I'm using his brilliance to put me in your seat, Whalen?" West asked. "Using the same hired gun to sell the opposition. The cynics would have a field day."

Iglesias flashed a sour look at West. "You'd prefer an ideologue?"

"Hell no," West interjected. "Between teaching and participating, I've been doing this for almost half a century. If I didn't know by now how this business works, and went around virtue-signaling, that would be offensive." She smiled at Iglesias. "You're the only honest person in this room. An honest broker."

Eileen poked her head into the office. "It's Mr. Lee."

Jones frowned.

"Shall I tell him to call back?"

"No, tell him I'm finishing up a meeting and to hold a minute."

"Okay," West said, "we're agreed. Whalen avoids saying anything about his open seat. No mention of successors; no endorsement."

Iglesias nodded. "We're going to say…"

Jones picked up the thought. "'I'm grateful for the years the fine people of the 24th Senate District allowed me to represent them. It's been an honor and a humbling experience to have their trust. These fine folks will be deciding who carries on and I'm not going to get in their way.' And so on and so forth…"

"That's the formal statement," West said, "but you will get the word out to your folks, the party people, that they should keep their powder dry. Stay on the sidelines. Right?"

"I will. I'll tell them the absolute truth. That wasting time and money running against you is a fool's errand. You're just too strong, Noreen."

She smiled. "You certainly know how to flatter a girl, Whalen."

As West and Iglesias filed out, Jones picked up his private line. "What?"

Lee explained.

Jones closed his eyes and cradled his head in his hand. "Cranston mentioned the women? The prostitutes? He went right there?"

"Marco was covered in blood. Cranston put the pieces together on Luna and the one in Wichita Falls. He has Marco pegged as a dangerous, so he wasn't making a huge leap on those two."

Jones blew out a sigh. "Jumped out a window? Okay, get him into the other wing. But keep him away from everyone. No wandering around the halls where someone might recognize him. No nurses, doctors, orderlies. Eyes on him twenty-four/seven. Got it?"

"I've had that discussion with Cranston. I say serious drug therapy. As in La-La Land. There's something I think you ought to know."

"No," Jones said moaning. "I don't think I need to know anything else."

"You're the triggering factor."

"The what?"

"Cranston says you're what sets him off. Why Marco is the way he is."

"I'm responsible for why he kills people?" Jones said, his voice going from elevated to a whisper. "That's fucking nuts."

"It's not that direct. More subtle."

"I'm not listening to any more of this shit."

"You need to listen, especially now that you're going to be in the news every single day for the next year or so. And then you'll be in the headlines running this state." Before Jones could object, Lee said, "The 'triggering factor' is what sets serial killers off. They live in their fantasies. They fantasize about killing. About how they're going to do it. What they're going to do and all the rest of it, but they don't do anything until something triggers them. You're Marco's trigger."

No response. The silence prompted Lee to ask, "You still there?"

"Did Cranston explain any of this?"

"Some...but you should talk to him."

"I'm talking to *you*," Jones said tightly. "Tell me what he said."

"At some point when you two were growing up, Marco made his life a contest with yours. Look," Lee said, frustration in his voice, "I'm not explaining this the way you need to hear it. To get all the details. The psychology. I'm probably butchering this."

"Go on," Jones demanded.

An extended pause. "Okay," Jones said resignedly. "When you 'shine'... That was the word Cranston used. When you 'shine' it sets him off. Look what happened when you took him with you on the campaign tour. You were getting all the attention. People falling all over you. That triggered him. The two latest ones came when you were getting coverage with the Hefner thing. Then you were called all kinds of great things by the President of the United States. Marco flipped out. If you line it up, it fits, and I'm guessing if you look back at his history, and those times he acted out, you'll find something connecting with something you did."

Jones lifted the receiver away from his ear and rubbed it along his leg, digging into his thigh. He felt his heart pounding and took a deep breath before returning to the call. "Marco's nuts and that's it. I'm sure as hell not going to blow my life up for him. You and Cranston make damn sure he's in a room he can't get out of. If that means keeping him in what you called La-La Land, do it."

Jones raised his arm to slam the receiver into the phone cradle, pulled it back to his ear and said, "See if you can find out if this latest shit has given Berger and his friends anything to work with. You were able to clean the other places because we found them before the cops did. Maybe if we know what they know, we can stay a step ahead of their game."

***

"Gentlemen," Layton said as he was secured to the table. "What a pleasant surprise." He smiled. "I'm flattered. You've come to see me even if I don't have anything for you."

"We have something for you," Berger said, sliding a file folder toward Layton.

Connor glanced at Berger and Ryan as Layton smiled, his eyes wide. He made a noise like humming or purring. He slowly opened the file. "Oh, these are not at all like the others." He spiraled into a world of his own thoughts, shuffling through the images, a smile, more a leer, animating his face; his eyes darting, taking in every detail; brushing his fingers across the surface of the photos.

Berger did not move a muscle. Ryan and Connor took their lead from him and sat stiffly. The only sound was Layton's purring and quickened breathing.

At one point the guard opened the door to the interrogation cell wide enough to peek into the room. Berger gave him a quick nod, which was returned by the guard who closed the heavy metal door.

This sound caused Layton to start. He drew his shoulders back but did not raise his head. He remained fixated on the photos. "Your boy has lost it," he said in a voice just above a whisper, as if he did not want to disturb his own reverie. "This is some crazy shit."

Ryan closed his eyes fighting his urge to reach across the table and hammer Layton's head down onto the steel tabletop over and over and over again. Berger felt Ryan stiffen and raised a cautioning finger.

Layton carefully arranged the photos in a pile and began leafing through them again. He placed each image over on its face after considering it carefully. He went through them all, squared the pile carefully, concentrating on aligning each photograph with the one under it, and went through them again. He lowered his hands into his lap, shivered, and grunted.

Connor pushed way from the table and stood in a far corner, one shoulder against the wall, his arms folded across his chest. The familiarity of Layton's reaction was pulling back into the small cell with the man. He was feeling suffocated and held himself tightly. Held himself from running out of the room.

"No, this is nothing like the others," Layton said, blinking rapidly, back from his reverie.

"But the same man?" Berger asked.

"Oh, yeah," Layton said, pointing at one of the images. "The eye. Removed cleanly. Neatly. The way it should be."

Berger nodded.

Layton was again leafing through the photos. "This place," he tapped one of the images. "Where is this? Some fleabag hotel?"

"It is."

"And those women. They're nothing like any of the others, right?"

Another nod from Berger.

"Working girls. Two of 'em at once." Layton leaned away from the table. "You better get to this guy quick. He's outta control and a lot of people are going to get hurt. He's not doing this for anything more than the kill."

"Why else would he be doing it?" Connor asked, anger in his voice.

Layton stared at Connor, squinting. His mouth pursed. His shoulder hunched. He let a long moment pass before answering: "We don't kill to kill. At least not me or those others I've read about, and I've read about a lot of us." He shifted his attention to Berger. "I'm not trying to understand what I did," he said as if answering a question. "I know why I did it. All the stuff we've been talking about." He smiled openly. "And the rush from knowing so many people were scared, and all of them looking for me. I liked it. A helluva rush."

Layton's attention back on Connor, he said, "This guy is not where he was before with the care in how he did what he did. The tying up. The other stuff. But always attentive to details. Neat. It's what he had to do to make himself feel good."

"To satisfy a need," Berger offered.

Layton bobbed his head. "And that isn't this," he said, looking down at the file folder into which he had placed the photos. "He's not thinking. He's not even trying to make it work for him. Something's snapped. Like I said, he's killing to kill and will keep doing it until you stop him."

Thursday-June 7

Ryan and Berger stood behind Smolders as he one-fingered his way through a raft of screen shots and settled on a page appearing to be a ledger sheet.

"Okay," Smolders said. "Here we are. This is the list of state cars." He pointed to the left side of the screen. "And those are the names of people they've been assigned to, and" – he moved his finger to the next column – "the plate numbers" – he slid his finger to another column – "that's the period of time the car is assigned. Never more than six months."

"Yeah," Berger said. "We have to apply for a continuance every six months. A pain in the ass, but I suppose it allows them to keep track of the cars and maintain them."

Smolders scrolled all the way to the bottom of the screen. "Look what I found." He placed his cursor over the name of Raymond Lee which was listed under the heading "Special Orders."

Berger stiffened. "Damn." He bent closer to the screen and read, "Permission for personal use." He squinted. "There's no restriction on lease time for these people."

"No," Smolders said. "Lee and the others on that list pretty much have unrestricted use of their cars."

Smolders pushed himself out of the chair. "I've got a lot more." He walked to the small round table in Ryan's office. Ryan and Berger followed and the men sat.

"I've got copies for both of you," Smolders said, his attention on three report binders. "You can read through this later but let me summarize." He opened his copy. "As unlikely as this is, Linares's people found something useful in the room at the hotel. In Wichita Falls."

Berger and Ryan sat bolt upright. Berger said, "In the room? That's a needle in a haystack deal. Gotta be a petri dish of DNA."

Smolders smiled. "Sometimes luck trumps everything else. They found hairs in the entryway. When the samples were submitted to find a match, Lee's profile popped up. His DNA is on file with the highway patrol. Came from a drug test."

Smolders leafed deeper into the binder. "After that little discovery, I asked fleet management to tell Lee it was time to give him a new car." He smiled impishly. "Offered him a newer model. I played a hunch. Jackpot! We found spots of blood on the driver's side floor of the car Lee had been using. On the gas and brake pedals. They were matched to the women found at the hotel."

Smolders flipped a page. "That last letter you all got from Layton?" He looked at Ryan and Berger, teasing with his pause. "Found some partials that match Lee. Only partials, but the likelihood they belong to anyone else is small. Good idea getting the warden to glove up his people," he directed at Berger. "It made a difference. We couldn't get anything from the other letters."

Smolders leafed to the back of the binder. "Linares found some CCTV footage taken from a couple of buildings near the hotel in Wichita Falls." He tapped his finger on still photos of a white sedan. "Caught these on Moran Avenue that runs in front of the hotel." He turned the page to an enlarged image of a license plate. "Can't make out the tag very well, but we definitely have a T and a Z."

"And," Berger said softly, as if he did not want to break the mood, "we know from the guest lists Lee was at the homes where the women were killed in Wesper, Laramie, and Mannix."

The men sat still. Ryan started to open the cover of the binder in front of him, then fell against the back of his chair. "Shit."

"Yeah," Smolders said. "Shit."

"We need to talk to Raymond Lee," Berger said. "Now."

"How do you want to go about this?" Smolders asked. Getting raised eyebrows from Berger, which he translated as "What?" he asked, "By the book? No explanation? Just bring him in? Or do we ask him to come in on his own?"

"On his own," Ryan answered. "Say we know he did some work on sex trafficking and his experience could help us with a case we're working on. No pressure. That'll keep him at ease."

"And when he realizes it's bullshit," Smolders countered, "which will be after we've asked the first question? What's the plan? How do we keep him from lawyering up, or walking out? You think the DNA matches are solid enough to hold him?"

"If he's our guy," Berger responded, "and now he's definitely number one on the list."

"We don't have a list," Ryan reminded.

"He's a person of interest," Berger amended. "And if he is our guy, he's got the ego of a psychopath. Huge, and he'll want to show us he can beat us. He'll relish that opportunity. He won't ask for a lawyer. I want to get him in here without word getting out we're looking at a person of interest. That will cue the rabid mob and we'll have the media camped out around this building. Plus," Berger hesitated a beat, "I can't help feeling there's something wrong with this."

Smolders put his hand on the binder. "This is some pretty solid evidence we've found the right guy."

"It is," Berger agreed, "but there are holes."

"Like?" Ryan asked.

"Lee is a former law enforcement officer."

"So was the Golden State Killer," Smolders said.

"But that guy had all kind of problems that were a tell for his behavior. In hindsight anyway. Lee has no blemishes on his record. Just the opposite. He's a decorated cop. He's close to one of the most powerful men in state politics who trusts him implicitly." Berger shook his head. "It doesn't feel right. Like I've said, these guys don't go from zero to sixty just like that," he said with a snap of his fingers. "It's an accumulation of things. Years of petty crimes. Arrests for sexual assaults or even voyeurism. Lee is squeaky clean. This is not computing for me."

"Maybe you're overthinking it," Ryan said. "There's good reason to consider him a person of interest and we need to pursue it."

"There is," Berger agreed. "I need to add more clarity for myself and a few hours with Lee will do that."

***

"'Dry Hole,'" Stephens said to Jones and Iglesias, holding up the editorial page of the *New York Times*. He laid it on his desk and read: "'A few thousand people gathered in states across the Southwest (and Alaska) to pledge their fealty to the nation's continuing dependence on fossil fuels. The operative word here is 'fossil.'

"'This was akin to paying respects to a retiring celebrity, or politician, whose time on stage has come to an end. As is usual at these kinds of affairs, the rhetoric was over the top. Variably called the "engine of progress" and "the driving force behind the nation's economy" the hyperbole describing these dirty and waning energy sources brought home the inevitable. The actor is leaving the stage.'"

"And more of the same," said Stephens after scanning the balance of the editorial.

"Look on the facing page," Iglesias suggested.

A smile animated the corners of Stephens' mouth.

"The editorial page editor, who I know from previous jousting matches," Iglesias said, "was kind enough to call me with a heads-up that the editorial was coming. I 'strongly suggested' that in the interest of fairness we should be allowed a rebuttal. As you see, we got one. That op-ed is co-authored by a geologist and a professor of economics. Impeccable credentials. It's reasoned, polite, and carefully sourced. A wonderful contrast to the editorial, which is a screed, plain and simple."

"Where do we go from here?" Jones asked.

"Truthfully," Iglesias said, "we're at the high point of our campaign. The iron is hot and it'll only stay that way for a while. We do have all kinds of things going on to keep things percolating at a steady, if not lower, boil."

Stephens asked, "Such as?"

"Such as every member of Congress working with us will be making remarks on the floor hitting our talking points." Iglesias ticked them off: "Economic boon of the industry. Jobs created. Down-the-line benefits like jobs in related industries. Trucking. Railroads. We can go to ports around the country where oil is loaded onto tankers and talk about jobs. Jobs to build the tankers. Jobs on the tankers. Jobs at the ports. Taxes paid by everyone. I have the numbers and will put them on a conveyor belt and dump them right into the mouths of our people." Iglesias smiled. "Want me to go on?"

A phone buzzed. "I think that's yours," Stephens said to Jones.

Jones mouthed "sorry" to Stephens and Iglesias as he answered his phone.

"You alone?" Lee asked.

"No," Jones said.

"Get alone real quick and call me back."

Jones gestured to the office door leading to the outer office as he stood. "This will only take a minute."

***

Jones walked hurriedly through the reception area and into a long marble hallway, the clicking sound of his steps echoing around the high-ceilinged corridor. He made for a door leading to a garden on the side of the Capitol, tapping on the face of his cell as he pushed into the open air. "What is it?"

"Two things. Berger and Ryan want to talk to me."

"About?" Jones asked, walking toward a wrought-iron gazebo surrounded by flowering poinciana bushes.

"Don't know. Ryan's deputy called. Said they want to talk to me about a case like one I had when I was with the highway patrol. They want to pick my brain."

"They want you to help them work one of their cases?" Jones asked, confusion evident in his voice.

"It's bullshit. A ploy. Used it all the time myself. They don't want to tip me off. Want to catch me by surprise. See if they can trip me up."

"But how could they possibly know anything?"

"I'm not saying they do, but I don't want to talk to them about anything, no matter what it is. So, call Slade and tell him to snuff this out."

"How the hell do I do that?" Jones screeched, alarming himself. He took a dep breath and studied his surroundings. "How can I do that?" he asked evenly. "I can't call the head of SBI and tell him I don't want his people talking to you. That's a random request. He'll ask why."

"I don't care how you do it, just *do* it. Nothing good can come from any sit down with them."

Jones walked around the gazebo. "I can't strong-arm Slade."

"This is simple. You own him. You control the purse strings. And isn't he appointed by the governor? Which means he can be removed by the governor, right? You're going to *be* governor. Remind him of that."

"A commission appoints the SBI director, but" – Jones stopped at the stairs of the gazebo and stared into the middle distance – "they wouldn't act without consulting the governor. I suppose there is that."

"Whatever, just do it. I'm not going to be a happy camper if I have to sit down with them tomorrow."

"For God's sake," came whining in the background of Lee's call. "Tell him."

"What the hell is that?"

"That's the other thing I want to talk to you about. Marco hung himself."

Jones felt give in his knees. He reached out and grabbed the handrail of the stairs leading to the seating area of the gazebo. "He what?"

"Allow me," the other voice squeaked from Lee's end. "This is Dr. Cranston, Senator. I'm so terribly sorry to be the bearer of this news, but when Michael arrived this morning he, uh…" Cranston cleared his throat. "He found your brother hanging from a sheet he tied around his neck and wrapped through the grating covering the windows."

Jones sat down on the stairs. The pause in the conversation prompted Cranston to repeat, "I'm so sorry."

"I'm not understanding this. Marco is…*was* in the secure part of your facility, where I thought this kind of thing is impossible."

"When we suspect a patient is suicidal, especially depressed or anxious, we have people checking in on them regularly. In this case…"

"In *this* case? You told me Marco was practically comatose the other day. Doesn't that qualify as depressed or anxious?"

"If he had been one of our…how shall I put this?"

"Jesus Christ," Jones expelled.

"If he had been one of our standard patients, we would have had staff checking on him regularly. He would have been on a 'watch list,' but if you'll recall, you asked not to have our staff interact with him. I made it a point to look in on Marco when I got in every morning, when I took my lunch break, and before I left every evening."

"I'm back," Lee said. "That was going nowhere."

"Now what?" Jones asked somberly.

"To get licensed, these places have to admit a certain number of indigent patients. We'll list Marco as one of them, give him a fake name, and..."

Lee directed himself to Cranston. "Do you have some arrangement with a funeral home?" A faint "yes" came back. "One that won't ask questions?" Another faint "yes."

"Unless you have objections," Lee said to Jones, "we'll get the body cremated and a false death certificate issued. You can destroy that if you want to and there won't be any trace of him."

"Fuck," Jones said. "Fuck, fuck, fuck. Poof, he's gone. All that shit he caused all those years, and... uh..." he struggled, "no consequences."

"You're going to have to handle questions from the family on your end, so be ready for that."

"Family," Jones said with a bitter laugh. "I keep telling you, no one will ask. That's not going to be a problem. Out of sight, out of mind." He stood quickly and began walking back toward the Capitol. "Poof, gone."

"What?"

"Nothing. How long will all this take?"

Lee's voice went in Cranston's direction. "How long will it take to get the body picked up, cremated, and the death certificate issued?"

"I'll see to it," came through to Jones. "Quickly."

Jones said to Lee, "Put Cranston back on."

A meek, "Yes?"

"I want this finished and done with by tomorrow morning."

"But..." came the pleading.

"No, no buts. You handle this yourself. No one else knows a thing. I want to hear from you in the morning that this has been taken care of."

"Do you want an urn?"

"Have you not been listening? Put Ray back on."

"I heard everything. Now, you talk to Slade."

***

"Sorry," Jones apologized to Stephens. "Did Gary have to go?" he said looking at the empty chair next to him.

Stephens nodded. "What do you think of his proposal?"

"The guy keeps hitting them out of the park." Jones scooted himself stiffly upright. "I have something I want to talk to you about."

"If that look on your face is any indication, I don't know that I want to hear it."

"It is a problem, but I think we can turn it to our advantage if we deal with it correctly."

***

"Len, this is Whalen."

"And Lincoln," Stephens said in the direction of the conference speakerphone.

"Got a minute?"

"Of course."

"I should've talked to you about this before," Jones started, "and something's come up reminding me how badly I've dropped the ball."

Slade made a noise signaling his concern.

"Raymond Lee, the investigator for my committee, has said some things now and again that should have raised red flags. It's been a gradual development which probably explains why the pieces didn't fall into place until...well, until right now." Jones shifted in his chair and stared into his lap. "But I've gotten ahead of myself. Let me back up. I got a call a while ago from Ray and he said Agent Berger wants to talk to him."

"About?"

"There was some confusion on that score."

"Confusion?"

"The call came from Sheriff Ryan's deputy. He said Berger and Ryan want to talk to him about a case Ray had years ago. They want to pick his brain to see if he can help them with a case they're working."

"Okay."

"Has Agent Berger talked to you about this?"

"About wanting to talk to Lee? No."

"I'm certain Berger wants to talk to him about the murders. He's heading up the taskforce and that's what you have him focused on. It makes sense, right?"

"I suppose," Slade agreed, his tone wary. "What do you need from me?"

Stephens said, "We'll get to that in a minute, Len. Let Whalen finish a few thoughts and it'll fall into place."

"Those first three girls who were killed? They all lived in my district. They were the daughters of donors to my campaign. Ray was with me on a fundraising tour when they were killed."

"Okay," Slade said, his manner light-years from "okay."

"Ray leaned on me to ask you to include him on that first taskforce. And again, after you announced the second one."

"We're combining them," Slade answered thoughtfully as if he was thinking out loud.

"I shrugged it off initially, but he's gotten aggressive about it lately. I'm not an expert on these things. You'd know better than I do, but don't these people like to stay close to their crimes? Haven't I read things about them wanting to insinuate themselves into the investigation so they can keep tabs on what's going on?"

"*These people*?" Slade asked, his voice raising an octave. "You think he's the guy?"

"Patience," Stephens cautioned. "We're getting there."

"When I think back to the circumstances; to the three young women being killed shortly after our fundraisers in the homes of their parents... well, yes, I think it's suspicious, at the very least. As I said, all this came together when Lee told me Berger wants to talk to him. Jesus, Len, I should have said something before. It just snuck up on me."

Stephens said, "This could be huge, Len. Whalen could be giving you your man."

"It's compelling," Slade admitted, "and worth exploring, but just being in the same place where they were killed is not much to go on."

"There's more," Jones said, his voice lowered, adding a compelling note to his words. "A lot more. He went off the clock about the time that woman was killed in Wichita Falls."

"Off the clock?"

"It's code. When the committee wants to take a look under the hood at one of the agencies we oversee, and we want to do it quietly, no hearings, stealthily, Ray takes care it. We call it an 'off the clock' investigation."

"So, you're saying…"

"I'm saying I would've had to approve something like that. I'm the only one who can authorize it. Nothing like that was going on at the time. I'd know. And there's something else. And I don't know exactly how to describe this." Jones paused. "Again, this is one of those things that came in hindsight." Another pause. "He's always been eccentric. I mean, he's a hard man. Someone who doesn't see a lot of gray in things. Black and white, but over time he's gotten, well… irrational, might be the best way to describe it. Every once in a while he'll rant."

"Rant?"

"He's bought into the whole deep state nonsense. People in government having their own agendas. Undermining official policy. Ranting about it. That's the best way I can describe it, but, again, it's all come in bits and pieces over a period of years. Bottom line, there's never been anything that pulled all of this together for me until he told me he got that call. It was like a light went on. Everything fell into place, and it made sense, to me anyway, and I thought you should pass along what I know to Agent Berger. It might help when he talks to Ray."

"We have to get *waaaay* ahead of this," Stephens said intensely. "Lee is a state employee for Christ's sake."

"And he works for my committee," Jones reminded.

Stephens continued, "There are so many ways this can go bad, I can't even begin to imagine the shit storm that could come down on us, unless we manage it."

"We're getting ahead of ourselves," Slade responded.

"That's the damn point," Stephens spit back.

The light dawned for Slade. "How do you want it managed?"

Jones said, "Call Agent Berger. Tell him what I told you about Ray being with me on those trips."

"And about Wichita Falls and the strange behavior," Stephens added. "That way we have one of our own contributing to bringing this guy down. We saw a problem and we took care of it."

"*If* he's the guy," Slade said. "And I'm guessing Berger knows most of what you've told me if he wants to talk to him. Plus, we're assuming he wants to talk to Lee about the serial murders. You said that wasn't clear."

"Focus on the big picture," Stephens said forcefully. "If Berger knows these things and that's why he wants to talk to Lee, great. But let's not leave it to chance. You're going to tell Berger you have this information from Whalen, and he wants you to look into it. That's the direction we need this to take. We have to be seen as out in front of it and not totally ignorant about what has been going on under our noses."

Jones added, "Make sure he knows I asked you to pass this along to him. Tell him I discussed it with Lincoln and we both agree, as do you, that we need to get answers to some disturbing questions. Let them know he's not all there at times. The ranting business. God knows what he'll tell them. That's important, too."

"We're going to need some solid evidence to keep him in custody," Slade said.

"Keep your eyes on that big picture," Stephens said. "I'm confident you can find a way to do whatever it is you need to do to put all of us in the right light on this."

"*If* one of our own is responsible," Slade answered. "But I get your point," he added quickly.

"One other thing," Stephens said. "No matter how we deal with this, it's going to cause a stir. We're cushioning the blow by taking control of the narrative, but we can cushion it further to make sure we have a soft landing. To do that, I've got something else for you to look in to."

"Okay," Slade said, the big picture now in clear focus.

"I have good reason to believe our fleet management operation is corrupt. I'd strongly suggest some forensic accounting."

Friday-June 8

"I got a call from Slade this morning," Berger said to Ryan as they walked into the interrogation room.

They placed a series of file folders on a single table in the middle of the room. Three chairs were arranged at the table. Two on one side facing a single one on the other.

"About?"

"This," Berger answered as he set up a whiteboard. "And I hadn't said anything to him."

Ryan stopped, his arms extended, poised to tape a photo of one of the victims on the wall Lee would be facing. "How'd he know?"

"Found out from, of all people, Senator Jones and the governor."

"How did they...?"

"Lee called Jones to tell him we wanted to talk to him, and Jones called Slade."

Ryan held up in hands in question. "And the governor?"

"Apparently, Jones was with the governor when Lee called."

"And?"

"According to Slade, Jones launched into a whole thing about Lee sliding off the deep end. How the guy has been losing it lately. And then Jones tells him about the fund-raising swing and Lee being with him, making the point that the women were killed in the cities along the way."

Ryan huffed and shook his head slowly. "So, Lee knows why we want to talk to him and he tells Jones. Why would he do that?"

"That doesn't surprise me. Jones is his boss and" – Berger glanced around the room – "this isn't a normal part of his workday. What does surprise me is what else Jones had to say."

"Like?"

"Like Jones said Lee wasn't at work the day the woman was killed in Wichita Falls."

Ryan stood in front of the whiteboard and watched Berger date the crime scene photos. "Jones decided now was a good time to tell Slade all this?"

"He said it came together for him when Lee said he was going to be talking to us." Berger looked at his handiwork on the whiteboard then turned to Ryan. "Weird, right?"

"Weird, right, but maybe it will sort out when we talk to Lee."

"That's the end game," Berger said and put a thick file on the desk, carefully arranging copies of the three trip itineraries and guest lists so Lee would see them.

"Unless you have a problem with it, I'm going to call Conner and ask him to come in. He might recognize Lee. Might've seen him with Luna. We can set him up in the viewing room."

"Good idea," Berger said, inspecting the set they had created for the interview pronouncing it, "Perfect."

***

"A 'burner'?" the man said, turning toward a wall of packaged prepaid cell phones.

Jones nodded.

"Any preference?"

"No."

Jones pulled down the brim of his hat and raised his eyes to scan the corners of the store for CCTV. Nothing. A good reason to hike into this Godforsaken neighborhood, he thought.

The man, obese and barely able to separate himself from the stool he appeared welded to, grunted as he reached for the item. He had to catch his breath before turning back toward the counter. "Here you go."

Jones hurried out of the convenience store and started down the side of the building toward his car, again scanning for CCTV. Two women were huddled near a dumpster. One asked, "Want a blow job? Five bucks. You can fuck both of us for twenty."

Back in his car, he wrestled with the plastic packaging, finally ripping it open with his teeth. Consulting a small piece of paper, he stabbed at the face of the phone as he drove away from the parking lot where his car stood out among the rusted, paint chipped, dented, and otherwise mortally wounded cars.

"Hello," came guardedly.

"Is it done?"

"Mr. ...?"

"No, don't do that. Just tell me if it's taken care of like we discussed."

"Yes, it's done. I used another poor soul's Social Security number and..."

"I don't need to know that. Are you alone?"

"Yes."

"Listen to me carefully. Ray is being questioned by the police this morning and..."

"Oh, my Lord!"

"Shut up and listen. There's nothing to worry about. The one we had to worry about is gone. Disappeared. Was never there. Even if Ray says anything there's nothing to corroborate it. Plus, you can't divulge any information anyway, right?"

A low wailing came back at him.

"For God's sake, there's nothing to be concerned about."

"Then, why are you calling?"

"Simply a heads-up. Even if it gets past a routine discussion between the police and Ray, believe me when I say you have nothing to worry about. I didn't want you to be surprised by anything you might hear. But if you do get a follow-up visit to check on anything, there's nothing there. Remember that. There's nothing there for anyone to find. Also, I want to thank you for everything you've done. I won't forget it."

***

Lee sat in his car and poked at his cell.

"Senator Whalen Jones's office," came the high-pitched voice of the perpetually cheerful Eileen.

"Good morning, Eileen. You must be getting annoyed having to screen my calls. This must be the fifth or sixth one."

"Not at all, Mr. Lee. I told the senator you called but he had to run to the floor for a vote and is likely to be there all morning."

"Please tell him I'm going into a meeting with Agent Berger and Sheriff Ryan and I'm not happy about it. Got that?"

"I do, sir."

Lee looked around the parking lot. *Slade must have ignored the call from Jones. If that was it, I'm going to make it my business to get his ass fried.*

Lee stepped into the bright, warm, but as yet not scorching sun. As he approached the multi-storied cement block building, he saw Ryan step out of double doors. "Thank you for taking the time to meet with us," he said, extending a hand, which was received by Lee who offered a "My pleasure."

Ryan pointed Lee toward the rear of an open reception area, past the receiving desk. "We thought it made sense to do this in an interrogation room instead of my office. More comfortable."

"Really," Lee said, stopping at the end of a T-branch. "A sterile room with no windows, blinking fluorescent lights, and rickety steel chairs more comfortable than your office? You need a better office." He eyed the corridor to his right. A kitchen and squad room were visible. To his left was a line was doors. He turned left. "Which one?"

"Last one on the right," Ryan said, trying to see if Lee's gait was recognizable as that of the man captured by the CCTV in Wichita Falls. His height was about right.

Lee stopped in front of a large, framed photograph of a small brick building surrounded by a porch. He leaned toward a plaque on the side of the photo and read "Original town hall and site of court chambers, coroner's office, and police headquarters."

"That's here, right?" Lee asked, inspecting the photo again. He pointed. "And that's the same elm tree that's out front."

"It is," Ryan answered. "A long time ago."

"You remember it?" Lee asked continuing down the hall.

"I do."

Berger was standing as the men walked into the room. He smiled and offered his hand. "Joe Berger." He pointed at the single chair on one side of the table.

"So, gentleman," Lee said politely, sat, crossed his legs, and smiled. "How can I help you?"

"First, thanks for agreeing to talk to us," Berger answered. "It is a bit of a drive here from Oklahoma City."

"Not too bad."

"You were successful a few years back with a sex trafficking case. Mind if we pick your brain on how you did that? It might help us with what we're doing."

"Which is" – he raised his chin in the direction of the wall behind Berger and Ryan – "trying to find out who killed all those women."

"Yes."

"Making any progress with that taskforce?"

"Not enough and we're hoping you can help us."

"How exactly can my experience with human trafficking be of assistance?"

"Let's get started and find out," Berger suggested.

Lee smiled at Ryan. "I can't believe this room is more comfortable than your office." He looked at the one-way mirror and back at Berger and Ryan. "Let's cut to the chase." He reached across the table, slid the trip itineraries and guest lists toward him, and took his time reviewing the pages. "Why don't we begin here?" he said, a challenge in his voice.

"I have a better idea," Berger said, reaching down toward the side of his chair. He lifted a computer to the top of the table, adjusted the screen, and tapped on the keys. "You're going to see a white sedan caught on CCTV near the location where Maria Luna was killed."

"Maria Luna?"

Berger lifted his attention from the computer. "I'm sure you heard about the woman killed at a motel here in Owen a few weeks ago. It's been the lead story in every news broadcast." He let the thought sit before turning and pointing at Luna's photo on the wall. "Ring a bell?"

"Okay. Got it."

"So, this image of a white sedan was recorded going in the direction of the Sleep Inn where the body was found. It's the only street running in front of the motel. Here," Berger said, tapping on the keyboard, "is that sedan going in the other direction a few hours later. Now…" More tapping on the keyboard. "There," Berger said pointing at the screen, "is that same sedan in images we pulled off CCTV in the parking lot of the hotel in Wichita Falls, where another woman was killed." He smiled at Lee. "You've heard about that one, I'm sure."

Lee nodded. "I have."

"Okay," Berger said, his attention back to the screen. "Then, you're going to see a figure walking down the corridor in that hotel and going into and out of the room where her body was found." Berger turned the computer toward Lee. "I've gone back to the beginning. Take another look. Hit the *play* button and let me know what you think."

Lee's eyes went to the screen. "Okay," he said, boredom in his voice. He leaned forward and watched without comment. He raised his head and announced, "The end."

"What did you see?"

"A white sedan like hundreds of thousands on the road across this state, and a grainy image of someone, couldn't tell if it was a man or a woman, walking down a hallway, ducking into a room and then leaving."

"Did you notice the license plate on the sedan?"

"I noticed there was one."

"We can make out a T and a Z on the license plate."

"You're saying 'plate.' There are two cars so that would be two plates that happen to have similar letters. Or numbers. Could be a seven and a two. Not much there, I'm afraid."

"We'll return to that. Let's talk about the image of the man."

"A man? You're certain it's a man? I couldn't tell. It's unfortunate you can't see his or her face or tell anything at all about the person because the quality is so bad."

"Still, you can tell from the tape, even if the quality isn't the best, he appears to be making a real effort to keep his face turned away from CCTV stations in the hallway."

"I didn't see all that," Lee said, his voice serious and intense. "You have a gift."

"The real gifts lie with our forensics team," Berger shot back. "They lifted some DNA evidence from the scene."

Lee shook his head. "DNA from a hotel room? Yeah, I imagine they did. A lot of it."

"George Layton," Berger said, moving forward in a challenging posture. "Do you know who he is?"

Lee furrowed his brow in question. "That's a hell of a leap from finding DNA to George Layton, but, sure, I know who he is. The Eyeball Killer." He looked from Berger to Ryan and back to Berger. He shook his head slowly. "You're going to have to give me more if you want something from me about him."

"In a minute," Berger said, letting the accumulation of evidence weigh on Lee.

"You do have a difficult time focusing, don't you?"

"The T and the Z are only found together on a unique category of license plates. It's on my plate. I drive a state government car." Berger paused. "It's on your car. You drive a state government car." He looked at the whiteboard where he had posted an image of the sedan. "So, we have a white sedan at two of the murder sites that looks much like those driven by government employees. In fact, we can confirm it *is* a government vehicle by the two letters on the license plate." He settled his attention back on Lee. "What does that tell us?"

"I said you have a gift, but," Lee said, eyes squinted in concentration, "you also have a problem."

"Which is?"

"Just a guess but there must be a couple of thousand government cars on the road on any given day. You have to narrow that number way down if you're hoping to make a case that the same person was driving that particular car in the vicinities where those women were killed. That's a hell of a challenge."

"We've already met that challenge," Berger hurled back at Lee. "We found DNA from two victims on the brake and gas pedals of *that* car." Berger pointed at the whiteboard. "That one." He stared at Lee. "Your car."

Lee folded his arms across his chest. "My car?"

"The car you drove for a couple years was recently replaced with a newer model, right?"

Lee didn't answer.

"The blood samples found in that car, your car, the older one, matches that of two women," Berger said, turning toward the wall behind him. Finding the images of Lila Nethers and Cindy Athens, he pointed. "Those two."

Berger spun the computer screen toward him, scrolled through the film, and turned the computer back toward Lee. "This person is wearing a hat. I'm guessing he must have taken it off in the room at some point." He stopped and waited a beat. "You're not disputing that this is a man."

"I already did."

Berger waited again before going on. "Anyway, when he did, he scattered some hair on the floor in the entryway. DNA was extracted from those hairs." He stood and approached Lee, leaned close to his face and said, "Ray, it's *your* DNA."

Berger circled the table and walked to the wall where he tapped the photos of Maria Luna, Eugenia Wilson, Lila Nethers, and Cindy Athens. "We've got you dead to rights on these three victims." He stepped away from the wall and walked back toward Lee. "And," – he reached down and tapped the guest lists still in front of Lee – "you were at the homes of the other three. Looks bad, Ray. Very bad. And, I have to say, stupid since you're a former cop and should have covered your tracks a lot better."

Ryan shook his head. "Not stupid, careless." He stared at Lee a moment before continuing. "You did a sweep of the Sleep Inn and made certain there were no cameras. Forgot to check the rest of the area." He smiled. "I know. I know. Not exactly the kind of neighborhood you'd expect to be riddled with CCTV, and it isn't, but you missed the junkyard up the way from the motel. Believe it nor not, that's where we got the tape."

Lee looked intently at Ryan determined not to show a reaction.

"But you know what was stupid?" Ryan said, pushing his shoulders forward. "Leaving your DNA behind in Wichita Falls. That was a serious slip up." He raised his hands, palms out. "I know. What were the chances of finding that kind of evidence in a hotel room contaminated with thousands of samples? But," he said with a shrug, "we did."

Berger sat down. "And the blood in the car. Reminds me of something Bundy said about getting careless after so many kills. 'It's like changing a tire. The first time you're careful. By the thirtieth time, you can't remember where you left the lug wrench.'"

"Quoting Bundy?" Lee said with a laugh. "You guys are reaching."

"Now, back to Layton," Berger said.

"Waste of time. Never met him."

"Your fingerprints are on stationery used to write letters to him about the other victims."

Lee spit out what could have been a laugh or a cough. "Oh, for the love of God, you've got to be kidding. Me, pen pals with a serial killer? You're *reaching*."

Berger shuffled through pages in the thick file folder and handed one to Lee, who studied it carefully. "First of all, this is a partial print," – he passed the page back to Berger – "and this is ridiculous. I don't know how you got that, but it tells me that all the rest of this is bogus. I never wrote a word to that idiot.

"Blurry images of a popular model of a car driven by millions of people. That T and Z could be a seven and a two. I'm not saying it was me, but for the sake of argument, say I went into that hotel room where you found those hairs. That doesn't mean I killed anyone. Hell, whoever it was on that clip you showed me wasn't in there long enough to kill anyone. DNA from those other girls? I have my car valeted all the time. Have it washed and vacuumed by people who are in and out of it. Your gifts are falling way short, Agent Berger."

"Good points," Berger conceded. He put a legal pad in front of Ray and slapped down a pen. "Write down all the places you had your car parked by a valet and wherever you had it washed and vacuumed."

Lee stared at Berger a moment before asking, "Why would I do that? I don't need to defend myself. You've got nothing."

"You've been on my side of the table a lot of times. If you offered someone the opportunity to confirm what they said and they refused, what would you think?" He pointed at the legal pad. "Do what an innocent person would jump at the chance to do." He stood and looked down at Ryan. "Let's give him some time to collect his thoughts and do the right thing."

***

"Do you recognize him?" Ryan asked Connor, who stared intently at Lee through the two-way mirror.

Connor shook his head. "Never seen him before."

"He's holding his own," Ryan said to Berger. "No sign at all he's the least bit concerned about any of this. And he's got a point about the... Well, about everything. The footage doesn't show anything conclusive. Any of it. And he's made a strong case for reasonable doubt on the other stuff. Imagine what a lawyer could do with it."

Ryan walked to the back of the room and looked at the caller ID on the screen of his buzzing cell. "It's Jones. Hello."

"Morning," Jones said. "Is this a good time?"

"Good as any."

"Did Raymond Lee come in to see you?"

"We've been talking to him. Taking a short break right now."

"I'm guessing you heard from Len Slade."

"Agent Berger did and he's here with me. Would you mind if I put you on speaker so he could join the conversation?"

"Not at all. Agent Berger?"

"Yes."

"Did Len pass along what I told him about Raymond Lee."

"He did, but I'd like to hear what you have to say in case I missed something."

"I'm feeling guilty I didn't put the pieces together before I found out he was going to be talking to you."

"Yes, Director Slade told me you mentioned that, but sometimes that's the way it happens."

"He was with me on a fundraising swing that took us through Wesper, Laramie, and Mannix where those women were killed."

"Being with you in those cities isn't especially compelling at this point," Berger pointed out. "Seeing this in the same way others will, especially a lawyer defending him, you were there, too. And just because he was there means nothing unless we have solid evidence tying him to those women. That's our challenge."

"I understand. I hope my contributions are not a case of 'too little, too late.'"

"It's all helpful."

"There is one other thing. For the past few months, it might be longer, I don't know for sure since I never spent much time with him, he has been acting strange. A little unstable. It's been a gradual decline."

"Director Slade said something about some strange behavior. Ranting he said you called it."

"Yes, that's the only way I can describe it. He was always a steady and reasonable person. One we could count on to be circumspect and prudent, then..."

"Hold on," Ryan said, "and sorry for the interruption, but what did he do for you? What were his responsibilities?"

"He doesn't do anything for me, really. He was hired as an investigator for the Public Safety Committee, which I chair. We oversee the Department of Corrections, the SBI, of course, Bureau of Narcotics and Dangerous Drugs, among other agencies. There are times when we need to gather information on our own, quietly, surreptitiously."

Ryan asked, "He doesn't work closely with you?"

"No more closely than he does with any other member of the committee staff."

"Really," Ryan said, with a look at Berger and Smolders. "Why was he with you on your campaign tour?"

"On occasion he provides security for members of the committee when we travel."

"*We* as in *all* members of the committee?"

"Primarily me as chairman, but if others request security, he provided it."

"Okay, back to the change in his behavior."

"He's gone from a steady and reassuring presence to a...a...well, I'd have to describe it as *unhinged*."

"Can you give us an example?" Berger asked.

"Just the other day he told me he had some information that could, and I'm using his words, 'take down everyone in the state house.'"

After waiting a beat for the other shoe to drop, when it did not, Berger asked, "That was it. He didn't elaborate?"

"No, he never does. He offers it as an aside. A remark as he walks away. The period at the end of a sentence. That sort of thing. Very matter-of-fact."

"And you never followed up with him? Asked him about the *rantings* to find out if you needed to pay closer attention? Maybe question whether he could continue doing his job effectively given his erratic behavior?"

"That's part of the mea culpa I'm wrestling with. I can only explain it by saying his behavior evolved slowly over time."

"As far as you know, he's never done anything violent or threatened anyone?"

"I've never seen that kind of behavior. Should I say something? Confront him when he begins acting strangely and see if I can get more from him? Would that be useful to you? I'd like to do whatever I can to make up for my obliviousness."

"No," Berger said earnestly. "We'll see what we can find out and get back to you."

"Whatever you say. Reflecting on everything I've reported to you, and after having this discussion, I have to say I don't think I'd be comfortable continuing to work with him. He appears to be a dangerous man. Am I overreacting?"

"We'll let you know."

"The sooner the better."

"Thank you very much for this."

"Does it help?"

"We won't know until we've had more time with him."

"Let me know if there's anything more I can do to help."

"We will," Ryan said and swiped off the call. To Berger: "I have an idea."

***

Ryan and Berger sat down and studied the list Lee passed to them. "Thanks," Ryan said, leaned forward and placed his arms on the table. Hands flat. "We just heard from Senator Jones."

Lee smiled broadly and spread his arms in front of him. "Terrific. I'm guessing he straightened all of this out and we're done here." He started to push away from the table and stood.

"No," Ryan responded. "Get comfortable. We have a lot more to talk about."

Lee hesitated as if uncertain what he had heard. "Like what?"

Ryan motioned for Lee to sit down. "He told us you were with him on a fundraising tour that took the two of you through the three cities where they" – he turned toward the wall behind him – "were killed." He pushed the guest lists at Lee. "He's going to make an excellent witness."

Lee put his hand on the guest lists and slowly slid them back to Ryan, then sat back in his chair.

"Need a minute?" Ryan asked.

Lee cocked his head and turned his shoulder. "I don't think you spoke to the senator, but if you did, I doubt he told you any of that. And let's just say..."

Ryan held up his hand. "Heard of an app called TapeACall?" He put his phone on the table. "I think you'll recognize this voice."

Lee's eyebrows jumped, his eyes narrowing, but he relaxed when the taped conversation settled into its rhythm.

Ryan cut off the call at its midpoint. "There's more, but I think that gives you a flavor for what the senator called us about."

Lee turned in his chair and crossed his right leg over his left knee and drummed his fingers on the table. "Did he know you were taping that?"

"Taping what?" Ryan asked with a smile and quick glance at Berger. "This is for the three of us."

"And?"

"And you're fucked," Berger said.

"No, not hardly." Lee nodded at the phone. "What you have there is no more solid than all this other shit."

"Let me ask you a question," Berger said. He stood and turned toward the wall behind his chair. "And it's not rhetorical so consider your answer carefully." He paced slowly in front of the row of portraits. "We can link you to four of the seven women with unimpeachable evidence. The remaining three, as a state senator and candidate for governor has now corroborated for us, can also be connected to you."

Berger stopped next to the whiteboard. He pointed at the eviscerated bodies of Cindy Athens and Lila Nethers. "DNA ties you to them." He shifted his attention to Eugenia Wilson. "Your DNA was found here. And," he said, pointing at the trussed-up body of Maria Luna, "we can put your car at this scene, and with Wilson, too."

Berger made a point of standing at the whiteboard for a moment before sitting down. "Imagine being in a courtroom as a defendant and the prosecution presents the evidence I did with a lot more detail and lawyerly talent. Those," – he gestured toward the whiteboard – "will be set up as sensational exhibits for the jury, the press, and everyone in the courtroom. And then there will be the expert witnesses, and, of course, that will include identifying you on the CCTV in the hotel by height, weight, and all the rest of it.

"You truly think you'll walk out of that courtroom a free man?" Berger held up his hand. "Don't give some smart-ass answer. Think about it. Take your time." He looked at Ryan. "Let's take a break." To Lee: "Want some coffee? A soda? Something from the snack machine? I'd let you get it yourself but we're going to have to ask you to stay in this room. I'll be locking it when we leave."

***

"That guy doesn't seem to be worried even a little," Connor said as Ryan and Berger walked into the viewing room.

"His kind never do," Berger responded and stood next to Connor. "I've studied hours of interrogation tapes of guys like this. When you're an empty husk, there's no soul to touch. No conscience to appeal to."

"Are you saying he is our guy?" Ryan asked. "You weren't so sure a while ago."

"The evidence is taking us there, but I still have something nagging at me that I can't shake. The pieces are fitting together, but I'm not seeing the picture clearly."

"What's next?" Connor asked.

"Honestly," Berger said and crossed his arms. "I'm not sure." He took a wide stance and stared through the two-way glass. "Any bright ideas on where we go from here?"

Ryan said, "He reacted when I hit *play* and Jones wasn't saying what he expected. It got to him. Only for a moment, but it did."

"And?" Berger asked.

"We didn't play all of the conversation. Let's hit him with the rest of it."

***

Ryan offered Lee a bottle of water. "You're going to need this. We'll be here a while."

"Thanks," Lee said and positioned the bottle in front of him.

"Have you thought about what I asked?" Berger said.

"Forgot what it was."

Berger smiled serenely. "C'mon, you can do better. Playing games with us is childish."

"This whole thing is childish," Lee said, pointing at the wall behind Ryan and Berger. He turned toward the whiteboard. "All this. I've been here. Done this. You can't really believe this bullshit is going to work. But if you do, it's insulting."

"Tell me, then," Berger asked, "professional to professional, do you think you could get out of a courtroom a free man with what we have?"

"Professional to professional, your strategy stinks." He laughed. "If you think you have enough to put me away, then why...?"

"Correction," Berger said. "We *know* we have enough. And it's an 'eye-for-an-eye' here in Oklahoma."

"You must be the 'bad cop,'" Lee said to Berger.

"Just stating the facts."

"Facts? You asked if I think I could walk out of the courtroom. You're asking me to make your case. You have huge holes to fill and you want me to plug them. It's a tired game anyone with an ounce of gray matter can see through. You need to do a better job at your job."

Ryan reached across the table and moved the bottle out of his line of sight. "Let's try this again. DNA is the Holy Grail. We've got you dead to rights on Athens, Nethers, and Wilson. The others not so much, but we have the CCTV on Luna. I'm thinking the prosecution will find a persuasive way to add the other three" – he pointed at the photos of the bodies of Churchill, Smithson, and Regent – "especially when they read the Layton letters to the jury. With all that, the profile of the Beast of Oklahoma will take shape. The outline will be filled in with detail." Ryan jabbed his finger at Lee. "It's you."

"Either you have enough for all of them or you don't have enough for any of them," Lee countered. "You can't play a hand you don't have. Going down this road is a waste of time."

"We've heard you're a scary person," Ryan said. "*Unhinged* is the word used to describe you. That's a pretty good hand to play."

Lee rolled his eyes. "Like I said this is a dead end."

Ryan held up his phone. "I don't think so." He placed it in front of Lee and tapped the screen. "*He's gone from a steady and reassuring presence to a...a...well, I'd have to describe it as unhinged.*"

Ryan stopped the recording. "Being called *unhinged* by the man you've been working for all these years, a respected public servant, is not good. There's more." He activated the app. "*Just the other day he told me he had some information that could, and I'm using his words, 'take down everyone in the state house.'*"

Lee let his head drop back and he stared at the ceiling.

"More," Ryan said scrolling ahead. "*'He offers it as an aside. A remark as he walks away. The period at the end of a sentence. That sort of thing. Very matter-of-fact.'*"

"The best part," Ryan said. "*'I have to say I don't think I'd be comfortable continuing to work with him. He appears to be a very dangerous man.'*"

"So, to sum up," Berger said. "You're fucked."

"I didn't say any of that."

"Really?" Berger said, his eyes wide. "A moment ago you were certain he was going to get you out of here."

Lee took a long sip of water. He looked at the whiteboard and pointed at Maria Luna. "Suppose I know something about that one."

"What do you mean *suppose*?" Berger asked.

"Suppose I can give you something to help you along your way." Lee took another sip of water. "And you give me something to help me on my way."

"On your way?" Ryan asked.

"To be perfectly clear," Berger said, "you're looking for immunity?"

"That's right. I'll solve your case for you. To start, I'll give you the person who killed six of those women."

"To start?"

"This goes way beyond those murders. I've got enough that you're going to want to get on the phone with the local prosecutor, or," – he waved his hand dismissively – "state attorney, DA, whoever, and give me what I need in exchange for the biggest break you'll ever get. It's a golden ticket you'll be able to cash in for whatever you want for the rest of your life."

"Let's not jump to any 'get out of jail free cards' or 'golden tickets,'" Berger said, skepticism in his voice. "We'll make those decisions after we hear what you have."

Lee looked up at a camera mounted in the corner of the room. A blinking red light indicated it was recording. "Turn that off." He pointed at the two-way mirror. "Any cops in there get out."

Ryan turned his attention to the mirror. "Smolders. Leave."

"And turn off any recording devices you got going in here," Lee said. "No Miranda rights. No lawyers. Just us," he said and gestured toward Ryan's phone. "Without Miranda, if you record any of this it's inadmissible. Nothing I say from this point forward is an admission of anything. We're just talking. If you try to use any of it…"

"We know the law," Ryan said. He dragged his chair to the corner, stood on it, pushed a button on the camera, and the red light went out. He returned to the table. "Go ahead. Make us believe you know what happened to Luna."

"What?" Lee said. "Now you're having doubts that I'm involved?"

Ryan shook his head. "No, but we need to hear it from you. Hear what you're going to tell the legal folks. Make us believe and we know they'll believe."

"Luna's scene matched the others. The first three," Lee clarified. "Whoever killed her had to know about the MO, and she was killed before any details were released. Right?" Lee let his words settle before adding, "Want me to go ahead?"

Berger and Ryan both nodded.

"That woman," – Lee pointed at Luna's photo on the wall behind Berger and Ryan – "was blackmailing someone. She had information that could have caused them a lot of problems. Maybe even stopped the roll of a career. She asked for and got a couple of substantial payments, but kept coming back for more. She lost her shit when we said, 'no more.'" Lee nodded at the whiteboard and pointed at the Luna crime scene photo. "That was staged to look like those other killings."

"And," Berger prompted Lee who had fallen silent.

"And it's time to speak to someone and work out a way I can help you and you can help me. We come to an understanding that gives you what you want and me my walking papers." His eyes went back to the whiteboard. "I can give you who killed every single one of those women."

Lee sat up in his chair, brought his hands together, and rested his elbows on the table. He looked from Berger to Ryan. "And that's a small part of the story. The *start* I was talking about. Who killed those women is not nearly as important as who is covering this up and why. Ever wonder why you were asked to keep your investigation hush-hush and not go to the media or public for help? There's a lot going on that makes the murders almost a sidebar. I can give you details reaching right into the Oval Office."

"Stop," Berger said and held up his hand. "Just stop. The Oval Office?"

"From the top of the heap here in Oklahoma into the Oval Office in Washington."

"Put a hold on the Oval Office for a moment," Ryan said with a note of derision. "Let's back up. Back to Maria Luna. She was killed because she was blackmailing someone?"

"No, she was killed because she lost her fucking mind," Lee said forcefully. "The thing is it was totally unnecessary. The idea was to draw a line in the sand so she wouldn't keep coming back for more, but she didn't recognize it was a negotiation. She got an offer and could have parlayed it into more for herself. But she went straight to Defcon Four and she caused her own death."

"Caused her own death?" Ryan said, lifting out of his chair.

Berger put a hand on Ryan's arm.

"You need more," Lee said with a nod at the crime scene photo of Luna. "She was bound. Her hands and feet weren't tied to the bedposts like the others. That was a mistake. Dawned on me later, but I couldn't go back. Too late."

Ryan and Berger, in a mind meld, stared at Lee.

Lee stared back. "Not enough?" He took a long sip of water. "Her eye. Didn't get that quite right."

***

"I was wondering if you'd stay," Ryan said to Connor as he and Berger walked into the viewing room.

"You told Smolders to leave so I figured it was okay for me to stay," Connor replied, his attention on Lee. "That motherfucker thinks this is some kinda game."

Ryan stood with his brother. "He's toast. We have to figure out if he has enough to leverage."

"Leverage?" Connor said incredulously. He turned toward Ryan. "You're thinkin' of cuttin' some kinda deal with him?"

Berger joined the two. "I think he's telling the truth. "Well," – he shrugged – "part of it anyway. The Oval Office and the state house? Jones did say he went off the deep end sometimes, or he could be crazy like a fox and just wants to keep us at the table, negotiating. I'm still having a hard time believing he's who we're looking for. It just doesn't fit."

"The evidence says otherwise," Ryan reminded.

Berger shook his head. "I know, I know. Really can't argue with cold, hard facts, but I can't shake my doubts."

Connor said, "The fucker killed Maria."

Berger answered, "Yes, he did. He knows things only the killer could know. The bindings. The eye."

Connor took a step closer to the glass. "I can't believe I'm looking at the person who killed her."

"I can't tell you how many times I've had that reaction," Berger said. "Especially with the ones who commit the most horrible crimes. They should be slobbering beasts with fangs, horns, and a tail. But this guy?" He pursed his lips and shook his head slowly. "I don't know."

Ryan asked, "You're ruling him out? Conclusively? We're supposed to overlook the evidence?"

"No, I'm not doing that. I know better. As with everything in life, there are exceptions to the rule."

"You're giving yourself some wiggle room."

Berger nodded. "Probably."

Ryan said, "He knows we're in here looking at him and trying to figure out what to do with what he's told us."

Berger laughed freely, startling Ryan and Connor. "Sorry, but speaking of 'trying to figure things out'... I'm supposed to be heading up a taskforce with all kinds of detectives, forensics experts, and" – he waved his hands – "telephone banks, war room shit, and here we are looking at a man who says he can solve this whole thing for us."

"Let's take the next step," Ryan said. "We call the DA and brief her on what we have. Let her know he's asking for a deal. Put that in her hands."

"Not so simple," Berger said. "Remember, there's another jurisdiction involved. A whole other state. Texas probably has its own set of rules that need to be figured into this."

"Fuck that," Connor said loudly, his words immediately absorbed by the padded foam soundproof walls. "If he don't get away with this by forcing you all into letting him go, he's gonna sit in Big Mac the rest of his life. Like Layton." His face red, Connor spun away from the glass. "Or he could get some kinda bullshit manslaughter thing. He's talking 'bout self-defense. Saying Maria attacked him."

Giving Ryan a quick glance, Berger said to Connor, "I'm going to call the DA and brief her. We're going to make sure that SOB" – he pointed at the glass – "doesn't get away with anything. And if he's telling the truth, we'll get the animal that's responsible for the rest of it. And a lot more."

Berger said to Ryan, "Go ahead and take Lee to the DA. By the time you get there, I'll have briefed her and you can get busy working out the preliminary charges to hold him. Then I've got to figure out a way to take care of the PR end of all this. Get this taskforce nonsense worked out." He shook his head. "Find a way to give everyone some credit and promise a big 'aren't we all wonderful' press conference. Maybe I'll use Lee's promise about a 'golden ticket.'"

***

"We're going to the DA's office," Ryan said, standing at the door of the interrogation room. He motioned Lee to him and reached for handcuffs in a leather holster at his beltline.

"Oh, come on," Lee said as he approached Ryan. "Is that necessary?"

"You want to talk to the DA or not? We aren't leaving this building unless we do it my way."

Lee held out his hands. Ryan snapped on the cuffs and the two walked down the corridor toward the rear door. As they pushed through into the sunlight both men blinked repeatedly adjusting to the brightness. Still in transition and squinting, Ryan felt a strong shove on his shoulders; so hard it snapped his head back painfully. He stumbled and fell forward onto the sidewalk. His head slammed onto the concrete, stunning him. He felt a tug on his belt. He rolled over, still trying to focus in the blinding light. He was also struggling to see through something streaming into his eyes.

"You fuckin' animal."

Ryan recognized Connor's voice and tried to wipe his eyes clear. An earsplitting pop caused him to turn away from the noise. The ringing in his ears and a jackhammering pain in his head kept him from gaining his balance. He rolled over and managed to push off the ground onto his hands and knees.

Ryan saw Lee on his back in the grass just off the edge of the sidewalk. He reached out and touched the body. Suddenly the fuzzy edges of the picture sharpened. Connor stood over the man, limp, the gun dangling from his fingers.

Ryan grabbed at Connor, clutching his pants at the waist. He pulled himself upright. "Get the hell out of here," he said, ripping the gun out of Connor's hand. "Go around the front. Walk away. Don't run. There are cameras there. None here," he said as his head continued to clear.

Ryan wiped the blood out of his eyes touching an open gash over his right eye. He fired another shot into a stand of trees at the back of the station house as he called frantically into the microphone epaulet, "ten/fifty-three behind the station house. Need help right now."

***

Berger slid the blue plastic curtains aside and walked to the bed. "How're you feeling?"

"I just killed a man. I have a splitting headache. Maybe a concussion. How do you think I'm feeling?"

"Sorry," Berger apologized weakly. "You want to talk about it?" He shook his head. "God, that sounds lame."

"He swung around, caught me with the corner of his cuffs," Ryan said, pointing at his eye. "Knocked me down, grabbed my gun, and we fought. The gun went off. That's about it, although I'm sure I'm going to be repeating it a couple of thousand times before the investigation is over. They already did a residue test and took away my gun."

Berger raised his chin toward Ryan. "The side of your face is all scraped up and your lip is swelling while I'm standing here. You look like you went ten rounds with Mike Tyson."

"I feel like it." He touched his lip. "Ouch!"

"Just when you think you've got a handle on things," Berger said in exasperation. "I was convinced he wanted to make a deal, but why'd he try to run if he did?"

Ryan raised his bed into the sitting position. "Because he knew his story wasn't going to hold up. Because he killed those women."

Berger shook his head. "No, that doesn't do it for me." He raised his hands defensively. "Okay, the evidence is there. Can't argue with that, and Luna is definitely on him. But there's way too much that doesn't make any sense."

"Like?"

"You really want to do this here? Now?"

"I can't go anywhere." Ryan touched his head. "Probably have to go through an MRI. I'm going to be here a while."

Berger retrieved a chair from the emergency room, pulled it next to the bed, and sat down. "I flat out don't believe Lee is our man. Not the one who killed six of those women. Luna, yeah. That said, we had enough solid evidence to hold him for three of those murders, so he felt he had to make a deal. He was willing to admit he killed Luna to bring us on board. I know nothing he said about her is admissible, but he convinced us he was telling the truth, right?"

"Right."

Berger scooted his chair closer to the bed. "Lee says he's got something that will be worth a plea deal. I'm not saying I believe the Oval Office or state house business, but I think he had something. You?"

"Okay, he probably had something to deal with."

"So why did he try to run? Where did he think he was going to go? How far would he get? Was he willing to kill you on the off chance he might get away? He was handcuffed. He was on foot. The place was bristling with cops." Berger shrugged. "What the hell?"

"Desperate people do desperate things."

Berger did not respond. He stared into the emergency room at flashes of green and white as the doctors and nurses rushed past. The chaos of frantic voices, rolling beds, and beeping machines provided a soundtrack eventually broken when Berger said, "I do think he had something important to trade."

"But you really don't think it was him? You're convinced of that?"

"When I asked him how he knew... How the *person* who killed Luna knew about the killer's MO before we revealed there was a serial offender, he said he didn't want to discuss it. He was telling us he knew all about the MO, and that tells me he knows who it is. He was withholding that as trade bait. Plus, he was so sure of himself and then" – he pointed at Ryan's bandage – "that. What the hell?"

Monday-June 11

Ryan stood with Berger and Slade as Linares and McDowell walked into the holding room. Slade was herding everyone together when Ryan's phone buzzed. He looked at it and gave Slade the 'one minute' index finger.

"Make it quick," Slade barked.

Ryan walked away from the group and to a corner of the room. "Hello."

"Thanks for taking my call," Jones said.

"I remember having a conversation about this. Said I always would take your calls."

"Yeah, well, I know you're about to go into the press conference."

"You caught me on the way in."

"This'll be quick. First, congratulations. A helluva job. How're you doing?"

"Healing."

"Good to hear." Jones cleared his throat. "Slade told me he's going to say something about my...um...I guess you'd call it my help with all of this."

"Help?"

"Yeah, that's what I want to clear with you. He's going to say a few words about what I told you about Lee. His being with me in those three cities, and then giving you enough to place him in Wichita Falls. Helping you push the investigation forward."

Ryan looked up at Berger, who was staring at him, a question on his face. Ryan rolled his eyes.

"I'm guessing you knew most of that already, but I'd like to think I did add something to the mix."

Ryan let his silence say what he could not.

"I wanted to give you a heads-up so you wouldn't be surprised."

"I would have been surprised," Ryan admitted.

"Anyway, again, congratulations."

Ryan tapped off the call without a response. He joined the group as they began filing into the media room and whispered to Berger, "Try not to look surprised or pissed."

***

The room was bristling. Overflowing. The barrage of clicking cameras continued until the five men sat and Slade stared down the front-line photographers who melted into the crowd.

"We asked you to show up a half-hour prior to the start of this press conference so you'd have time to review the contents of the press kits we've provided," Len Slade said from behind a podium. "The *who*, *what*, *why*, and *where* details are in the most recent release and the other materials you have. We also released a lot of this over the weekend. Many of you have reported extensively on it, so today we won't be rehashing, but we'll be happy to take questions."

A forest of hands shot up along with a burst of crosstalk.

"First," Slade said, motioning for calm, "I have a few words. The men with me, and others under their command, did a remarkable job of identifying the offender. I can't begin to express my admiration for the job they did. I'd also like to note at this time that we had invaluable contributions from Senator Whalen Jones."

Berger glanced at Ryan and mouthed, "What the fuck."

"As you know, Raymond Lee was an investigator for the Oklahoma Senate Public Safety Committee which is chaired by Senator Jones. The senator shared valuable information with me that we used to identify Lee as a person of interest, and it was instrumental in building a solid case against him. I, and everyone involved in this unprecedented effort offer our sincere thanks to Senator Jones."

"As usual," Slade said, "identify yourselves and your affiliation and who you have a question for. You..." He pointed.

"Reed Milsap, CNN. This is for Sheriff Ryan. I'm having trouble understanding exactly what happened with Lee. He attacked you and in the course of fighting for your weapon, he was shot and killed."

"Yes," Ryan responded.

"Where was he going handcuffed and next to a police station? Seems like suicide by cop."

"That's irresponsible speculation." Slade snapped. "We're working with local internal affairs and our investigation is telling us the man was trying to escape and Sheriff Ryan responded to defend his life." He turned his attention to Ryan. "Anything you want to add?"

"The only answer I have is the one I've given others who have asked, and that is 'desperate people do desperate things.'"

Slade selected the next questioner.

"Rhea Moore, *Tulsa World*. This is for Agent Berger. If I'm understanding the information you've provided, the murders you can conclusively tie to Lee are Wilson, Athens, and Nethers. Does that mean the other four remain open cases?"

"Yes and no," Berger said to sighs of dissatisfaction that pocked the room. "We are confident Lee is also responsible for the murder of Maria Luna. We have evidence placing him in the vicinity at the time she was killed. We can also place him at the locations of the first three murders. There is no DNA tying Lee to these three so we can't say conclusively he was involved, but we have strong circumstantial evidence saying he was. That makes him a person of interest."

"Next," Slade said, picking out a woman directly in front of the podium.

"Lettie Sangers, KOKI, Tulsa. This question is for whoever wants to answer it. Raymond Lee was a highly regarded member of the Oklahoma Highway Patrol, and an investigator for a senate committee. How is it that everyone, even those responsible for vetting him at his jobs, and for directing him while he was employed in these positions of responsibility, completely missed the fact he was a psychopath?"

Berger raised a finger. "Are you familiar with a book by Ann Rule, *The Stranger Beside Me*?"

Sangers, clearly caught off guard, shook her head.

"Then I recommend it to you." He reached into his back pocket and pulled out his wallet from which he removed a piece of paper. "I've kept this with me since I read Rule's book, which is about Ted Bundy. A man she knew well and worked with at, of all places, a suicide hotline. Bundy was by every account, including Rule's, very good at his job of talking depressed and anxious people down from the ledge. Rule said he appeared to be a caring, compassionate, and sensitive person. After finding out who the real Ted Bundy was, she wrote the following: 'Like all the others, I have been manipulated to suit Ted's needs. I don't feel particularly embarrassed or resentful about that. I was one of many, all of us intelligent, compassionate people who had no real comprehension of what possessed him, what drove him obsessively.'"

Berger carefully folded the page and placed it back into his wallet. "The same thing can be said about most serial offenders. They look and act exactly like you, Ms. Sanger, and like me," he said not trying to hide the annoyance in his voice.

The room was eerily quiet for a few seconds before the noise level ratcheted up.

Slade studied the room and glanced to his right where Iglesias, standing apart from the throng, nodded at him. "Okay," Slade said, "one final question."

"Tom Reed, the *Oklahoman*. This question is for you, Director Slade."

Iglesias took a couple of steps out of the shadows. Slade was prepped for his response.

"I understand the SBI is investigating contract abuse within the state government's fleet management office, specifically no-bid contracting. What can you tell us about that?"

Iglesias watched Slade raise his eyebrows and widen his eyes in surprise – as they had rehearsed. It had taken some negotiating to get Reed to agree to be a shill, but promising him an exclusive interview with Slade about the investigation into the contract abuse had done the trick.

"I can't comment on an ongoing investigation," Slade answered, morphing from surprise to command. Again, as planned.

"So, there is an investigation of contracting irregularities in the fleet management program. You're confirming that?"

"I can confirm we are looking at the possibility of irregularities."

"Does that explain the resignation of the Speaker of the State Legislature, Noreen West? Her husband owns the state's largest car dealership and has the contract currently under investigation."

"You're not listening," Slade said with noticeably less conviction than his usual dismissal of questions he did not want to answer. "I'm not going to comment about ongoing investigations."

Iglesias stared at Reed willing him to force the issue. *Demand an answer, dammit.* Iglesias felt his shoulders tense and he squeezed his hands into tight fists, his knuckles going white.

"How did you discover the contracts were being awarded to the same vendor year after year bypassing the bid process?"

Iglesias watched Slade run through the practiced reaction. *Pause. Give it some thought. Go ahead.*

"I received a call from Governor Stephens a few weeks ago. His staff found some irregularities in the line items in the draft budget proposal and brought it to his attention. I can't go into any more detail other than to say he handed the information to us and we're grateful. Thank you."

***

Berger, Ryan, and Smolders sat at a wrought-iron table in the bustling Capitol Building Health Nut Café. They leaned close to ensure the privacy of their conversation.

"How does it feel to be a political shill?" Smolders asked, a smile tugging at the corners of his lips.

"Dirty," Ryan said without displaying any sense of humor about Smolders' dig.

"I'm glad you warned me," Berger said. "If I'd heard that genuflecting to Jones without any warning at all, I would've fallen off my chair."

"You knew about that?" Smolders asked Ryan.

"I got a call from Jones before the presser. He told me what Slade was going to say. I think he was afraid I might look horrified or something."

"Did he tell you about the contracting thing?"

"No."

"What a shit show," Berger said, staring into his cup of coffee. "I still can't wrap my head around it. Slade put it to bed but... I don't know."

"I have to go with the evidence," Ryan said.

Berger hung his head. Ryan drummed his fingers on the table.

"What'd your brother say about it all?" Smolders asked Ryan.

"My brother?"

"He didn't leave with me. I read your" – he looked from Berger to Ryan – "report on what Lee said about Luna. Man, that had to bite Connor."

Ryan shrugged. "He hasn't said much."

Berger gave Ryan a sidelong look. "I'm going to put something on the table here and it's the only time we're going to talk about it. We need clarity among" – he looked from Ryan to Smolders – "us. It's over with this conversation. We leave it here. Good?"

"Yeah," Smolders said tentatively. He looked at Ryan for a signal of some sort to explain what Berger was saying.

"You took Lee from the interrogation room through the back door. Your brother was still in the viewing area when I left." Berger left the statement there and stared at Ryan.

"Connor killed Lee," Ryan said flatly.

Smolders' eyes widened. "Fuck."

Berger said, "I sure didn't shed a tear over Lee. He was scum but..." He took a deep breath. "It leaves a lot hanging out there."

Tuesday- July 31

Holly Madison pushed through the door into the concierge's suite and met the smile of a young woman who stood up behind a blond oak desk and greeted her with "Welcome to Gladwynne Tower, we're so pleased you'll be residing here with us."

"Thank you," Madison replied. "I'm looking forward to it. Is Mr. Riley in?"

"Give me a minute," the smiling young woman said and turned toward a door directly behind her desk. She disappeared momentarily, emerged, and swept her arm toward the open door. "Please."

A tall, slim man in a fitted suit was standing as Madison walked toward him. "Everything okay?" he asked.

"Yes, perfect. I'm planning on moving in this weekend."

"Terrific," the man said with surprising enthusiasm. "I'll email you the code for the freight elevator. It opens onto a dock at the rear of the building. Your movers can back their truck right up and unload.

Madison nodded. "Just two things. Please add my name to the mailbox in the lobby, and could you have one of your maintenance people take a look at my refrigerator. The right-side door doesn't close tightly." She lifted her right hand and brought her index finger and thumb close together. "There's a little space when you try to close the door."

"I'll do that right now," the man said and showing his diligence, lifted his phone and pressed a button. "Lily. Have Burton go to Ms. Madison's apartment and check the refrigerator. The door on the right side isn't closing properly." He rang off and smiled. "Anything else?"

"That should do it."

"Hope the move goes smoothly," he said as she turned and walked toward the door. As soon as she disappeared, the man sat heavily. *What a damn pain in the ass all of this has been. The police hold up on clearing his apartment. No, couldn't just get rid of all his shit. Had to rent a storage bay for sixty days before we can dump it. Stupid company policy about keeping the stuff for the family to claim.* He pursed his lips. *Can't even dump it, have to arrange for a sale to cover the storage fee. God! And those damn reporters! All over the place, wanting access for a few hours. Reporters and photographers. People on my ass about it. I usually rent these apartments in days, long waiting list, but who wants the Oklahoma Beast's apartment? Cut the rent in half and even then it took a month. God, I'm going to be glad when this is finally over.*

His walkie talkie buzzed. "Yeah?"

"It's Burton. Which door?"

"The one that won't close," the man said impatiently.

A moment then, "Oh, okay. Got it. The gasket on the right side is twisted. Keeping it from closing."

"Just take care of it."

Regis Burton opened and closed the door trying to flatten the bulge in the gasket. No luck. He tried to straighten the rubber seal with his screwdriver. Nothing. No easy fixes. He loosened the rubber seal, the panel swung open releasing stacks of money bound neatly with paper currency straps. Burton stood transfixed as a pile collected around his ankles. He reached down, lifted a few stacks, and put them on a kitchen island behind him. After piling all the stacks together, he shut the right-hand door and opened the left side. Upon removing the seal from that door, the panel fell forward releasing more bundles of money.

No one ever saw Regis Burton again.

Eighteen Months Later

"The Future is Now" dinner was a first. The first time a newly elected senator and governor joined together to fete the men and women who supported their candidacies. Only the most generous were on the guest list.

Befitting the occasion, the hosts welcomed this select group to the celebrated Vast restaurant on the forty-ninth floor of the Devon Energy Center, Oklahoma City's premier location. The setting was perfect. The city's lights below and the stars above sparkled through the sheet of windows surrounding the restaurant. A buffet table the length of the room was the axis around which the crowd revolved. Grass-fed beef carefully selected by the Oklahoma Beef Council; an assortment of imported cheeses; mounds of colorful vegetables: bell peppers, carrots, asparagus, grilled Brussel sprouts; a full display of salads: Caesar, spinach, arugula, wedge, and mixed greens; a pasta station with penne pasta puttanesca, wild mushroom ravioli with prosciutto. A separate wing of the table was dedicated to seafood: Key West shrimp, Maine lobster, salmon, halibut, cod, Chilean sea bass, and red snapper. A dessert table was piled high with cakes, pies, puddings, assorted cookies and chocolates, and a wide choice of ice cream and sorbets.

An open bar. Servers also mingled with silver trays and flutes of champagne, which, along with a generous wine selection, were available when diners settled at their tables, all arranged in front of the magnificent views of the city. The tables also offered a clear view of the dais where various guests of honor, including newly elected Senator Lincoln Shepherd and Governor Whalen Jones were seated.

Berger and Ryan stepped out of different elevators, the timing perfect, allowing them to eyeball each other.

"I didn't know Owen PD had a budget for dress uniforms," Berger teased Ryan. "Navy blue with epaulets and braids. And fancy silver buttons." He reached for the cuff of Ryan's coat. "Even here." He took a step back and made a show of inspecting the man. "What are those, patent leather shoes?"

"Exactly like yours," Ryan returned in kind. "At least I didn't have to stuff myself into a cummerbund and suspenders."

"Shall we?" Berger swept his arm toward the festivities. "I take it you also got a gold-embossed invitation to this soiree?"

"That and a follow-up call to make certain I understood it was not so much an invitation as a command performance."

"I got one of those calls, too."

"I'm going to make sure a few people see me and get the hell out of here," Ryan said.

Berger pointed at the buffet table. "We have to dig into that first."

Cleaning their plates after a second trip around the table, Ryan poked Berger on the shoulder, and they started toward the exit. A large man quick-stepped past them, closed the doors, turned to face them, and widened his stance. "The hosts," he droned in a monotone, "would appreciate it if you returned to your tables for the recognition ceremony."

Berger and Ryan asked simultaneously. "Recognition ceremony?"

The man pointed them back toward the room which had fallen silent. The lights dimmed and a single spotlight shown on the podium at the center of the dais. Gary Iglesias welcomed guests to "A night like none other in our great state of Oklahoma."

After an extended round of applause, during which Berger and Ryan returned to their table, Iglesias continued: "My name is Gary Iglesias and I have the honor and good fortune to be the MC for the evening. And with that, I'd like to introduce our newly elected Senator, Lincoln Stephens."

Ryan and Berger polished off multiple cups of coffee while Stephens humbly accepted the responsibilities entrusted to him by the good people of Oklahoma. He also laid out his priorities to improve the lot of all Oklahomans by increasing opportunities and promising a better life in the Sooner State. Applause lines came fast and furious and continued for more than twenty minutes.

Berger kept his eye on the door where the guardian had taken up residence. He and Ryan slowly accepted their fate and both made several trips to the dessert table. They looked up from their plates of chocolate cream pie when Jones took the helm, did the ritual "thank you's," announced his plans to make "Our great state of Oklahoma a shining example of what can be accomplished when men and women come together to raise all boats," which brought a "What the hell?" from Berger, and a responding shrug from Ryan.

Jones ran through a list of nominees for his cabinet beginning with "Dr. Drew Cranston, my choice for Secretary of Health and Mental Health."

"Isn't that the guy from Ottinger?" Berger asked.

Ryan nodded.

Jones continued, "Leonard Slade who has served us well as Director of the State Bureau of Investigation is my nominee for Chief Operating Officer."

Berger spit out what could have been a laugh or a cough and quickly covered his mouth with a napkin. He uttered a muffled, "Seriously?"

Ryan leaned close to Berger and managed to say through a soft laugh, "I hope he gets some media training."

"Where is Agent Joe Berger?" Jones called out.

Mouth still covered by his napkin, Berger gave Ryan a quick glance as if looking for confirmation that he had heard his name.

"Agent Berger?" Jones repeated.

Berger, unsure whether to raise his hand or stand, slowly raised his hand.

"Ladies and gentlemen," Jones said, "I will recommend the commission charged with finding our next Director of the Oklahoma State Bureau of Investigations put Joseph Berger at the top of their list. In fact, I strongly suggest it should be a short list with a single name."

Jones raised both arms gesturing for Berger to stand, which he did as applause undulated from the front to the back of the room. Over this applause, Jones said, "I'm certain everyone in this room recognizes Agent Berger's name. He is the man who took down the Oklahoma Beast."

"'Took down the Oklahoma Beast,'" Ryan said teasingly. "What a guy." His good humor was quickly chilled when Jones called out his name, urging him to stand.

With Berger and Ryan standing side-by-side looking like two deer caught in the headlights, Jones said, "Owen Sheriff Declan Ryan worked closely with Agent Berger throughout, and I'm suggesting this team continue at the SBI with Sheriff Ryan serving as Deputy Director."

"Before I release you to enjoy the balance of the evening, I have one final announcement. My first act as governor will be calling for a special election to fill my seat in the state senate. As unorthodox as this might be, I'm announcing my support for Monica Filer, who I've convinced to run for this seat. She did a wonderful job filling in for the late, great Roy Evans whose tragic and untimely death shocked us all. Fortunately, he had a competent aide in Monica who did a wonderful job in Washington. Where is Monica?"

Filer stood and the spotlight went to her.

***

"Son-of-a-bitch," Berger said as he elbowed Ryan, and cocked his head toward the door, which was clear.

"I think I'm beginning to get the hang of this," Ryan said as the two men hustled toward the arriving elevator. "A man told his son, 'You will marry the girl I choose...'"

The End

Thank you for reading.

The pleasure of a review or a kind word or two
would be most appreciated.

About the Author

John David Bethel is the author of award-winning novels, *Unheard of* and *Holding Back the Dark*. Other published novels include *Little Wars*, *Capitol Evil* and *Hotel Hell*. He has also been published in popular consumer magazines and respected political journals.

Mr. Bethel spent 35 years in politics and government. He served in the Federal Senior Executive Service as a political appointee where he was Senior Adviser/Director of Speechwriting for the Secretaries of Commerce and Education; Editorial Director for the U.S. Small Business Administration; and Assistant Administrator for the U.S. General Services Administration's Office of Communications and Citizen Services. Bethel also worked as press secretary/speechwriter to Members of Congress.

He graduated with Phi Beta Kappa honors from Tulane University and lives in Orlando, Florida.

For sales, editorial information, subsidiary rights information
or a catalog, please write or phone or e-mail
iBooks
Manhanset House
Shelter Island Hts., New York 11965, US
Tel: 212-427-7139
ibooksinc.com
bricktower@aol.com
www.IngramContent.com